# Skyfall

Tor Books by Catherine Asaro

THE SAGA OF THE SKOLIAN EMPIRE
*Primary Inversion*
*Catch the Lightning*
*The Last Hawk*
*The Radiant Seas*
*Ascendant Sun*
*The Quantum Rose*
*Spherical Harmonic*
*The Moon's Shadow*
*Skyfall*
*Triad* (forthcoming)

# Skyfall

## Catherine Asaro

TOR®

A Tom Doherty Associates Book
New York

SKYFALL

Edited by James Minz

A Tor Book
Published by Tom Doherty Associates, LLC
175 Fifth Avenue
New York, NY 10010

www.tor.com

Tor® is a registered trademark of Tom Doherty Associates, LLC.

Library of Congress Cataloging-in-Publication Data

Asaro, Catherine.
     Skyfall / Catherine Asaro.—1st ed.
          p.    cm.
     "A Tom Doherty Associates book."
     ISBN 0-765-30638-7
     1. Skolian Empire (Imaginary place)—Fiction.    2. Life on other planets—Fiction.
     I. Title.

PS3551.S29S58    2003
813'.54—dc21

                                                                    2003055985

Printed in the United States of America

0  9  8  7  6  5  4  3  2

To Aly's Writing Group:

Aly Parsons, with Al Carroll, J. G. Huckenpöler, Paula Jordon,
Simcha Kuritzky, Mike La Violette, Connie Warner,
and George Williams

For all your insights, your support, and especially
for your friendship.

# Acknowledgments

I would like to express my gratitude to the readers who gave me input on *Skyfall*. Their comments greatly helped the book. Any errors that remain are mine alone.

To Aly Parsons, Jeri Smith-Ready, and Trisha Schwaab for their thorough readings; and to Aly's Writing Group for critiquing scenes: Aly Parsons, Simcha Kuritzky, Connie Warner, Al Carroll, Michael La Violette, and J. G. Huckenpöler. A special thanks to my editor, Jim Minz, for his insight and suggestions; to my publisher, Tom Doherty; production manager, Fiorella de Lima; art director, Irene Gallo; publicist, Jodi Roscheff; copy editor, Nancy Wiesenfeld; Natasha Panza; and to all the other fine people at Tor and St. Martin's Press who did such a fine job making this book possible; to my excellent agent, Eleanor Wood, of Spectrum Literary Agency; and to Binnie Braustein, for her enthusiasm and hard work on my behalf.

A most heartfelt thanks to the shining lights of my life, my husband, John Kendall Cannizzo, and my daughter, Cathy, whose constant love and support make it all worthwhile.

# PART ONE:
# Lyshriol

# 1

# Roca

Her son was going to start a war.

Roca paced in the starport lobby, trying to ignore the hail that battered the glass wall to her left. Outside, a storm raged in the night. She felt like raging herself. She had eluded her bodyguards and escaped their trap, only to be caught on this backwater world by something as absurd as the weather. Most ports could easily operate under such conditions, but this one gave new meaning to the word "dilapidated." All ships were grounded until the storm cleared. If she could have used normal travel lines, she wouldn't have had to come through here, but the same modernization that made most ports so convenient also made it that much easier for Kurj's guards to catch her.

Kurj.

Her son.

Roca stopped at the window and pressed her palms against the glass as she stared into the storm. Its driving force reminded her of Kurj. Strangers often assumed he was her uncle or a much older brother, but in fact he was her firstborn son, her sole child. Although he was only thirty-five, he had already become a modern-day warlord, commander of the J-Force in the military. He had earned his rank by being the smartest, hardest, most versatile pilot in the J-Force. Roca had no doubt he did his job well, but neither the ambition nor the aggression that drove him were moderated by the wisdom of age.

Restless, she paced to a waist-high column with a holo above it that listed departures. No ships were leaving, not even freighters. The reports scrolling below the display predicted the storm would last for days. She couldn't believe that, in this progressive age, such an ancient problem could stop a port from sending out vessels.

Thunder cracked and a burst of rain pounded the window-wall behind her, as if to mock her thoughts. Frustrated, she crossed her arms. She had to get off this world. Soon. If her layover lasted much longer, she would miss the upcoming session of the Assembly. Her presence there shouldn't have mattered; Kurj had her proxy to cast her votes.

But it did matter.

In this session, the Assembly would vote on whether or not to invade the Platinum Sectors. Roca's people claimed that region in space, which abounded with ore-rich asteroids, but the Eubian Traders had taken control of it and refused to negotiate.

Roca wished now she had stayed on Parthonia, the world where the Assembly met. But it hadn't been unusual when she received an invitation to the inauguration of a premier on the world Irendela. As Foreign Affairs Councilor, she often represented the Assembly at such events. This wasn't the first time she had asked Kurj to cast her votes; he attended almost every session, more than her parents even, and though she and Kurj didn't agree on some issues, she had always trusted him. He was, after all, her son.

She wasn't certain what had made her suspect Kurj arranged the invitation so she would miss the upcoming Assembly session. She had no reason to believe he could have foreseen that the Irendela premier would request Roca stay longer to help mediate a political dispute. Whatever spurred her intuition, she had delved deeper into the tangle of links between Irendela and Parthonia. Her son had left no hard evidence, but she recognized his methods; he had deliberately manipulated events on Irendela to delay her return. He wanted her to miss the Assembly session because he intended to cast her votes *for* instead of against the invasion. To cast them herself, she had to appear in person; Kurj could block any web signal she used. And with the ballot so close, her votes could be the deciding factor.

Now, after all her work to escape Irendela, she was stuck. How could it be that she lived in one of the greatest interstellar civilizations ever known and she couldn't find a single ship out of here? If she didn't reach the Assembly in time, her son would start a war their people could never win.

Lost in thought, Roca just barely noticed the man headed toward her, his gaze downcast, his manner preoccupied. In the same instant she dodged out of his path, he looked up, saw her, and jumped to the side. They ran smack into each other.

Roca stumbled back, her face heating. "My apologies."

The man stared at her, a flush spreading across his face. "I'm terribly sorry."

She managed to smile. "Please don't be."

He cleared his throat. "I'm always clumsy around gorgeous women." Then he winced at his own words.

Roca shifted her weight. "Thank you." She knew she sounded chilly, but she had never been good at moderating her tone when she felt ill-at-ease. Alone here, with no bodyguards, she had lost the sense of emotional insulation she usually experienced.

However, she was also an empath. The fellow's mood was so strong, it came through the mental barriers she raised to protect her thoughts and respect the privacy of others. He felt mortified by his statement, convinced he sounded like an idiot.

"It's all right," she added, trying for more warmth.

He hesitated. "You look familiar. Do you act in holovids?"

Roca answered quickly. "I used to be a dancer." She hoped he hadn't realized her actual identity. Although it wasn't a secret, she preferred it kept quiet. Now, on her own, she particularly didn't want to be recognized. But perhaps her assumed identity as a performer would sidetrack him.

"The Parthonia Royal Ballet!" He snapped his fingers. "Of course. I saw you in *Harvest of Light*. You're Celina Lesson."

It took her a moment to recognize his pronunciation of her pseudonym, Cya Liessa. Then relief flowed over her. "Yes, I did *Harvest of Light* a few years ago."

"Excellent." He peered at her. "Do you know, I've never seen anything like that metallic gold color of your hair and eyes. In the performance, I thought it was makeup. But it's real."

Roca flushed. "Yes. It is real."

"Amazing!" He beamed at her. "I'm glad to have met you."

"You are kind, sir." She tried not to sound stiff.

After they parted, Roca breathed more easily. It felt odd to speak with a stranger; her bodyguards usually formed a bulwark separating her from the rest of humanity. Nor did she perform much now. She had to conserve her energy. She still had her youth; top-of-the-line nanomeds in her body delayed her aging, making her look twenty, though she was in her fifties. But the constraints on her life imposed by her duties as an Assembly Councilor left little time or energy for other pursuits.

She wasn't going to be performing any duties, political or otherwise, if she didn't reach Parthonia in time. More determined than ever, she went to a row of consoles against one wall. She took her ID chip out of a pocket in her jumpsuit and slid the small disk into a console. The holo of a pleasant-looking woman appeared above a horizontal screen, though the grainy quality of the image washed out details.

"Good evening," the fuzzy holo said. "What can I do for you?"

Roca squinted at it. "I need a flight out of this starport. As soon as possible. Now, in fact."

"I am sorry, Gentlewoman Liessa." The holo simulated regret. "No ships can leave the port."

"Surely you can manage something."

"I am sorry. No ships can leave the port."

"I would like to speak to a person."

"I will forward your request."

Roca knew what that meant; they would file and forget it. Right now, the port authorities probably had hundreds of such requests, as stranded travelers scrambled to make arrangements.

"Run code I4DE," she told the holo. It would find 14DE on her ID chip. Nice code, that. It could crack open the port security and erase the record of her inquiries.

As the holo vanished, a neutral voice said, "Cleanup done."

Roca retrieved her chip, then glanced around to make sure no one could overhear. Seeing she was alone, she turned back to the console and inserted a new ID chip. The holo reappeared—and bowed. "My honor at your presence, Your Highness."

"My greetings," Roca said. "I would like to meet with the person who schedules outgoing ships."

"One moment, please." After a great deal more than one moment, the holo said, "Director Vammond can see you. His assistant will meet you in the lobby. Look for a tallbot."

"Thank you."

"You are welcome, Your Highness. Can we do anything else for you?"

"No, that's all." Relieved, Roca erased her interaction with the system and pocketed her chip.

A humanoid robot was approaching from across the lobby, its body scuffed and dented. When it reached her, it bowed. "Please come with me." Its voice had no inflection.

They headed into a nearby corridor, the tallbot walking slowly at her side, its joints creaking. Roca sincerely hoped the ships in Director Vammond's port were in better condition than his assistants.


Vammond greeted Roca in an office barely big enough for the two of them. Consoles and shelves crammed it. He was standing behind a table covered with light-pens, palmtops, thread-cable, and machine parts. Gray streaked his brown hair, and he carried far more weight around his middle than would someone who could afford the treatments that kept people thin regardless of what they ate.

He bowed to Roca as the tallbot held the door open for her. "You honor my humble port with your presence, Lady."

"Thank you, Director Vammond." Roca heard the coolness in her voice. It wasn't what she intended, but she felt too tense to add more warmth.

He waved ruefully at the clutter. "I would offer you a chair, but I'm afraid I have no place to put one."

"Please don't worry." She waited until the tallbot closed the door, leaving her and Vammond in private. "Director, I would rather my identity remain confidential."

"Certainly." He hesitated. "I wouldn't have expected you to be traveling alone."

Roca felt the tickling in her throat that came when she was afraid. She *shouldn't* be traveling alone. She tried to project a lack of concern. "It isn't unusual, given how closely my staff monitors my itinerary." In fact, no one had any idea where she had gone. It was the only way to prevent Kurj from tracking her. His intelligence network spread across the Skolian Imperialate. She dreaded what he would do when he found out she had escaped his guards, but she was damned if he was going to manipulate her into letting him start a war.

Vammond didn't press the matter. He beckoned her to his console, moving aside so she could read the screen. "I think we can do something for you."


Roca ran to the freighter through torrential rain. The ship was in a remote location with no covered walkways or robot sleeves to take her to its hatch. Rusted equipment had blocked the magcar that brought her here. She didn't care. It mattered only that she had a way off this planet.

The freighter had no stairs for boarding. She hurried up a pitted ramp, but it ended a meter below the hatchway. Someone reached out of the hatch. Unable to see clearly in the rain, Roca grabbed the offered hand, and its owner hauled her into the ship. She stumbled forward, rain cascading off her jumpsuit. She didn't even have a jacket. Her hair had tumbled out of its roll and fell in heavy, soaking lengths to below her hips, plastered against her body.

"You're getting my deck wet," an irritated voice said.

Wiping rain out of her eyes, Roca peered at the person who had pulled her up, the captain apparently, since this freighter had no other crew or passengers. From the voice, she had expected a man, but it was a woman—a brawny, weathered, annoyed woman. Half a head larger than Roca, she stood over six feet tall. She wore her blond hair in a spiky cut, and her faded coveralls looked even older than her beat-up ship.

Roca pushed back her streaming hair. "My greetings. And my apologies for the mess."

The captain didn't crack a smile. "Right." She grabbed Roca's arm and hauled her into the bridge, though that seemed a generous description. The pilot's and copilot's chairs were crammed in the front, facing screens that had seen better days. Equipment covered the walls, obviously scavenged from other ships and cobbled together.

The captain shoved her toward the copilot's seat. "Strap in. We're leaving."

"Welcome to you, too," Roca muttered.

"Listen, honey." The captain looked her over as if Roca were an overpriced piece of equipment. "I don't know who you are, and I don't care who you fucked to get this favor. I'm taking you for one reason and one reason only; it gets me out of this hellhole. Don't expect special treatment here."

Roca stared at her, water dripping off her body. "I didn't have sex with anyone." She took a breath, reminding herself she needed this person's goodwill to reach the next port. "And I appreciate your willingness to take me."

The captain jerked her hand at the copilot's chair. "We won't be going anywhere if you don't strap in."

Roca bit back her tart response and squeezed into the seat. It took her several embarrassing moments to figure out what to do; this seat had none of the aides or automatic functions she took for granted on her yacht. She had to pull the safety webbing around her body and fasten it herself.

The captain wedged into her own chair and began her preflight checks. She seemed intent on her controls, but she spoke as if she had seen Roca's every move. "Haven't you ever strapped in before?"

Roca flushed. "Of course."

The other woman snorted. "You ready to go?"

"Yes." In truth, Roca didn't want to go anywhere in this ship. It was a wonder it continued to operate. But the captain had been willing to take off even knowing the weather blinded the port's outdated and poorly maintained safety systems. The freighter could take her to Skyfall, a backwater world in the hinterlands of settled space. Two days later, a supply shuttle was scheduled to put in to Skyfall. That ship would take her to Metropoli, one of the most heavily populated worlds of the Imperialate. From there, she could catch a flight to Parthonia, where the Assembly met.

Skyfall. Roca had never heard of it. Neither, it seemed, had anyone else. She and Vammond had been unable to dig up much about the planet except a schedule for the supply shuttle.

Unexpectedly, the captain grinned. It made her look like a predator. "We're off."

Roca managed a smile. "Great."

As the launch sequence started, Roca waited for the tower to give them clearance. When it remained silent, she tensed. From what she understood, the captain barely had time to make this side trip to Skyfall and still rendezvous with the buyers for her cargo. Any delays, and she might cancel the trip to Skyfall. Roca was desperate enough to buy the cargo herself or commandeer this craft, but that meant she would either have to access her personal funds or else convince the captain she had authority to take the ship. Either would require revealing too much about herself, a risky proposition that left her open to trouble, including kidnapping and assassination.

Roca could see the captain preparing to lift off. Hopeful, she said, "Has the tower cleared us?"

The other woman continued to concentrate on her controls. "What, are you a copilot now?"

"It's important we leave on time."

The captain glanced at her. "I'm not your servant, girl."

Roca stiffened. "It isn't necessary to be insulting."

The captain's voice fell into an exaggerated parody of Roca's Iotic accent. "Oh, well, do please hurry. I must be waited on and catered to."

Roca stared at her. "Why are you so angry?"

"We're leaving." The captain pulled on the stick. "Now shut up and let me do my job." The engines roared and—and the ship leapt off the tarmac into the pounding storm.

Roca had traveled all her life, but she had never experienced such a takeoff. G-forces slammed her into the seat, which had minimal cushioning and no smart-sensors to protect her body. She could barely breathe. The pressure seemed to go on forever, until spots danced in her vision and she wondered if she would suffocate.

The pressure stopped as abruptly as it had begun. Grateful, Roca gulped in air.

"You all right?" the captain asked.

Roca took a shuddering breath. "Yes. I am fine."

"Gods almighty." The captain made an incredulous noise. "You sound arrogant even when you're gasping."

"I don't understand why you are angry."

The captain remained intent on her controls. After a long silence, Roca tried again. "Did the port clear us for takeoff?"

The captain was reading a holoscreen above her head. "No."

Roca clenched the arms of her seat. "It's illegal to take off without clearance."

"Well, isn't that a shame."

The last thing Roca needed was to end up in legal custody. "You can't just break the law."

The captain jerked around to her. "Listen, rich girl. You wanted out of that port. We left even though they couldn't ensure our safety. That's breaking the law, honey. You think they're going to give us clearance and implicate themselves?"

"Oh." That made sense. "I see."

"Good for you. Now shut up."

Roca scowled. "Just think, if I hadn't put you to such inconvenience, you could have stayed in that lovely port, no doubt for days."

To her surprise, the captain laughed. "Got some spunk in you, eh?"

Roca was too annoyed to answer.

They fell quiet after that, the other woman intent on her controls. For all its decrepitude, the ship worked amazingly well. Roca had to admit the captain knew what she was doing.

"You've a good ship," Roca finally said.

"She goes." The captain sat back in her seat. "Probably nothing like what you're used to."

"It isn't polish that makes a ship valuable." Roca thought of her son's Jag starfighter, what many had called the fastest, deadliest, most aggressive craft in the J-Force. "It's the character it develops after years with the same pilot."

The captain considered her. "I wouldn't have expected that from you."

"Why?"

She shrugged. "You don't seem the type to notice old drums like this."

An alarm blared, warning of a malfunction. The captain immediately turned her attention to jury-rigging a repair. Sitting back, Roca silently urged fate to let her survive this trip. She was uneasy enough to lower her mental barriers and let the captain's mood wash over her. Normally Roca recoiled from opening her mind so much; it exposed her to mental injury and trespassed on the privacy of others. As much as she disliked it now, too much depended on the success of this mission for her to take chances in her judgment of the captain's intentions.

Her companion wasn't a psion of any strength, so it was hard to pick up much, but a sense of her thoughts came through. She resented Roca but would honor her word. She believed the cover that Director Vammond had created to protect Roca's identity. Roca flushed, already knowing the story; Vammond had described her as a runaway wife who had tired of her aging but wealthy husband and wanted to see her lover. It was a dismal tale, but if it helped her reach the Assembly in time, she could live with it.

Roca thought of her first husband, Tokaba Ryestar, an explorer who had scouted new worlds. Her parents had arranged the marriage in her youth. Roca resisted it at first, but she and Tokaba had soon discovered they suited each other. Kurj's birth overjoyed them. For the next six years they had lived a contented life.

Then tragedy hit, when Tokaba's ship crashed on a world he was exploring. Roca had never forgotten the devastating night they brought his body home. Nor had Kurj; at the age of six, a bewildered, heartbroken child had lost his beloved father to a violent death the boy couldn't understand.

It had taken a long time to recover, but eventually, several years later, Roca had remarried, this time choosing for herself. Darr Hammerjackson had been handsome and charming, everything a lonely widow could want. Roca swore to love him forever, certain she and Kurj had found an end to the loneliness.

The first time Darr had hit her, she hadn't believed he meant it. She learned the hard way how wrong she had been. Roca flinched at the memory, the flash of his hand, his incomprehensible fury. The impact of his rage on her mind had been even more debilitating than the blows. But Ruby Dynasty heirs didn't divorce. No public disgraces were allowed; they kept their private hells out of sight. In private, she had done everything she could to stop the violence, and when nothing worked, she had tried for over a year to accommodate the nightmare.

Then he had beaten Kurj.

That night, Roca had taken her nine-year-old son and left Darr. Nothing swayed her: no excuses, no promises, no threats. No one—*no one*—hit her son. She began legal proceedings the next day. In the years after, as she had recovered her sense of self-worth, she came to realize she should have protected herself with the same ferocity she protected her child, regardless of what five millennia of tradition dictated about the behavior of Ruby heirs.

Kurj had never revealed what Darr said to him that day, when the two of them fought. But it had changed her son. And that was only the beginning. As a Jag pilot, he had lived far too many horrors in the constant, undeclared shadow war between the Skolian Imperialate and the Eubian Traders. Over the years it had turned him into a hardened stranger. Now he was a phenomenon, the towering warrior prince respected by his officers, admired by women, and feared by many. But beneath his square-jawed, golden exterior, his rage festered, threatening to explode. In that, he had become like Darr, with an outward self-possession that hid his seething anger.

Roca exhaled. Dwelling on the past would help nothing. This looming threat of all-out war was insanity. Kurj was wrong if he believed they could win. He knew what they risked—and he welcomed that specter. If her son couldn't defeat his inner demons, he would expend his fury leading two empires into a star-spanning conflict that would tear them apart.

# 2

# The Dalvador Bard

---

Roca slept, ate, and spent her waking hours in the copilot's seat. There was nowhere else to go except for the minuscule head. She had little room to exercise, only enough to flex and stretch her cramped muscles.

Neither she nor the captain talked much. The woman grunted when Roca asked her name. It didn't surprise Roca; the less all of them involved with this illegal takeoff knew about one another, the less likely anyone could implicate anyone else.

Eventually Roca said, "Director Vammond said you were the only pilot willing to take off during the storm. I thank you for your courage."

"My courage?" The captain laughed. "Where'd you learn to talk like that?"

"Like what?"

She copied Roca's accent. "So disdainfully sophisticated." In her normal voice, she added, "Maybe sophisticated is the wrong word. You don't sound like the rich twitches on Capsize."

Roca stiffened. "I don't know Capsize."

"That port." The captain gave an irreverent grin. "You'd have to capsize before you'd be willing to put in there."

"It does seem antiquated."

"Antiquated. Gods. You talk like a dictionary."

Roca's voice cooled. "Do you always ridicule your passengers?"

"Aren't we touchy?" The other woman shook her head. "You have it all: wealth, privilege, status, family. But it's not enough, is it? No, you need a lover on the side. It sickens me." She slanted Roca a look. "How much did that body cost you?"

"I beg your pardon?"

"Oh, come on. No normal person has tits that big or a waist that small."

Roca didn't know whether to be shocked or awed. No one ever talked to her this way. It was a singularly unique, albeit equally unpleasant, experience. "It cost me nothing."

"Right. You just exercise a lot."

That was, in fact, what she did, even now when she rarely performed. But for all that she bridled at the implication, she knew what the captain meant. Many entertainers bodysculpted themselves. Although she had never changed her face or figure, she had undergone operations to improve her skeleton for ballet. One procedure altered the way her leg bones fit her hip sockets, giving her what dancers called perfect turnout. Doctors had redesigned the arches of her feet and removed a bone spur on her elbow. A computer node in her spine controlled augmentations to her skeleton and muscles, making it easier for her to adapt to variations in gravity, so she could dance on different worlds or habitats. As for her mammary glands, the only operation she had ever contemplated in that department was making them smaller, so she would be less top-heavy in a leotard.

She said only, "Think what you want."

The captain leaned back and crossed her arms. "Don't you ever wonder how it would be to live like the rest of us, the ninety-nine-point-nine-nine-nine-nine percent of humanity without your advantages?"

"What do you want me to say?" Roca asked. "That I don't deserve my life?"

"No." She shrugged. "I guess it doesn't matter."

"You resent that I've had privileges." Roca thought of her frantic attempts to reach the Assembly. "Some might say they are small compensation for the demands of duty."

The woman's gaze narrowed. "What duties?"

Damn. She had let the captain goad her into saying too much. "I support many charities."

"You know, I don't believe you're a Capsize twitch."

Sweat beaded on Roca's palms. "Why not?"

"You don't talk like them. They sure as hell don't care about duty." She studied Roca. "And you don't flash your flush. Capsize types, they compete to see who can put on a bigger show. Gaudy, cheap, overdone. You're the opposite, so refined, like you don't even breathe the same air as the rest of us. I'll bet you have so much, you don't even know you're rich."

Roca didn't know how to answer. She never thought about her wealth. She certainly had no intention of revealing anything about her private life.

"I'll tell you what else." The captain leaned toward her. "You're a load more arrogant than a Capsize twitch. I don't mean the arrogance people use to hide insecurity, but the kind where you're so sure of yourself you don't even realize it. Capsize types are always compensating, knowing they aren't the real thing. I'll wager you've never compensated in your life."

Roca blinked. "You think I'm arrogant?"

"Oozing it, honey."

Dryly Roca said, "Whereas you are humility personified."

The captain laughed. "Point to you."

"I'm glad I get one."

The captain's smile faded. "You don't need any more."

After that they fell silent. Roca didn't know what else she could say.

Soon they would reach Skyfall.


Sunlight poured over Roca as she and the captain crossed the tarmac of the Skyfall port. Roca felt heavy. The gravity was noticeably stronger than the human norm, and she walked carefully, relearning how to time her steps. The air was rich and fresh, exhilarating in its purity. She breathed deeply, savoring it. No smog. No irritants. No impurities.

Actually, that last wasn't true. Clouds puffed the lavender sky. Blue clouds. They were lovely, but strange. It meant the water here had impurities that made it blue. She hoped they wouldn't make her sick or turn any part of her blue.

The suns were dim enough to glance at. Two suns. Another oddity. The double star system surely destabilized the planet's orbit. The suns were beautiful, though, a rich gold. The big one hung like a great coin in the sky, half eclipsing its smaller, darker companion. Although both seemed darker than the star type considered ideal for human life, their combined output wasn't noticeably dim. Golden light suffused the landscape.

Roca doubted this system had developed naturally. The world had probably been moved here long ago and terraformed for human life. Her distant ancestors, the people of the Ruby Empire, had possessed a remarkable technology, managing feats of astrophysical engineering impossible today. That knowledge had vanished after the fall of the Ruby Empire five millennia ago.

"Pretty," the captain grumbled, as if offended that she had to admit such a thing.

Roca smiled. Skyfall captivated her. They left the tarmac and walked through the safety zone around it, out into the plains. Silver-green reeds as high as her hips rippled in every direction, each topped by an iridescent bubble the width of her thumbnail. Leaning over, she touched a bubble. It floated into the air and popped, showering her with glitter. Roca laughed with delight.

"Careful," the captain growled. "We don't know what this flora can do to a person." She looked around, shading her eyes with her hand. "Where is everyone?"

"Good question." Roca surveyed the port. It consisted of little more than the tarmac and a round, whitewashed house whose turreted roof resembled a bluebell turned upside down. Sparkling bubbles floated in the air along the path she and the captain had taken through the reeds. The only other motion was a small droid on the tarmac refueling the freighter. Although the Capsize port had notified no one of their travel plans, the captain had been in contact with the computers here. Surely *someone* human knew they were coming.

The captain scowled. "This is bizarre. Even an automated port should have someone in charge. A full-sized robot, for flaming sakes."

Roca motioned toward the south. "Look." About a kilometer away, a cluster of white houses with blue or purple roofs showed above the reeds. The towers of a picturesque castle rose up beyond them, topped by spires, with pennants snapping in the wind.

"It's a village," she said.

The captain squinted. "Or the set for some absurd holovid about our 'charming' past, as if it were romantic to have no central heat or garbage removal."

Roca could see what she meant. Idealists nostalgic for an old-fashioned life might have established the village. However, it could also be the real thing, descended from a colony of the Ruby Empire. Many of the lost colonies had survived the five millennia of dark ages that followed the collapse of the empire. Now that Roca's people had re-gained star travel and formed the Imperialate, they were gradually re-discovering the Ruby colonies.

Although Roca recalled no briefings about this world, news of re-discovered colonies usually went through Planetary Development or Domestic Affairs. As the Foreign Affairs Councilor, she dealt with two other interstellar civilizations—the Eubian Concord and the Allied Worlds of Earth—that shared the stars with her people of the Imperialate. However, the line between the Foreign and Domestic offices tended to blur when they were reestablishing relations with an ancient colony.

"It wouldn't take long to reach the village," Roca said.

The captain glanced at her. "You know people there?"

"No, I don't. But I doubt Imperial Space Command would have established a post like this if the natives were hostile." She waved at the pretty house that constituted the port. "This hardly looks like a defense installation."

The captain crossed her brawny arms. "Then why didn't anyone meet us, eh?"

"Maybe no one human received your messages."

The captain glared. "So the natives cooked them all and had a feast."

Roca gave a startled laugh. "I hope not."

"I'd just as soon be leaving."

The reminder that she would soon be on her own disquieted Roca. "You're certain the supply ship sets in here the day after tomorrow?"

"It's supposed to." The captain shrugged. "I fulfilled my part of the agreement. You're here. I can't hover around until your next flight comes."

"What if no ship shows up?"

"Not my problem."

Looking past her, Roca saw the droid was done refueling the freighter. The other automated functions of the port also seemed to have finished their maintenance. Well, she had agreed to this. She could hardly expect the captain to stay. Trying for a cheerful tone, she said, "Gods' speed on your trip. I hope you haggle the blazes out of your buyers."

The captain grinned. "You can be sure of that." Her features softened a micron. "Hope the, uh, marriage thing works out."

"Thank you." Roca thought of Darr all those decades ago, and of her son Kurj, who had suffered several broken bones from the beating Darr gave him. She had never married again. Right now the Assembly was pressuring her to wed a prince from one of the noble lines, the House of Majda. Roca dreaded the union, but its political advantages were too important to ignore.

She said only, "I'm sure it will."

"Well, so." The other woman set off for her freighter, easily pushing her way through the reeds, then walking solidly across the tarmac. At her ship, she looked back and lifted her hand in farewell.

Roca waved. The freighter took off in a blast of flame and exhaust, and soon disappeared in the great expanse of the sky.

The port house was as charming inside as out. It struck Roca as more like a home than anything else, with a living room, rustic bar, and doors to inner rooms. An emerald-green material paneled the room, neither glass nor wood, but something in between. She christened it "glasswood." Real paintings hung on the walls, rather than holoart, scenes of craggy mountains capped with blue snow.

Roca stood in the center of the room, uncertain what to do. She didn't want to trespass, but now that the captain had left, she had nowhere else to go except the village. The supply ship was due the day after tomorrow, but she didn't have a good sense of what "tomorrow" meant here.

She thought about walking to the village, but decided against it for now. She couldn't take chances. Given her questionable departure from Capsize, it was unlikely Vammond had notified the supply ship about her. If Roca wasn't here when it arrived, its pilot would have no reason to wait. Even if he expected her, she doubted he would tarry; other settlements depended on him to deliver their supplies in a timely manner.

Restless, she wandered about the room. She had just decided to go outside again when the front door opened, the old-fashioned way, swinging on hinges rather than shimmering away in a molecular airlock. A man stood framed in the doorway. He was about her height, husky, with curly black hair, dark skin, and brown eyes. Oil stained his wrinkled coverall. He froze in the process of taking off a heavy glove, staring at her in open astonishment.

"My greetings," Roca said, self-conscious. "I hope you don't mind my coming in. I couldn't find anyone when the ship landed."

The man continued to stare at her.

"The freighter," Roca added. "I'm afraid I don't know its name." She heard how strange that sounded.

The fellow blinked, then finished pulling off his glove. His mood leaked through to Roca despite her mental shields: surprise, puzzlement, uncertainty, and pleasure at having company. The friendly quality of his mind appealed to her.

"Goodsir?" Roca asked. "Is everything all right?"

"I'm sorry." He answered in an unexpected language. "I can't understand you. Do you speak English?"

It took her a moment to reorient. He was using a language from Earth, of all places. She had assumed her people settled this planet; it never occurred to her that the Allied Worlds of Earth might have found it first. The supply ship was Skolian, but it wasn't unusual for ships of both civilizations to service isolated settlements off the main travel routes. Although Skolians rarely spoke English, Roca had some familiarity with it, given her position as Foreign Affairs Councilor. It was among the languages she had chosen for the node in her spine.

"My English not so good," she said, "but I do some." As she heard more of it, her node would update her speaking ability. Having such an aid helped her learn languages fast, an invaluable asset to her job.

The man smiled, an expression of warmth and good nature. He spoke slowly, making it easier for her to follow. "I had no idea the supply ship was due in today. I thought it was two more days."

"It is." Roca smoothed her hands on her jumpsuit. "I am passenger on it, I hope."

"Ah." He closed the door and came over to her. "My name is Brad Tompkins." Extending his ungloved hand, he added, "Welcome to Dalvador Port."

Roca hesitated, trying to remember the custom his people had with hands. Her node came up with the answer; he was offering her a greeting in a manner that showed respect between two parties. She took his hand and moved his arm up and down. Apparently the gesture had the desired effect; by the time they released their grip, his tension had eased.

If she interpreted his responses correctly, the appropriate behavior now would be to give her name. She picked the names of two friends, a wife and husband she very much admired. "I am Jeri Christian."

"Hello, Jeri." He motioned awkwardly at his coverall. "My apologies for my clothes. I've been working on the flyer. It came down outside of Dalvador yesterday. Bad circuit, I think." He pulled off his other glove. "Or maybe I need to replace the conductor plugs."

His English had an accent compared to the "British English" Roca had learned, but the words were similar enough that she could follow most of what he said. Her node identified his dialect as "Californian," which wasn't a country on Earth she recognized.

"The port has damaged aircraft?" she asked.

"That's right. I'm hoping I won't need to order supplies." His expression warmed. "Would you care for a drink—water, juice, anything?"

After two days with the brusque captain, Roca found Brad's friendly nature like an oasis. "Water, thank you."

"Coming right up." He went to the bar, his relief so strong she picked it up despite her mental barriers. She unsettled him. He was glad to have something to occupy him, lest he pull apart his gloves with nervous twists.

He took out two glasses from under the bar. "The water is treated."

"Treated?" she asked.

He poured clear, sparkling water from a pitcher into the glasses. "Did you see the clouds outside?"

"They are blue."

Brad turned, holding their drinks. "As is all water here. It has a chemical in it, sort of like food dye. The natives have nanomeds in their bodies that break it down." He came over and offered her a drink. "It probably wouldn't hurt you to drink a little of the untreated stuff, but it might make you sick. This is treated."

Roca took a sip. It tasted wonderful, as if it came from a spring high in the mountains. "Is good."

He gave her a lopsided smile. "If you will excuse me, I'll go change."

"Please, yes, be comfortable."

Brad crossed the room and left through a glasswood door that glowed with a deep blue luster. When Roca was alone, she let her mind relax, giving it a chance to recover. She wasn't used to one-on-one interactions with strangers. For her entire life, she had been distanced from everyone except her family, as if she were in a crystal sphere.

In many ways, being an empath intensified the effect. She needed the distance. If her mental defenses became too strong, though, they muffled her mind and slowed her thoughts until she felt only partially alive. She couldn't shut out every emotion from every person; to stay human, she had to let herself be vulnerable to their minds. She noticed it most as a dancer, when spectators watched her perform. Scientists who studied psions claimed strong empaths picked up moods, magnified them, and projected them back to their audience. Roca never analyzed it; she knew only that when she felt a performance in her heart, she somehow linked more with her audience.

Yet even on stage she felt set apart, separated, performing, unspeaking and unreal, a fantasy to watch but never touch. In a way, her work as Foreign Affairs Councilor was another performance. She interacted with many governments, but her high status distanced her from people, a separation heightened by the formal protocols required by her duties. Intermediaries introduced her to her counterparts in other administrations and took care of any functions that involved less formal contact among their staffs.

Her title as a member of the Ruby Dynasty also created distance. The Ruby Dynasty and noble Houses were ancient. In these modern times of elected governments, only her family and the House of Majda wielded significant power, though the other Houses still existed, much as royal families continued on Earth. She had won her position as Foreign Affairs Councilor by election, but her Ruby title seemed to enthrall the public far more, until she felt as if her life had become more fantasy to them than reality, making the crystal sphere around her even thicker.

Here, with anonymity, she felt no distance. It unsettled and exhilarated her. The loss of that separation made her aware of how much it buffered her mind, but she also felt more connected to the people around her. Given her stumbling English, Brad probably couldn't tell she had the Iotic accent of royalty. Even the captain, who had recognized that her accent came from another social class, hadn't guessed enough of the truth to feel inhibited from speaking plainly. As aggravating as it had been, it had also refreshed Roca, like cold, bracing air. She reveled in this freedom she had never before known.

The door across the room opened, startling Roca out of her reverie. Brad walked in, smiling more naturally now, wearing blue trousers and a gray sweater that accented the width of his shoulders. With his dark hair and eyes, he resembled a nobleman in the House of Majda, except that they had straight hair and patrician noses. He had one other striking difference from a Majda lord—his friendly, open personality. The Majda held themselves so aloof that at times Roca wondered if they considered *anyone* else worth their time. It was one reason she dreaded marriage to Prince Dayj Majda, her intended.

Brad beamed at her. "I must say, you're a welcome sight."

"Thank you." She tried to soften her formality.

"I hope you enjoy your stay with us." He lifted his hand, inviting her toward the sofa. "If you'd like, I can take you on a tour later. We could visit the village."

"Yes. I like that." She settled on one end of the couch. "I wonder— how long is village here?"

He sat on the other end, leaning back, relaxing as if he had known her all his life. "We aren't certain. Six or seven centuries, maybe. It's called Dalvador, and this area is the Dalvador Plains. The name goes back thousands of years."

Roca wondered if he realized the significance of his words. A human settlement that old had to descend from the Ruby Empire, which meant her people would challenge any claim the Allieds made here. Did Brad know the history? Six millennia ago an unknown race of beings had come to Earth and taken away a small population of humans, moving them to the world Raylicon. Then the kidnappers vanished. Over the next millennia, the bewildered humans had developed star flight and gone in search of their lost home. Although they never found Earth, they established the Ruby Empire.

Unfortunately, the empire had soon fallen. It wasn't until a few centuries ago that the Raylican people had regained star travel. As they spread out across space again, they split into two factions, the Skolian Imperialate and the Eubian Concord. When Earth's children finally reached the stars, they found their siblings already here, busily building their two empires. Earth formed a third civilization, the Allied Worlds. As far as Roca knew, this was the first time the Allieds had claimed an ancient Ruby colony.

"This world," she asked. "Hold it many people?"

"Not a lot. We estimate two hundred thousand, all on this continent." Brad rubbed his chin. "The Dalvador Plains have relatively small villages, but if you cross the mountains to the Rillian Vales, you'll find larger towns. The Blue Dales are high in the northern mountains. Nomadic archers live there."

The names sounded like music to Roca. "Make you contacts with people?" Belatedly, her node suggested, *Do you have many contacts with the people here?*

"Some." His mood dimmed. "A resort company on Earth plans to develop the area, put up hotels, spas, that sort of thing."

It sounded like a good way to ruin a beautiful land. "People in village—know they you?" She meant to ask if the villagers knew about the resort, but it didn't sound right. After a second, her node suggested, *Do they know about this?*

"Most of them know me." Brad grinned, creasing the laugh lines around his eyes. "I enjoy their visits to the port. I'm the entire staff, so it's great to have neighbors."

Roca could see why they sought his company. "They are like you?" No, that wasn't right. She wanted to ask if they were generally friendly toward offworlders.

"Actually, they aren't much like us." His mobile face became thoughtful. "Their culture has backslid a lot. They have virtually no health sciences and know nothing about electricity. They no longer even have a written language."

None of it surprised Roca, except perhaps the lack of written language. This wouldn't be the first Ruby settlement to lose its technology during its millennia of isolation. She spoke carefully. "This world is old Ruby colony."

"Don't the Ruby settlers descend from your ancestors?"

She nodded, relieved he understood. "Yes. They are part of us. Family, you see. Such worlds we think as Skolian."

Brad gave her a rueful look. "I don't really know the politics. I just run the port."

"Is pretty world. I see why your businesspeople are wishing to develop it." She thought of the pristine countryside. "Is sad, though, if they hurt this land."

His face flashed with anger. "Yes! The company honchos just care about money. The people here don't understand. They think we come from some province over the mountains. The resort planners are going to rob them of their lands, lives, and world, and they don't have a clue."

"Can someone help?" She tilted her head. "Someone like you, who has caring for their world?"

"Lord knows, I wish I could. But if I hinder the developers, it conflicts with my job." He pushed his hand across his tightly curled hair. "I might be able to help a bit, though, if I'm careful."

"I wish luck to you." A distant rumble tugged at her awareness. She tilted her head. "Hear you noise?"

"What do you mean?"

The rumble deepened. "It come here."

Brad sat up straighter, his forehead furrowing. "I don't—" Suddenly he laughed, an open, hearty sound. "Hah! They must have seen your ship land. They probably think it was the supply ship."

"The villagers?"

"You got it."

Roca blinked. Got it? Her node had trouble with that one. Nor was she sure why villagers would come to the ship. Surely it didn't provision the native population. Even if people here had somehow acquired the credit to buy offworld goods, selling to natives was of questionable legality. Under Skolian law, it would tangle Brad in a morass of complications. She knew less about Allied laws, though.

"They come for supplies?" she asked.

"Some." Concern showed on his ever-changing face. "Medicine mostly." Then he paused. Even if she hadn't been an empath, she would have known he realized he had said too much. Awkwardly, he added, "And I, uh, can't provide them with medicines, of course."

Her voice cooled. "Of course." Well, it wasn't her affair. This was an Allied port, none of her business. "If not for medicine, why they come?"

His tension eased. "Chocolate."

"Chocolate?"

He chuckled. "A drink."

"Ah." Roca had never heard of the substance.

"Their Bard likes it. So I treat him to it."

"Bard?" The similarity to his name gave her pause. "A singer?"

"That's right. The Dalvador Bard." His smile morphed into a scowl. "The resort marketers call him the King of Skyfall because he lives in that castle in the village. They claim it adds 'romance' to the setting. But to name him a king, especially of an entire world, is absurd."

Remembering the idyllic castle, she could see why the planners had jumbled their cultural cues. "But he sings?" She wondered if he and Brad ever mixed up their names.

"He keeps the history of his people in ballads. I guess you could call him a singing archivist. His voice is incredible." Pleasure suffused Brad's mood. "With formal training, I'll bet he could walk into a job at any major opera company."

That piqued Roca's interest. "I regret I no hear him sing."

"You might." Brad had to raise his voice to be heard above the rumbling now. "He sometimes comes with Garlin to pick up the supplies." He paused. "The, uh, chocolate."

"Chocolate." Her tone cooled. This had nothing to do with her, but it troubled her to think that he so flagrantly broke the law. For all Brad knew, medicines that helped his people could kill the natives here.

As the rumbling surrounded the house, Brad stood up. His smile had vanished. "You disapprove."

She also rose to her feet. Her voice came out like ice. "Why I disapprove of chocolate?"

"Tell me something." He regarded her steadily. "Have you ever had to watch someone you care about die because you didn't have enough medical care to save them?"

"And if someone die from wrong care?" She met his gaze. "Or because expected supplies never come?"

He frowned. "I would never take resources meant for someone else. Nor would I dispense medicine without precautions."

"You are doctor?"

"I have some knowledge."

"Is not same."

"Tell that to the mother whose baby dies in her arms." His fist clenched at his side. "Tell the screaming farmer who has neither antibiotics to stop the infection in his injured leg nor anesthetics to knock him out while the town blacksmith saws it off."

Roca flinched. No mental shield, no matter how strong, could block his fierce emotions. He had witnessed the scenes he described. She spoke quietly. "I am sorry."

Brad loosened his fists. "I shouldn't have unloaded that on you." He tried to smile, but it barely qualified. "I really do give them chocolate. They will be disappointed to find I've none today." He started toward the door. "Come on. Meet the locals."

His regret flowed over Roca. As she went with him, the thunder outside grew even louder. Her pulse leapt. The walls were vibrating. She hung back as Brad opened the front door and stood framed in the entrance, his hands on his hips.

Outside, a blur of color sped past. Many boisterous people appeared to be riding large animals around the house. Brad started to *laugh,* for flaming sakes, as if the tumult were all a great show. He didn't seem the least concerned.

The riders congregated in front of the door, their mounts stamping and snorting. The animals looked like horses that had been bioengineered into a new species, an extraordinarily graceful one. Two clear, crystalline horns on their heads refracted the sunlight like prisms, sending sparks of color everywhere. They had hooves made from the same substance, and their coats shimmered, either blue or lavender. The lovely creatures were much more refined than she had expected given all the noise they made.

She had more trouble seeing their riders, so she moved closer, standing right behind Brad. The men wore simple clothes, white shirts and rough trousers dyed dark colors, either blue or purple. Embroidery bordered their collars and cuffs. All had on knee-boots. Their hair, neck length or longer, stirred in the breezes.

"Ho!" A young man in the front called to Brad. "You lost your chess match to Garlin! You owe us much chocolate."

Brad gave him a cocky grin. "I will win a match with you, Bard."

The man smirked. "I play not, man with the name of Bard misspelled in his own language."

Brad laughed. "So you've finally learned to spell my name."

The other fellow turned smug. "I am clever, eh?"

An older man was sitting on an animal next to the Bard. He spoke dryly. "And humble."

"Hello, Garlin." Brad waved at the older man. "You're the one who told him about the spelling, aren't you?"

The Bard glared at Garlin. "Don't tell him."

Garlin cocked an eyebrow at Brad. "It seems I have nothing to say."

"Ah, well," the Bard said. "Maybe Garlin did tell me. I've no time for spelling." He grinned again, unabashed and unrestrained, his face alive with pleasure. Roca *felt* his joy. His mind poured over hers, incredible, like a waterfall. Even with her family, who were all psions, she never picked up their moods this well.

Roca moved closer, trying to see this Bard more clearly. His odd coloring startled her. He had thick hair the hue of burgundy wine, but streaked gold from sunlight. His violet eyes were large and round. She couldn't be certain, but she thought freckles sprinkled across his nose. Although she supposed he had a handsome face, he wasn't her type. She preferred tall, dark, somber men. It was hard to resist his light and laughter, though. He mesmerized, drawing her nearer.

His mind glowed.

Why Roca dropped her mental shields, she didn't know. She had never experienced anything like his mind. It flowed into her with the power of an ocean and the gentleness of a breeze, like warmth and spring all mixed together.

The young man suddenly went still. Then he tilted his head, his forehead furrowed as if he were listening to a distant voice. Turning to Garlin, he spoke in a language Roca didn't recognize, persisting when Garlin shook his head. She loved the musical quality of his voice. Deep and resonant, it *chimed*. She could easily believe what Brad had told her, that this man was an extraordinary singer. The waterfall of his mind poured over her, sparkling, bracing, invigorating. Entrancing.

Suddenly the youth yelled, jarring Roca out of her trance. Dismayed, she realized she had walked out of the house. The riders jolted into motion again, spurred by his shout, rearing their animals as they added their own yells to the din. In her sensitized state, she reeled under the onslaught of noise and emotions. She stumbled back, confused, but she went off somehow and missed the doorway, backing into the wall instead.

"Jeri!" Brad's shout came through the din. "Over here!"

Roca saw him in the doorway a few meters away. She edged toward him, but too many riders were in the way. She had no idea what they were trying to do. One animal reared much too close to her, its translucent hooves pawing the air. She gasped, putting her hands above her head. The animal came down, slamming the ground with its hooves, and she glimpsed the Bard astride its back, his face wild. Holding up her arm to protect her face, she pressed back against the wall.

The Bard leaned down, hanging off his animal, and grabbed her arm. Someone else yelled and another animal reared so close that Roca felt its motion like a wind.

"*No!*" Roca fought to pull away from the Bard. She stumbled against the animal and its hair scraped her face, far less soft than it looked, its musky scent filling her senses. She lost her balance when the animal stamped its feet, but before she could fall beneath its hooves, the Bard dragged her up its side. With a great heave, he hefted her up so she was sitting on the animal in front of him.

"Stop it!" Roca yelled. As she struggled, she started to slide off, unable to adapt fast enough to the unfamiliar gravity. Even knowing how far it was to the ground, with so many other animals pounding the reeds around them, she kept fighting. *No one* touched her this way.

The Bard caught her before she fell, but as he grabbed her waist, his agitated mount reared again. Roca froze as their height above the ground more than doubled. The animal trumpeted its call to the sky, and another animal answered, then another. As the Bard's mount came down, he gave a shout of triumph. Leaning forward with his arms around Roca, he spurred the animal into a run.

With that, the entire party took off, thundering across the plains—taking Roca with them.

# 3

# The Broken Path

---

The plains went by in a blur. Roca jabbed her elbow into the ribs of the man behind her. When he grunted, she kicked her heel into his leg, then raked her fingernails up his arm. She didn't need to understand his vehement words to know he was cursing.

"Ai! Stop!" He finally spoke in English, shouting above the drumming hooves of the animals. "Don't do that." His mount had a remarkably smooth gait, much more so than a horse, enough to let him speak despite their fast pace.

"Take me to port!" She whacked his leg *hard.*

"Ow! Stop!"

"Back to port!"

"We cannot." He leaned closer so he could speak near her ear instead of shouting. "Garlin says I must learn to understand you port people better. I didn't want to, but I changed my mind. You must teach me about your people."

"Pah. You are rude boy. I make no diplomacy for you."

His hold shifted into an embrace. "But you have such wonderful passion."

She pushed off his arms as if they were a plague, making him lose his grasp on the reins. "Not for you."

"Hey!" He flailed for the reins. "I need those."

"I rather fall."

As he struggled to regain control of his animal, an unexpected sight startled her. His hands. He had no thumbs. His four fingers were about the same length, longer than hers and unusually thick. A hinge ran down his hand, starting between the second and third fingers and going all the way to his wrist. To hold the reins, he hinged his hand, folding his palm so his first and second fingers opposed the fourth and third, respectively. It worked with such efficiency, she thought the structure must have been engineered.

Roca peered at the other riders. Those she could see well had hands like the Bard. They all had violet eyes, too, and gold, platinum, or burgundy hair. It was odd. The people of the Ruby Empire had been dark-haired and dark-eyed, as were many modern Skolians, especially the nobility. It helped Roca hide her identity; her gold coloring didn't fit the imperial ideal. But the reflective skin, hair, and eyes she had inherited from her father served a purpose similar to the darker coloring of her mother's people; it protected against bright sunlight. Perhaps the settlers here had decreased their pigmentation because their world received less light. The human eye could adapt to a wide range of intensities, so the streaming golden sunshine didn't seem dim, but the amount was probably below the human norm.

None of that made this situation less alarming. "Bard," she said. "You break law. Take me back."

"Your English is hard to understand."

She snorted. "You understand fine."

Another rider pulled alongside them, the man Garlin. He resembled the Bard, but his features had an edgy, gaunt look and his hair was dark burgundy, streaked with gray instead of gold. Had he had access to treatments that delayed aging, Roca would have guessed him to be well into his second century of life. But according to Brad, these people had no health sciences. If this man had never known the benefits of modern biotech, he could be much younger, even in his forties.

Garlin spoke tightly in his language, his words directed to the Bard, though he was obviously angry at Roca as well. His mood came through to her with unusual strength, making her suspect he too was an empath, though nowhere near as strong as the Bard. He regarded her with antipathy, as if it were her fault that this hotheaded person had hauled her off under the bizarre pretext of improving Allied-Skyfall relations. Gods only knew what they would do when they found out she wasn't an Allied citizen.

"You Garlin, yes?" she asked. She wished she spoke English better, with more nuance.

Garlin gave her a chill stare.

"Of course he is," the Bard said. "He used to be my regent. He is also my cousin, the son of my mother's sister."

That puzzled Roca. Her node defined "regent" as someone who raised a child sovereign and performed his duties until the child reached adulthood. Yet Brad claimed this man wasn't a king.

She considered Garlin. "You guardian for Bard?"

He turned forward, guiding his mount across the plains.

"Garlin, you are rude to our guest." The Bard sounded annoyed.

The older man answered in their language. Roca had a feeling he better understood the trouble they had created for themselves by taking her. She wondered if Garlin had sensed that moment of mental recognition between the Bard and herself back at the port.

Aside from her family, the Ruby Dynasty, Roca knew of no one else with a mental signature as strong as this Bard. Such powerful psions were rare almost to extinction. Scientists had yet to determine why incubating them in vitro almost always failed. The more powerful the psion, the higher the fatality rate. But her people desperately needed Ruby psions. Only an analysis of this man's DNA would verify if he had the full set of Ruby genes, but certainly he had many. He might be a vital resource to the Imperialate, their most valuable find in decades. How she dealt with this situation could have far-reaching effects, particularly if he was a leader among his people.

This Bard was an enigma, one possibly dangerous to her. She needed to understand him, to compare him with her family, the only other psions with such power. She thought of her father, Jarac. The Imperator. As the hereditary leader of Imperial Space Command, he led the Skolian military forces. A stoic and kind man, he had an immensely powerful mind, but he lacked the finesse to detect subtleties in moods and thoughts. The Bard had less strength, but his mind felt robust, healthy, strapping, with a youthful quality and perhaps more finesse than Jarac.

Roca's mother, Lahaylia, the Ruby Pharaoh, had plenty of subtlety—and also an edge. Where Jarac was temperate, Lahaylia was fierce. Jarac relaxed now and then, but Lahaylia never rested. She loved her family deeply, without compromise or condition. A direct descendant of the ancient Ruby queens, she had founded the Skolian Imperialate. In contrast, the Bard seemed to have little sense of his power. It was instinctual with him.

Roca's sister, Dehya, had enough finesse for ten people. She had inherited their mother's dark hair and exotic eyes, but not her ferocity. Dehya was a thinker, lost in equations, a genius at the webs. As the older child, Dehya was first in line for the Ruby Throne, but Roca had always suspected her sister would have rather become a math professor. Dehya was too different from the Bard to compare the two.

There was Kurj, Roca's son. He and his grandfather Jarac were both huge and metallic gold. They had similar minds in their power and lack of nuance, but their personalities differed. Aggressive in his ambition, Kurj seethed with an anger Roca only partially understood. He had hardened after the violence with Darr, but it wasn't until his years as a Jag pilot that his rage crystallized and the barriers separating him from Roca became insurmountable.

Roca had no good comparison—but wait, she had left out someone: herself. She took after her father, tall and robust, gold instead of dark. She had inherited some of his mental power, but leavened with her mother's subtlety. Her interest in politics tended toward her mother. Her artistic bent probably came from her father, though he claimed to have the artistry of an iron brick. Although both her parents enjoyed her dancing, he seemed to understand more how it made her feel.

She might come closer in mental style to this Bard than the others in her family, but she hadn't found a good comparison. It left her without a way to understand him. He descended from stock that had evolved independently of hers, producing a psion unlike anyone in the Ruby Dynasty.

Roca became aware of the Bard behind her. He knew she was studying him. That startled her. Neither Kurj nor Jarac would have realized it. If Kurj had somehow guessed she was analyzing him, he would have tried to influence her conclusions. The Bard made no such attempt; he had just waited patiently.

"You are quiet for a long time," he said.

She leaned back so he could hear her better. "Why you tell me nothing about yourself?"

"You never asked." He traced his finger over her ear.

It unsettled Roca to realize she liked it when he touched her. She knew why; psions produced pheromones targeted for other psions. Nature compensated for their high mortality by driving them together with chemical cocktails, spurring them to make babies. But knowing that in theory and dealing with it in practice were two very different matters. Disconcerted, she pulled her head away from him.

Disappointment came from his mind, but he answered her unspoken question. "I am Eldrinson Althor Valdoria." After a pause, he added, "You may call me Eldri."

"I am Roca." Too late, she caught her mistake. Odd that she was so flustered. "I mean Jeri."

"Roca is a good name."

"Jeri."

He laughed. "Roca. I know."

"No you don't."

"I do indeed. I know when people lie."

That piqued her interest. "How?"

"I just do."

"Something they do? Their voice?"

"No. I don't think so."

"So how you know?"

He shifted behind her. "It doesn't matter how."

Roca had no doubt he felt it in their minds, especially hers, given the bond they were forming. She didn't think he realized what he was doing, though. "You have good English," she said.

His laugh rolled out, deep and chiming. "Better than you."

"True."

"Why can't you speak your own language?"

"Is not mine. I am Skolian."

"I have never heard of Skolians."

Roca frowned. The Allieds had better be able to answer for this, moving in here without telling the natives their origins. From what she understood, the Allied port had been here for three years. That was plenty of time to inform her people about this rediscovered colony.

It occurred to her that Eldri must have developed his fluency in English in only three years. Or less. "How speak you English so well?"

"I listen to Brad, the Reversed-Bard." He laughed at his joke.

"I listen to many. For years. I not speak like you."

"Why do you ask how I know things? I just do."

Softly she said, "Psion pick up language fast."

"Psion? I don't know this word."

"Empath. Telepath."

"I don't know those, either."

"Empath feel emotions. Telepath read thought from emotion."

His grip on the reins tightened so much that his knuckles turned white. "It is not true!"

His vehemence surprised her. She indicated Garlin, who was riding up ahead. "You feel when he has anger, yes?"

"Always." Now he sounded amused.

"You feel my mind at port, yes?"

Silence.

"Eldri?"

"No! I am not different!" His thoughts surged, erratic and upset— and his mind opened to her. For one moment she felt the deep-seated pain that caused his reaction. Then his natural barriers snapped back into place. Roca didn't understand what had just happened. She wanted to know more, but she held back, afraid if she persisted, she would alienate him.

They had been riding toward a line of needled mountains in the northwest. Looking back, she saw clouds of bubbles floating in the air, released by the riders as they crossed the plains. Glitter dusted the animals and people. It made her hair and Eldri's eyelashes sparkle.

"We go back to port," she said.

He spoke with reluctance. "Very well."

Relief washed over her. "Now, yes?" She didn't want Eldri to leave, though. "You stay a little, yes? We visit with Brad."

Eldri snorted. "He is too busy for visits. His flying machine broke again. He must fix it." He shifted her in his arms. "Come visit my home in the mountains."

"Why mountain? Village closer." Also safer.

Sadness came over him. "It is only a ride."

His response puzzled her. She picked up no more from his mind except his conviction that he couldn't reveal the truth. She didn't think it had anything to do with Brad or his flyer, but that was her only lead. "You no help Brad's flying machine?"

"We don't know how." Eldri brushed her hair back from her face. "But we would if we could. He is a friend. Besides, he lives in Dalvador. That makes him my responsibility, even if he thinks he belongs to this Allied Skolia of yours."

She blinked at his tangle of misunderstandings. "Brad come from Allied Worlds of Earth. I am Skolian. Is different." She checked her node for the words she wanted. "And if you are his liege, why you bedevil him?"

He chuckled. "We don't. We just play with him."

Roca doubted it amused Brad to have a Skolian citizen hauled out of his port. "Eldri. Tell this animal take us back."

"Lyrine."

"Say you again?"

"The animal. It is called a lyrine."

"Tell lyrine take us back. Brad worry."

To her surprise, he reined the lyrine to a stop. She twisted around to look at him, maneuvering her leg over the animal so she was sitting sideways. That would make it easier to jump down if he started up again. She was aware of the other riders gathering around them, milling among the drifting bubbles, but she couldn't stop looking at Eldri. Nor did he disguise how much she unsettled him. Or maybe she knew it from his mind; she was becoming so sensitized to him, she had trouble separating his moods from his behavior. She told herself it was pheromones, but she suspected her response went deeper than chemicals.

"Why stare you so?" she asked.

"I am sorry." Eldri brushed her cheek. "I have never seen a woman with gold skin or gold eyes." His touch on her eyelash was so tender she barely felt it. "They glitter. But they are soft. Not hard like metal."

"We shouldn't—" She broke off. He looked as if he could take her into him, mind and body.

"Nor have I ever seen a woman so beautiful," he added, as if it were the most original compliment ever uttered instead of one she had heard too often. She knew she should discourage him, but it was hard to remember that when he gazed at her this way.

Roca cleared her throat. "Pheromones."

"What?" His smile lit his face. And he *did* have freckles across his nose.

"We go to port." She felt like a repeating audio loop. "In two day, I leave on ship."

He touched a tendril of hair curling around her face. "Why?"

"A meeting of my people comes. I need be there. If not, we have war."

He didn't look surprised. "I too would go to war for you."

"Eldri, no." She tried again. "They not fight over me. Leaders of my people meet. We vote about war. I must vote no."

"Ah! A meeting of Bards and Memories. And you vote? This makes sense. You are a Memory. Yes, I see that. You are a woman of intelligence." He tapped her temple. "I feel it here."

Roca blinked. "Memory is title here of woman who leads?"

"Of course." He paused. "Are you sure you cannot miss this meeting?"

"Sure." Her node found the right word. "Absolutely sure."

His mind nudged hers, though Roca could tell he didn't realize it. Her instincts prodded her to strengthen her barriers, but she kept them down. She projected her mood to Eldri, both her concern that she not miss her ship and her interest in developing ties with him and his people.

He spoke carefully. "You would know my people better?"

"We would like that."

"I have a proposal."

"Yes?"

"Your ship comes in two days?"

"This is true."

"Be my guest tonight at Windward. It is true that Garlin says I must know your people better." He hesitated. "Or Brad's people. Or whatever he represents. Even if Brad pronounces his title wrong, he is the only Bard here from the place he calls Allied Worlds. And you are a Memory from a different province." He stopped as if confused by his own reasoning. "Anyway, let me offer you the hospitality of Windward. You and I will begin relations between our people. Tomorrow morning I will bring you back to the port. You will have plenty of time to meet your ship."

Roca reached out to his mind, trying to gauge his intent. She sensed no deception. It was a well-made offer, given the limited conditions they had to work with. But she shouldn't have linked to him; she also felt how much he wanted her. Erotic images of her without clothes were playing out in his mind. Her face heated. He certainly had a prodigious imagination. Rather than putting her off, though, as such fantasies would have with anyone else, his excited her.

Flustered, Roca snapped up her barriers, breaking contact. Eldri tensed, though she didn't think he consciously realized they had been in a link. His desire was simple arousal enhanced by his fascination with her, much as she felt about him. No political calculation tainted his interest, none of the sexually charged avarice that edged the minds of the men, and sometimes women, who coveted her. Power was one of the most potent aphrodisiacs in existence, far more than her face or dancer's body. Eldri had no idea of her power; he just plain wanted her.

He smoothed her hair. "Come visit my home."

Roca tried to stop imagining what he could do with that hinged hand of his. She moved his hand away from her hair. "I accept invitation. But only for business."

"Yes!" His smile blazed. "We can do that."

She gave him a stern look. "No personal. And we send message to Brad."

"Any message you would like," he promised.

Roca pulled a clasp off her belt that regulated the temperature of her clothes. She fooled with its chip until she managed to program in a message. She wished she could have kept better comm equipment, but she couldn't risk carrying anything Kurj could use to trace her.

She gave the chip to the rider Eldri chose, and the man headed back to the port. The rest of their group took off for the Backbone Mountains, thundering across the plains.

As they went, Garlin shot her a hard look.

The path crumbled under the hooves of Eldri's mount, and rocks clattered down the cliff. With her heart beating hard, Roca turned her gaze forward so she wouldn't see the drop-off to their right. The cliff went straight down for hundreds of meters. It astonished her that Eldri and his men took this so casually. She felt as if they were going to end up very dead, very soon.

They had climbed high into the Backbone Mountains. The stark peaks reminded Roca of spindles, and the upper ranges truly did resemble the skeleton of a giant. Their path wound along the edge of a mountain, following a trail barely wide enough for the lyrine to go single file. Another cliff rose on their left. The iron ringbolts driven into it would allow travelers to string ropes along the way or continue their trek when the winds became tricky, but nothing protected them from the drop-off to the right, no rail, fields, or cables.

Roca's body ached from the long ride. Although her jumpsuit had kept her skin from being rubbed raw, the material was wearing thin. Another hour of this and her clothes would shred. Eldri had given her one of the furred jackets they all wore now, but the cold still made her shiver. She thought with longing of the temperature chip she had sent to Brad that would have regulated her clothes.

Eldri wrapped her in his arms, the reins held loosely in his hands. His lyrine seemed to know the route without guidance. "Are you all right?" Eldri asked. He didn't seem the least bothered by the ride.

She shivered. "Is cold up here."

"Usually not this much." He sighed. "I should apologize for our weather's poor showing to my guest."

"Is not so ****" She had meant to say "terrible," but it came out wrong. Her node supplied the pronunciation.

"I don't know that word." He rubbed his cheek against her hair. "But I love how you say it."

Roca reminded herself to pull away. He had been persistent in his attentions during the trip. She told herself she didn't want his lips against hers, his breath warm on her skin, his hands on her body . . .

"No more," Roca muttered, to herself rather than him. At least he helped distract her from the danger of their route. The pounding of her heart came as much from the drop-off at their side as from his sensual voice.

"Why are you so cool?" He spoke near her ear. "You look like the suns but you act like ice."

"Do not do that." The way his breath tickled her ear was driving her crazy.

"I know a sun burns inside you," Eldri murmured. "Let me be your second sun. We can orbit each other for a while."

She couldn't help but smile. "Who is larger sun?"

"Neither." He nuzzled her hair. "We can be the same."

Roca sighed. "Is only dream." She didn't have the luxury of such dreams. She had too many duties.

A shout came up ahead, followed by an exchange of calls in Eldri's tongue. He lifted his head, his arms loosening around her.

"What is it?" Roca asked.

"A part of our path has collapsed."

Her shoulders hunched. "We stop?"

"I am not sure." He fell silent while they rode, listening as people called back to him. After a moment, he said, "I am sorry, Roca. Nothing like this has happened before."

"We go back to plains?"

"I think not. It will be dark soon. Navigating this path then would be deadly."

She felt the blood drain from her face. "Then what we do?"

"We cannot stay here. The lyrine must sleep, and if they do, they might step off the path. Also, the cold is more than usual. We haven't protection enough for the coming night."

"Good gods," Roca said. "Is terrible way to travel."

Eldri spoke patiently. "Perhaps your people can do it better. But this is the best we can do now."

Roca closed her mouth. He was right, it didn't help for her to criticize their lack of technology.

More shouts came back. The riders halted, their lyrine stamping on the path, breath curling up from their nostrils in the freezing air, making blue condensation. Roca had dealt with many cultures, but never anything like this. The situation was always controlled, with her staff setting up the meetings ahead of time.

Eldri called forward, and the riders relayed his words to the front of the line. They soon began moving again.

"They find new route?" Roca asked.

"There isn't any." He cleared his throat. "We have decided to cross the break."

"You make bridge?"

"No. We jump."

"*Jump?*"

"It is our best chance of survival."

Roca closed her eyes. "Gods help us."

Eldri answered in a low voice. "Yes."

The climb seemed to take forever. The animals would walk a short distance, then stop. Apparently they had to wait as each rider executed the jump. Every time the line moved again, Eldri exhaled behind her.

Then came the long stop.

Roca knew tragedy had hit before the call came back. Shock reverberated from the riders. Then the word reached them: someone hadn't made it. He and his lyrine had plunged down the side of the mountain.

Eldri leaned his forehead against the back of her head. His pain fell over her like a great weight.

"I am much sorry," she said softly. "Know you him?"

"Yes." His voice caught. "We grew up together."

"I am so very much sorry."

He said nothing, but she realized he was crying silently, his shoulders shaking.

After a while they moved again. Eldri lifted his head, but he spoke no more.

When they finally reached the break, Roca stared in disbelief. Their path here was more a ledge than a road, and it ended in a jagged breach. It didn't resume until several meters beyond, leaving a broken stretch longer than a lyrine. Garlin was standing on the other side, bundled in furs, coiling a rope that had one end tied to several ringbolts in the cliff. Dark blue clouds covered the sky and cast a pall over the waning day.

Garlin threw the free end of the rope across the gap. Eldri caught it, then tied a length around Roca's waist and his own. She doubted it was strong enough to hold them if they didn't make the jump, given what had happened to the rider they lost, but it was better than nothing.

"Ready?" Eldri asked.

She took an uneven breath. "Yes."

He backed his mount down the trail. Then he leaned forward and kicked with his heels. The lyrine surged up the path, its muscles bunching under them. With a great leap, it sailed into the air. Before Roca had a chance to breathe, its feet hit the other side and rocks went flying. As the animal stumbled, one hoof going over the edge, Garlin reeled in the rope, trying to pull them toward him.

Then the lyrine caught its balance and stepped unevenly down the trail. Eldri whispered in his own language.

"What say you?" Roca's voice trembled.

He too spoke shakily. "By Rillia's Arrow."

"I know not Rillia, but if his arrow bring us here safely, I thank him."

"I also."

"Eldri?"

"Yes?"

She breathed in, trying to settle her pulse. "How go we back tomorrow?"

"I will send people to bridge the break."

"You can do this? You say it never happened before."

"My rock-builders have made many bridges. They can fix worse than this."

She touched his arm. "My sorrow for your friend."

"Thank you." His answer was so quiet she barely heard. She felt the tears he kept inside, unable to shed them in front of his men.

They continued on, so other riders would have room to jump. The line of lyrine hugged the precarious path in the last light of the fading day.

# 4

# Windward

---

The castle rose out of the dusk. Roca had sagged over the neck of the lyrine, but now she sat upright, gaping. Windward was literally sculpted from the mountain, with ethereal stone spires, flying buttresses, and soaring towers. Her breath caught. No primitive culture had created this keep. It stood on an island encircled by a canyon so deep, she couldn't see the bottom. They were crossing an arched, buttressed span of rock that provided the only access to the fortress.

"Gods above," Roca murmured. Wide enough for four lyrine to ride abreast, the bridge led to a portcullis in the massive wall of the fortress. "This is incredible."

"You like my house?" Eldri asked.

"House?" She laughed shakily as they rode under the portcullis. "It is a monument."

"It is as old as all time."

Roca smiled. "All time?"

"Since before history." He waved at the sky. "Legend says the wind god came down before time began and exhaled his great breath on the mountain to make Windward."

"A good legend." Roca could almost feel the weight of the millennia in the magnificent walls. She didn't doubt the castle had endured for thousands of years. From what she had seen, these people had nothing close to the technology needed to carve a structure like this out of a mountain, isolate it on an island of stone, and have it survive for ages. The ancient Ruby colonists must have built Windward.

Light glowed within its windows, a welcome sight as night fell, its arrival hastened by the heavy overcast. When Roca turned her face up to admire the castle towers, snow fell on her cheek.

"Ah, no." She brushed the flakes off her face. In accepting Eldri's invitation, she had underestimated the problems of traveling in a primitive culture without the safeguards she took for granted. "Tell me this not snow season."

"Season?" Eldri asked.

"Winter."

"What is winter?"

"Cold time of year."

"Year?" He sounded bewildered.

Roca pulled back the hair blowing across her face. "Does snow come more at some time than other time?"

"It comes when it comes." He slowed his lyrine as a boy crossed the courtyard to them. "We never know what the weather will be. Snow, ice, rain, sun." After handing the reins to the boy, he slid off the lyrine.

Roca jumped down beside him, then staggered as pain shot through her already sore legs. Her landing also jarred because she felt too heavy; although her node was analyzing the gravity and helping her adapt, it could only do so much.

The "boy" who had come for the lyrine turned out to be a girl. She smiled shyly and led the animal away, toward a structure Roca guessed was a stable, mainly because other people were taking animals there. All the riders were accounted for—except one. Eldri stood watching the stablehands, his face shadowed as if he were searching for the animal— and rider—that were missing.

Roca laid her hand on his arm. "Are you all right?"

"Yes." He obviously wasn't, but he tried to smile.

Garlin came toward them, his long-legged stride eating up distance. He was about six feet tall, two inches taller than Roca, and he towered over the other men in the courtyard. Roca was the same height as Eldri, but she too stood taller than most of the men. The Lyshrioli people seemed shorter than Skolians, perhaps due to their diet or the heavy gravity.

Garlin spoke in their language, ignoring Roca. Eldri gave him a look that reminded Roca of how she felt when her bodyguards hovered about. It didn't surprise her that Garlin bothered him. The older man's tension snapped against her mental shields; Garlin regretted that Eldri chaffed under his watchful eye, but he disliked Roca too much to back off. Perhaps he feared she would replace him in influence with the Bard. She had seen that dance of intrigue played out again and again among the noble Houses, as the aristocracy jockeyed for power. She didn't trust Garlin. She wished it weren't so important she return to the port in two days; she felt drawn to Eldri's life and wanted to learn more.

Turning to Roca, Eldri held out his hand, palm up, hinging it as if to cup the air for her. "I am sorry your introduction to my home comes with such grief." Sadness had replaced his earlier cheer. "But I welcome you."

Roca took his hand. "Thank you." It felt odd to hold such thick fingers and only four of them.

Garlin spoke in their language, his voice low and taut, and Eldri shook his head. When Garlin persisted, Eldri scowled. Tightening his hold on Roca's hand, he took his leave of Garlin and led Roca away. As they walked to the great double doors of the castle, she felt Garlin's gaze like a laser burning into her back.

Many people joined them inside the castle. Their faces lit up when they saw Eldri. An older woman in a homespun tunic and leggings fussed about, taking his coat, drying him off, chattering in their musical language, making his face gentle with fondness. A white-haired man addressed Eldri with obvious respect. Others spoke as well. She needed no translation to see they were offering welcome and informing Eldri about the castle. Their affection and high opinion of him came through in their every gesture. She didn't yet know the social hierarchies here, but she sensed none of the distance between Eldri and his people that in her universe set royalty apart from commoners. These people dressed in simple clothes and had work-roughened hands, but they treated Eldri as one of them.

Torches and antiqued oil lamps lit the hall. Actually, the lamps probably weren't antique; they just looked that way to her. Although she doubted the plan of this building matched castles on other worlds, certain traits tended to repeat in human architecture, including windows and also artistry in great houses. Windward was no exception. Its arched windows were gorgeous, their borders engraved with intertwining lines and spheres, probably a stylized version of the bubble reeds in the plains. The openings were narrow, perhaps to make defending them easier. All had shutters in red, blue, green, or purple glasswood, which young people were closing throughout the hall. Roca could see why; the windows had no glass. Shutters provided the only protection against the storm.

People bustled around her and Eldri, drying the melted snow on their clothes. A huge fire blazed in a hearth at one end of the hall, defying the chill that seeped through the walls. Blue snow had scattered across the stone floor beneath the windows, as if the sky had fallen to the ground and collected in a pile. Two thoughts came to Roca, first that she understood the name of the world—Skyfall—and then that she didn't understand at all. The sky of this planet was lavender. Snow here matched the color of the sky as seen from Earth, not from "Skyfall."

Deep in conversation with his people, Eldri walked through the hall. He continued to hold Roca's hand, keeping her at his side. The curiosity of everyone around them washed over her like a fountain, soaking through her shields. Although she knew almost nothing of their language, she was developing a feel for its cadences and sounds, aided by her node. It sounded as if Eldri was making arrangements of some kind. She earnestly hoped they included warm, dry clothes for the riding party.

Roca suddenly felt as if her shoulders heated up. Turning, she looked past the people around her. Across the hall, Garlin was coming through the entrance, his hair disarrayed from the wind. A woman in a red robe walked at his side. He was watching Roca with a scowl, but when her gaze met his, he turned back to his robed companion.

Eldri slowed to a stop and took Roca's hands, drawing her to face him. "We will have a ceremony for Jacquilar in the morning. Then I will take you back to the port."

"Jacquilar?"

His voice caught. "The man who died."

She squeezed his hands, offering comfort with touch rather than words. His staff hastened off to take care of the arrangements, tactfully leaving their Bard alone with the unknown woman he had brought into his home.

Eldri curled his fingers around hers. "Tonight we will have a dinner in your honor."

She spoke gently. "You need not do this."

"But I must. I asked you here. It is not your fault we had a tragedy." He released one of her hands and raked his fingers through his hair, tousling the shoulder-length mane. "Never before has it been such a problem to come up here."

She ran her thumb over his thick fingers. "I wish I knew a way to make it better."

"You do just by being here." He lifted her hand and pressed his lips against her knuckles. Then he lowered her hand, turning it this way and that. "You have beautiful fingers. Strange, but pretty." A hint of his earlier mischief returned. "One wonders what you could do with them."

Roca flushed, remembering her fantasies about his hand. She disengaged her grip, feigning a coolness far different from what she felt. "Does one, now?"

"One does indeed." He led her over to a more private niche in the wall. "Surely we could learn—what is the word? Brad told me once." He paused. "Ah. I know. Anatomy. You must teach me your anatomy."

"Diplomacy."

"You have diplomatic anatomy?"

She barely managed to hold back her laugh. "I come here for diplomacy. Not anatomy."

"You break my heart, beautiful lady."

She slanted him a dry look. "Your heart is as strong as big, sturdy lyrine."

Eldri grinned, his grief seeming to ease, at least for this moment. He set her against one wall, in a carved archway that went nowhere. "Will you not give me a single kiss?"

"No."

He wasn't the least deterred. "You are an ice queen beyond compare, Roca. A matchless woman." He put his hand against the wall behind her, his palm near her head. "Can no man melt your heart?"

Roca couldn't help but smile. "Oh, Eldri, stop." She ducked under his arm.

"Come back," he protested. By the time he turned around, she had moved several paces away.

"We agreed," she said. "We do business here. No personal."

"I remember you saying this." His lips quirked. "I don't remember agreeing to it."

"You must behave."

Eldri sighed. "Very well." He approached her with more decorum. "Shall we have a conversation?"

Roca could tell he was hiding his sorrow behind bantering. She gentled her voice. "I wondered what call you this world."

He said a beautiful word, his voice chiming. Roca thought he must have incredible vocal cords, to create such melodic sounds. It happened when he spoke English, too, but much less so, perhaps because the phonetics didn't lend themselves as well to the music.

"Is a lovely word," Roca said. "Can you say again?"

"Lyshriol."

"Lyshriol." It sounded so dull and pedestrian on her lips.

Eldri smiled. "Something like that."

"So you not call this place Skyfall?"

He waved his hand in dismissal. "Brad's friends at Starlane Resorts call it that."

"Is wrong?"

"Not exactly." He paused. "It is hard to translate Lyshriol. It means something like 'the clouds have come to the ground.' "

Roca had to admit it was a clever interpretation by the resort planners. Skyfall resembled Eldri's translation, but at the same time it would have meaning to people from Earth, where the sky was the color of the clouds here. "Does it bother you that they say Skyfall?"

"What they say matters little."

"But when the others come, will not this bother you?"

"Others?"

"The people who want to build here."

"You talk in puzzles." When she started to answer, he shook his head. "Let us enjoy this night. Tomorrow is so soon."

Roca let it go. His sorrow had come closer to the surface of his mind, clear now despite her barriers. She wondered if she and Eldri could ever fully shield their thoughts from each other. The compatibility that linked them went further than desire or fascination. If only she had more time to know him. If only she wasn't supposed to wed Dayj Majda. If only.

Roca realized then that she felt more than Eldri's grief. Another anguish went deeper in him, the suppressed pain he had revealed in the plains when he had spoken with such vehemence: *No! I am not different!* He wanted to enjoy tonight, not because tomorrow would come too soon—but because he feared it would never come at all. It startled her that someone so alive and vibrant could feel such despair. He guarded that part of himself so tightly, she doubted she could pick up the reason for his dread even if she dropped her barriers all the way.

Outside, the snow continued to fall.

The dining hall made Roca's breath catch. Hundreds of white and green candles filled it with golden light. Clusters of red bubbles hung under rafters made from green glasswood. Mosaics in gold, blue, red, and purple glasswood patterned the walls in star designs that fascinated her. In places, their symmetry broke into scenes of mountains, suns, and plains. Roca couldn't be certain, but she thought some of the images included stylized starships in the sky, symbols probably long forgotten by Eldri's people.

The room was smaller than the hall where they entered the castle, but still substantial. A long table filled its center, made from blue glasswood that looked as deep as a sea when Roca gazed into it. A fire roared in the hearth at the far end of the hall, the flames gold, green, blue, and red, taking on the colors of the glasswood logs they were consuming.

The people of the castle and the riders from the plains poured into the hall together, filling it with their musical voices and bright clothes. The men dressed like the riders, and some had overshirts lined with fur. The women wore knitted leggings with fur-lined knee-boots, and tunics embroidered in glistening threads.

A shy girl had taken Roca to a chamber with sun and moon mosaics on the walls. She had given Roca a pair of leggings dyed a vibrant blue, and a gold tunic edged in blue and green embroidery. The leggings stretched to fit Roca's long legs and she managed to pull the fur-lined tunic down to her hips, but the clothes clung to her more snugly than to the other women, who were smaller. The boots hadn't fit at all, but Eldri had found a pair of his that she could wear.

Now Eldri sat at the head of the table, with Roca on his right. People filled the seats on both sides, and Garlin sat at the opposite end of the long table. No class distinction seemed to exist here; these were the same folks who took the lyrine to the stables, tended the hall, and set the tables.

Roca doubted many of them were over fifty and most seemed much younger. But they didn't *look* young. Garlin was one of the oldest adults, and Roca was beginning to think he hadn't reached forty. Everyone out of their teens showed signs of age: lines around the eyes, gray in their hair, drier skin that became leathery or loose on the eldest. Although she knew less advanced cultures had few means to delay aging, it stunned her to encounter such blunt evidence of that. She had never interacted with a culture this primitive. These people would be old and decrepit at an age when members of her own circle were just reaching the vigorous prime of their lives.

The servers were teenagers. They brought out pale stone dishes heaped with steaming entrées, then took their places at the table. Roca blinked at the food. It was all bubbles, nothing but bubbles in a multitude of sizes, shapes, and colors. A youth piled her plate high with fragrant spheres.

Eldri grinned at her. "Eat. Enjoy."

Roca managed a smile, aware of the others discreetly watching her. She picked up a utensil by her plate, a fork with two prongs extending from a cupped bowl similar to a spoon. Then she delved into her meal. She ate slowly, giving her nanomeds time to analyze the food. Nothing reacted enough to stimulate a rejection in her body. If her meds encountered a poison they couldn't neutralize or dispose of, they might spur her to vomit. It wasn't the most elegant process, but it worked.

The food confused Roca, but it tasted delicious. Some bubbles were sweet, some sour, others crunchy or chewy. One particularly succulent entrée was hard and spicy on the outside and meltingly smooth inside.

The man next to her sipped wine from his mug, which was made from the same white stone as the other table settings. After setting it down, he picked up a white cloth embroidered with green and gold stars and wiped his mouth. It surprised Roca, though she wasn't sure why. Then she realized, with embarrassment, that she had expected people in a less advanced culture to have less refined manners. Here the opposite was true, a reminder that she should avoid assumptions.

"Roca?" Eldri asked.

Startled, she turned just as a youth set a stone cup by her plate. The young man had the violet eyes ubiquitous among the Lyshrioli and pale lavender hair. Roca had never seen that color of hair occur naturally before, but it didn't seem uncommon here. She nodded to thank him for the drink, and he smiled shyly, blushing, which made the freckles across his nose stand out. Then he backed away, bowing.

Eldri leaned over to her. "You enchant my kin."

"These are your family?"

"Some. Others are friends." He indicated a girl farther down the table. "Chaniece is the daughter of my aunt's oldest cousin." He relaxed in his chair, nodding to the man on his left, beaming at others. Several people called out to him, and a man down the table raised his mug.

Roca smiled. "They like you."

His grin flashed. "They are a wise people."

She snorted. "And you are so terribly modest."

Eldri laughed freely, and gently, with no edge. "So Garlin admonishes me." He tapped the rim of her cup. "This is water. I asked them to boil it for you."

"I thank you, kind sir."

"Perhaps, if I charm you enough, you will thaw enough to acknowledge that I am tolerable, eh?"

Roca laughed. "You are incorrigible."

He smiled companionably. "That too."

Conversation flowed around them, drawing Eldri's attention. Roca understood little of what anyone said. Children chattered, and the younger ones ran around the hall when they grew bored with dinner. Everyone used the tongue common to this land, a language called Trillian. No one but Eldri spoke English, though Roca knew Garlin could if he wished. The Lyshrioli language was sheer joy, caressing her ears. Her node was processing it, but she doubted she could learn enough in one day to converse.

She obviously fascinated Eldri's people. Their moods flowed over her, soaking through her shields. Some of the women projected a friendly regard, looking forward to having someone new in their in-grown society; others resented Roca's favor with their Bard. Many of the men envied Eldri, including some who watched Roca with an appraising regard that disquieted her. Had she not been Eldri's guest, she wondered if she would have made it to her room alone that night, whether she wanted company or not.

Roca shuddered, remembering Darr, and her growing trust of Eldri faltered. As charming as he had been this evening, this was also the man who had hauled her off from the port. In his culture that might be considered a good-natured prank, but for her it evoked darker memories.

Yet despite all that, she enjoyed the festivities. She loved learning new customs and coming to understand people. She watched carefully, trying to adapt. Being an empath helped; she could catch nuances she might have missed otherwise. At one point she started to pick up a long knife by her plate. As she touched the handle, shock came from everyone around her. She left the knife alone and the concern of the people faded. It wasn't until after Eldri started using his own knife that anyone else picked up theirs.

The meal took several hours, with many courses, ending with sweet yellow bubbles in syrup. Everyone had wine, a potent brew that made Roca's eyes water. It only took one cup to relax her quite agreeably; her nanomeds weren't designed to stop her from getting drunk.

After dinner, Roca went with Eldri up a staircase against the far wall. Below them, young people cleared the table while the older folks gathered into groups to talk and tell stories. Mellow from the wine, Eldri took her hand in his. Had she been sober, she would have pulled away, but right now she couldn't seem to remember why it was important she remain uninvolved. His large palm hinged around hers, enveloping her fingers, leaving her thumb free. She rubbed his hinge, wondering why his ancestors had redesigned their bone structure. Did his feet also bend that way, with four instead of five toes? She imagined pulling off his boots and trousers to find out, and heat spread from her face down her body.

"Do you wish to wash before you sleep?" he asked as they walked up the stairs. "Chaniece can bring you water. I will have her boil it."

She gave him a mellow smile. "Just make warm. No need boil. Only what I drink." Her voice slurred. "I clean myself with blue water."

He leaned closer to her. "I will help."

Roca waggled her finger at him. "Behave."

"But life would be so boring then."

Roca slanted him an admonishing look, but it had a different effect from what she intended, making his gaze turn sultry. He didn't look the least admonished. It occurred to her that as tipsy as she was right now, she might be letting him know more of what she felt than was wise.

They had reached the landing at the top of the stairs. Roca gazed over the hall below. It enchanted her, bathed in golden light, crowded with people in rustic clothes, the furniture glowing in deep glasswood hues.

Roca sighed. "So beautiful."

"Yes," Eldri murmured. "It is."

She turned to find him watching her instead of the hall. His violet eyes mesmerized. Everyone here had eyes like that, but on him they looked different. She wondered why she had ever considered brooding men attractive. Right now, Eldri was gorgeous. His desire flowed over her, stirring reactions that should have stayed dormant.

"I go to my room now," she said unsteadily.

"Certainly." He opened the door on the landing and ushered her into a stone hall. After a short walk, they reached an arch with a curtain strung from tiny iridescent bubbles. The beads jingled as he pushed aside the strings. He escorted her into an antechamber with a cushioned bench running around its wall.

"This is where people wait who come to see me," he explained.

Roca peered at him. "I thought we go to my room."

"Well, maybe you could say that."

She stopped and folded her arms. "I not sleep with you."

"You could come in for just a moment," he coaxed. "We can learn each other's culture. Garlin always says I must do that with your people."

"Men," Roca grumbled. "You are same everywhere. I not go in there with you."

"Why not?" His mischief flashed. "Do you fear you can't control yourself around me?"

"Hah. You have ego as big as this mountain. I have no worry about me."

Eldri leaned closer to her. "I think you should prove it."

She poked her finger against his chest. "That trick is old as this castle. Almost as old as getting girl drunk."

"Just come in to talk. I won't grab."

"Pah."

"Really."

It was hard to resist when he looked at her with those big eyes of his. She cleared her throat, wishing she could clear her brain as easily. "Eldri, you have no interest in talk."

"Yes I do."

"Pah."

"Come in just for a few minutes."

"Famous words."

"Famous?"

"We go in, you say 'just a few more minutes' every few minutes."

Her finger was still against his chest, so she ran it around in a circle, aware of the muscles under his shirt. "Many 'few minutes' later, woman is in bed."

He smirked. "You think about only one thing, Roca."

"Me! Never."

He grasped her finger, which she suddenly realized had been rubbing his chest, more slowly now, like a caress. "Always."

She pulled her hand away. "Never."

"Come on, Roca," he murmured.

So tempting . . . maybe she shouldn't have drunk so much wine. "I don't believe you just talk a few minutes."

"I promise."

She meant to refuse, but somehow instead she said, "*One* minute. We see how well you keep promise."

He grinned at her. "Come on." Then he led her across the foyer to a purple glasswood door. It let them into a bedroom with stone walls, floor, and ceiling. Across the room, flames leapt in a fireplace. Throw rugs softened the floor, but the walls were bare except for two crossed swords above the hearth. To the right, in an alcove, tall windows looked out over the mountains, or they would have if their shutters had been open. On the left, quilts and embroidered pillows were piled on a large bed.

"Here." Eldri drew her into the alcove with the windows. "Be comfortable. The benches are cushioned. I will be right back." Then he took off across the room.

Roca squinted at him, then settled onto the bench and relaxed against a shutter. The cold from outside seeped through the glasswood. Had she been sober, it might have bothered her, but right now everything seemed warm, even the cold, though if she thought about it too hard, that made no sense. Better not to think.

Eldri reappeared with a carafe and two goblets made from ruby-red glasswood. He gave her one of the cups.

Roca turned the goblet over in her hand. "Pretty."

"Very." His voice had gone husky. He poured wine for both of them, then leaned the rim of his cup against hers. "May we weave many profitable and mutually agreeable relations between your people and mine."

"Yes." Roca tapped her cup against his, which had nothing to do with any of his customs or hers, but seemed a good idea. Then she took a swallow of wine. "Hmm. Good."

"Here. Have some more." He filled her goblet.

She gave him a dour look. "You know, Eldri, is not so easy to make me drunk."

"You already are drunk, my ice queen." His grin was so wicked, it was a wonder he didn't get arrested, though she wasn't exactly sure who would do the arresting.

She spoke with dignity. "I drunk not. Not drunk, I mean."

He took her goblet and set it on the floor with his own and the carafe. "There. Now neither of us will be drunk." Scooting closer, he slid his arm around her shoulders.

Roca pushed off his arm. "We have done our talk. Now I go."

He put his arms around her waist. "You know, other women long to kiss me. They dream about it."

She cocked her eyebrow at him. "Your humility astonishes me."

"Ah, but it is an honor to kiss the Bard . . ." His voice trailed off as he brought his lips to hers.

Roca fully intended to push him away. But somehow instead she put her arms around his neck and molded her body against his. As his embrace tightened, his kiss became more urgent and his hands wandered to her breasts. Nudging her backward, he stretched her out on the cushioned bench and lay on top of her.

Roca turned her head to the side. "I'm crazy," she muttered. Then she rolled him off of her body.

"Ai!" A loud thump reverberated through the alcove.

Trying to focus her blurred sight, Roca turned on her side and hung on the edge of the bench, peering down. Eldri was lying on the floor, looking annoyed. He sat up, wincing as he rubbed his shoulder. Then he glared at her. "You are colder than a rain of ice and hail."

"Hail *is* ice." Roca also sat up, wishing she didn't want so much to go to bed with him. It was wrong for so many reasons, she couldn't count them. But that was hard to remember when faced with his tousled, appealing person. "We are supposed to talk about relations between our peoples."

His grin came back. "We *were* exploring relations."

"Pah. I give you doubt benefit." She paused as her node corrected the idiom. "I gave you the benefit of a doubt. Now I go."

"Doubt benefit?" He folded his arms around his torso. "You know, it really is cold in here."

"Maybe snow still come down outside."

He stood up and unlatched one of the shutters. As he cracked it open, snow blew into the room. He shut it hard, grimacing, his shirt already covered with blue powder. Roca crossed her arms and shivered.

Eldri dropped onto the bench next to her. He wasn't smiling anymore. "I am very, very sorry." He looked very, very guilty.

She regarded him uneasily. "Why?"

"We cannot go down the mountain in such snow."

"No." He couldn't mean that. "We must leave tomorrow."

"It is too dangerous."

Roca swallowed. "Is only snow."

"Up here, snow can kill you."

She had traveled in every type of weather, but always with modern protections and the knowledge that if the unexpected arose, she would soon have a fix for the problem. Here she didn't know what to do. "Maybe it stop soon."

"It could." He pushed his hand through his hair, pulling it back from his widow's peak. "It never snows in Dalvador."

"We can manage the path down." Roca schooled herself to calm. She had a good cushion of time, over a day before the ship arrived. She could fool with some of the chips in her clothes to see if she could send a message to the port, though she doubted any had the range she needed. But Brad knew her location, assuming he had received her last message. If he could fix the flyer, he could come for her. But no matter what, she had to find a way back even if snow kept falling.

Eldri was watching her, a strand of hair curling across his cheek. He trailed his fingers over her lips. "Can you not stay longer?"

She took his hand in hers. "I wish it is possible." The depth of her regret surprised her. "But I must go back. Tomorrow, or morning of next day."

He turned sideways on the bench and extended his leg behind her. While she was trying to figure out why he had done that, he slid his arms around her waist from behind and pulled her close, her back against his chest. Roca knew she shouldn't let him take liberties, but he felt so very fine. His mind suffused hers with warmth, and she had been lonely for so long. Leaning against him, she told herself it would only be for "a few minutes."

"We need a plan," Eldri said.

"When snow stop, we go."

"The path could be dangerous."

"Can we manage it?"

"I don't know. I've never tried under these conditions." He paused. "If we dress warmly, take animals that know the path, and go slowly, I don't see why we cannot try."

Roca closed her eyes with relief. "Good."

He twined her curls around his hand. "I've never seen hair this way, like metal but soft. So many hues. Gold, copper, bronze, platinum."

"Is metal." Roca paused as her node updated her grammar. "It has metallic components."

"Why?"

Good question. She tried to remember the answer. "My ancestors make themselves that way. My father, even his skin look metallic."

"Yours does a little." He pressed his lips against her temple. "I *will* find a way to take you back tomorrow." With difficulty, he added, "After the memorial for my friend."

"Yes," she said gently. "After."

Eldri laid his forehead against her head. He was silent for so long, she wondered if he had fallen asleep. His mind felt quiet, his mood shrouded. Then she felt moisture soaking through her hair, and she realized he was crying.

Eventually he lifted his head. "Perhaps we should sleep."

It was the first time Roca thought he actually meant sleep. "I go to my room."

"Don't leave." He tightened his embrace. "I will sleep here, on the floor, with a quilt. You can have the bed."

"You will be cold."

He tried to regain his earlier mischief. "You could keep me warm." But his bantering sounded forced.

Roca turned and cupped her hands around his face. "I stay tonight, if it helps. But please, Eldri, no more love play. I know you feel my mind, even if you say you do not. I cannot hide my loneliness. You must not take advantage."

"Let me ease that loneliness."

"It is wrong."

"But why?"

"I cannot give you promises."

"I don't ask for promises."

"But you will."

His mouth quirked up. "Now who has no humbleness?"

She flushed. "Is not what I mean. We have . . . ach, I have not the words. A link of empathy. It make us become too close."

"Empathy?"

"Here." She tapped his temple. "In our minds."

His lips quirked. "It isn't your mind I want to hold."

"*Eldri.*"

"Why do you worry so? If we like each other, you can come back. You will, won't you?"

Roca hesitated. The better she knew him, the greater her reservations about revealing his mental gifts to her government. If they took control of his life and the colony here, he and his people could end up losing as much as if the Allied developers exploited Lyshriol. And there was Kurj, her son. She dreaded how he might react to a relationship between her and Eldri. She reminded herself of Dayj, the prince everyone wanted her to marry, but all she could remember about him right now was his chilly reserve.

"I can probably never come back," she said.

He grasped her shoulders. "Don't say this."

Gods knew, she longed to stay. But what she wanted was irrelevant.

Too many people would suffer if she shirked her duties. She didn't want to add to the hurt Eldri was already suffering because of Jacquilar's death, so she said only, "Perhaps anything can happen in this universe." She motioned as if to encompass Windward. "This place has magic."

He spoke in a low voice. "Then for one night, let that magic be real. If I never see you again, gift me with memories of you, the golden woman from above the sky, that I can hold forever close to my heart."

Roca was more tempted than she dared admit. And Brad was wrong—if Eldri realized they came "from above the sky," he knew she wasn't from some other province. Or perhaps she misinterpreted his pretty words, longing to believe he understood the situation and despite that, he still wanted her.

"Is wrong for me to stay," she said.

"Why is it wrong?" He slid one arm under her knees and the other around her back, then stood up, holding her in his arms. "Never worry about tomorrow."

"Eldri—"

"One night," he whispered.

Perhaps if he had continued to tease, she would have resisted. But his intensity caught her. As he walked across the room, Roca couldn't stop looking at him. When he laid her on the bed, she put her arms around his neck and drew him down with her. They sank into handmade quilts turned soft from many washings.

Eldri was strength and warmth, and he held her with a need born as much from grief as desire. They undressed each other with both urgency and care. Scars covered his body, but whatever battles had left those marks hadn't injured his heart. Unrestrained in his passion, he cracked the ice that surrounded her emotions. For the first time in years, maybe in decades, she felt no separation, no distance, no sense of standing behind glass, outside the circle of warmth a man and a woman could create.

They loved each other in the dim firelight, isolated in a mountain fortress, pretending for one night that no storms raged beyond their precarious refuge.

# 5

# Son of Stars

Kurj Skolia, son of Roca Skolia, had no equal.

Rumor claimed Kurj was more machine than man. His ancestors had settled a low gravity planet and engineered themselves with larger, stronger bodies than normal humans. He stood seven feet tall and had a massive physique. The military had enhanced his skeleton and muscle system, and he had personally arranged yet more augmentation. The biomech web in his body controlled his enhancements, with a micro-fusion reactor to provide energy. Nanomeds maintained his health and youth. Despite his size, he could move many times faster than an un-altered man. He thought nothing of crumpling a metal block in his fist. When he entered a room, he dominated it by the sheer force of his size.

He was a man of metal.

Kurj had inherited his coloring from his mother, Roca Skolia, who inherited it from her father, Jarac Skolia. His gold skin reflected light. His hair and eyelashes glinted, and his eyes were molten gold. His ancestors had engineered inner eyelids as protection against intense sun-light, and Kurj had inherited them from his grandfather. They covered his eyes with gold films. He could see through them, but to everyone else they were opaque, making him a cipher.

Kurj and Jarac could have passed as twins, if not for the gray in Jarac's hair. But no one confused them. Where Jarac was kind, Kurj was hard; where Jarac smiled, Kurj showed no emotion. As Imperator, Jarac headed Imperial Space Command, the military. His title was hereditary; he split the actual command among his senior officers. With a proclivity for peace, he chose commanders who understood but didn't relish war.

Roca was next in line to become Imperator, a title she would some-day assume by joining the Dyad, the power link that controlled the interstellar information network known as the Kyle web. Kurj was next after her, though he had far more interest than she in the title. He knew Roca intended to delegate authority much as Jarac did now, and that she shared her father's preferences for diplomacy over warfare.

Kurj had other ideas.

In his younger days, Kurj had flown a starfighter in the J-Forces, a branch of the military. He had fast become known as a ruthless and versatile pilot, earning rapid promotions until he attained the rank of Primary, equivalent to an admiral or general. At thirty-five, he was the youngest officer to hold such a high position. Now he oversaw all the J-Forces.

He had two obsessions.

His first was Eube, that vast empire his people called the Traders. Its aristocratic rulers based their economy on the buying and selling of people. The Trader Aristos enslaved over a trillion people on hundreds of worlds and habitats. Given the chance, they would conquer Skolia and subjugate her people as well.

As a pilot, Kurj had experienced Aristo inhumanity firsthand. The agony of their captives stabbed his empath's mind, even reaching from one ship to another. He *felt* Aristos savoring the deaths of the soldiers they killed. When his units had liberated Eubian captives, he felt the suffering behind their traumatized silences. He took it all in, shell-shocked and unwilling, until finally he could bear it no more. He raised impenetrable mental shields, cutting himself off from all emotion. Driven by his memories of a stepfather who had brutalized his mother as Aristos brutalized their slaves, he swore nothing could appease his hatred for the Traders except their destruction.

His second obsession was Roca.


"You *lost* her?" Kurj slowly stood up behind the massive desk in his office. "How the hell could you lose her?"

Sweat beaded the forehead of the man facing him, an J-Forces officer named Render. "We aren't sure how the Councilor gave us the slip, sir, but she disappeared two days ago."

Kurj restrained the urge to grit his teeth. "I want every operative you have on the search. Find my mother. Understand?"

"Yes, sir!"

"And one more thing, Quaternary Render," Kurj added in a deceptively quiet voice.

Render stared at him. Prior to entering Kurj's office, the man had held the rank of Secondary, roughly equivalent to a lieutenant colonel in other branches of the military. Kurj had just demoted him to the lowest rank in the J-Force.

"Yes, sir?"

Kurj watched the man through the gold sheen of his inner lids. Render couldn't see his eyes, only an unbroken shimmer. "If you find my mother—and she is unharmed—you may manage to stay out of prison."

Render swallowed. "Yes, sir."

"Good. Dismissed."

Render saluted, crossing his clenched fists at the wrists and raising them to Kurj, his arms out straight. Then he left—fast.

Alone now, Kurj paced along the window-wall behind his desk. Lost in thought, he only glanced at the spectacular landscape outside, far below his office in the Orbiter, the space station where he worked. Military experts had developed its biosphere to provide an optimum working environment for the powers of Skolia, but today he barely noticed the rolling hills, lush forests, or ethereal city.

Where the blazes had his mother gone? She must have discovered his plans. If she showed up at the Assembly and voted, then those factions that opposed the invasion would win. If he cast her votes for the invasion, he still might lose but at least he had a chance.

It worried him far more, though, that Roca was out there alone. She could take care of herself, yes, but the risk of her traveling without bodyguards was too great.

The true value of the Ruby Dynasty lay not in their heredity, but in their minds. Only Ruby psions could create and power the Kyle web, a computer network in Kyle space, a universe outside of spacetime. Physics as humans knew it had no meaning there, including the speed of light; as a result, the web made instant communication possible across interstellar distances. The Traders had no Kyle web because they had no Ruby psions. The Trader Aristos commanded a powerful military, but their communications were slow. That one disadvantage was all that kept them from conquering Skolia. And Skolia had only five Ruby psions, including Roca. Just five.

Once, after an on-planet battle, Kurj had found a Trader girl huddled in the ruins of an installation. She had been a provider, one of the slaves Aristos tortured for their pleasure. He would never forget her inability to talk, even to move, except to shake. He had wrapped her in a blanket, but she had only cried and struggled to escape. Her mind had been wide open, with no barriers to mute her emotions. Unable to blockade his mind from hers, he had lived her terror. She had no concept of kindness; she expected only cruelty from him.

He had taken her to a hospital, and eventually the doctors had restored her physical health. But they couldn't heal her emotional wounds. She had remained withdrawn and silent, never able to form normal human relationships. The memory of her lovely face and ravaged mind was only one of hundreds that haunted Kurj. The thought that his mother might fall into Trader hands was more than he could endure. If the Aristos had taken her prisoner, he would annihilate every last one of them even if it took his entire life and all the resources of ISC.

Kurj took a deep breath, trying to calm his thoughts. Chances were Roca would show up at the Assembly, angry at him but very much free and alive. He would see to it she never evaded his security again.

Settling behind his desk, he activated its screen and chose a holo from thirty years ago, when he had been five. The image formed above the desk, luminous and three-dimensional, a tableau of his parents standing together, smiling. His father, Tokaba, held his five-year-old son in his arms, Kurj, a laughing boy with curly gold hair who in those days had rarely lowered his inner lids.

The image soothed Kurj. Tokaba had been the finest man he had ever known. When Kurj's anger threatened to explode or his wish for vengeance against the Traders became too intense, he found peace by thinking of his father.

He brought up a new holo, one of his mother dancing. She was balanced on one foot, high on her pointe shoe with her other leg straight out behind her. She stretched one graceful arm forward and the other to the side, her head held high. Her formfitting costume started out dark blue at the feet, turned into the pinks of a rising sun up her leg, and blended into yellow on her torso and arms. Her hair was flying out behind her, streaming along her body, so many shades of gold and bronze, with a metallic luster, incredibly thick, grown for decades. She had been performing *Loss of the Sun,* a solo choreographed for her by the artistic director of the Parthonia Royal Ballet.

Kurj switched off the holo, unable to face the conflicts it caused him. Looking at her, he saw a lovely woman. As a small boy, he had loved her the way a child adored a loving parent. He wanted that innocence back. He despised himself for noticing her beauty. Nor would he ever forget the last time she had danced *Loss of the Sun.* After the performance, she had come home and found her second husband and her son trying to kill each other.

As much as Kurj had loved his first father, so he had hated the second. Darr Hammerjackson. Roca had met Darr when Kurj was eight. Before the marriage, Darr had made himself everything a lonely widow would want; afterward, he had shown the truth, a monster hungry for Roca's power. Even at such a young age, Kurj had seen how Darr threatened, manipulated, and strove to control Roca, and through her, the immense power she wielded. He knew the games Darr played with violence and with her emotions, building on her conviction that her duty as a Ruby heir bound her to him. No divorce. No disgrace.

Kurj had lain in bed at night, supposedly asleep, while Darr hurt his mother. The memories seared. She had thought she protected her child by shielding her mind, but his empathic link to her had been too strong. He had lived every painful blow, every hateful word.

He remembered vividly the day he realized he had grown taller than his stepfather. Kurj had been clumsy then, shooting up fast, struggling to adapt to his large body. Darr was berating him more than usual, ridiculing him for knocking over a vase. Agonized from knowing how Darr brutalized his mother, Kurj had finally snapped and attacked his stepfather, first with his fists, then with shards of the vase. He had felt Darr's anger that his unwanted stepson dared defy him, felt Darr's bitter jealousy that Roca loved her son more than her husband. Kurj fed on that rage, driven into a fury fueled by shame. If he had just been a little stronger, a little faster, a little smarter, he could have killed Darr.

He would never forget what Darr had said to him that day: *You're a sick, dirty boy. You want her for yourself, don't you? You want to fuck her, you bastard. You should leave and never come back. Go, before your sickness corrupts everything decent.* That moment had devastated Kurj's life, ruined the innocence of his love for his mother, and haunted him from that day forward.

He could do nothing more to Darr; his stepfather had died in prison. But Kurj would purge the universe of the Trader Aristos, who thought it their gods-given right to treat mass numbers of humans the way Darr had treated Roca. No matter what it took, even if it killed him, he would destroy the Traders. No one would hurt his mother again.

Especially not her own son.

# 6

# Hidden in Blue

---

Roca drifted awake, content. Her face felt icy, but the rest of her was warm. She stretched under the heavy covers—

And rolled into a warm body.

Sweet memories of the night washed over her, vivid and sensual. Pressing sleepily against Eldri's back, she put her arms around his waist.

"Ummm . . ." He turned over and gathered her into an embrace. "You really are here."

She kissed his chest. "So are you."

He gave a drowsy laugh. "This *is* my castle, after all."

"A beautiful castle." Just like its owner. "Do you think it stopped snowing?" Her node had been at work while she slept, updating her facility with English.

"I've no idea." He nudged her onto her back and slid along her body, pulling the blankets over his head. Then he began to suckle her breast.

"Oh . . ." Roca closed her eyes, her hands entwined in his long hair. When he slid his palm lower on her body, she groaned. What he did with those hinged hands ought to be outlawed. Anything that felt that good couldn't be legal. His desire flooded her mind, until she couldn't separate it from her own.

Eldri kept at it until Roca lost control. Their minds were already blended and her peak burst over them both, intensified. He struggled to hold back, but then, suddenly, he pulled himself up along her body, bringing his hips between her thighs with a powerful thrust. Almost as soon as he entered her, he cried out. She felt his release as strongly as her own, a wild burst that took away her thoughts.

As Eldri collapsed on top of her, Roca gulped in breaths. She had forgotten how good it felt to be that crazed with desire and have it so soundly satisfied.

"I am glad I soundly satisfy you," he murmured smugly.

Her face flamed. "Stop listening."

"Listening to what?"

"My mind."

"Don't know what you mean."

"Then how did you know how I felt?"

"It is obvious." Mischief flared in his voice. "How could you not be pleased with me?"

She thumped his head. "This is certainly swollen."

Eldri laughed. "That's because you make me feel as if I could take on the whole world." His voice softened. "You are no ice queen, Roca. Not in your heart. Under that armor, you burn."

Roca didn't know how to answer. She had never before experienced such an intimate link with anyone, not even Tokaba, her first husband, whom she had loved deeply. Eldri scared her. After Darr, she had never risked opening her heart again. She wasn't ready for this. Her link with Eldri existed on many levels, sexual, yes, but emotional and mental as well, and less defined qualities she barely understood. She needed time to stop fearing the nascent connections they were discovering with each other. More than ever, she wanted to stay.

But nothing had changed: she had to leave.


They held the memorial service outside Windward.

The snow had stopped, and the overcast sky pressed down like a lid of blue-gray pewter. Dark blue fog wreathed the castle. The riders from Dalvador and the residents of Windward gathered in a ten-branched star pattern on the bridge that arched across the chasm to the castle. Roca stood in one branch with Eldri, Garlin, and a Dalvador couple.

A woman in a long red robe spoke the service, her voice like wind chimes. She wore her hair in a coil on her head, but when she finished, she took down the coil and let the wind whip the long tresses around her shoulders, a tribute to the rider who had lost his life while on the way to what the Lyshrioli also called the Castle of Winds.

Garlin spoke next, his voice deep and melodic. He stood at the edge of the bridge, with only a stone rail separating him from the chasm. Roca knew Eldri's people could never have carved that perfectly cylindrical rail. Its ancient supports rose straight out of the bridge, all one solid piece with no seams.

When Garlin completed his eulogy, Eldri went to stand with him. He cast a handful of glittering dust over the chasm, in place of ashes from the body, which they had been unable to retrieve. The glitter drifted down, sparkling dimly in the overcast day. Only the keening wind broke the silence.

Then the Lyshrioli began to sing.

Fifty people joined in the hymn, singing in the incomparable Lyshrioli language, their voices rising in the clear mountain air, chiming like bells, caressing a bittersweet melody so beautiful, it brought tears into Roca's eyes.

And when they finished, Eldri sang alone.

Roca knew then that even Brad's extravagant praise hadn't come close to describing the vocal gifts of Dalvador's Bard. Eldri's voice soared into the air, filling it with such purity, such incredible clarity and power, that no ecstasy they shared in bed could match this moment.

It would be a crime for anyone—including her people—to contaminate the rare splendor of these people.

Eldri pulled his fur-lined jacket tighter around his body. "Garlin forbids us to leave." His breath condensed in the air of the stable, making puffs of blue.

Leaning on the half door of a stall, Roca rubbed the nose of the lyrine butting her hand. "How can Garlin forbid us to leave? Do you not rule here?"

He crossed his arms on top of the half door. "Rule?"

Roca wished she could go inside the stall, where the animal had made a nest out of the softened stalks of glasswood piled there. It had pulled the stalks up around itself in a way a horse could never do, and now it stood surrounded by their warmth.

"Your title of Bard," Roca said. "It means you lead, yes?"

Eldri's forehead furrowed. "I sing. I keep our history."

"These people treat you as their leader."

"Not leader. Judge." He rubbed the lyrine's nose. "They bring me disputes. I try to settle them. Garlin did it until a few years ago. He still advises me."

Dryly Roca said, "I'm sure he does."

"Why do you say it like that?"

"He troubles me. Why does he dislike me so?"

Eldri hesitated. "I am not sure. He wanted me to take you back to the port right away." His face reddened. "He says I let my loins think for me."

"Your loins?" When her node provided the translation, she blushed. "Never mind."

His laugh tickled her ears. "Perhaps we should go back to my room and investigate what he means."

Much as she would have liked to, she couldn't banter with him now. "Eldri, we must return to the port. The snow has stopped. We should leave as soon as possible."

"Garlin says to stay. And he is wise."

She scowled at him. "Garlin wants you to think he is wiser than you. That way, he retains power."

"You say I should not trust Garlin." He leaned closer, his lips near her ear. "He says I should not trust you."

Roca sighed and moved into his arms, though their heavy jackets kept them from coming too close. "I have to go back."

"I do not understand why it is so important."

She searched for the right words. "If I do not vote, my people may have a war. A terrible war. Many would die. Millions. Perhaps billions."

He pulled back and regarded her uncertainly. "I do not understand 'millions' or 'billions.' "

"Think of how many people live in Dalvador and the Rillian Values."

"Very, very many."

"Yes. Very. Now imagine five times as many as that." She wasn't sure if he could; she had no idea what mathematics he knew.

He only paused for a moment. "All right."

"That is a million people." Her breath made plumes in the air. "Double, triple, quadruple that number and you still won't have all the people who might die. Do you begin to see?"

He blanched. "It is too many."

"Yes. Too many."

"And you can stop this?"

"I think so. But I must be there. Otherwise my son will vote to go to war."

"Your son?" His embrace turned rigid. "Where is his father?"

Softly Roca said, "He died."

"Ai, Roca, I am sorry." Relief also came from his mind.

"It happened many years ago."

"Is the boy all right? I didn't mean to keep you from him. I had no idea."

"He is no boy." Roca thought of her indomitable firstborn. "He is a man, grown and strong."

Eldri's forehead furrowed. "You are not old enough to have a son that age."

So. Here it came. She had to tell him sooner or later. "I am older than I look, older than Garlin, even."

He gave her an uncertain smile. "You play with me."

Roca shook her head. Then, remembering he might not recognize the gesture, she added, "My people age differently than yours."

He looked doubtful. "This son, he is a warrior?"

"A warlord. A great one." She shivered, though her jacket kept out the cold. "I love my son, Eldri, but he also terrifies me. I must return home before it is too late."

"It sounds so strange."

"Please help me."

He rubbed his hands up and down her arms. "Garlin says it may snow again."

"It isn't snowing now."

"I do not comprehend all you say." He held her shoulders. "I understand only what I see and touch. But I know you speak truly when you talk about this desperation you feel."

Her voice caught. "I wish it could be otherwise."

"If you leave now, you must come back." Longing filled his voice. "We have so much to discover about each other."

She took his hands, afraid she was giving him hope where none existed. "I will try."

He took a deep breath. "Very well. We shall go."


The first flakes fell when Eldri and Roca had ridden a third of the way down the mountains. The storm rapidly grew worse. Snow drifted down and the world became a wash of blue, all the sky, air, and ground. Soon it was impossible to see either the cliff rising to their right or the drop-off on the left. Cold seeped into their clothes, through their leggings, socks, trousers, fur-lined shirts, jackets, and gloves. It seemed to penetrate Roca's bones. The lyrine slowed until it was barely moving through the swirls of blue. Finally it stopped and would walk no more.

Sitting behind Roca, Eldri rested his forehead against her head. "We can go no farther. It is not safe. If we try, we will join Jacquilar."

She couldn't accept defeat. "The snow may stop again."

"It may." Eldri lifted his head. "But it is too thick on the ground now. It would be dangerous to go even if it stopped."

Roca knew he was right. With reluctance, she said, "I have more than a day yet until the ship comes. If we cannot go today, then perhaps tomorrow morning."

"It may clear enough by then."

She could tell, from his mind, that he had doubts. She twisted around to look at him. "What do we do now? Return to Windward?"

"I am not certain. I have never been caught out in snow like this before." Reaching back, he checked the ropes and spikes fastened to the saddlebag across the back of the lyrine. "I have survival equipment, but in this weather it won't be enough."

Roca tried to imagine what else they might do. "The path becomes narrower back up the mountain, yes?"

"Yes. It does."

"Is it safe to go that way now?"

"Probably not." He brushed at the snow that had gathered on the fur of his hood. "The Eira Lysia Meadows are to our north."

"Can we get there from here?" Meadows sounded far more secure than this path.

"The lyrine knows the way, I think." He paused. "I remember an old cottage. It is a ruin, but it might protect us from the storm."

"We can try." Roca turned back around and scratched the lyrine's neck. "Can you take us to safety?" she murmured.

Eldri put his hand over hers, offering comfort, then took the reins and urged the lyrine forward. At first it refused to move. Then Roca felt Eldri's thoughts, a gentle pressure directed toward the animal. She doubted he realized what he was doing, but the lyrine responded, stepping forward.

So they went, continuing in the blinding wash of blue.

They were moving in a trance, lost in a universe without definition, two people and a lyrine amid swirling blue snow. The wind had risen, Roca wasn't certain how long ago. Eldri kept his arms around her waist, his hands clenched on the reins. He offered no hint that he recognized the way. The lyrine seemed to know, though how it could tell, Roca had no idea. She understood so little about the animals.

A dark patch in the whirling snow formed in front of them. They came up against the mounded ruin before Roca even realized they had reached a building. She stared numbly through the storm as Eldri jumped off the lyrine. Rousing herself, she slid down next to him, stiffly, her body aching. Gripping the reins and Roca's hand, Eldri led the way forward, past a crumbling wall.

The wind suddenly died. For the first time in hours, since the blizzard had started, Roca could see farther than a few hand-spans. The daylight was dim, but enough to show they had entered the remains of an empty cottage. It had three walls, a roof, and most of its fourth wall. Snow had piled up against the walls, but they gave welcome relief from the storm.

Eldri pulled his jacket tight, shivering. Blue ice encrusted the hair that had escaped his hood. "I was beginning to wonder if it was here anymore." He tried to grin. "Do you like my new castle?"

Roca managed a bow. "It is lovely, Your Highness."

"Highness?" He laughed unevenly. "What does that make us in the plains? Lownesses?"

She smiled. "I never thought of it that way."

"You have heard this title before?"

"People use it for me."

"Do you live in a high place?"

Roca shook her head, scattering snow off her hood. "It is only a title. Is it so unfamiliar? Last night, when you called me an ice queen, I thought—" She didn't finish, uncomfortable with his words even if he had only been teasing. They came too close to the truth.

Eldri flipped his hand, which Roca gathered was the Lyshrioli equivalent of a shrug. "Brad's people, they talk about kings and queens. They tell me this is like Bards and Memories, except a king marries a queen. They even say I am king of Lyshriol." He looked alarmed. "I hope they don't tell Lord Rillia that. He might not appreciate them saying I am Bard over him."

That intrigued her. "Who is Lord Rillia?"

"Bard of the Rillian Vales. They have more people there than we do in the Dalvador Plains." His teeth were chattering. "I am Bard of Dalvador, but he is lord of all the lands, including mine."

Roca wanted to shake the resort planners. The least they could have done was get their facts straight before they started playing with local cultures. She wondered if they even cared that they might endanger Eldri if they treated him as if he ranked above the true leader here. "Do you know Lord Rillia?"

"Of course. He and my father were friends." He rubbed his palms together, making his gloves squeak. "Unlike Lord Avaril."

"Who is Lord Avaril?"

"He lives in the Blue Dale Mountains." His face paled even more than from the cold. "He swore he would kill my father. Now he says he will kill me."

"Good gods, Eldri. Why?"

"He wants to be Bard in Dalvador." Eldri wrapped his arms around his body. "He might have killed my father. We don't know."

She spoke gently, remembering his kindness when she had told him about her first husband. "I'm sorry your father died."

"All my family did." He sounded subdued now. "It was on this mountain during an avalanche. Possibly it was an accident. Such things happen here."

"Possibly?"

"Many rumors claim Avaril caused it. He is my cousin, the son of my father's brother." Eldri stamped his feet in the snow. "If everyone in my family dies, he becomes Bard."

It sounded all too familiar. The long histories of the Skolian noble Houses included their share of titles gained through assassination. If that was what had happened here, though, it hadn't succeeded. "But you survived."

"I was only a few months old, so they left me at Windward when they went riding. Garlin had to stay home and take care of me because he had misbehaved. He was sixteen." Eldri was trying to sound unconcerned, but his bewildered pain was obvious. "The avalanche killed everyone, my parents, sisters, brothers, uncles, aunts, cousins . . . Garlin is my family now."

"Ai, Eldri. I am so sorry." Roca threaded her arm through his. Although she suspected Garlin had taken advantage of the situation over the years, it seemed unlikely he had helped cause the tragedy. From what she understood, titles here went through the male line, unlike in many Skolian cultures where it went through the female line. As a son of Eldri's aunt on his mother's side, Garlin wasn't in the line of succession. If anything happened to Eldri, Garlin would lose the power he wielded now as the Bard's chief adviser.

"Someday I will have a big family again," Eldri said. Ice glittered on his eyelashes and he could barely get out the words.

Roca moved closer to him. "You are so cold."

"Aren't you?"

She grimaced. "Very."

"You look warm." He was obviously trying to achieve the same state, without success.

"Will you be able to sit out this storm?"

He had a strange look, as if she had cornered him. "I don't think so. I don't understand. Why does it not bother you?"

Roca's foreboding was growing. At first she had thought the people here were physically better able to resist the cold, but now she realized they were just more used to it. Up to a point, she didn't handle it as well as they did. But the nanomeds in her body monitored her physiology, and right now they were working overtime to keep her temperature at survival level. She felt the cold bitterly, and she would be ravenous after a while, but she could live for hours, maybe even days, as long as she had shelter.

The same might not be true for Eldri.

"Can we reach Windward from here?" she asked.

"I don't think so." He crossed his arms and hunched his shoulders. "You were right about the path being unsafe."

"I have an idea." She hesitated, uncertain how he would react. "It has to do with the way we share our emotions."

"What?" His laugh was shaky. "That is crazy."

Why did he deny it so vehemently? His panic sparked like fire whenever she suggested he might be different. "I know you feel it."

He wouldn't look at her.

"Eldri, listen. The traits are hereditary. If you and Garlin are cousins, he may have some of it, too."

He still wouldn't meet her gaze. She focused on his mind, gently, a visitor asking permission to enter. Although he didn't sense her on a conscious level, he didn't instinctively retreat either. She gathered impressions from him, enough to know he and Garlin had always been close, much more than she would have guessed from their strained relations these past two days. They did share their moods, though it frustrated Eldri that Garlin seemed less attuned to him than the reverse.

"Try to reach him," Roca urged. "Let him know we are here. I can boost your signal."

"Boost my signal?"

"Make your call to him stronger."

His look turned doubtful. "That sounds very strange."

Roca dug her hands in her pockets and scrunched her shoulders against the cold. "It is better than doing nothing at all."

He grimaced. "Garlin will be angry when he finds us."

"I've no doubt about that." More quietly, she said, "I'm sorry I caused this trouble."

"Roca, no, you caused no trouble. You only accepted my ill-timed invitation to come here." He pulled her closer, as much for warmth as for affection. "Very well. Let us try this idea of yours."

She closed her eyes, leaning into him, her arms around his waist, with only the faintly keening wind for company. His mood suffused hers, but she sensed nothing.

Just as she was beginning to think they would fail, she felt a stirring of his mind. He reached out on instinct, with no training, no idea how to proceed. But he did reach out and Roca helped him, using her skill to direct and augment his undefined call. Whether or not he made contact, she couldn't tell; she had trouble sensing Garlin clearly even when he was nearby. His animosity toward her swamped his other emotions. She had no idea if he would recognize their cry for help.

Sometime later Eldri's hold loosened. Roca opened her eyes to see his pale face. Snow encrusted his eyebrows.

"I am so very cold," he whispered. Then his eyes glazed over and his face went blank.

"Eldri?" Roca shook his arm. "What is wrong?"

No response.

"Eldri!"

He stood unmoving, his mind diffuse. Mentally, she suddenly felt odd, as if she stood on the edges of a storm. She had the curious sensation that static had muddled their connection.

Suddenly he focused on her. "Roca . . . ?"

She took his hand. "What happened?"

"Happened?" He sounded lost.

"You blanked out." His mental static was gone now.

"*No* . . . nothing wrong." He looked around. "I need to sit."

"It would be better if we kept moving."

Eldri didn't seem to hear her. He went to a wall and slid down to sit in the snow. Roca bit her lip, knowing he would get cold faster that way. But he looked as if he would pass out on his feet. She was becoming more and more alarmed, afraid Garlin wouldn't arrive in time, if at all.

With misgiving, she settled on the ground next to him, in the snow, with drifts on either side. He put his arms around her and they squeezed as close together as possible.

Then they waited.

# 7

# Mind Demons

---

"Eldri, no." Roca grasped his arm as he walked back to the wall. Over the past few hours, she had needed to prod him to his feet more times than she could count. "You must keep moving."

He spoke leadenly. "I need sleep."

"We cannot." She dragged at him when he tried to sit down. "Keep walking."

He swayed on his feet, his face drawn. Then he wearily took her arm and stumbled away from the wall, plowing through a drift of snow, making blue powder cascade off his knee-boots.

Together, they began another trek around the cottage. He said nothing, just plodded, his eyes downcast and glazed. Roca didn't believe she would ever feel warm again.

And night was coming.

A shout came from outside.

Roca stiffened. "Did you hear?"

Eldri kept plodding.

Another shout.

"Listen!" She shook his arm. "I heard someone."

He stopped, his eyes focusing. "Yes. I think so."

They started toward the broken wall, where snow was sifting in from the storm. Before they made it halfway, a figure shoved past its broken edge, someone taller than most Lyshrioli men, long and lanky in his heavy clothes and hooded jacket.

"Garlin!" Eldri jerked forward, then stumbled and nearly lost his balance.

Roca caught his arm, giddy with relief. He snagged her around the waist, grinning now, and limped toward Garlin, pulling her along. More people were pushing through the break in the wall, crowding into the cottage.

Garlin grabbed Eldri and pulled him into a bear hug, drawing him away from Roca. As the cousins embraced, she stood to the side. Relief overflowed Garlin's mind—and anger. He didn't even look at her.

The other people in the rescue party kept glancing in her direction. She recognized many of them from dinner last night. From their minds, she gathered that she and Eldri were in better shape than anyone had expected. No one seemed hostile; in fact, they wanted to rejoice with her. But they took their lead from Garlin.

The cousins finally separated, laughing and talking at the same time. The rescue party gathered around, their voices rising like a swell of music. Someone handed Eldri a ceramic jug. When he uncovered it, puffs of blue condensation rose into his face. He drank with steam wreathing his cheeks, and Roca watched from outside the circle, shivering, her hands scrunched in her pockets.

Suddenly he lowered the jug and looked over the heads of the people around him. Catching sight of Roca, he motioned her over. As everyone turned, she came forward, self-conscious, aware of their guarded responses to her.

When she reached Eldri, he hugged her against his side with undisguised enthusiasm. "They can take us back!" His voice had regained some strength. "They tied ropes together so we have a line all the way to Windward. So much rope! They used every coil, sheet, and line in Windward. We can follow it through the snow."

She managed a nod, too cold to do more. He pushed the jug in her hand and fragrant steam rose into her face. As much as it relieved her that they would soon be warm at Windward, it also meant she would end up no closer to the port than she had been this morning.

The supply ship would arrive in less than a day.

The hall where they had dined last night looked much different today, empty, with only a fire roaring in the hearth, no people. Garlin had sent away everyone except Roca and Eldri. Woolly bolts of cloth were strewn across the table, along with half-done tapestries and glasswood cups.

Garlin strode along the table, whipping off the long scarf he wore around his neck and tossing it onto a high-backed chair. Watching him, Roca and Eldri stopped at the end of the table. Eldri pulled his blanket around his shoulders tighter and took another sip from his mulled wine. Roca set her blanket on the end of the table. She wasn't so cold now; the soup they had given her had helped replenish the energy used up by her nanomeds, which were working full-time to keep her warm.

Eldri started toward Garlin, his gait stiff from their bout with the storm. He stopped abruptly when Garlin spun around and glowered at him. Then Garlin stalked back down the length of the table to him. He spoke in their language, his words astoundingly beautiful despite his anger. Eldri listened with a patience that astounded Roca. He answered when Garlin demanded a response and otherwise stood quietly. She had the sense it wasn't the first time this scene had played out.

After several moments of this, Garlin walked in a measured gait to Roca. His icy gaze could have frozen her far more than had the storm. He spoke in English. "Did you enjoy your game?"

"I play no game," she said tightly. She hadn't liked the way he had spoken to Eldri and she had no intention of accepting such treatment from him.

"You don't call it a game?" His voice had an edge like a knife. "You have done nothing but display yourself since the moment you saw Eldrinson. So cold, so perfect—" His gaze traveled down her body and back to her face. "So *blatant*. Well, you got what you wanted. Now I suggest you leave him alone, before you do more damage."

"Garlin, wait." Eldri came over to them.

Roca met Garlin's gaze steadily. "It threatens you much that he care for another person?" In her anger, she was losing her command of English. "You cannot control him forever. He is adult now, not child."

"Roca, don't." Eldri tried to step between them, but Garlin pushed him aside.

"Haughty words," Garlin spat at her. "For one so young."

Her voice chilled. "I suggest you worry about your own maturity. Or lack of it. I have son your age."

He jerked his hand in dismissal. "You offworlders lie so easily. Did it mean nothing to you that you could kill Eldri by tempting him to cavort around the mountain in this weather? Did you ever once think of him instead of yourself?"

Roca gave him a regal stare. "Did you ever once think I might have good reasons for my actions?"

He made no attempt to hide his incredulity. "For three years I have dealt with you people, you 'planners' and 'marketers.' For three years I have listened to you talk about our lives and lands as if they were nothing but goods for your use."

Eldri inserted himself between them. "She isn't in that group. She comes from another one."

Garlin glared at him. "You trust them too easily."

Roca bit back her response. Exhausted from their ordeal and shaky from the cold, she knew if she stayed longer, she might say things she would regret. Taking a deep breath, she turned and walked to the stairs. But they were only a few meters away, which wasn't enough to let her anger subside. The first few steps led to a landing; then the stairs turned at a right angle and ran up the wall to a second landing.

"Wait," Eldri said as she climbed the first steps.

"Let her go," Garlin said. "She is bored with her new toy."

*That's it.* Roca was tired of his insults. She swung around on the first landing, her hand clenched on its railing. "You overstep yourself, Garlin."

He came forward, past Eldri, to the foot of the stairs, his anger like sparks, crackling against her barriers. "You come here, so full of condescension. You play with Eldri as if he were no more than a toy to entertain you, though among our people he claims great respect." His voice rose, powerful in the hall, with the astonishing richness only the Lyshrioli could attain. "And you presume to say *I* overstep myself?"

"Stop it!" Eldri strode past him and climbed the first two steps. "Both of you."

Roca braced herself against the waves of hostility from Garlin that flooded her mind. She could barely control her voice as she spoke to him. "Among my people, you could be imprisoned for speaking to me in that manner."

"Please," Eldri said. "Don't tear at each other this way."

Garlin never took his gaze from Roca. "Among my people, you are nothing."

"Stop!" Eldri said. "You are the two people I—I most—I—" His eyes suddenly lost focus. He grunted—

And then he fell.

Caught off guard, Roca froze. Garlin reacted faster, lunging to catch Eldri as the younger man toppled down the stairs. Eldri's body had gone rigid. As Garlin eased him to the floor, Roca started down the stairs, her fear for Eldri swamping her anger.

His entire body jerked, his torso arching, his arms and legs moving violently back and forth. A convulsion wracked him from foot to head. Garlin pulled off his jacket and eased it under Eldri's head, to keep him from cracking his skull on the stone floor. Then he shed his overshirt and put it under Eldri's legs. He turned Eldri on his side and knelt by his cousin, staying back just enough to keep from being hit by Eldri's jerking limbs.

The seizure seemed to last forever. To Roca's mind, it felt like a raging fire, buffered by her defenses but threatening to overwhelm them. When Eldri's face turned blue, her breath caught with fear. For a moment she thought the seizure had ended, but then he began to jerk again. Garlin remained by his side, his face agonized, his hands hovering in the air as if he wanted to help but could do nothing more.

Roca had no formal medical training, but her node stored some knowledge. Eldri was having a generalized tonic clonic seizure caused by an overload of neurons firing in his brain. People sometimes put an object in the person's mouth to keep him from biting his tongue, but Skolian doctors advised against it. Garlin's quick response suggested this had happened before, enough that he had learned what to do.

Finally, mercifully, Eldri's body went limp. He seemed to collapse into himself, his muscles releasing their vise-lock on his body. For a moment the three of them remained frozen in a tableau. Then, in the same moment that Roca stepped forward, Garlin laid his hand on his cousin's shoulder.

Eldri's eyelashes fluttered up. "Garlin?" he whispered.

Garlin's voice cracked as he spoke in their language, and his reassuring tone had the sound of desperation. As Eldri's eyes closed, his face went slack. For one horrible instant Roca thought he had died. But no, he was breathing, the rhythm shallow but regular. Her surge of relief was so intense, it almost hurt.

With great care, Garlin slid one arm under Eldri's legs and the other around his back. Then he lifted his cousin and stood up, holding Eldri's limp body. When he turned to Roca, she saw the same guilt in his eyes that she felt in her heart. Had their argument done this? She couldn't speak, couldn't ask that damning question.

Garlin carried Eldri up the stairs and she followed. Eldri was sleeping now; the firestorm in his mind had ended.

In Eldri's suite, Garlin laid him on the bed and pulled off his boots. As he drew the quilt over his cousin, Eldri opened his eyes and spoke. Roca recognized none of the words except her name.

Garlin stiffened. He straightened up and stood, staring at Eldri, his face frozen. Then he turned to Roca with a leaden gaze. "He wishes to speak to you alone."

She answered quietly. "Thank you."

He just shook his head. Then he left. Roca watched him go, wishing she knew how to heal this pain. Turning back to Eldri, she sat next to him on the bed. "Are you all right?"

His lashes drooped. "Now you know."

"Yes," she murmured. "Do you have the seizures often?"

He opened his eyes, struggling with the effort. "More as I am older.

Every ten or twenty days. Lately . . . every few days. It is why we came to the mountains. I improve here." His voice was fading. "Happens more if I become upset . . ."

"I am so sorry," she whispered.

"Not your fault." He gave up the struggle and let his eyes close. "The demons have come all my life . . . long before you and Garlin didn't like each other."

"Demons?"

"Garlin says they shake my body."

"Ai, no." Roca felt as if her heart ached. What else would he believe, in a society with so little health care, one where they became old in their thirties? She hated to think what he must have felt, spending his life convinced angry spirits wracked his body with such violence, growing stronger each year.

She spoke softly. "There are no demons, Eldri. You have a medical condition, a treatable one. I think it is epilepsy."

"I do not know this word."

"It means your brain has a problem."

He smiled wanly. "When I was young, Garlin said similar. I often got into mischief. He would intone about my behaving myself. But really, he liked fun, even if he tried to be stern . . ." His voice trailed off.

After a moment, Roca realized he had fallen asleep. She watched him for a while, smoothing the hair off his forehead when he stirred. He looked younger in sleep, hardly more than a boy.

Brad Tompkins had asked if she had ever had to watch someone she loved die because they lacked medical care. She remembered all too well her self-righteous response. Gods, she wished she could take back those words. Of course she had never suffered such heartbreaks. Everyone in her circle had the best medical care possible. Eldri lived on the other side, in the bleak struggle to survive an illness with no cure among his people, no treatment, no explanation.

The severity of his attack frightened her. Having so many of his neurons fire at once had to be like a storm sweeping his brain. And psions had extra neural structures. She had never known an empath or telepath with epilepsy before, but she could see how having so many more neurons could worsen his condition. His seizure had lasted longer than the one or two minutes predicted by her node. Her files listed a condition, status epilepticus, in which the seizures didn't stop, but kept on going. Mercifully, Eldri's had ended. But if he experienced such severe attacks often, increasing in frequency as he grew older, then without treatment he had no chance of a normal life. It was no wonder he wanted to live his life with such intensity now, fearing he might die tomorrow.

He could be right.


Roca walked down the Vista Hall, a long, narrow room that overlooked the northern mountains, behind the castle, on the side opposite the approach from the plains. The windows here were twice the height of a person and wider than she could stretch her arms. Normally they let in copious sunlight, but today most had their shutters closed. At the end, one pair was open, letting light and freezing air pour into the hall. Outside, across the canyon that surrounded Windward, a secluded valley nestled in the cliffs. The Backbone Mountains rose above it like gigantic, contorted needles.

Garlin was sitting on a bench by the window, with one foot up on the cushion, his elbow resting on his bent knee. He faced away from Roca, gazing at the snow-covered peaks, his hair blowing back from his face.

His resilience daunted her. He had on only a fur-lined tunic, trousers, and boots, with no other protection from the icy wind. She wore heavier clothes and a jacket, and her nanomeds had boosted her metabolism, but the cold still bothered her. She had never faced weather like this without the computer-regulated warmth of garments that included their own climate-control systems. Eldri and his people lived this way every day, with no heating except fireplaces, no electricity, and only marginal plumbing. It brought home with inescapable bluntness just how much she took for granted.

She let the tread of her feet alert Garlin to her approach. He didn't turn as she reached him, but she felt his recognition. Although he had nothing resembling Eldri's luminous mental gifts, he was an empath.

When she stopped next to him, he continued to gaze at the mountains. Then he said, "How is he?"

"He sleeps." Roca came around and sat on the bench facing him. "Will he be all right?"

He finally looked at her. "Yes, I think so." His pain showed clearly on his face. "This time."

Roca chose her words with as much care as if they were blown glass that might shatter. "In my life, over the years, I have developed a certain cynicism. Many people have wished to make use of what they thought I could give them, either physically or from my position among my people." She spoke quietly. "If I have judged you unfairly because of that, I apologize."

He regarded her, the wind tossing his hair around his face. "The people who have come to Dalvador, these resort planners, do not treat us well. I have watched them make their plans with little concern for Eldri or our people, as if we were quaint displays to use for entertainment rather than the custodians of this land. Eldri understands it less, but he *feels* it. When you came, so beautiful it hurt to look at you—" He pushed back his blowing hair. "If I have made unfair assumptions about your motivations, I too apologize."

"Perhaps we might start over, fresh."

"Yes." He sounded weary. "Let us try." He moved his head in the direction of Eldri's room. "If not for ourselves, then for someone who matters more than either of us."

Now that his animosity toward her had eased, Roca sensed what she had missed before. She felt the depth of his love for Eldri, his only family; she heard it in his voice and knew it in the lines that furrowed his face. Perhaps she might have seen before, had she been less armored against the pitiless intrigues that drove the powerful and the wealthy among her people. Eldri and Garlin were like their world: primitive, beautiful, harsh, and pure.

"How long has he been this way?" she asked.

Garlin answered quietly. "All his life."

"Even as a baby?"

He nodded. "The demons first came the day his family died."

"They aren't demons." Roca willed him to believe her. "It is called epilepsy. Our doctors can treat it. We can relieve his seizures, maybe stop them."

Garlin gave her an incredulous look. "You people from Earth, or Skolia, or wherever it is, you speak glib, impossible words. The planners for this resort tell their fantastic stories with such ease, I question whether they even comprehend what 'truth' means."

She met his gaze. "I'm not lying to you."

"How can you do what no healer or maker of magic has managed throughout my cousin's entire life?"

"It is no magic I offer." Roca didn't know the right words for this. "My people understand medicine better, that is all."

His voice hardened. "If you raise his hopes and then crush them, I will see that you pay for causing him pain."

"I cannot promise miracles. But we may be able to help." She glanced out at the cloudy day and towering mountains. As long as she was trapped here, she could do nothing for Eldri. Looking back at Garlin, she said, "Please know that when I asked Eldri to—"

"Eldri?" His anger sparked so fast, she almost saw fire jump off him. "Do not presume to call him such."

Roca blinked. "He said that was his name."

"He *asked* you to address him that way?"

"Well, yes." She hesitated. "Is that wrong?"

"No." He turned away from her and stared at the valley, his tone taking a new chill, though this time it seemed more to hide his own pain than push her away. "Not if he allows it."

Roca bit her lip. Although she had noticed Garlin used Eldri's nickname, she hadn't realized until now that Eldri allowed her a familiarity he had granted to no one else but Garlin. She spoke gently. "Please believe that I would never have asked him to go down the mountain if it wasn't vitally important. I would never be that cavalier with his safety."

"Why vital?" He turned and narrowed his gaze at her. "Do you report to these resort people?"

"No. I have nothing to do with them." She shivered in the gusts coming through the window. "If I am not at the port tomorrow, I am not able to leave with the ship. If that happens, I will miss an important meeting among my people."

"A meeting?" His manner remained guarded.

"I am not sure of your language, but Eldri thinks I am similar to what you call a Memory."

Garlin raised an eyebrow. "Memories are mature women."

"As am I."

"You look like a girl."

She knew he didn't mean it as a compliment, which was refreshing, though she doubted he would believe her if she told him. "It is the truth that I have a son your age."

He shook his head, apparently one of the few gestures his people and hers shared. "It is not possible."

"I age differently."

"Then why do you make yourself look so young?"

It startled her that he intuited it was a choice rather than a natural process. She would never reveal how much she resented that "choice." Her contract with the Royal Parthonia Ballet stipulated that she must maintain her appearance and youth. Although she danced far less now, she hadn't stopped completely, and every dancer with the Parthonia Ballet had to sign such a clause. The reasoning was blunt; the more beautiful the dancers, the more tickets the ballet sold. If Roca aged, they would fire her.

Parthonia was a premier company; for every one of its dancers, a hundred others were waiting for their chance, just as brilliant, just as beautiful, and just as driven. She could be replaced that easily, Ruby title or no. She loved her art, but years of having her worth based on appearance rather than character or intelligence had drained her. In some ways, it had been a relief to curtail her performance career when she became Foreign Affairs Councilor.

Even if she had known Garlin better, she wouldn't have felt com-

fortable telling him. The age difference between her and Eldri made her
self-conscious, even here, where no one understood.

She said only, "It is part of a contract I signed."

"I do not like this word 'contract.'" Garlin frowned. "The resort
people use it. We have no such thing. We do not 'sign.'"

Roca wondered how she could explain legal documents to a people
with no written language. "You make agreements among yourselves,
yes?"

"Of course."

"How do you verify them?"

"You say you are a Memory, yet you do not know this?"

Ah. Now she saw. "A Memory remembers the agreement."

"Of course. You do not do this?"

"Not myself, no. My assistants do. But I am part of our governing
Assembly. They meet soon and I must be there." She wished she knew
how to convince him. "My people may have a war. Many will die. I
could stop it, but not if I am here when the Assembly meets."

Garlin had tensed. "This war—will it come here?"

"I doubt it." Skyfall had neither strategic nor commercial importance. In fact, its value as a resort came from its distance, both physical
and metaphorical, from the centers of civilization. But Roca feared many
other worlds would suffer the ravages of the first open interstellar conflict
ever fought by humanity. Now her people skirmished with the Traders
in shadow battles; this would take it into an unprecedented full-scale
war.

"Please," she said. "If there is any possibility I can reach the port
tomorrow, I must try." According to the estimates made by her node,
days here lasted twenty-eight hours, fourteen of night and fourteen of
sunlight. It left her so little time.

"Does Brad know you must meet this ship?" Garlin asked.

"Yes, definitely."

"Perhaps he will send his silver bird for you."

"The flyer?"

"He calls it that." Garlin rubbed his chin. "You say it is no magic
your people have, and Brad says this also, but his flyer is a metal room

that floats, having light without candles and warmth without fire. His house is the same. If this is not sorcery, what is it?"

"Technology."

"I know not technology."

"Your people must have, once."

He spread his hands apart, his palms to the ceiling.

Roca gathered he was indicating confusion. "Have the people here no legends of great machines in times long past?"

"Our myths are of gods and goddesses."

"From the sky?"

"Sky. Moons. Suns. Stars."

She motioned upward. "Your ancestors came down from the sky just like my people do."

He smiled wryly. "Brad does. He tries not to, though."

"Not to?" Roca wasn't sure what he meant.

Garlin sighed. "Not to come down from the sky. Always this flyer of his has problems. He has to send for parts."

Roca didn't like the sound of it. "How long does that take?"

"He tells the supply ship what he needs. The next one brings his supplies."

"How long between supply ships?"

Garlin thought for a moment. "My friend's son was just born when the last one came. The boy walks now."

She stared at him, aghast. "That could be *months*."

"Can you send a message for someone to come sooner?"

*If only.* She could do nothing without access to the webs. Two ways existed to communicate across space: by starship, which could take days, even months for a remote outpost like this; and through the Kyle web, which was almost instantaneous. But the Allieds had no access to the web; they used it only by arrangement with Imperial Space Command. Brad couldn't swing an arrangement like that on such short notice. Eventually the Allieds would probably petition for access here to the Kyle web, but for now, the supply ship was Brad's lifeline to other worlds. Roca didn't miss the irony, that her family created and maintained the Kyle web, yet she had no entry into it when she needed it most. She couldn't even contact the port because she had ditched her wrist comm on Irendela to make it harder for Kurj to find her.

"The ship is my only way to send a message," she said.

He tilted his head toward the window. "It snows again."

"No." Roca felt as if walls were closing around her. Snow drifted down from the sky, turning the world blue, making it hard to distinguish where the land ended and the air began.

"Even if it stopped this moment," Garlin said, "the path down the mountain wouldn't be safe for several days." The regret in his mind was genuine. "And I have seen weather such as this before. It will not stop snowing, I don't think, for many days."

Roca held her hand up to the window, letting flakes gather on her palm. They dusted across the bench and Garlin's legs, light blue powder, so beautiful, so bitter.

Her voice caught. "I have to try."

"If you leave here, you will die." In an unusually gentle voice, he added, "You must stay. I am sorry."

Roca stared out at the snow. "So am I."

# 8
# Legacy

In the observation sphere, Kurj felt as if he touched a piece of his soul, a part he had never truly understood. The sphere curved out from the hull of the Orbiter space station like a transparent bubble. Space surrounded him in its infinite beauty, the fire of stars, the spumes of nebula, and the mystery of secrets known only to the cosmos. He stood with his hands resting on a clear railing and gazed at the great void. Despite what many people believed, space was no more "empty" than his heart: void was a label others used to define what they couldn't see.

The view stirred his memories of flying a Jag, the exhilaration of joining his mind to the EI brain of his ship, plunging into the magnificent reaches of the Kyle web in another universe. When he accessed that web, he could contact any place in human space that also linked into it, letting his mind expand throughout the far-flung settlements of humanity.

A memory stabbed him: hurtling through space with his squadron, his mind submerged in the web, he had sensed another squad. Eight enemy fighters were headed their way. Traders. Six of the pilots were slaves, but with so much Aristo blood, they were hardly less cruel than their owners. One was an Aristo, his insatiable mind thirsting for the agony of psions. Kurj had *felt* his cruelty, his pleasure in killing, his desire to inflict pain, until finally Kurj vomited. To this day, it made him ill to hear the whir of the miniaturized droids that cleaned a pilot during battle.

But what had horrified him most had been the eighth "pilot." The man was a psion, a slave, a provider. The Traders had bound him into his ship, with two Aristo copilots in control. They used him to locate the telepathic Jag pilots, torturing him to force his compliance. With no training to defend his mind and no natural protections, the provider had been in agony. His screams had reverberated in Kurj's mind, drawing him into a link so intense, Kurj had lost his identity, becoming that anguished pilot. Tears had poured down his face. Pulling free of the link had taken a mental wrench so severe, it had forever scarred Kurj's mind.

When Kurj's squad engaged the Traders, he destroyed the ship with the provider first. In that instant he wasn't fighting an enemy, he was freeing a human being from a torment that would have otherwise killed him in a pain greater than Kurj could have imagined if he hadn't lived it. His squad defeated the Traders that day, but in his mind he had kept fighting that battle, along with the hundreds of others like it, ever since.

Kurj pushed away the memories. He became aware he was no longer alone in the observation sphere. His grandmother had come. Still shaken, he turned to see her several hundred meters distant, sitting in a transparent chair across the rounded chamber, gazing out at space, a raven-haired sovereign on a crystal throne.

Kurj walked across the sphere, using a transparent path that ran through its center. Lahaylia Selei, the Ruby Pharaoh, wore her hair down today, letting it loop over her chair, arms, torso, and legs, as black as space but liberally streaked with white. It had grown a long time, over three hundred years; his grandmother was the oldest human being that had ever lived.

He stopped beside her throne and stood looking at the stars, his hands clasped behind his back. It seemed appropriate, in view of the magnificent cosmos, that he kept his uniform simple, with none of the medals, ribbons, or other symbols he had a right to wear. His khaki pants tucked into dark boots and his pullover sweater indicated no sign of his rank except for the single band of a Primary around each of his upper arms.

Lahaylia motioned at the view. "This is your legacy, Kurj. The stars. Not the warships."

"No?" Anger edged his voice, born of the years he had spent fighting an enemy that was bigger, stronger, and as cold as space. "Without those warships, none of us will inherit anything."

"It takes more than ships."

He turned to her, a pharaoh descended from the queens who had ruled a mysterious, ancient empire. She evoked those matriarchs, with her dark hair, long limbs, and classic features. But instead of dark eyes, she had green ones, startling in their vivid hue. The lines around her eyes and white in her hair were the only signs she had lived 322 years. No one knew her potential life span; she was the first human to have had the benefit of age-delaying biotech from the moment of conception. How long could a human live? Early nanomed technology had been crude, but in the 322 years since it had improved.

In those centuries, she had founded an empire.

The people of the Imperialate worshiped her. She was a symbol, their exotic forever-queen. But Kurj sensed the truth: she had grown weary. She pushed herself too hard, working in the Kyle web she had created, centuries ago. Striving to protect her empire, she spent days at a time wired into the great command chair that linked her body to the ever-evolving network. He feared the time was coming when she would give the medics an answer to the question of how long a human could live.

He spoke with atypical gentleness. "You should rest."

Lahaylia glanced at him, her slanted eyes a deeper green than usual today. She spoke in a too quiet voice. "Yes. I should."

The finality of her tone sent a chill up his spine. "I meant sleep." For a race as long-lived as theirs, the concept of death became distant, easy to forget, making it even harder to accept.

"Ah, Kurj." She spoke softly. "I've had a life most people would only dream of. It has been a good one, even with all the struggles and heartache. It is your time now."

A lump seemed to form in his throat. His grandmother was one of the few people he could talk to without barriers. She didn't fear him. It devastated him, knowing he could stop ships, armies, even wars, but not the passing of the people he loved. He wanted to tell her what he felt, but he had no words to express such emotions. So he answered simply. "Say no more."

She nodded. They watched the stars wheel past as the Orbiter rotated. After a while she spoke again. "Is she home yet?"

"No." None of his vast intelligence networks had located his mother. His fear for her had been with him every moment since she vanished. Sometimes he could submerge it in his daily concerns, but it never left his mind.

"She always was a stubborn one," Lahaylia said.

Kurj glanced at her. "My mother?"

"Yes. And I will tell you something else."

"What is that?"

She spoke evenly. "You cannot force her to do what you want. That includes trapping her on Irendela so you can change her votes in Assembly."

Kurj was glad the nanomeds in his body prevented him from flushing. "I would never change the votes of a Councilor."

She just arched her eyebrow. Then she went back to watching the stars wheel past. He didn't try any more denials. They wouldn't fool her.

Eventually she said, "I was born a Trader slave, you know."

Kurj frowned. She spoke casually, as if commenting on the weather instead of dropping a bombshell. It couldn't be true, of course. She couldn't have kept such a well-guarded secret for over three centuries. Perhaps she was making a terrible joke. But he knew her. She wouldn't joke so about the Traders.

"Grandmother." Kurj waited until she turned to him. "You descend from the queens of the Ruby Empire. Many doctors have verified your DNA." They constantly examined her, especially as she aged. "You cannot have been a slave."

"Of course I can."

He waited.

Her gaze darkened. "You know of the Rhon project."

"Of course." It was his heredity. Centuries ago, Doctor Hezahr Rhon had isolated the mutations that created Ruby psions, the most powerful empaths and telepaths known. Humans on the world Raylicon had just been regaining space travel, emerging from five millennia of dark ages. They needed powerful psions. It was the only way to resurrect the ancient machines; the people of the Ruby Empire had developed an arcane discipline combining mathematics, neuroscience, and mysticism. Their machines accessed universes based on thought rather than spacetime. But Kurj's ancestors had lost that knowledge; nothing had survived the millennia except three Locks, those mysterious command centers that could create and power a Kyle web. Only a Ruby psion could activate them.

Rhon had pursued two goals: to create and to protect Ruby psions. It was an ancient dilemma; the stronger a psion, the more sensitive their mind, and the more pain they experienced when other people suffered. Rhon had meant to ease the anguish they endured, but that noble, well-intentioned goal became one of the worst failures in human history. It created the Aristos, a race of anti-empaths with no capacity for compassion. When an Aristo picked up pain from a psion, it stimulated the Aristo's brain, producing an ecstasy they called "transcendence." Psions projected their pain more; the stronger their minds, the more intense the effect. Aristos brutalized them with obsessive cruelty. They enslaved empaths and telepaths and called them providers.

They craved the Ruby Dynasty beyond all reason.

Now, centuries later, the Aristos ruled the Eubian Concord, an empire built without the inhibition of compassion. All their subjects, trillions of them, were slaves. Providers made up only a tiny fraction of those populations; most Trader slaves lived comfortable lives as long as they followed the precepts set out by their owners. But none had freedom.

As a Jag pilot, Kurj had defied the Traders. Linked to his ship's EI brain, strengthened by technology that allowed humans to endure immense accelerations, he had become phenomenally versatile in battle. But Jag pilots had to be psions—and hypersensitizing psions during combat exacted a terrible price. Kurj could never lose the memories of the soldiers he had engaged, not only the Aristos and almost Aristos, but the many slaves who had no choice but to fight, or who nurtured hopes of a better life if only they could distinguish themselves in combat. It was impossible to demonize an enemy when he felt their humanity. He wept with them, screamed with them—and died with them.

Kurj had flown a Jag for eight years, longer than most Jagernauts, and he would never lose the guilt of having outlived so many of his contemporaries. Jag pilots also had a higher suicide rate than personnel in any other branch of the military. He survived by barricading his emotions until he became a fortress no one could breach. He could no longer open his heart, but his defenses made the pain bearable. Almost.

To Lahaylia, he said only, "You were born in the Rhon Project." They had created her using preserved DNA from ancient Ruby Pharaohs.

"Actually," she said, "I wasn't."

"I've seen the records."

"It's true, the history of the Skolian Imperialate has been arranged to explain my birth in such a manner." She shrugged. "In a sense it is true. Rhon envisioned my birth. But he never succeeded. It is prohibitively difficult to make psions in vitro."

"Prohibitive, yes." It perturbed him to have his view of the universe disrupted this way. "But not impossible. You are living proof."

"The Aristos created me."

Kurj stiffened. "No."

"It is true."

"It cannot be."

She regarded him steadily. "They had no ethical compunctions. None. They tried thousands of times, even millions, and in all those attempts they produced only two viable fetuses, myself and a boy, my mate. We were to be the ultimate providers." A deep rage stirred within her and she let him sense it. "The boy killed himself when we were teenagers. He preferred death to a life of torture." Her voice grated. "Nor could he bear to know the Aristos intended to breed our children for the same. He took his own life rather than live that nightmare."

He didn't know where to put these revelations. "You knew the boy?"

"We were together every day of our lives." Darkness shadowed her eyes. "Until he died."

Now he knew what lay under her simmering rage; she had loved the youth. "Did you know what he planned?"

"Yes. I tried to talk him out of it. But what could I say? I had considered the same." Her fist clenched on the arm of her throne. "After he died, I no longer cared for anything. I planned, I listened, I let my owners think I was stupid." Her voice hardened. "And when the day came, I killed them."

Feeling the steel of her will, Kurj knew she had done as she said, though he had no doubt it had been far more difficult than she implied. "And then?"

"I escaped. And founded the Imperialate." Her gaze never wavered. "On that day I swore I would destroy the Aristos."

Her revelations shook the foundations of his life. His nightmares meant nothing compared to hers. With clarity, he saw what she was telling him. "You will vote for the invasion."

"Yes."

"If my mother doesn't vote against us, we might achieve a majority. The invasion will proceed."

"We have no guarantee."

"But it is possible."

Grim satisfaction showed in her eyes. "Yes. It is. But listen well, Kurj. If Roca arrives in time and the vote goes against us, you *will* respect it. I will not ever have you betray her again. Do you understand?"

He nodded once, in respect. "Yes."

A deep voice rumbled behind them. "Make sure you remember."

Kurj turned with a start. Jarac was standing behind them, a gold giant, his gaze hard on Kurj.

"Grandfather," Kurj said.

Jarac inclined his head with more reserve than usual, but when he turned to Lahaylia, his metallic gaze softened. As always, it unsettled Kurj to see him; it was like looking in a mirror, except Jarac usually kept his inner eyelids raised, leaving his gold eyes visible. Kurj didn't realize he had retracted his own inner lids until they came down now.

He could still see well, but it gave the world a gold sheen.

Lahaylia held out her hand to her consort. Jarac stepped forward and stood next to her, across the throne from Kurj. A stab of loneliness went through Kurj. He would never know the companionship they enjoyed. Too much fire burned within him to leave room for the love of a wife. He chose his companions according to how little they interfered with his life and how well they pleased him in bed.

Jarac cocked his eyebrow at Lahaylia. "You and our grandson are plotting to overthrow the galaxy, eh?"

She frowned at him. "We vote to protect ourselves."

"Less drastic ways exist."

"And less effective."

"A war will destroy us," Jarac said.

Kurj wished he knew a way he could add fire to Jarac's heart. How could they look so alike and have such similar minds, yet come to such different conclusions? "We must fight them, Grandfather. If not today, then tomorrow."

"Perhaps tomorrow we will be ready." Jarac remained calm. "Or perhaps tomorrow we will find peace with them."

"Never will they make peace with us," Lahaylia said.

Kurj thought of the horrors he had lived and what his grandmother must have endured. "No peace is worth what we would give up. They will take us only as slaves. Nothing else."

"Not if we have enough strength." Jarac pushed his hand through his graying hair. "But if we engage them before we are ready, they will break us."

Kurj's voice rumbled. "I will never break."

"That which cannot bend, breaks," Jarac said.

"I would die first."

Lahaylia laid her hand on Kurj's forearm. "Do not speak so. You will live a long and full life." Her features gentled. "The stars may be your heritage, but it is *you* who are our legacy."

Kurj smiled slightly. "A strange legacy, that."

Both she and Jarac smiled, a rare moment with his formidable grandparents, one when he felt accepted for himself, without evoking apprehension or alarm. He had known few such times as an adult.

Yet nothing eased his worry. Roca had outwitted him, but in doing so, she had risked herself. He claimed he would never break, but he had lied. If he was responsible for injury to Roca, it would destroy him. He had wanted her kept from the Assembly, but not at risk to her person. Never that.

If anyone harmed her, he would annihilate them.

# 9

# The Amphitheater

Eldri drifted in a pleasant dreamlike state between sleep and waking. Eventually reality intruded and hazy memories came to him. He didn't recall much of his attack, but he knew he had spoken to both Garlin and Roca.

Roca.

His contentment vanished. She knew. Misery swept through him. He must repulse her now. She would never wish to look upon his face or endure his company again.

In Eldri's childhood, Garlin had striven to keep his seizures a secret, but they had happened too often to conceal. Eldri's attacks terrified people, made them want to flee. He had been forced to make a choice: live as a recluse or accept that people would dread him. He chose a life of partial seclusion. Garlin spread rumors that he was chosen by the gods, that he convulsed because they touched him. Eldri knew perfectly well no such thing happened. More likely, demons possessed him. He usually awoke feeling sore, often with a headache. Sometimes he bit his tongue during the attack and it hurt for days afterward.

And yet . . . Eldri recalled no shock from Roca, only concern. It seemed impossible. She had even named the demons that plagued his life. He didn't recall the word. Epsily? Was it possible that his miraculous guest, this person from the sky, could help him? She came into his life so unexpectedly, like a gift. She was gold like the suns; perhaps they had sent her. He had never really believed all those deities existed, but perhaps he should pay more attention, especially to the sun gods,

Valdor and his younger brother Aldan. He didn't want them taking her away because he had neglected the proper rituals.

His smile curved as he remembered the "spells" Roca wove with her incomparable body. She was the tallest woman he had ever met, with legs that went on forever. Thinking of her, he opened his eyes. No light leaked around the shutters on the windows; either the suns had yet to rise or else the snow had become thick and stolen the day's illumination.

As his eyes adjusted, he saw Roca snuggled under the quilts near him, fast asleep, her lashes sparkling against her cheeks even in the dim light. It startled him; if he repulsed her now, surely she would have chosen other sleeping arrangements. He marveled to find such a woman in his bed. He could tell she didn't like praises to her beauty. Maybe she had heard such words too many times and no longer believed the sincerity of those who spoke them. Or perhaps her appearance had brought her injury. But if she would have let him, he would have composed a thousand ballads and sung his elation to the brother suns.

She was smart, too. In fact, he didn't understand much of what she told him. No matter. He liked to surround himself with intelligent people. It helped make up for his own deficiencies.

A familiar sorrow threatened him. How long would he have with Roca? He had become resigned to having his life curtailed, but every time he adjusted to the severity of his attacks, they worsened. If they became much more frequent, he didn't see how he could go on. At times, he wondered if it might be easier to end his life by his own choice, in his own way, rather than waiting for the day he didn't recover from an attack.

It frightened him, even more now because he had Roca. She had been here for such a short time, and she needed to leave. But surely she would come back. He felt how much she wanted him. And she was like him. Incredibly, he and Garlin weren't the only ones with such strange, sensitive minds. But Roca wasn't like Garlin. Her icy emotional armor hid a luminous sun. She glowed, as gold inside as without. Next to her brilliance, Garlin was an ember. Eldri hoped it didn't always cause his cousin this great pain, knowing Roca could be so much closer to Dalvador's Bard in her mind. He wanted Garlin and Roca to like each other.

Roca stirred under the covers and his body immediately reacted. He didn't know how she worked this magic, but he felt dizzy with needing her. It was quite pleasant, though nowhere near as good as the actual consummation. If she had no longer wanted him, he couldn't imagine that she would have undressed and joined him in bed. He drew her into his arms and folded his hand around her breast. Amazing that a woman could be so well endowed and not fall forward when she stood up.

Roca laughed softly, her eyes closed. "What a romantic thought."

"A fine morn to you," he murmured.

"And to you." She curled closer, her hands wandering on him. "Dancers shouldn't really be that big."

"You are a dancer?"

"Hmmm . . ." She had no trouble reaching the places she wanted to touch; someone had undressed him while he slept. "Never asked me to make 'em smaller, though. Sells tickets . . ."

"Ah." He had no idea what she meant. His mind was blurring into a sensuous haze.

Then Roca pulled away.

He tried to tug her back. "Come here, beautiful lady."

She braced her palms against his chest. "I don't want to overdo it."

He brushed a kiss over her ear. "Why not?"

Her lips parted, tempting, but she kept pushing him back.

"Come on," he murmured. "What is wrong?"

"I . . . well, I don't want you to have another seizure."

"You mean like yesterday?"

"Yes." She sounded subdued.

"Making love never caused them before."

"You're sure?"

"Positive." He went back to kissing her. He could tell she liked it, especially when she started to move against him.

So they greeted each other, moving together under the soft, warm quilts. He savored the warmth of her body against his, their limbs entangled.

Sometime later, as they drowsed, she said, "Morning is coming."

"Hmmm." Eldri stretched, half asleep. Belatedly, he realized what she had said. "How do you know? It is dark in here."

"My spinal node has an atomic clock. It keeps time."

He wondered if he would ever understand the things she said. "What is 'spinal node'?"

She was quiet for a while, and he sensed she was thinking of how to respond.

"It is part of my memory," she finally said.

"Ah." Now he understood. "Where you store what you learn."

"Well, yes." She sounded surprised. "Exactly."

Eldri pressed his lips to her temple, this time in respect for her duties as a Memory. "We should begin our preparations to go down the mountain."

Her mood brightened. "Do you think we can make it today?"

"I don't know," he admitted. "I haven't much experience with travel in such weather. It never snows in the plains."

"Well, we can try."

They climbed out of bed, shivering in the icy air, and dug garments out of the tube-narrows against the wall. For some reason, Roca seemed surprised he stored his clothes by stacking them in a vertical tube. She exclaimed over the blue glasswood and its gilded mosaics, though it all looked quite ordinary to Eldri.

"And this!" She pointed to a design of a blue and green sphere circling two larger gold ones. "What does it represent?"

"The gold orbs are the two sun gods." Eldri rubbed his arms to warm them. The fire had died to embers, and it was too early for the maid to have built a new one. "The green is Lyshriol."

She seemed to expect his answer. "The star system."

He wasn't sure what she meant, but her recognition implied her familiarity with the sun gods, supporting his theory of how she had come to him. He had no clue why Valdor and Aldan would send him such a treasure when he had been so remiss in attending them, but he would remedy that from this day forward, performing any expected rituals. He didn't actually remember what most of them were, but he could ask the Memory.

They returned to the warmth of bed and dressed under the quilts, laughing and kissing. Eldri thought of it as a dream. Then they tumbled back out and put on jackets. Roca went to the alcove and opened the tall shutters. As soon as snow blew inside, Eldri knew the storm had returned. Saddened, he stood with her, gazing outside while powder blew over them. Falling snow blurred the world. It must have been coming down all night; the drifts were so deep now, they buried the bottom of the castle. Everywhere, in every direction, he saw nothing but snow.

For a long time Roca gazed at the silent snowfall. Eldri stood behind her, his arms around her waist, watching the storm that had gifted him more time with her, but was breaking her heart. He couldn't imagine the great war she described. He had only one enemy, Lord Avaril, and his men had fought only skirmishes with Avaril's small army. This pain in Roca went much, much deeper.

"I am sorry," he said. "I wish I could make it stop."

She said nothing, just turned and put her arms around him, burying her face against his neck. "Fate is capricious, that it offers me so great a treasure, but exacts such a terrible price."

He went very still. "What treasure would that be?"

She drew back to look at him. "You are a miracle, Eldrinson Valdoria."

He touched her cheek. "It is you."

"How many people will die because of it? Thousands? Millions? *Billions?*"

"Don't," he murmured.

"No one knows where I am. I hid my trail." She shook her head. "Another ship may not put in here for months, maybe even longer. The port has no link to my people."

"I will take care of you."

"And who will protect you when my son finds us?"

"What do you mean?"

She spoke dryly. "He avenges first and asks questions later."

That didn't sound promising. "I will make offerings to Valdor and Aldan."

She sighed. "I wish it were that easy."

"Roca, we will make it work out."

She cupped his cheeks with her strange hands, her fingers so slender and delicate, her "thumb" to the side. Her palms felt warm against his cold skin. "You are a wonder."

"It does not trouble you, what you saw yesterday?" He made himself ask the question he had been avoiding. "The attack?"

"It troubles me greatly. The longer your condition goes untreated the worse it could become." She considered him. "Do you know what triggers the seizures?"

"I am unsure what you mean."

"What causes an attack?"

That was easy. "Stress. Tension."

Mischief flickered in her face. "Then we must make sure you are happy, hmmm?"

Eldri grinned. "I like your healing advice." He brought his lips to hers and showed her just how much.

But as much as he rejoiced at having her with him, foreboding plagued him. His time with Roca was a fragile dream that could soon shatter.


The web shimmered.

Humanity knew it by many names: Kyle web, psiberweb, Kyle space network, other ever more abstruse designations. Kurj experienced it as a lattice extending in all directions, awesome in its central regions, where its nodes reached their greatest numbers and concentration, but fragmented near its edges.

His command chair on the Orbiter served as a portal into Kyle space. His body remained in the chair, but his mind occupied another universe, one defined by thought rather than position or time. The vertices of the lattice provided doorways to and from real space. Their proximity to one another had little correspondence to the location of the telepathic operators, or telops, using them; instead, the more similar the thoughts of the telops, the closer their vertices in Kyle space.

Any telepath with sufficient training could become a telop. They could use the web, but they could neither build nor maintain it; such functions required a more powerful mind than almost any telops could claim. As a Ruby psion, Kurj did have the strength, but he had no access to the power link that created the web. He chafed at its denial: control the web and he would control an empire. The Assembly claimed it ruled Skolia, but he knew better.

His grandmother, Lahaylia, had created the web using an ancient Lock, her mind acting as its Key. She had maintained the web on her own for decades, struggling as it grew larger and more unwieldy. No other choice existed; without the web, her fledgling empire would have fallen before it ever had a chance to rise.

Then she had found Jarac. No one had known what would happen if he became a second Key. What little they had deciphered of the ancient glyphs in the Locks suggested that joining two Ruby psions into a power link would overload it and kill them both. But Lahaylia had reached her limit. She needed help or her empire would collapse. So Jarac joined her—

And so he survived. Together they formed the link that powered the web. The Dyad.

Jarac had taken command of the military, becoming Imperator. The job could only be done well, to its full extent, by someone with access to the power link that allowed communication across the stars; as Imperator, Jarac could spread his mind throughout the far-flung reaches of his interstellar military forces. Thus two Keys ruled the Skolian Imperialate: Pharaoh and Imperator.

Lahaylia and Jarac had very different minds. They existed together in the Dyad without interfering. Kurj desired to become a third mind in that link, but he feared the consequences to his grandparents. He and Jarac were too alike. That Jarac fit well with Lahaylia could mean Kurj would, too, but it might also be that minds as similar as his and Jarac's couldn't occupy the link at the same time. Or the power surge from adding a third Ruby psion might overload the link and short-circuit the web. At times like this, when Kurj was deep within the lattice, becoming part of it, his drive to harness its power tormented him. He struggled to rein in his ambition, aware that it could endanger his grandparents, two of the very few people he could admit he loved.

Now he searched, haunted by knowing that his resolve to control his mother's votes in the Assembly had made her vanish. He skimmed the lattice, looking for a sign. Any sign. Echoes of her visit to Irendela bounced everywhere, but then her trail became strange. Every time his spy network found a lead, it faded away. She had disguised her escape too well.

Today he repeated procedures he and his people had tried many times before. He hunted for back doors she might have used to slip through his spy network. He traced her finances, but found no record of her travel. A search on Cya Liessa produced millions of references to her dancing. Too many people adored her. He couldn't wade through it all. He sent thought-spiders to collate the data, attaching them to an outer shell of his mind as he browsed Kyle space. His node sifted through the data and listed references in order of their relevance to her recent activities. It all looked useless, but Kurj tagged a few comments for review later.

A gold ball approached him. Kurj paused, waiting within a lattice cell.

His grandfather's thought reverberated: **Kurj.**

His answer rumbled: **Grandfather.**

**The Assembly begins.** The gold ball spun away, into the web.

So it was time. Roca had to be hiding, waiting for this moment. He had his EI spiders on alert throughout the web, ready to stop her if she tried to attend the Assembly session through Kyle space. He also had human operatives in every starport on Parthonia, the world where the Assembly met, and he had posted agents in the session hall itself. If she came, he would catch her.

And if she didn't come?

No, it wasn't possible. She would be there.

As Kurj moved through the lattice, it grew rich and complex, with so many nodes he could no longer distinguish them individually. He had reached the systems that networked Parthonia, the capital world of Skolia. He thought of the Assembly session and one node swelled in size.

A large amphitheater formed around Kurj. He was attending as a simulacrum, with his body still on the Orbiter. Projecting his image into the Assembly, he appeared behind a console, what they called a "bench," though it was actually a virtual reality workstation. With his brain linked into its system, he would experience the session as if he were actually here. He could even smell the air and brush his hand across the bench where his simulacrum formed.

People overflowed the amphitheater. The controlled pandemonium of Assembly sessions always struck Kurj as inefficient. Tier after tier of seats ringed the central area, and above the tiers, balconies held yet more people. They filled every seat, including VR benches such as where Kurj sat, high in a balcony. It all ringed a dais that could rise or descend according to where a speaker wished to address the audience. Mechanical arms on every level also made it possible for speakers to move to the center of the amphitheater to address the assembled representatives.

Kurj found no trace of Roca. If she revealed herself on the web, his people could track her signal. They would let him know immediately. To attend the Assembly in person, her ship would have to land on Parthonia. It would be prohibitively difficult for most people to evade his on-planet security, but if anyone could manage such a feat, it was Roca.

She hadn't yet arrived.

The speeches were interminable, divided about equally between supporters and opponents of the invasion. Kurj had sent his best J-Force officers to speak, and they presented their case well. Platinum was crucial to modern technology. Although nanobots could construct Bose-Einstein platinum substitutes, the process was extraordinarily time-consuming and expensive. Mining proved easier, and the Platinum Sectors abounded with ore-rich asteroids. Skolia had long challenged

Eube's claim to that region, a dispute that had heated as the need for rarer metals grew. Skolia's forces had to take action now to reclaim its asteroids, before the Traders strengthened their position even more.

When the speeches finally ended, the Assembly prepared for the ballot. The number of votes held by each delegate depended on the size of the population that had elected them and their status within the Assembly. The First Councilor, Skolia's leader, had the largest bloc. The next largest went to Councilors of the Inner Circle: Stars, Intelligence, Foreign Affairs, Industry, Finance, Judiciary, Life, Planetary Development, Domestic Affairs, Nature, and Protocol. Ten years ago, Roca had won election as a delegate for Parthonia. She had risen in the ranks of the Assembly until two years ago she had attained the coveted position of Foreign Affairs Councilor.

The Ruby Dynasty and House of Majda had the only nonelected positions with significant voting blocs. They inherited their seats rather than winning them through election, a remnant of that ancient time when the dynasty ruled. Every noble House claimed votes, but only the Ruby Dynasty and Majda carried blocs large enough to affect most tallies. The Ruby Pharaoh and Imperator each held almost as many votes as members of the Inner Circle, and Roca, Kurj, and Dyhianna had smaller blocs associated with their titles. When Roca's votes as a Ruby heir were added to those she held as the Foreign Affairs Councilor, she wielded one of the largest blocs in the entire Assembly.

She still hadn't arrived.

Kurj leaned forward when the Councilor of Protocol called the vote. As the ballot progressed, the tally showed on a holoscreen above the podium. Kurj didn't like the numbers. The vote against the invasion was higher than he expected, well over fifty percent. When Protocol called his aunt Dehya, his mother's scholarly sister, she voted against the invasion, a disappointing but not unexpected development. Kurj voted for the invasion, canceling her bloc but doing nothing to shift the balance in his favor.

Then Protocol called Roca's vote.

Kurj stood behind his console, knowing he appeared solid and huge. A red light on its front provided the only indication that he was present as a holographic simulacrum. His voice rumbled throughout the amphitheater, amplified by the console audio. "In her absence, Councilor Roca has authorized me to cast her votes."

A clerk at a console on the dais spoke into her comm. "Proxy choice verified."

Protocol addressed Kurj. "What is her vote?"

He spoke clearly. "All in support of the invasion."

A tumult broke out, voices everywhere raised in disbelief. Roca's preference for peaceful resolution was well known. The First Councilor was standing by the podium on the dais, a tall, lanky man with dark hair. He opened his mouth with undisguised shock, and for an instant Kurj thought he would protest. Then he closed his mouth in an angry line. No changes could be made; the vote was final.

Kurj stood, patient.

"Your vote is recorded," Protocol said. She sounded stunned.

With a nod, Kurj resumed his seat. The balance of the tally moved solidly in favor of invasion.

"Jarac Skolia, Imperator of Skolia," the moderator said.

Kurj's grandfather stood, towering behind his VR bench just as Kurj had behind his. Seeing him, a giant of gold metal, gave Kurj an idea of how imposing a presence he made himself. Jarac looked around the amphitheater, his gaze sweeping the tiers as if that alone could press everyone into their seats. When it reached Kurj, Jarac stared at his grandson for a long, hard moment. It was one of the first times in Kurj's life that Jarac had looked at him with his inner eyelids closed.

Then the Imperator spoke, his words rolling out. "I cast all votes against."

Once again startled voices arose in the amphitheater, a wave of sound. Few people expected the Imperator to go *against* the vote when so many of his top officers—indeed, his own grandson and daughter—went in favor of invasion.

Protocol cleared her voice. "Your vote is recorded." As Jarac took his seat, the tally moved toward a balance, though it was still slightly in favor of invasion.

Protocol turned to Lahaylia. "The Ruby Pharaoh of Skolia."

Lahaylia rose to her feet, regal and tall, her hair piled high on her head. The amphitheater became silent. Kurj could see people leaning forward in their seats to better see and hear their legendary ruler. She spoke in a clear, resonant voice. "All in favor."

The rumbles in the amphitheater resumed, though with less agitation this time. The tally swung solidly in favor of invasion.

Protocol called for the last voter, the First Councilor, the leader of the Assembly, the government, and all Skolia. He stepped up to the podium and turned slowly in a circle as the dais rose high in the center of the amphitheater. Looking out over the assembled representatives, he spoke in a ringing voice. "I cast all my votes against."

Kurj inhaled sharply as the tally changed, careening back in favor of those who opposed the invasion. He didn't breathe as the numbers changed.

Then it was finished. The tally was done.

By a mere two votes, the Assembly had voted to invade Eube.

Kurj had won.

He also knew, without doubt, that he had lost far more than he gained—for Roca had never arrived.

# 10

# The Price of Miracles

The days passed with bittersweet pleasure while Roca waited for the snow to clear. She and Eldri spent their time together. He showed her Windward, an ancient castle as cold and drafty as it was beautiful, but filled with the warmth of the people who lived there.

Eldri had no more convulsions, but several times Roca felt him blank out. He would stare into space, then come back to himself, disoriented, with no memory of what had happened. It frightened her. Had he received treatments as a young child, his condition probably could have been controlled, even cured. But the convulsions had apparently grown worse over the years as he suffered the long-term effects of repeated, severe, and at times continuous seizures.

"Come on," he told her on the third morning. "See the Reed."

"The Reed?" She laughed as he pulled her with him, running down a hall on the second floor of Windward. They sped around a corner—and barreled into a man whose arms were piled high with blue sheets. Laundry went flying, and Roca and Eldri jumped back while the fellow swore, his voice chiming on each cuss word.

Mortified, Roca lunged for the sheets. Eldri went for them at the same time and they banged their heads. The man was laughing now, the lines around his eyes crinkling. Eldri glared at him, but as a youth would scowl at an elder who found him amusing rather than as a sovereign to one of his subjects.

After Eldri and Roca untangled themselves, they helped the man pick up the laundry. He and Eldri chatted, their voices rising and falling in musical cadences, their emotions trickling past Roca's barriers. Eldri enjoyed the fellow's company, having known him since childhood. The older man was glad to see him, gratified even, though Roca couldn't tell why.

Eventually she and Eldri continued on their way, at a more sedate pace. Roca took his hand. "You surprised him."

He intertwined his fingers with hers. "I suppose it is odd for people to see me dash about. Usually I stay in seclusion."

"Because of the convulsions?"

He nodded, his face pensive. Then, suddenly, he grinned. "Look, Roca!" He pulled her into a recessed stone archway. The door within it opened into a circular chamber only a few paces wide.

Roca walked inside. The stone room contained nothing, and its unadorned walls were unnaturally smooth. "What is it?"

"A temple for Jaliece Quar." Eldri came up next to her. "Goddess of the Reeds."

"Ah, I see." She craned back her head. "It is a reed." The chamber rose through many levels of the castle, up into the west tower. "Actually, I think it is a transport tube."

"Transport?"

She turned to him. "You know that cylinder in your room where you store your clothes?" When he nodded, she said, "Haven't you ever thought it inconvenient?"

He blinked. "Well, no."

"It would be easier to hang clothes from a pole."

"Whatever for?"

"You don't have to take everything out to reach the garments on the bottom."

"The tube opens halfway down," he reminded her. "You only have to take half the clothes out to reach the bottom."

"But then the ones on top fall down." She indicated the temple. "The people of the Ruby Empire used tubes like this to suspend things. The design of the cylinder in your room probably derives from that same principle. But it lacks the technology to float garments or move them up and down, just as this can no longer move people up and down."

Eldri hesitated. "You speak as if you know the builders of this castle."

"They were my ancestors."

He touched a tendril of hair curling around her face. "So it is true. You descend from the makers of this place."

"Well, yes." For some reason, she felt as if she had given him the wrong answer, though it was true.

His face paled. "I thought so."

"You did?"

"From now on," he vowed, "I will observe the rituals. You have my oath."

"Rituals?"

"For the goddesses and gods of the sun, wind, and reeds." He paused with his hand near her cheek, as if he wished to touch her but was unsure she would allow it. "Are you a sister or daughter?"

"Of who?"

"Valdor and Aldan, the sun gods."

"Ah, no. Eldri, no." She put her hand on his arm, letting him feel her solidity. "I'm a person, just like you. Nothing more. People built this castle. Not deities."

"Even so." He held up his fingers. "Every ten days, I will make a flame in a reed as thanks."

She peered at his hands. "That is eight. Not ten."

"Eight?" He glared, apparently already forgetting his intent to be deferential. "Whatever could 'eight' mean?" He sounded far more irate than puzzled, and she suspected he knew perfectly well what it meant.

"Your fingers." She counted them. "Eight."

Glowering, Eldri made two fists and uncurled each finger as he counted it. "One, two, three, four, five, six, seven, ten."

"Of course!" Roca beamed at him. "You count in base eight. It makes perfect sense. Eight fingers, base eight."

"You sound like Brad," he grumbled. "And you make no more sense than him. Ten is ten. Not twelve." He took her hands and indicated her ten fingers, including her thumbs. "Twelve."

"We call that ten."

"It *isn't* ten." Eldri crossed his arms. "You are as bad as those resort planners. They never listen, either."

Her smile faded. "When I return home, I will see what can be done about them." The Assembly had to dispute Earth's claim here, lest it set a precedent of giving Skolian territory to the Allieds.

"Stay, Roca." He lowered his arms. "Don't leave."

She swallowed. "Please don't ask me that."

He didn't answer, only took her hand and walked with her out of the Reed. The day's light seemed to dim around them.

On their fifth day, Eldri took Roca up to the battlements atop the highest tower. Bundled in heavy jackets and trousers, they stood in the wind under a vivid lavender sky with no trace of clouds. Valdor, the large sun, was a huge golden coin hiding Aldan, his smaller brother. The mountains spread around them, spectacular in their jagged, dangerous beauty.

Far below, young people were clearing snow off the bridge that arched to the castle. Beyond it was the plain of windswept stone that visitors to Windward had to cross to reach the castle. Cliffs bordered both sides of the plain, rising higher as they came closer to Windward, until on its east and west sides, they towered straight up from the chasm, making it impossible to reach the back of the castle from this side.

Across the plain, Roca could see the end of the path that led up here from Dalvador. Two great statues bracketed it, each carved in the shape of a winged beast with curved horns. From a strategic point of view, she could see why Eldri's ancestors had put a fortress here; it was almost inaccessible. But she didn't understand *what* it protected. Windward had no city, no farms, no population of any kind except its staff.

"Eldri, look." She pointed toward the path. "Do you see?"

Squinting against the sun, he shaded his eyes. "Riders!" He grinned at her. "We have visitors."

"That means we can leave here, yes?"

"I think so." Jubilant, he heaved open the glasswood door to the tower. They ran down the steps inside.

At the ground floor, many of Eldri's men joined them. They all jogged across the courtyard, through the melting snow, and out under the portcullis. Garlin was already on the bridge, surrounded by soldiers from the castle, all in disk mail and leather armor dyed a dark purple. As Eldri came up to Garlin, the older man handed him a belt with a finely tooled scabbard. The sword it held had a crystalline pommel made from the same prismatic material as lyrine hooves.

"Saints above." Roca gaped as Eldri took the weapon. "You aren't really going to use that thing, are you?"

He glanced at her as a man helped him into his armor. "You must go inside the castle."

"You can't think we're in danger from those few people." She knew nothing about combat here, but surely some principles were universal. They wouldn't all be standing out here if Eldri genuinely believed they were about to be attacked.

"We do not know who they are." He paused as his man finished outfitting him. "Probably friends, but they could be enemies. We will see." He strapped the sword belt around his hips.

It astonished Roca that he wore the weapon so easily. It had to weigh a great deal, with its great length and wide blade. "Eldri, that thing is dangerous."

Garlin spoke dryly. "That is the idea, Lady Roca."

Looking around, she realized all the soldiers on the bridge were similarly armed, many with daggers as well, and a few with weapons that resembled curved axes. She frowned at Garlin. "And if those people coming here are friends?"

He shrugged. "Then we will invite them inside."

Eldri drew her aside and indicated the castle. "Look."

Gazing up, she saw archers lined up along the battlements atop the castle wall, partially hidden behind merlons, between the crenellations. She arched an eyebrow at Eldri. "Are you always this friendly to visitors?"

He adjusted the belt around his hips. "Rumors say Lord Avaril plans to attack."

She hesitated. "Isn't it dangerous for you to fight?"

"I cannot live my life hiding."

"You could die."

His lips quirked upward. "I promise not to."

"Eldri! It's not a joke."

"I know." After a moment he added, "I had a seizure during a battle once."

She couldn't believe he said it so calmly. "How did you survive?"

"My opponent ran away. He thought I was possessed."

Roca heard the pain under his attempt to sound amused. Before she could respond, Garlin came over. "Lady Roca, you must return to the fortress now."

She wanted to stay, but she knew they would insist, just like her bodyguards. Annoyed, she stepped back toward the castle, still gazing out over the windswept plain. Across the open area, about a kilometer from where she stood, a group of riders were exiting the mountain path, riding between the towering statues.

"I only see ten lyrine," Roca said as the group came out onto the plain. "They don't look dangerous." Certainly not compared to all Eldri's men bristling with their weapons.

Eldri squinted at them. "I can't tell if those are my men."

*Magnify,* Roca thought. Her node accessed her optic nerves, and the riders seemed to jump in size. "Well, I'll take a launch off a lily pad!" She took off running across the bridge, unmindful of the slush that splashed on her boots and trousers. Her response startled Eldri's men enough that by the time anyone grabbed for her, she had already passed.

It took her only minutes to cross the kilometer-wide plain. The riders were dressed like Eldri's men, but without armor, and they carried no weapons. A man reined in his lyrine and jumped down while the other animals milled around him. As Roca dodged among the lyrine, the fellow wove his way to her.

"Brad!" She was so glad to see the port administrator, she threw her arms around his neck as soon as she reached him. He hugged her back, laughing, with no attempt to restrain his relief.

Suddenly a hand grasped Roca's arm and yanked her away from Brad. Startled, she swung around to find Eldri gripping her so hard, the veins in his hand stood out. He stared at Brad with no hint of a smile. Roca sighed. Apparently male territoriality was the same in all cultures.

Eldri's men had no such reservations about their visitors. Still in full armor, but with their weapons sheathed, they gathered around the newcomers, boisterous and laughing as the riders jumped down from their lyrine. Everyone mixed together, calling out names and slapping each other on the back.

Eldri spoke to Brad with chill formality. "You have ridden a long way."

"I'm sorry I didn't come sooner." Brad gave Roca a look of apology. "I tried to fix the flyer, but I don't have the parts. And I couldn't raise you on my comm equipment."

Roca winced. "I didn't have any with me." Before he could ask why not, she said, "Can you get parts for the flyer?"

"I sent an order with the supply ship." He started to say more, then stopped, the vertical lines between his eyes deepening.

"What is it?" Roca asked.

"It will be a year before another ship comes."

"A year?" Her stomach seemed to drop. "No ship puts in here for another *year?*"

"I'm sorry." Brad blew out a gust of air. "The pilot of this one waited several hours, but he couldn't delay any longer."

"Gods almighty." This was even worse than she had feared. "Pray they can find me."

"Who?" Brad asked.

Garlin was glancing around at the milling people. "Perhaps we should continue this inside."

Brad smiled at him. "Hello, Garlin. You look as annoyed as always."

Unexpectedly, at least to Roca, Garlin laughed. "And you," he told Brad, "will soon lose more chess games."

Brad chuckled as they all headed for Windward. His breath made blue puffs in the air. "We had quite a ride here. It took most of the day to bridge that collapsed section of the path."

Roca couldn't hold back her shudder. "We jumped it."

"Good Lord, why?" Brad asked.

Garlin answered. "It was too late in the day to go back." He walked at Brad's side with ease, seeming far more pleased than Eldri to see the Allied man.

Roca felt Eldri's confusion. His natural inclination to like Brad was marred by the image, vivid in his mind, of Roca hugging him. Roca wanted to assure Eldri he had no reason to worry, but she knew an open acknowledgment of his discomfort would hurt his pride.

Eldri spoke quietly. "We lost Jacquilar at the break."

Brad's smile vanished. "Eldrinson, I'm terribly sorry."

After a respectful silence Garlin said, "Brad, can you stay long?"

"Not too long. I can keep in touch with the port from here, but I should get back. I don't like to leave it automated." He glanced at Roca. "I had to make sure you were all right. Your message said you would only be gone a day. When you didn't return—and given the way you left—" He cleared his throat, avoiding Eldri's gaze. "I thought I had better check."

Roca could tell Eldri was upset. "I am fine," she assured Brad. "Everyone has been an excellent host." That wasn't completely true for Garlin, but it would do. "The snow kept us here."

Brad gave her an odd look. "Your English has certainly improved."

"I have a node optimized for languages."

His eyes widened. "Those things are expensive."

Roca didn't think this was the time to explain. They were crossing the bridge now, so she motioned at the melting snow all around them. "I take it the storm was unexpected."

Brad nodded. "It's hard to predict the snows."

"Lyshriol has no seasons?"

He gave her a startled smile. She wasn't sure why until she caught a flash of his thought—she had used the true name of the world rather than the one chosen by the resort planners.

"This planet has no axial tilt," he said as they passed under the portcullis. "And its orbit is circular. So no seasons. Climate variations mainly come from changes in altitude and churning of the atmosphere. It's always summer in the plains and winter up here. Snowfall this heavy is unusual, but it happens."

"No tilt and a circular orbit?" Roca asked. "That doesn't sound natural."

"It probably isn't." He motioned at the sky. "Eventually those stars will tear apart the orbit."

Roca glanced at the suns. Aldan had moved out from behind Valdor, showing as a small disk next to its more golden brother. They were probably K stars rather than the human standard of G, as typified by Earth's sun. From what she had seen, it took them about three and one-half hours to orbit each other.

"This world must have an interesting history." She gave Brad a pointed look. "A *Skolian* history."

He raised his hands as if to defend himself. "Jeri, I just run the port."

"Jeri?" Eldri snorted. "Her name is Roca."

"Uh, Eldri—" Roca started.

"Jeri is a false name," Eldri added, glaring at Brad as if daring him to argue.

Roca knew Eldri was asserting his familiarity with her, but he didn't understand what he could reveal. Roca was an unusual name and a well-known one.

Sure enough, Brad laughed. "Well, hell, maybe you're Roca Skolia herself. You know what they say, that she is the most beautiful woman alive, as radiant as gold, with eyes that shimmer like . . ." His voice trailed off as he stared at her.

"Skolia?" Eldri asked Roca. "You said the name of your province was Skolia. It is your name, too?"

Roca glanced at Eldri, and he inclined his head, understanding her unspoken request. Then he gestured to the riders and soldiers with them. Everyone dispersed, leading away their lyrine, the people of Windward deep in conversations with their visitors, who brought excitement into the community of this isolated mountain fortress. Roca gave Eldri a look she hoped conveyed her gratitude. Although no one at Windward understood English, some from Dalvador might. If she wanted off this world as fast as possible, she might have to take chances in revealing herself, but she had to minimize them.

Roca stopped with Eldri and Brad. Garlin also stayed, standing at Eldri's side. The four of them were alone now in the trampled snow of the courtyard.

Although Roca answered Eldri's question, she spoke to Brad. "Yes. Skolia is my name."

His face paled. "Roca *Skolia?*"

"Yes."

"This is significant?" Garlin asked.

Brad was staring at her. "Gods, why didn't you tell me?"

"Why do you think?" she said.

He narrowed his gaze. "It is an unusual claim."

"One punishable by death, if false," Roca said. The Assembly guarded its Ruby psions with a tenacity that bordered on obsession.

"If you truly are Roca Skolia," he said slowly, "then I am in one blazing mess of trouble."

"You have done nothing wrong," Roca said.

"Why would you be in trouble?" Eldri asked.

"Roca Skolia is a queen among her people," Brad said.

"Queen?" Eldri put his hands on his hips. "Like this 'king' your resort planners call me?"

"Something like that," Brad said.

"Good." Eldri grinned at Roca. "Then we are well matched."

Brad spoke carefully. "Eldrinson, I don't think you understand."

"Lady Roca." Garlin waited until she turned to him. "When the resort planners call Eldri a 'king,' they give the impression that a true sovereign would have a great deal more power than anyone here possesses. Is this true among your people, too?"

She understood what he was asking: did *she* have that kind of power. She said, simply, "Yes."

"Oh, God," Brad said. "I'm dead."

"Administrator Tompkins." Roca used his formal title, trying to jar him out of his panic. "No one will blame you."

"Like hell. I've watched your father and son on the news holos. And yes, now that I look for it, I see the resemblance." He took a deep breath.

"It's just not anything I would ever have imagined for a visitor to my port."

"Can you help me?" Roca asked. "I must return to Parthonia."

"My communications work at light speed. It would take years for a message from here to reach another world." Brad raked his hand across his tight curls. "I was chosen for this position with the understanding that I could adapt to life here without much support until our presence became better established. It was expected I could go for long periods on my own."

"We must have some recourse," Roca said. "Some way to access the webs."

"Can you create a Kyle web node?" His excitement jumped at the thought.

"Only a member of the Dyad can do that."

"Dyad." Despite the cold, he was perspiring. "You mean the Imperator and Ruby Pharaoh, yes?"

"That is right."

"Your parents."

"Yes. My parents." As much as she disliked revealing herself, it might be the only way to convince him they had to try every extreme to get her off Lyshriol. She had hidden her trail too well; the same twists and turns that freed her from Kurj's scrutiny had also stranded her.

Roca dreaded what Kurj would do to Eldri if he found her here. At best, her son had a controlled animosity for the men in her life. No one could match his memory of his father, Tokaba Ryestar. He considered no man good enough for his mother, especially after Darr.

The closer she and Eldri grew to each other, the more she feared for his life.

# 11

# Warlords of the Snow

---

Roca danced with the other women in an exquisite hall, a room with onion-shaped arches everywhere, all adorned by carvings that resembled frozen lace. Intricate mosaics designed from glasswood covered every surface like stained glass, but deeper in hue, less translucent. Roca whirled and spun, exuberant, letting herself go as she hadn't done for years. The women wore dresses today, with blue or violet skirts that swirled when they turned.

She didn't understand their speech, but she read their tone, body language, and moods. They drew her into ever more complicated steps, their voices trilling with delight that she learned fast. Although she could handle the gravity better now, she misjudged some of the steps and lost her balance, flailing her arms. Laughing and teasing, the others caught her, making it into a game. They called out with approval when she kicked her leg higher or arched her back farther than anyone else.

Over and over the dancers broke into four pairs, eight women in a set. The patterns were all based on powers of two. In fact, now that she thought about it, everything on Lyshriol came in pairs: two suns, two moons, two sets of two opposing fingers on two hands, two sets of two opposing toes on two feet. She smiled, thinking of Eldri and herself. Two lovers.

The men stood around the edges of the hall, watching, drinking, and laughing among themselves. Musicians in one corner played drums, reeds, bells, chimes, and harps. Other folks sat at round tables, intent on a game that involved rolling small bubbles of various colors. Children

ran through the hall, shaking rattles at one another and bouncing hardened bubbles.

Sometimes a woman in the dance would tease one of the men,
waving a scarf at him until he waded in and pulled her out of the crowd,
stealing kisses from her. Sometimes he took her out of the room altogether. Roca hoped the men would join the dancing, but they showed
no inclination to do so. Searching for Eldri, she caught sight of him
standing under an archway with Garlin and several other men. He
waved, but stayed put.

So Roca danced, abandoning herself to the sheer pleasure of move-
ment. It touched her deep inside, as it had her entire life. Her Assembly
duties may have forced her to curtail her dancing, and the grind of the
Parthonia Ballet may have dulled her joy in performing, but the love of
her art would always be in her heart. This magical time became a warm
place in the cold reality of her life, a reality that could all too easily
freeze this lovely but vulnerable dream.


Eldri and Roca lay sprawled on his bed, still in their finery from the
dance, eating sweet-poms, small blue bubbles that tasted like heaven.
Roca gazed dreamily into the fire in the hearth, where glasswood rods
burned with red, blue, and green flames.

Eventually she laid her head on the quilt and closed her eyes. Having two sets of visitors in only a few days, first the Bard showing up
with his people, then the non-Bard and his party arriving yesterday, had
sent Windward into a whirl of parties. It was fun, but exhausting. She
ought to rest now; tomorrow they would head back to the starport to
see what could be done about this frustrating mess of her being stranded
here.

Eldri nuzzled her cheek. "You are an incredible dancer."

"You should dance with me."

"*What?*" He sounded scandalized. "Do not make such jokes."

She opened her eyes halfway, her lashes shading them in a gold
fringe. "Don't men dance here?"

"Of course not. What a question."

She smiled drowsily. "You look as if I just suggested you run naked through Windward."

"Better that than dance," he growled.

"Really? Why?"

He seemed bewildered by the question. "That is like asking why a man isn't a woman. A man who dances is—well—female."

"I think it's sexy."

"Please do not tell me that men dance among your people."

"All the time." She yawned. "The Parthonia Ballet has more male than female dancers."

His mouth fell open. Then he snapped it shut. "No wonder you must come here to find a genuine male person."

Roca laughed. "It is just different customs." She snuggled closer to him. "But you most certainly are a genuine male person."

"Come dance for me some more," he murmured.

A knock came at the door.

Eldri ignored it, pulling Roca against him. Another knock came, louder than the first.

"Bah," he muttered, letting her go. "Enter," he called in his own language.

An older man opened the door, his face creased with lines. As he spoke, his voice sharp, Eldri went rigid. Roca caught little of what the man said, but she recognized the word "lyrine."

Eldri moved off the bed, fast and urgent. "I have to go."

"What has happened?" Roca asked. She stood up next to the bed as Eldri strode to the tube-narrows that held his clothes. "What is wrong?"

He yanked out the boots he wore with his disk mail. "A party of riders comes up the mountain."

Roca felt the blood drain from her face. "From Dalvador, I hope."

"I don't think so." He swung around to her. "Not hundreds of men in armor astride war mounts."


Roca stood with Brad atop the highest tower of Windward. Late afternoon sunlight slanted across them, bringing no warmth. They were in a lookout, an area only a few paces across, protected by merlons carved in the shape of bubble reeds. Freezing wind pulled at their heavy clothes and the hoods of their jackets. It was hard to believe that only yesterday she had stood here with Eldri, watching Brad come up the mountain.

Their new visitors terrified her.

Hundreds of warriors astride dark lyrine were climbing the path, the only viable approach to—or escape from—Windward. Cliffs to the east and west would block the army from surrounding the castle, which meant they could only occupy the barren plain in front of it. However, on the other side of the castle, more warriors were descending the supposedly inaccessible mountains. With her augmented optics, Roca saw men rappelling down the cliffs, anchoring their ropes with spikes they hammered into the stone. It had shocked Eldri; apparently mountain climbing was unheard of among his people. Until now. Lord Avaril had just invented it.

The men on the cliffs had no access to the castle, but their presence also made it useless for Windward's inhabitants to try bridging the chasm *behind* the keep. If Eldri's people found a way to sneak out the back, the invading army could just as easily break inside. Avaril had thoroughly trapped them.

People were running across the courtyard below, battening, locking, and securing everything. She wished she could help, do anything, but when she and Brad had offered, everyone politely urged them to stay back. They claimed it was because Roca and Brad were incarnations of Lyshrioli deities, the Suns and Night, and as such had to be protected and revered. Roca suspected it had more to do with her and Brad getting in the way because they had so little experience with castle operations.

She studied the massive wall around Windward. Several meters thick and many stories high, it was topped by protected walkways, with towers at the corners. Although it differed from castle walls she had seen on other worlds, it served the same basic function, to protect its inhabitants and keep out hostile armies. She prayed it performed its purpose well.

"I need to do something," Brad muttered.

She felt the same way. "They want us out of the way."

"I can't believe this is happening." He dug his hands deeper into his pockets. "An interstellar leader shows up at my port and what do I do? Get her caught in a local war."

"You did nothing wrong," Roca said.

He gave her a dour look. "Tell that to your Imperial Space Command when they show up."

Roca knew he was right; if she died here, Kurj would raze Windward to the ground, along with half the mountain range. Brad would be history. "Can you reach the port with your comm?"

He didn't look optimistic. "I can contact the EI there. I've already sent a message. But Avaril has probably also invaded Dalvador, and even if he hasn't, Eldri's people aren't likely to look for any message from me. They don't understand my equipment and wouldn't trespass in my home anyway."

Roca nodded, disheartened but unsurprised. Eldri's men were taking positions on walkways and in towers, concealing themselves while they studied the enemy forces. "How will they fight?"

"I can't say." Brad hunched his shoulders against the cold. "Even if I knew ancient warfare, which I don't, they probably have their own strategies here."

"The strategy is the same everywhere," she muttered. "Kill."

To their left, on a large tower, several people walked out onto a balcony. They gazed at the approaching army as it poured between the two statues guarding the end of the path up from Dalvador. The balcony was lower than where Roca stood with Brad, and far enough away that she couldn't pick up the mood of the people there. But it took no telepathy to guess their thoughts; Avaril's army far outnumbered the forces at Windward. The castle's best defense was its impregnability, but Avaril could wait them out until Windward's people starved or surrendered.

"I hope we have enough food," Roca said.

"Maybe they will come to a truce, eh?"

"Maybe." She doubted it, though, given Avaril's advantage.

Eldri and Garlin joined the group on the balcony, both of them in leather armor and disk mail. Compared to the cybernetic armor Roca was used to seeing on soldiers, theirs looked excruciatingly fragile. They were holding their helmets, which were designed like wild beasts and would cover their heads and upper faces, with openings for the eyes.

As Avaril's army spilled onto the plain, a man separated from the general mass and headed to the castle. He wore armor and mail similar to Eldri's men, except the leather was dyed red. Stopping at the foot of the bridge, he waved a red scarf over his head.

"What does that mean?" Roca asked.

"I haven't a clue," Brad said.

On the balcony, one of Eldri's men waved a purple flag.

"Maybe they're challenging each other," Brad said.

"I think they want to talk."

He looked doubtful. "Why?"

"The women dance with scarves." She recalled the party this morning. It seemed an eternity ago now. "When they want to catch a man's attention, they wave it at him."

"This is no courtship," Brad said dryly.

Garlin was leaving the balcony; below, Avaril's man waited at the bridge. Several meters back, a taller man stood in the midst of several warriors, his head held high and his gaze narrowed at the group of people on the balcony. He had wine-colored hair of the exact same shade as Eldri, and he seemed about Eldri's height.

A discordant grinding echoed through the mountains, the sound of the portcullis raising, then lowering. A moment later Garlin appeared in view on the bridge.

Brad swore. "Is he nuts? They could kill him."

"I think they're going to negotiate." Roca watched as Garlin crossed the bridge to Avaril's man.

"I hope so," Brad said. "But we need a backup plan."

Roca studied the scene below. "If Eldri's people destroy that bridge, no one can reach us. The chasm is too wide to jump." Twisting around, she indicated Avaril's warriors in the northern mountains. They had gathered in clumps on snowy ledges and the snow-drenched valley behind Windward, but none had tried crossing the chasm to the castle. "They can't manage it even with their ropes and spikes."

"But then we couldn't leave."

"We could build a drawbridge."

Brad considered the thought. "It might work. But they would need explosives to destroy the bridge down there. I don't know if they have them." He rubbed his chin. "I might be able to help."

Roca smiled. "You blow things up?"

"Actually, usually just the opposite. I'm an engineer." He studied the bridge where Garlin and Avaril's man were talking now. "You're right that the bridge is our weak point. Avaril's men could bring across a battering ram and smash their way in here."

Roca leaned out to see better. The tower was high enough to let her peer over the castle's outer wall, but the portcullis was directly below, making it hard to see. "It would be difficult, I think. But not impossible."

Brad hauled her back, his face alarmed. "Don't do that! I get hives thinking of you falling."

"I won't." She hoped it was true. "I doubt they could bring a battering ram up the mountains. They would have to make it here."

"Nothing up here but snow and rock. We're above the elevation where plants grow." Brad indicated the people working in the courtyard below. "They have to carry in all the food."

Roca tried not to think about those limited stores. "Avaril's people might throw boulders at the castle."

"They would need a catapult, a big one, which has the same problems as a battering ram."

Roca scowled. "None of this makes sense. What does this keep defend? Not Dalvador. Avaril's army came up from *that* side of the plains. It would be easier for them to reach Dalvador than here."

"Dalvador has its own defenses."

"Then why attack this castle? Why is it here?"

Brad spoke slowly. "I'm not certain, but I believe it's more a temple than a fortress. It stands on the border between Dalvador and the Rillian Vales like a—" He paused, thinking. "Like a sentinel that watches over both sides of the world, at least the world as the people here know it."

Roca remembered how Eldri had taken her to the reed temple. "So if Avaril captures Windward, it gives him symbolic dominion over Eldri's people."

"Yes." His voice quieted. "Windward is hallowed to these people. I've been on Lyshriol for three years and never been invited. This is my first visit."

Roca understood what else he was telling her, how much it had meant for Eldri to bring her here. She hoped the Dalvador Bard didn't live—or die—to regret his decision.

Garlin was returning to the castle, while Avaril's man headed back to the army. As Garlin disappeared from view, the portcullis rumbled. Roca dug her hands into her pockets. "I know what else Windward has that Dalvador lacks."

Brad glanced at her. "What?"

"The Dalvador Bard."

His expression turned bleak. "He is the only one between Avaril and the title."

"Why is Avaril so intent on killing Eldri's family?" Roca curled her fists in her pockets. "Is he really such a monster?"

Brad squinted at her. "Actually, one might argue that Avaril has more of a claim to the title than Eldrinson."

That gave Roca pause. She wanted to hate the man who threatened her lover, and she couldn't imagine Eldri trying to kill anyone's family. But she was hardly an unbiased observer. "Why would Avaril have more of a claim?"

"Avaril's father was the oldest son of the man who served as the Dalvador Bard two generations ago. Eldrinson's father was the second son." His voice took the cadence of a storyteller. "Many years after the Bard lost his wife, he fell in love with a younger woman. Then his oldest son betrayed him. He impregnated the woman and demanded her hand in marriage. His enraged father disinherited him, which made his second son the heir. That was how Eldrinson's father became Bard. The older son did marry the woman, but she died in childbirth, leaving him even more embittered. He taught his rage to his child—Avaril." Brad exhaled. "And so Avaril Valdoria swore to avenge his parents."

Roca pulled her jacket tighter. "Your people have a saying, yes? The sins of the father—?"

"Shall be visited upon the son. Yes." A grimace creased his face. "Let us hope this castle is as unassailable as it looks."

She shivered. "Let us hope."


People filled the dining hall: Garlin, Eldri, soldiers, women and men from the castle. Young people moved among them, serving food and drink. Everyone wore heavy clothes, fur-lined boots, and jackets or cloaks. Only a low fire burned in the great hearth; they were already rationing the glasswood they used for everything but couldn't grow here. Roca and Brad waited on a bench against the wall, out of the way, a few meters from the long table where Eldri and Garlin conferred with several advisers.

Roca crossed her arms. "We should be over there."

"Garlin refused," Brad said.

She rose to her feet. "Garlin needs to trust us more."

At first Brad looked as if he would caution against interfering. Then he stood next to her. As they approached the table, Garlin glanced up and frowned at them. Following his gaze, Eldri looked too.

Roca stopped at the table. "We would like to help."

"This concerns Windward," Garlin said. "Not you."

"We are here, also," Roca answered.

He waved his hand at the room full of people. "So are they. I do not see them interrupting us."

"We have knowledge they don't."

Garlin scowled at her. "This is not about offworlders."

"It is about defense," Eldri said mildly. "Theirs, too."

"We might be able to offer insights," Brad added.

"I think they should stay," Eldri said.

Garlin's urge to send them away was almost palpable, so much so that Roca wondered everyone in the room didn't feel it. But apparently

Eldri's wishes superseded his. He motioned curtly at two chairs across the table, set back from his group. "Be seated then."

As Roca and Brad settled into the chairs, Roca looked around. Three other people were at the table: an older man with gray hair and a craggy visage; a portly woman, also with graying hair, though surely she was only in her early thirties; and Shaliece, the Memory in the red robe. Shaliece watched them all, her concentration never wavering. It unsettled Roca; she felt as if a holovid camera were recording her every move.

The others resumed their discussion. They spoke in Trillian, but Brad translated for her. The two of them were far enough away from the others that as long as he kept his voice low, it didn't disrupt the conversation.

"They are shocked by Avaril's army," he said. "They knew he was gathering men, but they had no idea he had so many."

She felt their bewildered dismay. "What did Avaril's man say?"

"He gave Garlin terms for surrender."

Roca scowled. "Why should we surrender?"

Brad indicated Eldri, who was gesturing with vehemence as he spoke. "He asks the same question. It is a standoff. We can't get out and Avaril's army can't get in. They wonder if Avaril can breach the walls." He paused. "Personally, I think he would need flyers to get in here or some other technology they don't possess."

"What do they say?"

Brad waited for an appropriate opening, then spoke to the others in Trillian. The older man responded, and Brad translated for Roca. "The walls are strong, probably enough to keep out Avaril." He paused. "They measure time differently here, but I think he is saying they have enough stores to last about a standard year, and that only with careful rationing."

"A year?" She held back her apprehension. "Surely Dalvador will send reinforcements before then."

He relayed her question and translated the answer. "Apparently Avaril has other forces that have engaged the armies of Dalvador and Rillia. Or so his man claims. We have no way to verify it."

Garlin spoke to Brad in English. "Can you ask your port for help?"

"I've sent messages." Brad tapped the palmtop on his belt. "With a good line of sight from a tower, I can reach the computers. Unfortunately, no one in Dalvador knows to check for messages or how." He glanced at Roca. "I sent a message offworld, but it won't travel any faster than light speed."

The Memory held up her hand. She spoke to Brad in a melodic trill; then, in perfect English, she said, "But it won't travel any faster than—" and tilted her head.

Brad spoke slowly. "Light speed."

She nodded and folded her hands on the table.

Roca smiled at Shaliece. "You speak English well."

Everyone at the table froze. The older man rose to his feet, his lips pressed in a line. Eldri spoke quickly, putting his hand on the man's arm, nudging him back into his chair.

Roca glanced at Brad. "What did I do?"

It was Eldri who answered, his voice gentle. "The Memory will not speak unless her hand is up. It otherwise disrupts her memory of events."

Roca spoke to all of them, with Brad translating. "Please accept my apologies. I am new here and meant no offense."

Eldri's face lit in a smile. "None taken." Then he added, "The Memory doesn't actually know English, but she can replicate what she hears perfectly. Sometimes when she hears new combinations of sounds, she needs to check their pronunciation."

Garlin leaned toward Roca. "What does light speed mean?"

"It means," she said dourly, "that it will take years for Brad's message to reach anyone." It sounded even more depressing out loud.

"I don't see what good that will do," Eldri said.

"Neither do we," Brad admitted. "But we must try."

Eldri inclined his head in acknowledgment. As he and the others resumed their discussion in Trillian, Roca spoke to Brad in a low voice. "Did you bring any weapons to this planet?"

"An EM pulse-gun."

She sat up straighter. "Do you have it with you here?" He could fight off a good number of warriors with such a weapon, as long as its ammunition and charge lasted.

He shook his head. "Garlin, Eldri, all these people—they've been my friends for years. I would no more draw that gun on them than on my own family."

"So you left it at the port."

"Yes." He rubbed his eyes. "I thought of bringing it, but I knew I didn't need a pulse-gun to make Eldri behave." He tapped the pocket of his jacket. "I did bring my smart-knife. But it won't help much against an entire army."

Although his response didn't surprise her, she wished he had thought to bring the gun. It was true, a pulse-gun was far more than he would need under most circumstances here, but someone in his position had to look at every possible danger. She glanced over the hall, so full of people who hoped Eldri and Garlin had a solution. "What do you know about this Avaril fellow?"

"Eldri's people don't like him. They don't believe he has any right to a title his father lost." Brad paused. "He is a personable man if you can get past his hatred of Eldri's family. But the Dalvador people love Eldri. The thought that Avaril would kill their Bard horrifies them."

It horrified her, too. "I wish we had your gun."

Brad spoke quietly. "Lady Roca, I would do my utmost to defend you and the people here. But attacking Avaril's men is another story. It violates so many interstellar contact laws, I can't even count them."

Roca gave him a sour look. "You Allieds have too many rules. Those warriors want to kill us. I would shoot them now and worry about interstellar contact laws later."

"Yes, you could kill a good number of them before they caught you or the gun ran out of power. Then what?" He spoke in a low, intent voice. "One pulse-gun can't destroy an entire army, even one armed with only swords and bows. You would be lucky to escape with your life, and it would be like stirring a hornet's nest out there."

Roca winced at the image. She indicated Eldri and his advisers. "What are they saying?"

"That we must prepare for a siege."

She made an incredulous noise. "This is surreal."

"No kidding."

Roca wasn't sure what he meant, but his tone mirrored what she felt. "Why is Garlin frowning?"

"He and Shannar are talking about blocking the bridge."

"Shannar?"

He indicated the older man. "Shannar Ervoria. He knows military procedures better than anyone else here."

"Have they considered destroying the bridge?"

Brad leaned forward to catch their notice. When Eldri inclined his head, Brad spoke in Trillian. Shannar answered, with Brad translating. "The bridge is too solid to break."

Roca considered what she had seen. Eldri's people knew how to smith metal swords and tools. She knew too little about forges to guess if the one here would have anything useful, but it was worth checking. As much as she hated the thought of destroying that extraordinary bridge, they had to consider it. "Can they make explosives?"

After Brad translated, much discussion took place. Finally he said, "It doesn't sound like it."

"Perhaps you can help them make some." Roca said. "Gunpowder, maybe?"

"What is 'gunpowder'?" Eldri asked in English.

"For a bomb, sort of," Roca said.

Garlin frowned. "And what is 'bomb'?"

"You know," Brad said. "Boom. Rocks and people go flying."

Garlin arched an eyebrow at him. " 'Boom'?"

"We could pour burning oil," Eldri said. "Or drop boulders."

With Brad translating, Shannar said, "Oil might have uses. But we have no boulders here large enough to affect that bridge."

"I cannot see my people starve!" Eldri pressed his palm against his breastbone. Then his eyes glazed and he stared into space, his face blank.

The gray-haired woman leaned forward, her forehead creasing as she addressed Eldri in Trillian. He showed no sign of hearing. Shannar started to speak, but Garlin held up his hand, motioning for silence. They all waited.

Brad spoke under his breath in a voice only Roca could hear. "What the hell just happened?"

"He had a seizure," she murmured.

Eldri blinked several times and looked around. Garlin and the others resumed their discussion, making an obvious effort to act as if nothing had happened.

"He has seizures?" Brad asked.

Roca nodded. "How well do you know Eldri and Garlin?"

"Garlin, well. We often play chess." He paused, rubbing his chin. "Eldrinson comes by much less often. He lives in seclusion, except when he sits as a judge or sings at festivals. His people say he is—" He spoke a Trillian word. It sounded flat, without the chiming of Lyshrioli vocal cords. "It means something like 'touched by the gods.' "

She sighed. "That seems to be what they call it here."

"Call what?"

"Epilepsy."

His gaze widened. "You think he has epilepsy?"

"Yes. I do." She watched Eldri, who was listening now while the others talked. "A few days ago he had a generalized tonic clonic seizure."

"Good Lord. You mean a *grand mal* attack?"

She checked her node for English, but "grand mal" was under French. Big sickness? She found a better explanation in her medical files. "Yes, that is right. But that term isn't used by your doctors now."

"I had no idea."

"His condition looks serious to me, maybe life-threatening. I'm not certain he can survive without treatment."

"I feel so damned helpless. We *have* the technology to do wonders for these people, but our hands are tied."

Roca felt her face flush. "I am sorry for my comments at the port about the, uh—the chocolate."

"Ah, well." He looked weary. "You had a point, even if I didn't want to see it. If we gave Eldrinson medicines without fully understanding his condition, we could do more harm than good."

She knew he spoke the truth. But that mattered little right now. It could be a long time before they had any means to help Eldri. Avaril might not have to kill the Bard at all.

Eldri's own body might do it first.

# PART TWO:
## Siege

# 12

# Miracle of Snow

---

The days passed, one after another, melting together for Roca into a dreamlike routine. Windward went on strict rationing. They lit few fires and never shed their heavy clothes. Everyone ate sparingly. Instead of dreading the snow, Roca hoped for it now, to replenish water for drinking and washing. Everyone waited, barricaded within the castle while Avaril's army camped outside. They prayed for the Dalvador army to come to their rescue, while no doubt Avaril's men prayed for its destruction.

Even if Dalvador could have sent an army, Roca doubted it could reach Windward; Avaril's men controlled the path up here from the plains and probably any other approaches as well. If the Dalvador army cut off his supplies, his climbers could bring them in through the northern mountains. Roca was developing a healthy respect for Avaril Valdoria; he was all too successful at this business of siege.

Yet for all the deprivations and fear, the days also brought joy. She and Eldri laughed, shivered, and made love, ensconced under the quilts on his bed. She loved his mischief, his teasing grin, the sensual way his lashes lowered when he wanted her. Their minds blended so easily. He had become part of her, an oasis in the loneliness she had lived with for so long that she had stopped seeing it.

He had no more *grand mal* seizures, but he experienced the less drastic type, blanking for a minute or two, then coming out of it, disoriented and dazed. For the most part, though, he seemed well, making her hope she had overestimated the severity of his condition.

Today he had gone to see Brad's group working on explosives. So far very little had come of the effort; Brad had too few resources and too little knowledge on the subject. But he and his people kept trying. Roca didn't go with Eldri, though. She had barely forced herself through her dance exercises this morning. Now she sat in the dining room with several women, dully poking at her lunch. She was truly weary of bubbles. People ate nothing else here. The food came in every color and consistency, sweet, sour, big, little, soft, hard, but it was all *bubbles.* What she wouldn't give for a big, thick steak.

One of her companions spoke, a friendly girl of about twenty with pink hair streaked by gold. To Roca, her speech sounded more like wind chimes than words. She wasn't sure what the woman said, but it had to do with food.

Roca gave her a wan smile and struggled to communicate in her fractured Trillian. "I no bubble know." She had meant to say she wasn't used to the food, but from their baffled expressions she gathered she hadn't succeeded. Trillian sounded so flat when she spoke it anyway.

One woman was watching her with particular concern, Channil, the gray-haired matron who served as an adviser to Eldri. She laid her hand against Roca's cheek, then felt her forehead. Roca couldn't understand her, exactly, but she thought Channil was asking how she felt. Roca didn't know how to tell them she couldn't keep eating their food. What could they do? They had nothing else. If a diet of bubbles made her sick, too bad.

Channil clucked at her and stood up, taking her arm. Roca let them lead her upstairs. They changed her into a nightshift and tucked her into bed, convinced she was ill. Roca supposed she was, though she had no cure for food poisoning, other than her nanomeds, which apparently couldn't deal with this constant diet of bubbles . . .

It was dark when Roca woke. She just made out Eldri in the dim light, changing for bed. Muddled, she rubbed her eyes. "Is it late?" She lapsed naturally into English with him.

"Very." He came to the bed. "How do you feel?"

"Tired." She closed her eyes. "I don't think I can eat your food, either."

He sat on the bed, still in his trousers and a green shirt with belled sleeves. "Tarla says you have missed your menses."

"Who?"

"Tarla. The woman who cleans our rooms. She says you have had no cycle since coming here. It has been enough time, hasn't it?" His voice sounded odd, as if he didn't know whether to be frightened or elated.

Roca sat up slowly. "I can't be pregnant. My nanomeds prevent conception."

He began to unlace his shirt. "Nanomeds. You use all these words that make no sense. When men and women make love, Roca, they have babies."

She touched his cheek. "I can't."

He pulled off his shirt and set it on the table. "Then why no menses? You have this sickness. And you are tired." His voice caught. "Will you give me a child?"

"I'm sorry." She felt how much he wanted this. "It isn't possible."

"Maybe these non-meds of yours do not work here."

"Chemistry doesn't just stop working."

He made an exasperated noise. "Chemistry. Brad likes this word too. He says it is mixing things up to make other things. It makes no sense. He claims the chemistry of life here differs from his world. Maybe it has made your med-things stop working."

"The differences in chemistry are what makes me sick."

He finished undressing and slid into bed, drawing her into his arms. "Very well. We will accept what you say. You cannot become pregnant. When you have gone nine months with no menses and are as big as Windward, we will discuss this 'chemistry' again."

She smiled, molding against his body. "Perhaps we should explore this idea about making babies some more."

He laughed softly. "We are most diligent, yes?"

"Hmmm." However queasy she might have been before, she felt remarkably diligent now.

Later she drifted to sleep amid dreamy visions of bubbles.

———————

Roca had more and more trouble keeping down food. She slept for increasingly longer periods. One afternoon she dreamed Brad was talking to her, his voice relentless, refusing to abate when she tried to block it out of her sleep.

She slowly opened her eyes. Brad was seated on a stool by the bed. The room was dim, its shutters closed tight against the cold. No flames licked the hearth; rationing had grown so tight, no fires were allowed now in bedrooms during the day. Across the room, Eldri was hovering in the window alcove with Channil, the matron who had taken Roca under her wing.

"Lady Roca?" Brad spoke kindly. "They asked me to talk to you. They thought it might make you more comfortable, since we're both offworlders and share knowledge unfamiliar to them."

"Hmmm . . ."

He tried again. "Is that all right with you?"

"Yes . . . fine." Tired. She was so tired. "Go ahead."

"Channil says you have missed two menstrual cycles now."

"Two?" She tried to wake up. "You must explain to them. No matter how much Eldri wants me to be pregnant, it cannot happen."

"Are you sure?"

She sat up, pulling the quilt around her body. Her shift offered no protection from the icy air. "The food makes me sick. The water, I think, too. I don't always boil it."

He started to speak, then stopped.

"What is it?" she asked.

"I have a girlfriend in Dalvador."

She strained to orient her groggy mind on his change of subject. "You must be worried, with Dalvador under attack."

"Yes." He hesitated, seeming flustered. "Do you remember what I said about the people here having nanomeds in their bodies that break down impurities in the water?" When Roca nodded, he said, "Well, I have them now, too."

"Did your doctors synthesize it for you?"

"No. I have the same ones as the natives."

She struggled to focus. "I don't understand what you're trying to tell me."

"My girlfriend and I." He was stuttering. "Lady Roca, please forgive my mention of personal matters. But the nanomeds can be passed from woman to man, or vice versa. During, ah, intimacy."

Oh. She was suddenly more aware of Eldri in the alcove, and grateful too, for his tact in waiting out of earshot. "Then I must have them too."

"Yes."

She pushed her tousled hair out of her face. "You think I've picked up meds from Eldri that interfere with my contraception?"

"It's possible."

"Pray that isn't true." She couldn't begin to imagine what would happen if she returned home pregnant, especially by a man her government and family would consider an illiterate barbarian.

Nor was that all. Even in this egalitarian age, when men had achieved equality with women in most facets of life, the noble Houses remained anachronisms, following matriarchal customs of the ancient Ruby Empire. Roca wasn't sure how Eldri's culture had taken on patriarchal qualities, but an isolated colony could evolve a great deal in five millennia. It wasn't unusual for a woman in her position to marry a younger man, but with Eldri she pushed the age difference too far even for the Imperial Court. And those were the very people who would find his background the most scandalous—especially General Vaj Majda, Matriarch of the House of Majda, who expected Roca to wed her nephew.

And yet for all the mess, muddle, and chaos it would create, her heart leapt at the thought that she might be carrying Eldri's child. She had all the signs, not only "morning" sickness that lasted all day, but also fatigue and soreness in her breasts. It was a treasured but tenuous gift, one she feared would disintegrate under the force of reality.

Roca looked past Brad to where Eldri stood with Channil. She suspected the older woman was a midwife. Raising her voice, she spoke in halting Trillian. "Channil, check me, can you, for babe?"

The midwife came forward. "Yes, Lady. I can check."

Channil shooed the men out. Eldri hesitated at the door, looking back, an unbearable hope in his eyes. Channil had to push him through the doorway.

Roca lay back down on the bed, exhausted. During her first pregnancy, she hadn't been worn-out this way. She had felt wonderful. If this was a second, it was going nowhere near as well as the first.

Channil examined her with gentleness and unexpected expertise. Roca knew she shouldn't be surprised; humans would never have survived through all the ages if they had needed modern doctors to have babies. But it frightened her to think of giving birth with so little medical care. If she had complications, she or the baby could all too easily die.

Channil pulled the covers up over her legs. "You are a healthy young woman."

"What think you?" Roca asked in Trillian. "A babe?"

"I think so." Channil sat next to her, her face kind but concerned. "It will be easier to tell in another thirty days. For now, you must rest."

For all her apprehension, Roca felt a delicate joy. "Why look you so much worry?"

Her chiming answer was hard to follow, but Roca thought she said, "You do not carry this one so well."

"This one?" Roca asked.

"It is not your first."

"No. Not first." She hadn't known a midwife could tell so much. But then, she had never known a midwife.

"Did you have trouble the last time?" Channil asked.

"None."

"This time is difficult, I think. You must keep down food."

"I try." Softly Roca added, "Send you Eldri in?"

The matron smiled. "That I can."

As Channil left, Roca sat up, smoothing her hair. A moment later, Eldri appeared in the doorway.

Roca spoke in Trillian. It somehow seemed appropriate. "Come in."

He closed the door and came to the bed, his step uncertain. His voice chimed as he spoke his language. "How are you?"

"Well." Roca laid her hand on the bed. "With me sit?" At least, she thought she said that.

His grin flashed as he sat against the headboard and pulled her into his arms. "Your Trillian is not so good."

"What say I?"

"That I should sit on you."

Roca laughed and switched to English. "I need more practice."

"Perhaps a bit." He hesitated. "What says Channil?" Despite his attempt at nonchalance, his hope leaked through to her.

Roca answered softly. "She thinks you are right."

"Roca! A child?"

"I had thought not, but it seems I am wrong."

"I knew it!" He grinned. "It is wonderful."

Roca swallowed. "I hope so."

"Are you sad?" He held her close. "I would like to be glad."

"It is incredible," she whispered. "And it terrifies me."

He pressed his lips against her temple, and she closed her eyes. She felt his happiness. The idea of a child didn't put him off, despite his youth. In fact, from what she had seen here, he was older than most Lyshrioli men when they became fathers. Perhaps he felt more pressure to start a family than a man his age would among her people.

"When would you like the ceremony?" he asked.

"Ceremony?"

"The wedding."

Her eyes snapped open. "What wedding?"

"For us."

"Uh, Eldri—"

"We must marry."

"Why must we marry?"

"To make our child legitimate."

Good gods. How to explain? The union of a Ruby heir had nothing to do with love and everything with politics, heritage, and duty. Her marriage contract would be like a treaty between major powers. This planet was part of the Allied Worlds, and marriages made in Allied territory were binding under Skolian law. Lyshriol might even be a Skolian world. If she wed Eldri, it would be legal—and it would create an interstellar crisis.

Roca didn't know how to begin. But before she could say anything, he spoke with difficulty. "You needn't explain. I feel it in your mind."

"I am sorry." She regretted it even more, knowing that by admitting he had picked up her mood, he was showing her a trust that came hard to him, after a lifetime of hiding his differences.

"Let us just sit here for a while," he said in a low voice.

"Yes." Roca drew him closer.

As they held each other, she tried to think of a way they could stay together. The Assembly was desperate for Ruby psions. They would need to verify his DNA, but Roca was certain he had most if not all of the Ruby genes. To be a psion, a child had to inherit the recessive genes from both parents. Roca had two of every one. Even if Eldri had some unpaired, he could pass them on to his children. Precedent existed. Roca's first husband, Kurj's father, had barely been a psion, but he had carried many of the genes unpaired. With the help of doctors, he had given them all to his son, matching every one from Roca. It made Kurj a Ruby psion, though his father manifested almost none of the traits.

The Assembly would rejoice if they could use Eldri to breed Ruby psions, but she feared they would treat him like a stallion they owned or a laboratory animal to study. They would never countenance his marriage to one of the Imperialate's most powerful women. Nor would the inner circles of Skolian authority tolerate a man with Eldri's primitive background gaining access to such extensive interstellar influence.

Roca could insist on the marriage; the Assembly would be hard-pressed to refuse her. She wielded considerable power in her own right. But the resulting battle could split cracks in the political landscape, setting her against the Assembly, even her family. It would weaken the government at a time when they particularly needed strength, given that they might soon go to war. She gritted her teeth, trying not to think of the vote she had missed.

Eldri spoke in a low voice. "Your moods confuse me. Am I deluded to believe I feel your mind? Now you are so very sad. You believe we can never be as one. Tell me I am wrong. Tell me I am crazy."

She swallowed. "You are not crazy."

"It is the flaw I have, is it not? The convulsions. That is why you refuse me."

"Eldri, no, never. Epilepsy isn't a flaw. It is a medical condition." She hurt inside, knowing he saw himself as lacking when he had so much to offer. "You had your first seizure the day your family died, yes?"

"That is what Garlin says."

"They were probably psions. The traits are inherited. Your mind would have been linked to theirs." She gentled her voice, feeling his discomfort with reminders of the family he had lost before he had a chance to know them. "When they died, violently, so many at once, it probably caused a trauma to your mind."

It was a moment before he answered. "I do not understand this word, 'psion.'"

"Someone who feels emotions and thoughts."

Silence.

"Eldri?"

"There are others like me?"

"Yes," she murmured.

"Before you, I thought I was the only one. Maybe Garlin."

"Our child will be like us."

He spoke in a low tone, full of pain. "Our child will suffer the cruel spirits as well?"

She cupped his face in her hands. "Eldri, no. Your seizures are symptoms of an injury, not part of being a psion. They have no connection, except that as a psion you may be more susceptible to seizures."

"Our child will not suffer them?"

She hesitated. "I can make no promises. You may pass on a greater susceptibility to seizures. But the chances are good that our child will be fine."

"Like Garlin?" Hope leaked into his mood. "His mind is like mine, but he has never had a problem."

"Yes. Like Garlin. But stronger."

His mood became tender. "This child is a miracle."

"Yes," she agreed softly. "A wonder."

"I composed a song, just in case it was true about the baby."

Her mood lifted. "Ah, Eldri, I would love to hear it."

He sang for her then, in Trillian, his voice heartbreakingly beautiful. She listened in joy, but also sorrow, knowing he hadn't asked the questions she most dreaded—for he didn't know them.

Roca was having too much trouble with the pregnancy. She and Eldri had too many differences, not just their hands or coloring, but also in biochemistry. They came from different stocks of genetically engineered humans. For all the midwife's experience, she had nothing resembling the knowledge she might need to assist in such a pregnancy and birth, if complications arose. To make it worse, they were in the middle of a siege, with dwindling supplies of food and fuel. Even if she and the child survived, she saw no way out of the tangle of political or social convolutions that would ensnare them—no way to stop reality from crushing their fragile miracle.

# 13
# Cyber Slums

---

The orbiter served as home to the powers of an interstellar empire.
Imperial Space Command had found the space station adrift in
space, a dead relic from the Ruby Empire—or so it had appeared. Then
the techs awoke it, reviving its ancient Lock, which could power a Kyle
web. Centuries later, Kurj had named the station the "Orbiter" because
it orbited throughout the Imperialate, never staying in one place. He
christened its idyllic city "City" and he called the valley where he lived
"Valley." The names made perfect sense to him, though they seemed to
amuse his grandmother. His grandfather understood.

ISC replaced most of the Orbiter's technology, but they left the
Strategy Table. Modern engineers had yet to reproduce the transparent
composite used in its construction. Lights glittered within its massive
top and blocky legs, illuminating the gold, copper, brass, silver, and
platinum components, all visible like the mechanisms of a gleaming,
antique clock.

Today, military personnel packed the Strategy Room, seated at the
great oval table or standing by the metallic walls. Officers on other
worlds attended as VR simulacra. All four branches of ISC were represented: the Imperial Fleet, Advance Services Corps, Pharaoh's Army, and
J-Force.

The Fleet had originated in the navy on Raylicon, but now it dominated the ISC space divisions. Banner Highchief commanded. When
Kurj had first heard her name, he had gritted his teeth, imagining the
atavistic culture that produced it. He had no romanticism for barbarism.

He should have avoided assumptions, though; Highchief was a towering cyber-warrior from a high-tech culture. Hard but fair, she had a dry sense of humor he appreciated. Although in private she expressed doubts about the invasion, in the Assembly she supported him.

The Advance Services Corps scouted planets. Kurj recalled how they had tried to recruit his father, Tokaba Ryestar, a civilian explorer. Tokaba had refused. When Kurj had been a small, laughing boy, Tokaba had often swung him around, saying he would much rather toss his golden child in the air than shoot people. Kurj didn't miss the irony: his father had declined to support ASC; now the ASC Commandant had voted against the invasion. Regardless, he treasured his memories of Tokaba. Recalling his father's love of peace was all that constrained his drive to obliterate the Traders, indeed, all that held his ambition for power in check.

Kurj himself headed the J-Forces, the fiercely independent pilots who faced the Traders one on one, without the mental static of crewed ships to interfere with their mind-intensive operations. He had risen through the ranks, ruthless and driven to this command. Today he controlled one branch of the military; someday, as Imperator, he would control them all.

The Pharaoh's Army had existed for five millennia, during the Ruby Empire, through the dark ages when technology crashed, and now in the interstellar age. Vaj Majda commanded. As the Matriarch of Majda, she came from a long line of warrior queens. Tall and dark-eyed, with iron-gray hair and an aristocratic face, the forceful Majda—General of the Pharaoh's Army—had given Kurj his strongest support for the invasion.

Kurj considered the Majda. Even he had approved the Assembly's choice of her nephew, Prince Dayj, as Roca's consort. The union would increase political stability, strengthen ties between Majda and the Ruby Dynasty, and enhance the prodigious wealth of their Houses. He suspected the Assembly also hoped Roca would weaken his links to the militaristic side of Majda. He knew better, but he kept that to himself.

Personally, Kurj found his future stepfather insufferably arrogant. Dayj had, however, one exceedingly admirable quality; he obeyed the conservative traditions of his House—which meant he kept his mouth shut and stayed in seclusion on Raylicon. That made him perfect for Roca. As a Councilor, she couldn't live on Raylicon, so Dayj's presence would be nonexistent in her life.

A voice spoke on the comm in Kurj's ear. "Primary Skolia, the First Councilor is on-line."

Kurj subvocalized his response: *Understood.* Sensors in his throat interpreted and transmitted the answer to his ear comm.

The simulacrum of the First Councilor formed across the table, so lifelike he looked solid. Kurj added his voice to the murmur of acknowledgment. "My honor at your presence, sir."

The First Councilor nodded, his dark eyes scanning the room. As the elected leader of Skolia, he was the supreme commander of ISC, even over the Imperator. Kurj thought it an absurd division of power. The Imperator should rule; without him, Skolia would fall to the Traders.

A woman's voice rang through the Strategy Room. "Imperator Skolia." The great platinum doors opened—and Jarac entered.

Kurj rose to his feet along with everyone else. Towering and massive, Jarac strode to a heavy chair embedded in the far wall. As he sat down, techs fastened him into the cyber-throne, plugging its exoskeleton into his neck, spine, wrists, and ankles. It linked him to the War Room, giving him full access to any data needed by this council. He would become the focal point of the meeting, its central command unit. Its Key.

Kurj wondered how Jarac felt about the Assembly overriding his vote against the invasion. Jarac had long supported the division of power that put the First Councilor over him, but Kurj thought it must bedevil him now, knowing that if he had full command, he could refuse to lead the invasion.

The woman spoke again: "Her Highness, the Ruby Pharaoh."

They all remained standing. The pharaoh's simulacrum formed at the head of the table, along with those of the officers who served as Operations, Communications, Plans, Intelligence, Logistics, and Security. After she settled into her chair, everyone else also sat down.

So began the meeting to formalize their invasion.

Kurj had his recommendations ready: send in the J-Force first. The split-second response times and accelerations of space warfare were beyond normal humans, but the Jagernaut-ship combination could handle them. Robot drones would fight most of the combat, but the creativity of human minds added an edge that could mean victory.

"Jagernauts can succeed where drones alone would fail," Kurj told the assembled council. "Both in space and on-planet."

Jarac's voice rumbled. "Settled planets and habitats must remain untouched. I want no civilians hurt."

Kurj gritted teeth. Certainly he intended to protect civilians. But Jarac insisted on too many limitations; it would curtail the ability of ISC to act as a coherent force. He didn't understand his grandfather. The Imperialate couldn't survive if it lost its technology, and for that they needed platinum. Without the Platinum Sectors, Skolia would fall. Kurj had won this time, on the invasion, but what about the next time? And the time after that?

The day would come when he had to challenge Jarac.

Submerged in the web, Kurj cloaked his identity and became a dark, anonymous figure. His slum-spiders were following leads on systems buried so deep, he would have never found them with normal searchers. But he had designed these searchers himself, and they went where respectable spiders never ventured.

Kurj didn't like what he found.

He had uncovered nothing about "Roca Skolia" since she vanished, but references to "Cya Liessa" abounded. In one cluttered info-shack he listened while two avatars "appreciated" her dancing.

**Never heard of ballet,** one said.

**Who cares what you call it?** the other answered. **Take her out of the fucking costume and "dance" all night. Now THAT would be art.**

Kurj sent a fire-pulse through the net and scorched the infostructure for their shack. It collapsed around them in a conflagration of error messages.

He followed another lead to an erotica site, where his mother topped the list of *female artists to see naked*. He torched the list and made sure they couldn't rebuild their database there.

In an underground seraglio hidden by illegal psiware, he uncovered a site dedicated to rape scenarios of celebrities, with VR technology that allowed a user to experience the simulations. His mother was listed under "less well-known gems," along with files of her dancing that had been doctored so she was wearing nothing but a slave collar.

Kurj was gripping the arms of his chair so hard, his fingers spasmed. He incinerated the entire site, bringing down its server and every site linked to it. Then he sent the data to his Intelligence people. They would take care of it. If the creators of this site had any connection with Roca's disappearance, he would dismember them with his own hands.

He couldn't take any more after that. He withdrew from the web and slumped at his desk, his head in his hands. Every day he awoke knowing he had provoked her disappearance. For all of his conflicted feelings about Roca, he loved her. No matter what her faults, she had been a wonderful mother. If she had died—or worse—it would kill him.

Whoever had taken her would pay for their crime.

# 14
# Song of the Heart

The days passed in a blur. Roca slept often, letting her body adapt to the many changes she was experiencing. She didn't know how much her physiology varied from Eldri's, but given her exhaustion, she suspected the differences were considerable. Her body was trying to compensate.

Although she could handle the stronger gravity reasonably well now, no longer mistiming her motions or stumbling, it added to her fatigue. She still managed her dance exercises every morning, wearing leggings and a sweater against the cold, but she had begun to question whether she could carry their child to term. She needed more help than they could give her at Windward. Every dawn she awoke praying the Dalvador army had arrived, and every day she learned the same disheartening news: the siege continued.

Eldri's seizures worsened. At first he had only the mild type where he blanked for a minute or two, then came back to himself, disoriented but otherwise unaffected. He often knew it was coming by a pain in his abdomen, though he had trouble describing the feeling, sometimes calling it nausea, other times an ache. During the episode, his fingers might jerk, but usually he simply sat. She felt his seizure like mental static, followed by blankness. The frequency of the seizures increased as the siege continued and supplies ran low.

He tried to hide his *grand mal* seizures, but Roca knew: they burned like a fire racing across her mind. One day she found him arguing with

Garlin in his office. As she entered, Eldri stiffened and fell to the ground, going into one of the worst convulsions she had seen.

Dismayed, Roca dropped to her knees next to him on the rug, whose plush thickness protected his jerking limbs. Garlin knelt on the other side, but they could do little more but watch, helpless as Eldri jerked. It was several minutes before he went limp; within moments, he was asleep.

Garlin spoke stonily. "You should leave."

"No." Roca looked up at him. "I shouldn't leave."

He spoke wearily. "Lady Roca, he doesn't want you to see."

"I live with him." She shook her head. "I feel it, Garlin. These big seizures come every six or seven days now."

He stiffened, clearly about to deny her words. But then his shoulders sagged. "Sometimes every five."

She swallowed. "How bad are they?"

"A minute or two. One went on for much longer." His voice shook. "I thought it would never stop, that he would die from lack of air and the strain on his body."

Roca's voice caught. "We must help him."

"Somehow." The sorrow in Garlin's voice made her wonder how she could have ever doubted his motives.

He carried Eldri to his suite and put him to bed with Roca's help. For a while, they both sat vigil, but as the day grew into evening Garlin had to leave, to tend other matters at Windward. Alone with Eldri, Roca climbed onto the bed and sat against the headboard. She held him while he slept, his head nestled against her hip.

And she cried.

"Surrender?" Garlin stared at Roca. "Are you insane?"

She stood with him in the Vista Hall by an open window. Chill air blew her hair around her body. In her side vision, she could see Brad standing by the bench.

"Is it less insane to sit here in Windward while our supplies run out and Eldri grows worse?" She twisted her hands in the fur shirt she wore over her swelling abdomen. "What if he hurts himself during a convulsion? What if one day they don't stop? We have to get help." She pressed her hands against her belly, her heart filled with the blindingly intense love that had gripped her since she first felt the child move within her. "We have to get me help, too. I can't give my baby the right nutrition. Gods only know what I should be doing that I'm not. Is it that bad to surrender? Better to be their prisoners than dead."

"Lord Avaril wishes to be Dalvador Bard. He cannot do so as long as Eldri lives." His voice had an oddly gentle tone, unusual for him. "He probably would have spared you if you hadn't been pregnant. He would have kept you for himself, but you would have lived. Now you carry Eldri's heir. Avaril can no more let you live than Eldri."

Roca closed her eyes, feeling the icy wind. Then she glanced at Brad, sending a silent plea for help in her gaze.

Brad came forward. "There must be something we can do."

"You have suggestions?" Garlin asked.

"Are you sure we can't climb down the chasm around the castle?" Brad asked.

Roca suspected Garlin's answer would be the same as the other times she and Brad had asked, but she kept hoping he would think of something new. "Perhaps it has some unknown outlets."

"No," Garlin said. "It just ends. And it is a long way down. I doubt even I could make it from up here."

Brad gestured at mountains outside, and the warriors encamped there. "Are you really so certain you can't sneak a messenger out through that blockade?"

A shadow passed over Garlin's face. "We have tried. Three times."

That caught Roca by surprise. "Do you think they got through?"

"Nay, Lady." He answered harshly. "The first time, Avaril sent the scout's severed head back to us. The second time he sent the man's intestines. The third, his heart."

"Good God." Brad blanched. "That's sick."

"But effective. We have sent no more scouts." Garlin's voice quieted. "I regret the two of you are caught in our war."

"I knew when I came here that I might have to deal with life-threatening situations." Brad glanced at Roca. "But none of us could have imagined this, with a Ruby heir."

Softly she said, "Nor could have I."

Roca went down the drafty staircase, with its cracked stairs and stone walls. It ended in a rough-hewn doorway that opened into a room built from blocks of stone. Stripped to their waists, wearing heavy trousers and boots, their chests slick with sweat, Eldri and another man were practicing with their swords, those monstrosities Roca could barely lift. Torches on the walls cast flickering light over the two men and made large shadows on the walls. Metal clanged, echoing in the underground room.

Mesmerized, Roca sat on the lowest steps. Although Eldri could often sense her presence, today his practice absorbed his attention. She loved to watch him move. He fought with deadly grace, parrying and lunging with an expertise that took her breath away. But it frightened her, too. He and his opponent were holding back to avoid injury, but gods knew they could still skewer each other.

After a while they stopped, heaving in huge breaths. They picked up their shirts from the floor, talking and laughing as if they had been doing no more than playing sports. It wasn't until Eldri turned toward the door that he saw her.

He hesitated, and she sensed he knew how much she worried about his fighting. "Roca. How long have you been there?"

"About half an hour." She couldn't help but notice his gleaming, muscled chest as he wiped down. "You were impressive."

The other man glanced at Eldri, trying to hide his smile, and inclined his head. He nodded to Roca with the same respect, then went up the steps, leaving her alone with Eldri. Although she appreciated his discretion, it made her uneasy to think that if Eldri had a seizure here, on the hard stone floor, no one would hear her call for help.

Eldri sat next to her. "How goes the babe?"

She took his hand and set it on her belly. "Can you feel it?"

"Feel what—ah!" Eldri jerked back. "He kicked me!"

She laughed. "A fine, strong son."

"Do you feel it, too, that we have a son?"

Roca nodded. "Sometimes, late at night, I lie with my eyes closed and the light of his mind fills mine."

"I feel this also." He put his arm around her waist and drew her against his side, resting his other hand on her abdomen. "I learned a word from Brad once. Angel. That is our son."

Roca chuckled. "Little boys are rarely angels. I'm sure Garlin can testify to that, having brought you up."

"Ah, well." His laugh rumbled, with a vibration on the end. "Is that why you came to see me train, so you could inform me that my son will misbehave as much as me?"

Her smile faded. "Doesn't it worry you that you might have a seizure while you are fighting?"

She expected him to deny it, but instead he said, simply, "Yes."

Roca focused on him, trying to understand his mood, gestures, motivation, everything about this man she was coming to love. "If you stopped, you would feel you were giving up. Giving in, both to Avaril and to the epilepsy."

"I have never made those exact thoughts in my mind." He spoke slowly. "But yes—fighting, whether outer or inner demons, is something I must do. Otherwise, why live?" He pressed his lips against her temple. "And I have so much to live for now."

She turned her head, bringing her lips to his. It was a gentler kiss than they usually shared, the fires of their passion banked for this moment. After they separated, Eldri put his arm around her shoulders and they sat looking into the arms-room with its flickering torches.

"I have a question for you," Roca said.

"Hmmm?" He leaned his head against hers, resting after his workout.

She finally spoke the words she had practiced all morning. "Do you still want to marry me?"

For an instant he seemed to freeze. Then he slowly lifted his head, turning to look at her. "Yes. If you will have me."

Her voice caught. "I will."

Eldri took her hands. "What changed your mind?"

"Life seems so short these days." She curled her fingers around his. "It is too precious to waste on politics and fear."

His face gentled. "I will make you a good husband."

She raised his hands and kissed his knuckles. "And I will be a good wife to you, for however long we have left."

His grin burst out, like the suns above the mountains. "Do not look so gloomy. I will trounce Lord Avaril. You will see." Mischief brimmed in his gaze. "And you know, Roca, only men are supposed to kiss the hand that way." He planted a resounding kiss on her knuckles.

"Hah!" She rained kisses all over his hands. "There. That is what happens when you tell me I cannot do something because I am a woman."

"Ah, well, I must say it more often, then." Laughing, he drew her closer, though they couldn't find an easy way to hug with her belly between them. It didn't matter. These last months, for the first time in years, Roca felt happy.


Garlin performed the ceremony. Normally a Bard would give the vows, but Eldri was the only one available. So Garlin stood in for him. Shaliece, the Memory, donned her red robe to record the marriage, her violet eyes following every move and gesture.

Roca felt as if events were swirling around them, gossamer and indistinct, hard to see clearly because they were in the midst of it all. Her throat tickled with a nervous anticipation she had never known in her first wedding. She came into the dining hall with Channil, descending the stairs. Eldri entered across the room, with Garlin at his side. The bone-chilling cold discouraged finery, and everyone dressed in layers of heavy clothes. Eldri and Roca met at the head of the long table and stood facing each other. He didn't smile, but his eyes had a glow she had never seen before. When he took her hands, his own were shaking.

Neither the Blue nor Lavender Moon shone tonight, so no moonlight leaked past the slits in the shuttered windows. With the fuel rationing, they had lit only a few oil lamps, giving the hall a dim golden glow that softened its harsher edges. The people of Windward gathered around, a few holding precious candles that flickered in the drafts.

Garlin stood before them, tall and proud, and spoke, his Trillian words rolling like deep-throated music. Holding Eldri's hands, Roca gazed into his eyes, feeling as if she floated with the musical words and antiqued candlelight. After Garlin finished, Eldri and Roca knelt before him. He held together his third and fourth fingers and touched each of them on the crown of the head. Then he drew them back to their feet. Eldri took Roca's hands again, always gazing at her. He took a deep breath—

And he sang.

His voice soared, evoking a treasury of images for Roca: the forests of her home on Parthonia, with droop-willows shading mansions of pale blue stone; brick-red deserts on the dying world Raylicon, beside the Vanished Sea, beneath a stone-washed sky; the infinite reaches of interstellar space, where stars blazed and celestial bodies rotated in an unending dance. His incomparable voice swelled until tears ran down her face.

When Eldri finished, Roca wiped her palm across her cheeks, smearing her tears. The Memory stepped forward, making a special effort to remember every detail of this moment. Then everyone crowded around, congratulating them, the women crying and kissing Roca on the cheek, the men thwacking Eldri on the back. It astounded her that they offered such friendship. Their emotions flowed like a benediction.

So it was done. She and Eldri had just changed interstellar history. If they died in the siege, but Brad lived, he could tell her people. If no one survived, if the news of her marriage went no further than Windward, she and Eldri would still know they had joined their lives, minds, and love on this extraordinary night.

# 15

# The Long Table

---

Useless.

Kurj had been in the web too long; it took a great toll on the body and mind to spend days submerged in that alternate space. Stalking the mysteries of another universe, searching its endless twists, became his reality, until he forgot he lived as a man of flesh and blood.

Intravenous lines fed him. He blamed his melancholy on having spent so long here, in the web, without rest or solid food. But he continued to search. Today he sifted through inconsequential nodes on fringes of the web so far from the centers of activity that he wondered why he bothered.

Even here, he found reviews of Roca's dancing. People chatted about her performances, giving opinions on her artistry, style, and technique. Most comments were positive, glowing even, but not all. Kurj deleted the disparaging reviews. He knew it was foolish; people had a right to dislike his mother's dancing. They were idiots if they couldn't see her genius, but that wasn't his problem. Even the critical reviews were courteous, without the sexually explicit or violent material he had incinerated in the cyber-slums and slave dungeons. But what the hell. He deleted the bad ones anyway.

He was preparing to leave the web when one of his Evolving Intelligence spiders spun up, whirling like heated copper.

**Yes?** Kurj asked.

I have found another reference for Cya Liessa.

**I will look tomorrow.**

This one may be important.
**Why?**
It dates from after her disappearance.
Kurj shrugged. **So do all of these.**
This person claims to have seen her.
He froze. **Show me.**

Kurj strode into the office of his security chief and slapped a holosheet on the man's desk. "I found this message in a rickety old network, one so dated, it had only one link to the Kyle webs. It's from someplace called Capsize, wherever the hell that is."

His startled chief picked up the sheet. Kurj knew the message on it by memory: *You won't believe who I saw last night at the port. Cya Liessa! The dancer. She's even prettier in person.*

"Saints almighty." The chief gaped at him. "This is nowhere near where we thought she had gone."

"Follow it up." Kurj planted his huge palms on the desk, his adrenaline surging. "Run down every flaming damn link to this message. *I want the location of that starport.*"

"There." Eldri pointed down at Avaril's army, which filled the flat area before the castle.

Roca pulled up her hood against the cold. The rich smell of its fur lining inundated her, so familiar now. She and Eldri were outside, in the tiny lookout area of the highest tower. The Backbone Mountains sheered up on all sides, a sharp and jagged range, surreal in its spindled peaks. Snow covered the higher summits, but only a dusting remained at Windward. The drifts from so many months ago were long melted and gone. The path to the plains had become a conduit for Avaril's men to bring in supplies. Roca tried not to think about how depleted the castle stores had become.

"There it is again!" Scowling, Eldri pointed at a group of men by a campfire. "Can you make out anything?"

Roca focused, using her enhanced optics. "What did you see?"

"A flash, like metal."

She scanned the camp, resolving details. One man was cooking over the fire and two were sitting, talking. "Someone is rubbing a sword, cleaning it maybe."

"That wasn't it." Eldri shifted restlessly. "It was larger than a sword."

Another man walked into the scene—and Roca gasped.

"What is it?" Eldri asked.

Roca squinted at the man. "You."

A pause. "What did you say?"

She watched the newcomer sit with the warriors at the fire. "A man down there looks like you." She studied the fellow. "Same hair, though with some gray. About your height and build. His face is similar to yours."

"Does he have a scar?" Eldri's voice had become strained. "It stretches from his left eye to his chin?"

Roca studied the man. "Yes, actually." She turned to Eldri, seeing only a blur. "Do you know him?"

"He is my cousin. Avaril Valdoria."

"Gods, Eldri." As her eyes readjusted, her new husband came into focus. "You could be brothers."

"Brothers shouldn't try to kill each other." His face creased in lines of tension. "I gave him that scar not long ago, when his men ambushed mine in the foothills."

Knowing that the man who wanted to kill her husband looked so much like Eldri made it worse, leaving no doubt this was kin against kin. She thought of her own family, so full of love and anger, tenderness and violence. "I wish I could help."

"You can't. But I thank you for the sentiment." He gestured toward the plain. "You saw nothing unusual? No metal?"

"I'll look more. Maybe it moved." Roca peered down at the army again. When she magnified the scene, it decreased her field of view, so she widened her search.

The settlement had become a village. At first only men had lived there; apparently women didn't fight in armies here. It seemed odd to Roca, who descended from the queens of the Ruby Empire, where men had been owned and never went into combat. Modern Skolians considered their culture egalitarian, but remnants of its ancient roots remained even in this modern age.

From what Roca understood, the population here had suffered a high mortality rate among female babies thousands of years ago, creating an imbalance of men and women. Eventually it had evened out, but during the era when men outnumbered women, they had assumed more authority, giving the culture both matriarchal and patriarchal elements. Inheritance of titles went through the male line; land went through the female line. Only women were scholars; only men served as judges. Men never danced, but it was a great achievement to sing well. A woman's ability to dance commanded great respect, but she would sing only for fun, never as a vocation. When the women and men combined their talents, they created a remarkable beauty of motion and music.

The protocols of life here seemed less formal, without rigid social distinctions. As the months of the siege had passed, women had filtered into the camp below, girlfriends and wives of the warriors perhaps, or camp followers.

"Did you find anything?" Eldri asked.

She scanned the camp. "The women are gone."

"You are sure?"

"I don't see any."

"This is not good."

Roca turned to him. "Why would Avaril send them away?"

"I would if I planned for my army to attack."

She pressed her hand against her abdomen, instinctively seeking to protect her child. "But how? They can't get in here."

Eldri glanced at her swelling abdomen, his face taut. "I cannot say. You saw nothing else unusual?" When Roca shook her head, he frowned. "I am certain something new was there. Metal."

"I'll try again." Turning back to the camp, she surveyed its layout. "Nothing. Just a lot of—good gods, what is that?" A large structure stood half-hidden against a cliff. She had missed it the first time because it was set so far back and made from the same stone as the mountain. Solid and round, it stretched as long as three people. Metal bands encircled its girth.

"What?" Eldri asked. "What do you see?"

Roca described it. "They must have brought materials up from the plains. They haven't been cutting that rock out of these mountains. We would have noticed." She pulled back and focused on him. "Does it sound familiar?"

"Yes." Eldri spoke grimly. "A battering ram."

No one expected Roca and Brad to stay out of war councils anymore. Roca sat next to Eldri at the table, and Brad sat near Garlin. Shannar, the military expert, was next to Channil, the senior midwife at Windward and the closest they had to a chief physician. Shaliece, the Memory, also sat with them, focused and attentive.

Over the past months, Roca had come to respect these people. Life here was rough and uncompromising, but it also had an integrity she valued. She wished she could distill its positive qualities and pour that essence into the cold, glittering Imperial Court. The man the Assembly had intended her to marry, the reputedly incomparable Prince Dayj, could learn a lot from these people. Not that he would; Roca knew her former intended would never view Eldri's people as anything more than inferior beasts. The irony was that Eldri probably had the blood of the ancient Ruby queens and kings flowing in his veins, far more than Dayj.

It had taken her a while to realize how much Brad disconcerted the inhabitants of Windward, who had never met him before. He apparently resembled a god from Lyshrioli mythology, a fertility prince no less. The god's hair was the night sky, so the people here found nothing strange in the idea that he came from "the stars." None of them had dark hair, skin, or eyes, and his coloring fascinated them. He took it in stride, though he seemed flustered to be considered the incarnation of a deity. Roca could imagine that with his good nature, good looks, and reputation for fertility, he hadn't had any trouble wooing his girlfriend in the village.

Right now, however, he was scowling at Eldri as he spoke in Trillian. "Yes, the port is only one house. But it represents something much larger. If Avaril's men murder a Ruby heir, the repercussions will be so severe, you can't begin to imagine them."

Garlin regarded him dourly. "Would you care to tell Avaril?"

Eldri's frustration was so strong, it felt like fog against Roca's skin. "You make dire proclamations," he told Brad. "But you offer no viable alternatives."

"We're working on the explosives," Brad said.

"Do they explode?" Garlin asked.

Brad grimaced. "Not much. Yet."

Although Roca didn't speak Trillian well, she had improved over the past months. "What about other idea—tunnel through chasm walls to escape into northern mountains?"

The Memory held up her hand. When Eldri inclined his head, she said, "I have retrieved my Memories of every route mapped over the ages. Avaril's mountain climbers have blocked them all."

"I do not understand this 'mountain climbing.'" Shannar glared at Brad as if he had invented the activity rather than just given them the terminology. "What sane person would hammer spikes in a wall and swing from them on a rope?"

Eldri cocked an eyebrow. "It works, Shannar. Cousin Avaril may be a harsh man, but he is not stupid."

Roca's baby suddenly gave a hearty kick. She rested her hand on her abdomen, aware of a pain with no connection to the child's robust activity. It devastated her to know how much death threatened his incipient life. "Have we news of the plains?" she asked. "Maybe the Dalvador army comes here now."

"We've seen no one on the trail," Garlin said.

"If only we had a carrier pigeon," Brad muttered.

The Lyshrioli looked at him blankly.

Shaliece lifted her hand. "Could you repeat 'pije'?"

"Pigeon," Brad said. "A bird. It carries messages."

"What is 'bird'?" Eldri asked.

"A small animal that flies," Brad said.

"Perhaps we could build one," Roca suggested.

Brad pushed his hand through his hair, which had grown out in fluffy curls. "I've been thinking for a while about how I might cobble something together. If I cannibalize my palmtop and smart-knife, I could provide computerized direction to several small fliers. But I would hate to lose my equipment."

He had already mentioned the idea to Roca, and she understood his hesitation. Without his palmtop, he couldn't communicate with the port, and he wanted the knife for protection. But the time might be coming when they needed to take desperate chances.

"What would be the purpose of such fliers?" Garlin asked.

"To carry messages to your people in the plains," Brad said. "According to the computers at the port, no one has read the ones I've sent there."

"What new could these fliers tell anyone?" Shannar demanded, crankier than usual. "That we need help? I imagine they already know that. They haven't heard from us for ages. They don't come because they are fighting the rest of Avaril's army. It is the only explanation."

Eldri frowned at him. "Shannar, it is not a bad idea. Brad wishes to help." Dark circles showed under his eyes. "Maybe the battering ram won't work." He didn't sound hopeful.

"Maybe it will." Shannar stood and began to pace. "It is time to destroy the bridge to Windward."

"Easily said," Garlin told him. "Not easily done."

Shannar glared at Brad. "What about your 'bombs'?"

"We can try," Brad said. "I doubt the explosives we've made so far are strong enough to destroy something that massive."

"I cannot allow this." Eldri crossed his arms on the table. "I am the one Avaril wants. I should give . . . give myself . . ." His voice faded.

Shannar frowned. "Are you suggesting a surrender?"

Eldri stared at the table, his eyes glazed.

"Bard Eldrinson?" Shannar asked.

Garlin lifted his hand, palm out. "Wait. The sun gods speak with him."

Shannar raised his eyebrows and Shaliece shifted in her seat. Brad started to speak, then stopped when Roca shook her head. She suspected everyone at the table knew perfectly well no deities were involved here.

Eldri slowly raised his head and looked around. He stared for a long moment at Garlin, as if trying to recognize his cousin.

"Eldri?" Garlin's voice was gentler than when he spoke to anyone else.

"I am . . . fine." Eldri rubbed his eyes.

It tugged at Roca to see Eldri's bewildered expression. She wanted to protect him, to take him away from these people and their impossible demands. But she held back, knowing his pride wouldn't allow him to acknowledge what he considered a frailty.

Garlin resumed their discussion as if nothing had happened. "No surrender. Avaril won't take prisoners."

Eldri didn't answer, he just rubbed his eyes, still dazed. Shaliece seemed uncertain about whether or not she should record this. Roca's unease grew. Usually Eldri recovered faster, at least enough so he could listen while others talked. He seemed lost now, unable to respond at all.

In the same moment that Roca laid her hand on Eldri's arm, to suggest a break, Garlin stood. "Thank you all for your counsel," he said. "I will let you know when we will consult again."

Brad and the Memory rose to their feet, followed by Shannar, who moved as if he creaked. When they hesitated, Garlin spoke abruptly. "Leave. Now."

Shannar glared at him. "Well, and fine, we will come back when you decide to be civil." Then he stalked out of the hall. Shaliece bowed to Eldri and also left, her robe whispering on the floor. Brad still hesitated, and Roca could tell he wanted to ask after Eldri. Garlin responded with an implacable look, crossing his arms. Taking the hint, Brad bowed and took his leave.

"Garlin." Eldri stood up slowly, careful but more focused now. "You didn't have to insult them."

Roca also rose, awkward with her extra bulk. According to her node, she was over seven months into her pregnancy. "Eldri, perhaps you would like to rest."

He gave her an inimitable frown. "Stop hovering over me."

"Ah, Eldri." Garlin pushed back his shaggy mane that swept from his widow's peak down to his shoulders. "Sometimes when you look like that—"

"Like what?" Eldri's anger flashed. "Like—like—"

By now, Roca recognized the signs immediately. In the same instant that she grabbed Eldri's arm, Garlin lunged toward them. Eldri grunted and collapsed, knocking Roca against the chair. It scooted along the floor and she toppled over, falling heavily to the stone floor. She cried out, instinctively wrapping her arms around her belly as she hit the ground. Eldri landed on top of her, heavy and limp, then rolled off to the side.

Roca groaned. She was aware of Garlin kneeling to check on her, but she was too shaken to notice more. She lay on her side, her heart beating hard. After several minutes, she slowly pushed herself up into a sitting position, holding her abdomen with one arm. To her immense relief, the baby gave a vigorous kick, as if to protest the unceremonious way he had been dumped on the floor. With gratitude, she absorbed the feel of his mind, as radiant as before.

Mercifully, Eldri's convulsion had ended. He lay on his side now, his eyes closed, his hair disarrayed, blood trickling out of his mouth, his head cushioned on Garlin's jacket. Garlin was checking to make sure he had no broken bones.

"Ai, love," Roca murmured, leaning over Eldri. "How are you?"

His lashes fluttered. He blinked at her, then closed his eyes.

Garlin looked across Eldri at her. "Are you all right?"

"I think so." She checked the sore spots where she had hit the floor. "I will have bruises. But the baby is all right."

"That is his second attack in three days." Garlin sounded as if he were breaking inside.

Roca brushed back Eldri's hair, keeping her touch light. He was sleeping now. "The third, if you count the one he had while we were talking with Shannar."

Garlin spoke bitterly. "Avaril may win without having to do anything at all to achieve his goals."

"Have the seizures ever been this bad before?"

"Not like this. Usually he improves at Windward. Sometimes he has none at all. That was why we came. All he wanted was a little relief." His voice caught. "He never complains. But his attacks are growing worse. He can't live this way."

"Ai, Garlin." Roca had never seen him like this, his pain open, his emotional armor cracking. "Instead he got a siege."

"If Avaril caused the rock slide that killed our family, he may have killed Eldri that day, too. It has just taken longer." His words came out low and agonized. "I would wish Avaril to suffer as he has made Eldri suffer. I should not. But I do."

"I, too." Roca knew it wasn't an appropriate sentiment for a Foreign Affairs Councilor; she should strive to understand both sides of the events that spurred this war. But faced with her husband's dying, she had no objectivity.

"Do you know why coming up here helped him?" she asked.

"The air, we thought." He pulled off the scarf around his neck and used it to wipe saliva and blood away from Eldri's mouth. "It is clearer. Less humid."

Roca went through the files in her node, but found nothing about dry air as a treatment. "I don't know. It seems unlikely."

"I can think of no other important differences."

"What about changes in lifestyle? Food? Pollen?"

Patiently, Garlin said, "What is pollen?"

"Plants make it. They reproduce that way."

"Like glitter in reed bubbles?"

"Essentially."

He shook his head. "No plants grow up here. So no glitter. But the attacks are much worse."

Roca recalled how she and Eldri had been covered in glitter all the way across the plain. He had shown no distress then. "Perhaps he's worse now because he's under so much strain."

Garlin's fist clenched on his knee. "It was my idea to come here."

"You couldn't have known."

"I feel so—" He fought with the words. "So godsforsaken helpless."

"You must not blame yourself." She could feel how much it hurt him to be unable to help Eldri. "He is alive today because of the care you've given him his entire life."

He considered her. "I would not have expected you would acknowledge such."

"But why do you say that?"

"When first you came to us, I thought nothing could thaw your heart." He lifted his hand, palm up, then turned it down in a gesture she didn't recognize, though she had a sense it meant he retracted his words. "With Eldri, though, you are different. He and I, we always shared a *knowing,* but it is nothing compared to what he has with you." His face gentled as he looked at Eldri, though with sorrow as much as affection. "Always I have been first in his life, closer to him than anyone else." In a low voice, he said, "It hurts to become second."

Roca could tell how much it cost him to make that admission. She thought of Garlin spending his life tending Eldri, never having a full life of his own, knowing the cousin he loved might die anytime. She spoke quietly. "I am honored to be part of your family."

His mouth quirked in a smile, making him look ten years younger. "Ah, well. You are a diplomat."

"Foreign Affairs," Eldri said groggily. He sat up between them, rubbing his eyes. "Is that right, Roca?"

"Yes." She tried to smile, too, though moisture gathered in her eyes. "Councilor for Foreign Affairs."

A ghost of his mischief sparked. "Am I a foreign affair? But no, we are married. Now it is legitimate."

Roca laughed. "Ah, love, behave yourself."

He put one hand on her arm and one on Garlin's arm. "You are the two people I love most in this world. It pleases me that you seem to get along after all."

Roca felt her face redden. "Were we that prickly before?"

Garlin winced. "Perhaps so."                                    •

Eldri put an arm around each of their shoulders. "This is better, yes?"

Garlin managed a strained show of cheer. "Yes, I think so." But Roca felt his sadness. They both knew the truth.

Eldri was running out of time.

# 16

# A King's Supper

---

Sulpher," Roca said, walking down an aisle between long, narrow tables in the kitchen. "The yellow powder for explosives."

"It smells like rotten eggs," Brad explained. "I need to find more of it."

Garlin sighed, ever patient. "What are eggs?"

Brad grinned at him. "Birds have them."

Garlin gave him a deadpan look. "Ah. Well, in that case, we can find them with your notorious 'pigeons.'"

Brad laughed, at ease with Garlin in a way Roca had never managed, even now when she and Garlin had stopped distrusting each other. She looked around the huge kitchen where the four of them were walking. "You need more charcoal, too, yes?"

"It would help," Brad said. "But at this point I'll experiment with anything."

"I do not understand," Garlin said. "You mix powders and they explode, just like that?"

"You need heat and pressure, too," Brad said.

"I still don't like this idea to destroy the bridge," Eldri grumbled. He motioned at the dried bubbles heaped on the tables, dark red, dusky yellow, and orange, or the clusters of blue or green bubbles hanging from the glasswood rafters. "When this is all gone, we must be rescued or surrender. How, without our bridge?"

"We can build the drawbridge," Roca said.

"That did actually sound like a good idea," Eldri admitted.

"I also need to plan how we will use explosives inside the castle," Brad said. "In case we can't stop Avaril outside. We don't want detonations to weaken the foundations here."

Roca peered at the table on their left. Vials were scattered around, all filled with powder, some covered with translucent bubble skins, but most open to the air. She stopped to examine them and everyone gathered around her.

"Can you come up with solutions?" Garlin was asking Brad.

"Thinking up solutions is what I do for a living," Brad said. "My doctorate is in mechanical engineering." When Garlin glared, Brad laughed. "Getting a doctorate is like learning a trade here."

Roca picked up a vial. "Anyone know what this is?"

Eldri peered at the white powder. "Salt."

"Oh." She set it down. "Can't do much with that."

"You most certainly can," Eldri said crossly. "You make food taste better." He gave the kitchen a sour look, including a cook several tables over who was preparing food. "I used to love coming to Windward because the meals were so good. Now, with all this rationing, these heartless cooks will use no salts. They want it for preserving." He scowled. "Avaril has much to answer for."

Brad smiled. "I think you will survive without salting your food. Besides, it raises your blood pressure."

"Blood pressure," Garlin said smugly. "I can figure that one out."

Roca considered Eldri. "When we first came up here, were the cooks seasoning the food?"

"I think so. It certainly tasted better."

Brad gave her a dubious look. "Lady Roca, you are a most admirable woman with a most admirable intellect, but I don't think it is possible to demolish a bridge with table salt."

Her lips quirked upward. "You say that so nicely."

"You want to blow up our bridge with salt?" Eldri asked, incredulous.

Roca shook her head. "Garlin and I were talking earlier today about why your seizures improve up here."

Garlin took a vial and poured its white powder into his palm. "We use salt in Dalvador, too. That is no different from here."

A hope was stirring in Roca, one she hesitated to entertain, lest reality dash it to pieces. "These salts." She motioned at the vials. "Are they all the same?"

"I can ask." Eldri called to one of the cooks.

A heavyset man with a blue apron and large stomach came over. He spoke in Trillian, his voice a melody of bass notes. "Pleased to see you, Bard Eldrinson."

"Thank you." Eldri indicated the vials. "We were wondering what these seasonings were."

The fellow seemed puzzled by the question, but he gamely studied the vials. He moved the two covered ones aside. "These two are challine. The rest are plain salt."

Roca picked up a challine vial. "It looks like salt."

"Well, it is, of a kind," the cook said. "We don't have much, though. It comes from the spas."

"Spas?" Roca asked.

"Mineral springs." Eldri motioned toward the north. "In the valley that Avaril's men have occupied. The water tastes good, and I love soaking in the spas." Sourly he added, "That is, when people aren't attacking my castle."

The cook crossed his beefy arms and frowned as if Eldri were a misbehaved boy. "It is bad for you to drink it."

"I like it," Eldri said. "It makes me sleepy."

"Ah, gods," Roca murmured. "I wish we had a chemist."

"What is it?" Brad asked.

She lifted the challine vial. "I think sodium bromide and potassium bromide can be used as anticonvulsants. I don't know what this is, but if something Eldri drinks or eats puts bromide in his system, it might help control his seizures."

"Bromide. Sodium. Potassium." Garlin looked frustrated. "These are real words?"

"They're names for salts," Roca said.

"Aren't bromides toxic?" Brad asked.

Roca hesitated. "Maybe it depends on the quantity or how it's made." She showed the vial to Eldri. "Do you have challine at your home in the plains?"

"I've no idea." He glanced at the cook. "Do you ever come to Dalvador?"

"I used to live there," the man said. "But I never worked in the kitchens of your home." He considered the vial Roca held. "This much is true; challine is an uncommon seasoning. If I had to guess, I would say your cooks in Dalvador don't use it."

Eldri nodded. "Thank you, Goodsir."

"My pleasure." The cook bowed to him.

After the cook returned to his work, Eldri picked up the other challine vial. "Could it be? Could something as simple as salt make my life bearable?"

Roca feared to offer too much hope. "Perhaps. But we can't be sure."

"We must find out, eh?" His face flashed with his old mischief, which had been absent all too much lately. "I shall tell the cooks they must salt my food again."

Roca set her vial on the table. "Did it ever make you sick?"

"Some," he admitted. "But if it controls my attacks, it is worth it." He thumped the table. "I am decided. I will try."

Brad turned in a circle, surveying the kitchen. "Think we can find any potassium nitrate here?"

Garlin groaned. "Sometimes, Brad, I think you make up these words just to bedevil me."

Eldri strode into the bedroom just as Channil was finishing her exam of Roca. The midwife glared at him. "Do you always explode into places uninvited?"

Eldri hesitated. "Uh—it's my room."

Channil shook her hands at him, shooing him away.

"It's all right." Roca sat up on the bed, pulling down her fur-lined shift.

Eldri approached the bed cautiously, with a wary glance at the midwife. "Is everything all right?"

Channil crossed her arms. "Your wife needs more sleep, young man."

Eldri turned red. "I, uh—yes, of course, ma'am."

Channil made a hmmmph noise. To Roca, she said, "More sleep. No more falling down." Then she bustled out of the room.

Roca watched fondly as Eldri flopped onto his stomach next to her. "And how are you today?"

"Wonderful." He grinned. "I've been watching Brad blow things up. It is very entertaining."

Roca laughed. "So his experiments are working?"

"Hardly. They never do what he wants." Eldri relented a bit. "Perhaps he makes progress. The bombs only fizzle half the time now."

Roca wasn't sure teaching Eldri's people to make bombs was progress, but it was better than letting Avaril slaughter them. "How are you feeling?"

He rolled onto his side, facing her. "Do you know that in the eleven days since I started the salt, I haven't had any big attacks and only a few of the small."

Every day he went without a seizure felt like a gift. "I am glad, love."

His face gentled. "Say it again."

"I am glad."

"No. The other."

She grinned. "The other."

Softly he said, "Roca."

She slid down next to him. "I am glad, my love."

"Do you truly love me?"

"Truly." She didn't think she had known what the word meant until she met Eldri.

He laid his hand on her abdomen. "It hurts to love you and this child."

"Hurts? But why?"

He swallowed. "Because the harder you love, the more it will crush you to lose it."

Roca entwined her hand with his, five fingers with four. "Whatever happens, know that I will do everything I can to make it possible that we can stay together."

His mood lightened. "Good. It will give me more opportunity to do this." Sliding his hand under her shift, he tickled her side.

Laughing, Roca pushed his hand away. "Eldri—"

"Bard Eldrinson!" The cry came from outside. "Come! Hurry!"


Warriors paced the top of the huge wall that surrounded Windward, protected by reed-shaped merlons. Roca, Eldri, and Garlin crowded into the lookout of the high tower. Leaning into a narrow opening, Roca studied Avaril's army in the plain below. They were guiding a battering ram on wheels, pushing it toward the bridge that arched across the chasm to Windward.

Eldri leaned next to her. "What can you see?"

"I can't figure out how they plan to use that thing." Roca magnified the scene with her optics. "They need a way to drive it forward, but I don't see any mechanism."

"Maybe they will just push it."

"That won't give enough force." She pulled away from the opening, awkward now, clumsy with her girth. "I don't think they've finished it yet."

Garlin was leaning against the wall next to them. "It might be a test, to see if they can get it across the bridge."

Roca regarded him uneasily. "They're managing just fine."

Eldri stood up straighter. "Garlin, I want the men to step up their training sessions. I will work with them again later this afternoon."

Garlin laid a hand on his shoulder. "I will do it."

Eldri pushed off his hand. "I will be fine."

"If you overwork yourself, you may have more attacks." Garlin spoke awkwardly, obviously aware his words could hurt. "Having one in front of your men now could hurt morale."

Eldri crossed his arms. "I would be no Bard if I hid while my men prepared for battle."

The mention of his title startled Roca. Although many cultures associated song with battle, this was the only one she knew of where the ability to sing historically accurate ballads had become a prerequisite for commanding an army. She hoped Avaril Valdoria had an atrocious voice. It would be fitting retribution for this man who would be Bard.

"You mustn't push yourself," Garlin told Eldri.

"I haven't had an attack in days," Eldri said.

"That doesn't mean they have stopped."

Roca almost urged Garlin to let him be, to let Eldri save his pride; then she wanted to urge Eldri to protect himself. She held back, knowing neither man would relent. Instead she said, "Eldri, can you do your extra workouts with Garlin?" Besides supervising his men's training, Eldri also trained one-on-one with selected partners, to hone his craft. "If you have a seizure, Garlin knows how to deal with it."

Eldri shook his head. "I must work with my men. Otherwise, why should they follow me?"

"And if the convulsions start again?" Garlin asked.

"Then they come." Eldri nodded to them. Before they could protest further, he took his leave, going down a narrow staircase to the shielded pathway that ran along the top of the wall. Roca wanted to go after him, but she held back. Through the doorway, she could see him walking. Each time he passed one of his men, he stopped for a moment to talk before continuing on his way.

Garlin watched until Eldri turned a corner. "The crime of it," he said, "is that he is a natural leader. The men would follow him from here to the moons if he asked."

"If he has a convulsion during battle," Roca said, "he's dead."

"And if he survives because he holds back when others fight?" Garlin spoke heavily. "He couldn't live with himself."

Roca knew he was right; if they interfered, Eldri would never forgive them. She wondered if fate were laughing at them. It offered all of humanity a new hope in Eldri, one of the strongest psions ever born— and then would take his life before he ever had a chance to realize his gifts.

# 17

# Bridge of Sorrows

---

There." Brad set the delicate contraption on Roca's upturned hand. The hollow glasswood body was so small, it fit in her palm, but the wings had a span longer than her forearm. She and Brad had used the skin of red and blue bubbles to make them. He had scavenged components from his palmtop and smart-knife and even torn out tiny computers in the clothes he had worn up here that long-ago day he had come to see if she was all right.

A breeze from the open window picked up the flier, and Roca barely managed to grab it before the wind carried it away.

Brad closed the shutters. "I hope it can reach the plains."

"I too. Who knows how long it can stay aloft." Roca flicked her thumb against the switch on the flier. The gadget fluttered up, wheeled around the chamber a few times, and drifted to the floor. She laid her hand on her abdomen, thinking a child would love such a gadget.

As Brad retrieved the flier, a tiny holo of Eldri activated above it and began telling them Windward needed help.

"It looks good," Roca said as the message finished.

"We can make ten of these fliers," Brad said. "Actually, we can make as many as we want. But to run the holo, I only have enough components for ten."

"We could send written messages on the rest."

"Who would read them?"

That gave her pause. It was too easy to forget the Lyshrioli had no written language. They didn't even understand the concept. She sighed.

"If only we could attach a Memory to the fliers. That would solve everything."

"The components have memory." Brad shrugged. "They could hold hundreds of text messages, but no one here could decipher them."

"I meant Shaliece. *The* Memory." Roca smiled. "I suppose she is like a computer. Her recall is incredible."

Brad nodded. "I've wondered if the original colonists here were trying to design human computers."

"I wish I could spend more time learning the culture." Roca would have liked to hear her sister's opinions on it. Dehya's genius with computers never ceased to astonish Roca. "It's remarkable."

"And in danger of vanishing." His anger flashed. "The resort planners intend to develop this world. If it has inconvenient wars, they may just take over and get rid of the leaders."

Roca scowled at him. "I thought your people had all these rules to protect new worlds."

"We do." Dryly he added, "So many, in fact, that corporations can use some of them to run circles around the others." He ran his finger down the flier's wing. "But only within limits. It's true, with the right approvals, the developers can get permission to meddle. But no one would allow me to kill the people."

She thought of his pulse-gun, useless in the port. "Even if you were defending yourself?"

He hesitated. "The boundaries are always gray."

She wondered if he realized just how gray. "Your laws are moot, here, anyway. This should be a Skolian world."

"And if it was?" His expression darkened. "What would you do? Kick out the developers and send in your military?"

Roca wanted to deny it, but she couldn't. ISC always set up a base on a new planet before it allowed civilian contact. If they weren't careful, their effect here could be as deleterious as the resort planners. With care, she said, "Normally, yes."

"Normally?"

She spoke quietly. "I am a Ruby Dynasty heir."

That seemed to throw him. After a moment he said, "We've been here so long, sometimes I forget what your title means beyond this world."

She thought of her marriage to Eldri. "Sometimes, so do I."

"Will you help Eldri's people?"

"I certainly intend to try."

"What about your family?" He spoke cautiously. "I imagine your new husband will surprise them."

That was certainly a masterful understatement. It wasn't a subject she wished to discuss with anyone, even herself. She wanted to enjoy however little time she and Eldri had left rather than brooding on a future they might never see.

Roca motioned at the flier. "If we send out ten with holos, a few might reach Dalvador."

"Changing the subject won't make it go away," Brad said. When she only looked at him, he held up his hands. "Right. The fliers. We'll have one chance with them. The first time we send out any, it will probably catch Avaril off guard. After that, I imagine his archers will be ready to shoot them down."

"We need decoys, to help the holo fliers get through."

"It shouldn't take long to make them, now that we know how." He shifted his weight. "But Lady Roca—when we launch the holo fliers, we lose our means to communicate with the port."

Roca also dreaded cutting their last link to home. "Let's just hope it works."


Standing at a window on the second story of Windward, Roca could watch Eldri's men training below. They were working in the "narrows," a long portion of the courtyard bordered by low walls. Stands for an audience stood along one long wall and tables along the other. She had wondered at the purpose of the narrows when she first came to Windward. Now she knew.

In peacetime, the warriors here stayed in shape by holding competitions in swordsmanship and archery. Healers used the tables as stations where they could treat injured men. But today was no game. Eldri and his warriors trained with a fierce concentration broken only by the clang of swords, the thunk of arrows, and the grunts of men. Healers waited with supplies, and pallets lay on the ground near them, ready for anyone hurt during the exercises.

Eldri's prowess with a sword mesmerized Roca. Even from so far away, she felt his intensity. Years of training had honed his skill; now he moved on instinct, as if the sword were a part of him. It was a bittersweet joy to watch, like seeing a beautiful dance, but one as deadly as it was graceful.

Her heart was tearing in two. Eldri would fight if—no, when—Avaril's army attacked. If he had a seizure, he would probably die; it was unlikely he would be lucky enough to frighten away his opponents again. And he knew it. Yet still he intended to lead his men. She wanted to rage against his determination, his pride, the integrity that made him refuse to stay back when others went into battle.

But nothing would change his mind.


Rolling over in bed, Roca opened her eyes into darkness. The shutters in the window alcove across the suite were cracked open, letting in air and hints of the pristine light that heralded the suns, though the strip of dark sky she saw wasn't yet touched by the gold, pink, and red of dawn.

She didn't know what had awoken her. Eldri lay at her side, deep in sleep, one hand under his cheek. The castle was quiet. People were surely stirring, but in here she heard nothing. On a world with no birds, the dawn came in silence. Lyshriol needed no musical animals; in its Bards, it had singers of unmatched beauty.

A distant clanking interrupted the silence, followed by a call from the courtyard. Roca slid out of bed and padded across the cold stone floor to a window that overlooked the courtyard. When she pushed apart the shutters, breezes blew across her face, less chilly today than usual.

Three men were running across the courtyard, outfitted in leather armor and mail, their hair streaming out, two holding helmets. One shouted to someone out of her sight. She didn't understand his words, but the alarm in his voice needed no translation.

Roca turned—and saw Eldri standing by the bed, his face blurred with sleep as he pulled on his trousers.

"What is it?" she asked.

"I don't know." He fastened his clothes, his fingers fumbling. "But they wouldn't sound an alarm without reason."

She went over to him. "Eldri—"

He took her hands. "Stay here. Don't go outside or even downstairs. We don't know if Avaril realizes I have married. Go to Brad's suite and hide. If they think you are Brad's woman, they may spare you."

She stared at him, hearing what he didn't say. He feared he would die today. She squeezed his fingers. It seemed surreal, impossible, that the heir to an interstellar empire had to see her husband go out with no more protection than primitive armor and a sword. "Take care."

Eldri kissed her, softly, urgently. Then he strode out the door, tying the laces on his shirt.

A crash vibrated outside. Roca ran back to the window, but she saw only Eldri's men gathering below. Another crash came, thundering from beyond the great wall that protected the castle.

"Gods almighty," she muttered. It sounded like Avaril's people were using the battering ram.

Roca threw on her clothes and ran out into the hall, headed for Brad's suite. She had only gone halfway when she saw him striding toward her. They met in front of a niche with the statue of a woman holding a bow and quiver, the archer-goddess Sauscony, now a part of Lyshrioli mythology, but probably a remnant from the ancient era when star queens had settled this world.

Roca spoke fast, breathing hard, her hand over her abdomen. "We need to send out the fliers."

"They're in my suite." He jumped as another crash thundered through the keep. "I have to get the explosives."

Her hope leapt. "Can you collapse the bridge?"

·"I don't think so. But we can use them in other ways." He took a deep breath. "Can you send off the fliers?"

"Yes. I'll take care of it."

Brad clasped her arm. Then they both took off, Roca running for his suite. She burst through its antechamber and into the room beyond, which was set up like the one she shared with Eldri. Piles of fliers were scattered on tables, strewn across the window alcove, and heaped on the floor. When she threw open the shutters in the alcove, cold wind gusted past her, blowing the fliers off the benches.

Roca scooped one up and flicked its switch, then threw it out the window, into the gales of the Backbone Mountains. It sailed away on the currents of air. She grabbed another and sent it off, then another and another. After she had released the ones in the alcove, she ran back into the bedroom and gathered up armfuls of the fliers. She sent every one out the window into the wind. A cloud of fliers soon stretched across the sky, above the mountains, headed toward the plains of Dalvador. Whether or not any would make it, she didn't know, but they had a good start.

All the time she was tossing mechanical birds, the ram continued to crash against the portcullis below. As soon as she sent out the last flier, she ran across the room and threw open the shutters of a window overlooking the courtyard. Eldri's warriors had gathered below, on walls, in towers, and at windows, archers up high and swordsmen below. The archers were shooting at Avaril's men, but the wind limited their efforts, endangering their own people whenever a gust sent an arrow intended for their foes at a friend instead.

Another crash came—and the great gates in the courtyard shook. A gargoyle carved into the rock above the entrance split off from the wall and smashed to the ground.

"Saints help us," she whispered. Roca had never believed in the pantheon of goddesses, gods, and saints worshiped by many Skolian peoples, but now she prayed to them all, for Eldri, for his people, for the unborn child she carried.

Then she saw him. Eldri. Fully outfitted in armor, he was striding across the courtyard, stopping often to encourage his men. A tall man in a helmet strode at his side, his height marking him as Garlin. Then Eldri donned his own helmet, the stylized head of a beast.

Eldri's people had rolled a staircase made from glasswood up to the great wall, next to the gates. A line of women and men extended from the courtyard up the stairs, and they were passing barrels to the warriors on top of the wall. Flame suddenly leapt up from a barrel held by two men at the top. When they tipped it over the wall, Roca realized they were raining burning oil on the attackers below. Shouts erupted from outside the castle.

Roca suddenly glimpsed Brad on the wall, just as he hurled an object through one of its crenellations. An explosion boomed outside the castle, probably on the bridge in front of the portcullis, in the midst of the invaders. Men screamed and Roca flinched, feeling ill.

The assault continued. The attackers had obviously succeeded in building machinery that moved the ram with enough force to make it effective. Whatever else Roca thought of Avaril, she had to acknowledge his ability to innovate; he and his people achieved wonders with basic engineering. The ram hit again—and a great crack split the gates, though they were made of glasswood layered until it was as thick as two men's bodies. Another crash resounded and a second crack appeared, rending the gates from top to bottom.

Down below, Eldri shouted to the men up on the wall. They dumped one last barrel of oil, then began a fast retreat. The people on the stairs ran down ahead of them, clearing the way so everyone could reach the courtyard. The civilians raced for the castle while the warriors took up formation in the courtyard.

Roca no longer felt the icy wind that whipped back her hair and plastered her clothes to her body. Her awareness strained toward the defenders as they prepared to protect the castle. She felt their determination, their fear, their battle fury, and their desperation.

With a great crash, the ram hit the gates again—and the massive portals split in two. One half toppled forward into the courtyard, and the other fell back onto the bridge. Warriors on both sides scattered, running madly as the portals fell. Avaril's men retreated across the bridge, but that reprieve lasted only seconds, while the gates slammed into the ground, the crash thundering throughout Windward as it sent up clouds of debris. Then the invaders surged back and poured through the break, through the swirling dust, jumping over the wrecked port-cullis and gates.

Eldri's men leapt forward, and the clang of swords filled the court-yard. It was a nightmare. Roca almost threw up when one man chopped the arm off another directly below her, blood spurting. The archers tried to pick off the attackers, but in the melee of fighters, with the gusting wind, it was hard to get a clear shot.

Suddenly an explosion went off in the midst of a phalanx of invaders working its way forward. Roca clenched the windowsill, her nausea surg-ing at the sight of what happened to the men caught in the blast. Another bomb exploded, but this one fizzled and had little effect.

Men had collapsed throughout the courtyard, some dragging them-selves out of the battle, but too many lying completely still. Avaril's warriors continued to pour in; far fewer of Eldri's men were coming out of Windward. Tears welled in Roca's eyes. Brad and his hastily assem-bled team of proto-engineers couldn't have many explosives left. Long after Windward's defenders had depleted their numbers, weapons, and energy, Avaril's much larger army would keep on coming.

Roca couldn't find Eldri in the chaos below. She glimpsed his hel-met among a mass of men by the western wall, but it vanished as the battle roiled across the courtyard. Another time she thought she saw him lying crumpled and broken against one wall. She cried out as an-other man fell, blocking her view, and she pressed her hands against her abdomen, praying her child wouldn't suffer such a brutal death. She couldn't believe Eldri lay in a broken heap under another dead man. It couldn't be him. It couldn't.

She couldn't accept such an end for the man she loved.


When Roca first heard the thunder coming from beyond the castle walls, she feared Avaril's men were using the battering ram again, though *why,* she had no idea. The relentless invaders were already pushing their way through the courtyard, cutting down Eldri's men. It wasn't until the fighting lagged in the courtyard, with men turning their heads upward, that she realized the roar she heard came from the sky.

Leaning out the window, her hair streaming in the wind, she craned her neck to look. She had been at Windward so long that for an instant she reacted as would a Lyshrioli woman, shocked to see a great gold and black beast soaring above Windward, its voice raised in an unnatural roar. Then her perception shifted—and for one brilliant, incredible moment she wanted to shout her relief at that great metal creature—a Skolian military shuttle.

Then the ship fired.

Its beam sheered off a tower, one far from the window where Roca stood. Another shuttle roared into view from behind the castle, looming over the battle. Warriors scattered, running for their lives as the ship blasted the courtyard with the exhaust of its landing. Roca shouted, her protest lost in the noise. They must have pinpointed her position—and were eliminating any threat they thought existed to that location. In "rescuing" her, they would destroy the very people who had protected her all these months.

She whirled around and took off, racing out of the suite. Her feet pounded on the stone floor in the hall. When she flung open the door to the stairs, shouts in the dining hall swelled in crescendo. She strode onto the landing at the top of the stairs—and froze, clenching the rail as she stared in horrified disbelief at the scene below.

Unaware of what was happening outside, Eldri's men were still locked in combat with the invaders, the battle crashing throughout the hall. Several warriors were on the table, fighting back and forth, swords flashing as they parried and attacked. One of Avaril's men suddenly found an opening in his opponent's defense and stabbed him through the heart. Roca cried out, but in the tumult, no one heard.

The double doors of the hall slammed open. The dining hall was supposed to be inside the castle, but sunlight streamed into the room, coming through the destroyed wing beyond. A gold giant stood framed in the doorway like an avenging metal god, a man seven feet tall, indomitable and massive, towering over every other man in the room. He wore the harsh uniform of a Jagernaut Primary, black leather embedded with computers, more machine than clothes. His skin, hair, and gauntlets all glinted, hard and unforgiving. He had drawn his gun, a huge

Jumbler that glittered black in the sunlight. His eyes showed no whites, only unbroken shields of gold, as if he weren't human at all, but a machine.

Her son had arrived.

# 18

# God of War

---

Roca saw Eldri.

He must have jumped on the table just before Kurj threw open the doors. Eldri had lost his helmet somewhere, and his disarrayed hair was wild around his head. He stood with his feet planted wide, his body half turned to the door, his sword held out, blood dripping off the blade, his eyes wild, his chest heaving from exertion. He looked as much the atavistic barbarian as Kurj looked a warlord of the stars.

How Kurj knew Eldri was more than just another fighter among hundreds, Roca had no idea—but in that moment, when he and Eldri locked gazes, she saw the recognition in their faces and felt it in their minds. Time seemed to slow as Kurj raised his Jumbler in both hands, his arms straight out, pointing it at Eldri. And in that moment Roca knew, without doubt, that her son was about to commit the equivalent of patricide.

"KURJ!" She shouted her words. *"Don't shoot!"*

Both Eldri and Kurj whirled toward her. Their reaction was so intense that for an instant she saw herself in their minds, her gold hair wild from the wind, untamed around her body, her face flushed, her eyes frantic. Desperate to stop them, she started down the stairs—and in her hurry, her foot caught on the top step. She flailed, yanked forward by the weight of her body. With relentless, unforgiving momentum, she toppled down the stairs.

The walls went by in a blur, too fast for Roca to comprehend fully. It hurt, hurt, *hurt,* every time she hit the steps. She wrapped her arms around her swollen belly, curling up, trying to protect the baby. Then she crashed into the lower landing and smashed against the railing on its other side.

Suddenly Kurj was bending over her, his voice buried in the roar in her ears, the roar of her pain, the roar of her own blood.

"*Mother!*" He grasped her arm. "Gods almighty."

Roca groaned, her body wracked by a brutal contraction. "Kurj, you mustn't—" Her eyes watered as the contraction worsened. "Mustn't shoot him—ah, *no*."

Other people were crowding into the hall, Skolian soldiers striding among the Lyshrioli warriors. Kurj shouted orders, calling for a doctor. Roca could barely hear for the roaring in her ears.

"Mother, you can't die." His words sounded so strange. She hadn't heard the cold, clipped tones of Iotic in months.

Roca grabbed his sleeve. "Kurj! You must not hurt him."

"Who?" His gaze hardened. "Who did this to you?"

"Listen!" She dug her fingers into his arm. "These people have protected me—ah!" She squeezed her eyes shut as another contraction hit.

"Primary Skolia!" A medic knelt next to Roca and did a quick exam. "She's gone into labor. We have to get her to the port."

Roca spoke through clenched teeth. "Won't make port." She could see Eldri now, down in the hall, struggling with Kurj's soldiers. They were holding him back, keeping him away from her.

"Let him go." She could barely talk past the pain. Medics crowded around her, bringing an air stretcher and blocking her view.

"No!" Roca shook Kurj's arm. "I won't leave!"

No one listened. They loaded her onto the stretcher and went down the stairs.

Then she saw who else was in the hall.

Avaril.

He was standing by the table, surrounded by his men, his sword lowered, his face stunned as he watched her. Skolians filled the room, no longer attacking Eldri's men, but keeping them back. Eldri struggled against the Jagernauts who were holding him, his face flushed.

"Let him go!" Roca ordered as the medics carried her past the Ja-gernauts. She used her strongest Assembly voice, which had cowed more than a few delegates.

The startled Jagernauts, normally unflappable and impassive, re-leased Eldri before Kurj had a chance to countermand the order Roca didn't have the authority to give. Eldri lunged forward and ran alongside the stretcher as the medics kept going. His Trillian words poured over Roca like water. "Where are they taking you? Who are these people? Our son!"

She grabbed his hand and answered in Trillian, one of the few languages Kurj could neither understand nor translate. She longed for Eldri to stay with her, wanted it intensely, but it was impossible. Kurj was already moving to separate them. She spoke fast. "I swear I will find a way to come back. *I swear it.* Remember that." Another contraction hit and she cried out, her grip tightening on his hand.

Then Kurj was dragging him away. The medics ran out of the hall into the ruins of the courtyard. The remains of the battle went by in a blur, as Skolians backed Lyshrioli warriors against the walls. The medics sped onward, taking Roca to the shuttle, and Kurj easily caught up with them.

The hatch of the ship loomed into view so fast, Roca hardly knew they had reached it before they were inside. She pushed up on her elbow, forcing out her words through another contraction. "No—can't take off—the acceleration—"

"No acceleration." The medic eased her onto a robot-gurney. "We're only going to the port."

Craning her head around, Roca saw the airlock shimmer closed, leaving a solid hull. She felt only a gentle lift as the shuttle rose into the air. Then she could think no more, caught in the grip of another contraction so intense, her nanomeds couldn't ease the pain.

The doctors moved fast, preparing her for birth. She was vaguely aware of Kurj hanging back, flattened against the hull behind her head. Medics draped her body, giving her privacy, but nothing could hide her agonized face. Kurj's panic surged against her mind. He had faced every horror of war without flinching, but now, in this, he was terrified.

Another contraction wrung her body and Roca screamed, her mind blanking to everything but the need to *PUSH*.

"It's coming!" a medic shouted. "Harder!"

She pushed again, tears streaming down her face. Again—

With a huge release, the pain ended. Roca gasped—and in that instant she heard a cry, a great protest to the universe. Straining up on her elbows, she looked past her draped knees to see the medics holding a baby, a boy, while they cleaned his face and body.

"Ah, gods." She collapsed back and groaned with another contraction. She hadn't finished; she still had to deliver the afterbirth. All she could think was that the baby should be held by his kin, not strangers.

"Kurj." She croaked out the name. "Your brother—take your brother."

"What?" He jerked away from the hull. "You want me to *hold* it?"

"Y-yes." Roca could say no more, caught in the wrenching delivery of the afterbirth.

Mercifully, it soon ended. Finally she was free of pain. She was dimly aware of medics cleaning her, but she could think only of the baby. Her son. Eldri's son.

Suddenly she remembered—gods, no, she had asked *Kurj* to take the baby. In that terrible instant, she remembered Kurj raising his Jumbler to Eldri. Frantic, she twisted around—

And saw a miracle.

Kurj was standing behind her with his feet planted wide, an indomitable giant. Cradling the tiny baby in his arms, he swayed back and forth in a rhythm humans had known by instinct since the beginning of their species.

Roca fell back on the pallet, wondering at the power of birth, that it could disarm even Kurj. By everything that mattered in love and fatherhood, it was Eldri who should be holding the baby now, Eldri who should have witnessed this miracle, Eldri who should be bonding with his son. But if the magic of this moment convinced Kurj to let his half brother live and thus made possible the day when the boy could know his father, she would accept that blessing.

"My son," Roca whispered.

Another flutter of activity, and Kurj was putting the swaddled baby in her arms. Roca bent her head over her child. "Is he all right?" She looked up at the people clustered around her. "My fall down the stairs, did it—?"

One of the doctors answered, a woman with graying hair. "He is fine, Lady Roca. Healthy and hale."

"Thank you," Roca whispered. She held the infant against her body, looking down into his wide blue eyes. "So beautiful. You are such a beautiful boy." He stared up at her, and she knew he recognized her voice.

"He is—astonishing." Kurj knelt with one knee on a seat that jutted out from the hull, bringing his eyes level with hers. Incredibly, his gaze was tender when he glanced at the baby. But it turned into steel when he shifted his attention to Roca. "Was it the man with the red hair? The wild one on the table?"

She tensed. "You will not harm my son's father."

He said nothing.

"Kurj." She recognized his expression. He had looked that way the day he had tried to kill Darr. "Listen to me."

"I will take care of you," he said.

She scowled. "I am perfectly capable of taking care of myself. I did after I had you and I will do so now."

"This is different."

"You heard me, Kurj." She felt as if she were talking to a stone wall. "You will not hurt his father."

A muscle twitched under his eye. "You didn't want Darr hurt either."

"Darr has nothing to do with this." She willed him to listen. "Eldri never hurt me. And I married him of my own free will."

"You *married* him?" Kurj stared at her. "That barbarian with the sword?"

"Yes."

"So." He sounded like he was gritting his teeth.

"You won't hurt him."

He said nothing.

"Damn it, Kurj. If you kill the man I love, I will never be able to bear your presence again."

"Love?" He sounded more bewildered than angry. "You cannot love such a man. You are a Ruby heir."

"And he is my consort." Roca was growing desperate. She was so very, very tired. And the baby was nuzzling her shirt, wanting to nurse. She couldn't do it in front of Kurj. She needed privacy, needed to be away from his deadly contradictions, his unbending love and anger. "Promise me you will never hurt Eldri."

"Who is Eldri?"

"My husband."

No answer.

"Kurj!"

His face remained impassive.

"He is a Ruby psion," Roca said.

Nothing in his face relented. "Absurd."

"It is true."

"A wild tale, Mother."

Roca knew she couldn't keep this up. Kurj might think she spoke from desperation, but he would soon learn the truth. The proof in Eldri's DNA would give her more to negotiate with. Until then, she had to make sure Kurj didn't kill him.

"Make me a bargain," she said raggedly. "If I swear I will never return to him, swear you will never harm him."

He clenched the gurney. "You love him that much?"

"Yes."

"And you would never see him again?"

"Yes." She wanted to choke on the word.

He averted his eyes. "Very well. I agree."

"Look at me."

He raised his gaze.

"Now promise," she said.

He said nothing.

"Kurj."

It was a long moment before he answered. Finally he forced out the words. "You have my word."

"You must not betray my trust."

"Never again." He spoke bitterly. "I did once. This happened."

"You should keep your promises because it is right. Not because you want no more brothers."

His voice suddenly cracked. "Gods, I thought you died. I thought I had killed you."

His emotion startled her. He so rarely let her see how he felt, and he had walled his mind off from her. She spoke more gently. "Can we not find a way to trust each other?"

He started to answer, then shook his head, as if he couldn't bear to reveal any more emotions or even let himself feel them. Instead he touched the baby's head. "What will you call him?"

"Eldrin," she murmured. "Eldrin Jarac Valdoria. For his father and mine."

He wouldn't meet her gaze.

"Kurj."

He slowly raised his gaze to hers. "Would that I could make the universe perfect for you. But I cannot. I can only do my flawed, bitter best."

She swallowed. "I fear your vision of perfection."

No answer.

She spoke softly. "Are we going to war with the Traders?"

"The invasion plans are under way."

"So you won."

"By two votes." He sounded weary rather than triumphant.

"Two votes." She wanted to grieve for the deaths those two votes would inflict on humanity. "I hope you are proud of it."

"Proud?" This time he didn't try to hide his pain. "I have no pride in destruction or death. But I will do whatever is necessary to protect my people and those I love."

"I know." A tear ran down her face.

She felt too worn-out to say more. These people believed they were taking her to safety, comfort, the life she was destined to live. But regardless of what they wanted to think, they were ripping her away from the home she loved.

# PART THREE:
# Father of Webs

# 19

# Homecoming

The docking bay alone was larger than a battle cruiser. Roca stood on the platform at the end of a high catwalk, cradling Eldrin as she watched the ships, cranes, and machines below. The frigate that had brought her to the Orbiter sat clamped in its docking pad. Kurj had just finished registering with the port authority; now he was striding toward a lift that would bring him up to this platform.

Eldrin stirred in his sleep, and pressed his hinged, four-digit hand against her arm. She smiled at him, her sadness easing. He had slept through the takeoff from Lyshriol, ensconced in a bubble that protected him from acceleration. He seemed similarly unimpressed now with this space station. In her more objective moments, she realized that although he was a hearty, healthy child, he wasn't *that* different from any other child born throughout the history of the human race. But most of the time she marveled that she had somehow, incredibly, given birth to this child who was so much more extraordinary than any other baby ever born.

She wished his father could be with them.

Kurj boarded the lift, which wasn't much more than a metal square with a rail. As it rose from the ground, he waved to Roca, but he let no emotion show on his face. It didn't fool her. Behind that impassive demeanor, he hid a heart capable of far more feeling and forgiveness than he let himself acknowledge. She just wished he could forgive himself. It wasn't his fault she had made flawed decisions in her life, that Darr had hurt her, or that the Traders wanted to do the same to the entire Imperialate. Kurj took the responsibilities of an empire onto his shoulders until she thought he would break under the weight.

The lift stopped at the platform and Kurj pushed aside the rail. "All set?"

"Yes." Roca had little else to say. She had hardly spoken to him in the three days it had taken to reach the Orbiter. He didn't push. He knew he had gone too far when he threatened her husband. For all her thoughts about forgiveness, she knew that if he had hurt Eldri, she could never have forgiven him.

Roca glanced at the tiny child in her arms. Would he too turn hard someday? Over the decades, she had seen the joy in Kurj turn to stone. Given time and a gentler life, he might have healed after Darr. Instead he had become a Jagernaut. Nothing could take away the hells he had lived since then.

"We all have our personal hells," he said softly.

She looked up with a start and found him watching her, his eyes unshielded. His height disconcerted her after she had lived for so long among the Lyshrioli. She didn't even reach his shoulder.

"We should go." She heard the chill in her voice.

"All right." He mentally withdrew and his inner eyelids lowered.

They crossed a catwalk to the arrivals gate. The rotation of the Orbiter produced a lower apparent gravity than what Roca had become used to on Lyshriol, and it felt strange now. However, her internal systems had a memory of dealing with the Orbiter environment and her body was adapting quickly.

Had she and Kurj come on a commercial flight, they would have disembarked in a lounge with all the amenities travelers took for granted. This gate was spare, dedicated to military personnel rather than civilians. Roca had never been in this area of the Orbiter. Soldiers did double takes as she and Kurj passed. She felt their astonishment at his large size and her appearance. Many recognized Kurj, though not all. A few wondered if she and Kurj were brother and sister. Mercifully, only one person assumed they were a husband and wife with their child.

The magrail station was a few hundred meters from the gate, down a carpeted hall. White Luminex walls lit the corridor, and panels of swirling holoart. The lovely effect surprised Roca; she hadn't realized ISC would seek to make its port areas attractive for its soldiers. Given the utilitarian aspect of the gate itself, the designers had only been partially successful, but at least they made the attempt.

A magcar waited at the platform like a huge bullet. As she and Kurj settled inside, facing each other across the small cabin, the baby began to fuss. Roca cooed to him, but he kept twisting in her arms. She could tell from the vague impressions in his mind that he wasn't hungry. He wanted something else, she wasn't sure what.

"It's all right, beautiful boy," she murmured. He flailed his small fists, his face scrunched up. So she sang to him, a Trillian ballad Eldri had often crooned to her when they lay curled in bed. The baby quieted immediately, his body relaxing as he snuggled against her, his eyes closing.

"That's a beautiful song," Kurj said.

She looked up, startled. Absorbed in her link with the baby, she had forgotten he was there. "His father used to sing it to me."

Kurj stiffened and turned away.

Roca wanted to entreat him to give Eldri a chance. But she knew Kurj; if she pushed, it would only make him more adamant against her husband.

They shot through tunnels in the Orbiter's hull, which housed the military command centers of the station. Then the car whirred into the main habitat. The spherical Orbiter had an inner surface area of over fifty square kilometers, divided into two hemispheres, Ground and Sky. Ground consisted of meadows, hills, and mountains, with the ethereal City in its center, its diaphanous beauty hiding an underlying strength. It reminded Roca of her sister, Dehya, whose delicate beauty hid a great strength of character.

It never ceased to amaze Roca that the great blue dome of Sky took up half the living area. The Sun Lamp moved across it during the day, and lights sparkled at night, like stars. Although lovely, it was a remarkably inefficient use of space. But the Orbiter housed many powerful government figures; to provide for them, it was designed for beauty rather than efficiency.

The "gravity" created by the Orbiter's rotation pointed down at its equator, which bisected Ground and Sky. The rotation poles pierced the horizon where Ground and Sky met. As a person walked from the equator toward the poles, gravity decreased and the ground sloped upward, until one became weightless at the poles and the "ground" was vertical. They could walk just as easily on Sky, if they wished.

The Ruby Dynasty lived in a valley about halfway to the poles. Roca's father, Jarac, had chosen that region because the lower gravity was easier on his huge size. Twenty years ago, Kurj had named the area Valley, just as he named Ground, Sky, and City. Jarac agreed they were sensible names. Roca's mother had wanted to know if they intended to name space "Space" and their ships "Ship." Roca didn't think her son or father had caught the joke, though, given how seriously they considered the idea.

"Why are you smiling?" Kurj asked.

She glanced up, softening despite her anger at him. "Do you like it here on the Orbiter?"

"Yes. I do." His inner lids raised, revealing his eyes. "I've always liked it. I don't feel so heavy."

She knew he meant more than gravity. "You work too hard."

His lips quirked up. "You always tell me that. And how I should settle down with a nice girl."

"Well, you should."

His eyes glinted. "I don't like *nice* girls."

"Kurj!"

He laughed. "Sorry." In a more serious voice, he said, "I am just so very, very glad to see you alive and well."

In truth, she felt the same way about being alive. "We feared Avaril's army would kill us."

"They might have if you hadn't sent out those robot birds. Otherwise, we might not have made it in time. We were having a hard time fixing your location on the planet."

"I'm glad it worked."

"Why were those people attacking the castle?"

"They wanted Eldri."

At the mention of his stepfather's name, his expression hardened. The baby stirred in Roca's arms, crying in his sleep.

"Look." Kurj's face relaxed. "He feels our tension."

"It is because he is a psion." Roca regarded Kurj steadily. "Possibly a Ruby psion."

His inner lids came down. "Impossible."

"No." She willed him to see the truth. "I know you sense the baby's mind." The mental bond he had formed with Eldrin at the birth was undeniable. Kurj treated him with a gentleness Roca had never seen him show anyone else. It gave her hope for both of her sons.

"How could it be?" Kurj said. "It means his father carries the genes of a psion."

Her gaze didn't waver. "Yes."

"That barbarian can't have them."

"Why not? What does his culture have to do with his DNA?"

His jaw stiffened. "It's too incongruous."

"Nevertheless, it is true."

He looked away, out the window.

The walk through Valley soothed Roca's agitation. The beauty of the secluded vale, with its pastoral hills and glens, comforted her. Sky arched far above, a reassuring blue, the Sun Lamp halfway from its zenith to the horizon. Kurj walked at her side, silent, as the two of them had often been with each other these past few days.

They went to the house where Roca lived when she visited the Orbiter. Entering the front room, she saw a massive gold man standing at a table by the far wall, glancing through a holobook she had left open there a year ago, the last time she had been here. She had an eerie moment of dislocation, entering the room with Kurj only to find him already here.

Then her mind readjusted and her mood warmed. "My greetings, Father."

Jarac turned with a start. "Roca!" He strode forward—and stopped halfway across the room, staring at the bundle in her arms.

Eldrin stirred and opened his eyes, trying to look around.

Roca's father blinked, his unshielded eyes like liquid gold with black pupils in the center. "Is that the baby?"

"Your grandson." Roca's pulse leapt. Would Jarac accept him?

Her father came the rest of the way over to them and peered at Eldrin. "He certainly is small."

Roca smiled. "That he is." Especially compared to Jarac.

Her father poked a finger into Eldrin's fist. The baby looked up, his big blue eyes scanning the gold face above him. Jarac spoke in a kind voice. "What do you see, little man?" His words took on a singsong quality. "Do you know your grandhoshpa? Well, you are a fine boy, eh?" He waggled his finger in Eldrin's tiny grip.

Kurj made an exasperated noise. "I have never understood why otherwise rational adults speak gibberish to babies."

Roca slanted a look at him. "I talked that way to you when you were a baby."

Kurj cleared his throat, his cheeks reddening under their metallic cast.

"Look at that." Jarac beamed at his infant grandson. "He turns his head to watch my face when I move."

Relief flowed through Roca. Her father wasn't rejecting Eldrin. It had probably helped that she sent messages ahead, letting her parents know she was alive—and a mother again. She could tell how much her father wanted to press her for news about what had happened. That he approached the situation with such tenderness made her want to hug him.

"Well, so." Jarac laughed as Eldrin gurgled at him.

Roca extended her child to her father. "Would you like to hold him?"

Jarac hesitated. "He's so small. I might break him."

Roca couldn't help but laugh. "I've seen holos of you holding me when I was this size. You never broke me."

With great care, he took Eldrin into his arms. "Well, and look at you, eh?"

She glanced around the room. "Where is Mother?"

"In the web." Jarac smiled at Eldrin, the lines crinkling around his eyes, more wrinkles than Roca remembered. With a start, she realized how much gray threaded the bronze mane of hair that swept to his shoulders. It was the most noticeable difference between him and Kurj; his grandson kept his hair clipped close to his head in metallic curls with no trace of gray. She would never understand how her older son and her father could otherwise look so alike and yet be so different. As a small child, Kurj had been similar to Jarac in temperament, but the years had hardened her son in a way that had never happened to her father.

Jarac tickled Eldrin's nose with his huge finger. To Roca, he said, "Your mother doesn't know yet that you've arrived."

"Actually, she does," a regal voice said behind them.

Roca almost jumped. Turning, she saw her mother, Lahaylia Selei, in the archway of the room. Gray streaked the black hair that fell to below the pharaoh's hips, its length a trademark of Ruby Dynasty women. She resembled a Majda queen, with her high cheekbones, slanted eyes, and elegant nose, but her eyes were vivid green instead of black. She came forward, willowy yet strong, with an imperial carriage.

"Mother." Roca went to her, wanting to throw her arms around this woman who had held her as a child. The Ruby Pharaoh's ingrained formality discouraged shows of emotion, but for all her mother's reserve, Roca felt her love, and her gratitude that her daughter had come home. It flowed over Roca.

"I am glad to see you, Daughter," her mother said.

"And I you," Roca answered.

Lahaylia glanced at the baby that Jarac held. "You have brought us a grandchild."

Roca tensed. Would her mother also accept Eldrin?

Lahaylia went to her husband, and Jarac beamed, showing her Eldrin. "Look, Lahya. He is beautiful."

The Ruby Pharaoh gazed at her grandson. "So."

"I named him Eldrin Jarac Valdoria," Roca said. Then she added the last name, her voice firm. "Skolia."

Jarac froze, his smile vanishing. Kurj stiffened at her side, even already knowing what Roca believed. Lahaylia didn't move.

Then, slowly, the Ruby Pharaoh turned to her. She spoke in a deceptively quiet voice. "What did you say?"

"Prince Eldrin Jarac Valdoria Skolia." Roca used the title deliberately.

Anger flashed in her mother's eyes. "The Skolia name may be taken only by a Ruby psion. For anyone else to dare claim it is a grave insult to our family."

"He is my husband's son. That makes him a member of the Ruby Dynasty." Roca's stiffness eased. "Mother, I'm not sure if Eldri is a Ruby psion. The geneticists will have to examine his DNA. But I think he is." Her hope surged despite her attempts to remain cool. "I really think he is."

"So it is true." Lahaylia's voice cooled. "You married the father." She didn't seem to have heard anything beyond Roca's first sentence. "How could you commit such an abomination?"

This wasn't going the way Roca had hoped. "I love him."

Her mother made an incredulous noise. "What does that have to do with anything?"

Roca scowled at her. "He is a good man."

"He is unworthy of you."

"His people might argue I am unworthy of him."

Lahaylia arched a perfect eyebrow. "I hardly think so."

Roca was aware of Kurj listening with the same concentration he used to size up combat situations. Although she spoke to Lahaylia, her words were as much for him. "It doesn't matter to you that this man may be a Ruby psion?"

"A far-fetched proposition," the Ruby Pharaoh said.

"But true."

"Perhaps."

Roca refused to back down. "You will see."

"It makes no difference, Daughter."

"No *difference?* He would be priceless."

"Certainly he would. We could make much use of him." Lahaylia crossed her arms. "He would still be unworthy to become your husband."

"He isn't a thing to 'make use of,' " Roca said angrily.

Jarac spoke. "Lahya, if she loves this fellow, we should be happy for them."

Roca could have hugged him. Her mother had other ideas. She frowned at her husband. "Pah." She made that one word an imperial rebuke that would have struck fear into the most stalwart soul.

Unlike the rest of the universe, however, Jarac didn't blanch under the force of her disapproval. Instead he smiled, the lines around his eyes crinkling. "Loving one's spouse is a good thing, Wife."

Although she gave him her most regal, aloof stare, gentleness underlay her gaze. But when she turned to Roca, her frown returned. "Have you informed your betrothed about this marriage of yours? Perhaps you have forgotten him—Prince Dayj Majda, nephew of the Majda Matriarch?"

"Or course I haven't forgotten." Roca wished she could, but that was another matter. "Reparations have been made."

Roca had spent the past months going over files in her node, studying precedents. While en route here, she had sent a careful message to the House of Majda. She phrased the news of her marriage in a manner that court protocol specified as an apology in situations that precluded an open statement of regret. Her betrothal to Dayj had never taken place, so technically she owed Majda no explanation. But implicit promises had been made. Majda had been grooming its prince to become a Ruby consort. In reparation, Roca had deeded the Matriarch a lucrative shipping company, one Vaj Majda had long coveted. To Dayj, Roca sent a jeweled box with two art figurines considered priceless. It wouldn't diminish what she had done, but it conveyed a message that he and his House would recognize, an apology of the highest order.

Lahaylia, however, looked unimpressed. "No reparations are going to appease Vaj Majda." She crossed her arms. "And I am sure the prince who had expected to carry your name and sire your children will be enthralled to know you have given birth to another man's child."

Eldrin's face scrunched up and he began to cry.

"Lahya, stop." Jarac gently handed Eldrin to his mother. As Roca soothed the crying infant, Jarac drew his wife away, to a window across the room. Light from the Sun Lamp slanted through the window, il-luminating the two potentates as if they were in a gilded portrait. Roca wondered how they could look so beautiful and be so infuriating, though this time it was only her mother.

With a hearty cry, Eldrin turned toward Roca's breast. She cuddled him close. "Are you hungry, sweetings?"

Kurj spoke hurriedly, his fierce demeanor replaced by alarm. "If you need me, I will be in the other room."

Roca nodded, her attention focused on Eldrin. As Kurj made a quick retreat, she crossed the room, murmuring to the baby. She left her parents in the other room, deep in discussion, and secluded herself in an alcove. She felt Eldrin's relief at being comforted. Some people believed a baby this young had no real personality, but she could already sense his moods and needs.

She nursed him, knowing this moment of peace wouldn't last. Had her mother accepted the marriage, or even remained neutral, it might have mitigated Kurj's hostility toward his stepfather. She had thought if Lahaylia knew Eldri was a strong psion, perhaps even a Ruby, she would be more open to him, but it seemed a futile hope now. Without the Ruby Pharaoh's blessing, the marriage had no future.

No matter. She had no intention of divorcing Eldri. Even if it turned out she couldn't see him again, she could protect him with her title. Otherwise, she feared ISC would demand control of his life, taking his freedom, dignity, and self-determination. An unknown native of a primitive world had few defenses against an interstellar empire, but they would think long and hard before they dared touch the consort of an heir to the Ruby Throne.

Whether her family liked it or not, Eldrinson Althor Valdoria was a member of the Ruby Dynasty.

# 20

# Aftermath

Kurj sat sprawled at his desk, intent on the holos rotating above its glossy surface: graphs, plans, reports, details of the planned invasion. Only five days had passed since he had found Roca, but in that time his team had done a great deal of work. He had spent hours today scrutinizing their reports. His EI strategists continually communicated with those of other officers, just as he communicated with the officers themselves. He had sent so many messages through the Kyle web today, his mind ached.

They had so far spent over eight months planning the invasion. Had they intended a fast strike, they could have gone in long ago. But they had to prepare for the possibility of a protracted, debilitating war. This would be no quickly undertaken and quickly won conflict; they could be embarking on a course that would lead to years of warfare across a region of space that encompassed hundreds, even thousands, of human settlements.

Finally he closed his files and EI shells. As he leaned his head against the back of his smart-chair, it shifted to make him more comfortable. For a short time he simply sat with his eyes closed, recharging his systems.

When he felt fully powered again, he went back to work. The files he brought up now had no connection to the invasion. The helices and diagrams showed the mutated DNA that produced a Ruby psion—him, to be exact. It wasn't just one gene, but many, corresponding to a wide range of traits, most associated with empathy and telepathy.

"Node **A** attend," he said.

"Attending." The deep voice belonged to the EI that ran the computers in his huge office. Dehya, his aunt, had designed it for him, at his request. He had set his spy programs against it himself, to check its security. It was the only system he knew of that his spies had never cracked.

"Find me the medical records on Eldrin Jarac Valdoria," Kurj said. He refused to give the Skolia name to his half brother.

And yet, as much as he sought to distance himself from the child, he couldn't stop thinking about him. In that incredible moment when he had held the newborn, his universe had flipped upside down. Was it a form of insanity that made him shaky inside when he saw that baby? No matter how much he tried to deny the emotions, they refused to go away.

The intensity of his response unnerved him. He had always kept an iron control on his emotions, lest they throw him about like driftwood on a storm-lashed ocean. His passions were too strong to let free. Yet, somehow, Eldrin reached that inner core. For some inexplicable reason, Kurj wanted to see the boy, hold him, say things just as ridiculous as those nonsense words his grandfather used. It was absurd and inappropriate, but nevertheless, he couldn't stop feeling that way.

"Medical records located," the EI said.

"Copy them into my memory stacks," Kurj said.

"The records are confidential."

Kurj waved his hand. "Never mind that."

"I haven't permission to copy them."

"I'm giving you permission."

"Only Roca Skolia or her doctor can give permission."

"So change the access protocols."

"That isn't allowed."

Kurj frowned. "I'm allowing it."

"You should not have the authority to do such."

"Node **A,** do what I tell you." Unfortunately, Dehya also tended to program some annoying traits into EIs, such as this resistance to overriding other people's security protocols. Every time he fixed this one, it tried to evolve back to its original parameters. He would have to run a personality check on it again.

"Medical records copied," **A** said.

"Good." Kurj leaned back in his chair and it shifted to accommodate his weight. "Bring up the analysis of my half brother's DNA."

The holos above his desk disappeared, replaced by new ones, similar but not identical to Kurj's DNA.

Kurj studied the diagrams. "So is the baby a Ruby psion?"

"The analysis is incomplete," **A** said. "But yes, it looks like he has the full complement of Rhon genes."

Kurj blew out a gust of air. He genuinely hadn't believed his brother could be a Ruby. No wonder his mother had acted rashly toward the Skyfall man. His pheromones would have muddled her judgment. Kurj didn't believe she loved him. She couldn't. It was impossible. The scum wasn't good enough for her. Of course, no one was good enough for her, but this barbarian was about as far from suitable as possible. At least Dayj Majda had impeccable heredity. The fact that Dayj never let anyone forget that didn't make him any easier to tolerate, but as long as he stayed in seclusion, it didn't matter.

Kurj frowned at the holos. "Is it possible the father of this child is not a Ruby Dynasty psion?"

"Yes," **A** said. "For him to be a Ruby psion, he must carry two of every Ruby gene. If he has only one of any of them, he won't manifest the full traits, but he can still pass the genes to his son."

"That isn't what I meant." Kurj knew perfectly well a child could be a Ruby psion even if his father wasn't; he was living proof of that. "I meant, is it possible he isn't part of the Ruby Dynasty. Is his marriage to my mother legal?"

"No written contract exists."

That sounded promising. "Is an oral agreement enough to make it legal?"

"Yes, if the bride, groom, and witnesses testify and have their statements verified by physiological monitoring."

"What would invalidate their testimony?"

**A** paused, working. "If monitoring determines that any of the parties are lying; if one or more of the parties has a previous contract that precludes the marriage; if the contract violates Skolian law; or if any of the parties involved are mentally incapable of agreeing to a contract."

"Interesting." Kurj swiveled his chair around to look through the window that took up the entire wall behind his desk. Far below the window, Ground sloped away, rolling down to City, which glowed like a gem in the distance. The sight soothed him, all the more so because his mood had lifted.

He knew how to rid their lives of Eldrinson Valdoria.

Windward lay in ruins.

Eldri and Garlin spent the morning walking through the castle with Shannar and the Memory, taking stock of the damage. Eldri felt as if he were withering inside. He had lost everything: Roca, his son, Windward, and so many of his men that he hurt every time he thought of it. In the five days since the battle, he had gone through the motions of life, but his existence seemed like a barren plain, a place that would never again see joy.

A group of people entered the courtyard through the broken gateway. Eldri frowned, squinting at them. His warriors were escorting several unfamiliar men. His stomach dropped when he recognized the man in their center. Avaril Valdoria.

Eldri stopped, his hand going to his sword. He touched nothing, of course; he had no weapon at the moment. In truth, it mattered only to his pride. His men wore swords, disk mail, and armor, all of them well equipped to defend him. Even that wasn't necessary; one of Avaril's men had tied a red scarf to his staff, the traditional request for a truce.

Eldri glanced at Shannar. "I would see my godsforsaken cousin leave Windward."

"He will soon be gone," Shannar said. "His army is broken."

"So is ours," Eldri muttered. "He will rebuild."

Garlin drew in a weary breath. "And so will we."

Shaliece spoke. "Shall I accept their request for truce?"

"Yes, I suppose." Eldri nodded to her. "Take extra care in recording all he says and does."

She inclined her head. Then she pulled off the violet scarf around her waist and raised it high, making the cloth ripple in the wind.

They fell silent as the warriors escorted Avaril to them. Eldri's men kept their hands on the hilts of their swords, but no one drew a weapon. To do so after both sides had raised their colors would have been unforgivable.

Avaril regarded Eldri with undisguised distrust. The wind blew back his hair, showing more of the gray. "Cousin."

Eldri only grunted. He had no intention of making whatever Avaril wanted to say any easier.

Avaril's mouth tightened. "Must we continually fight?"

Eldri crossed his arms. "It is you who chooses to fight."

"It is you who usurps the rightful heir."

"Our grandfather chose his heir," Eldri said. "You may hate that choice, but nevertheless, he was within his rights."

Avaril started to reach for his sword, then took a breath and relaxed his arms. "You can argue your supposed rights forever. It will not change the truth."

"I don't need to change any truths," Eldri said tightly. "No matter how many of my men you murder, your claim will never be valid."

Avaril's gaze flashed. "You have no shame. The immorality of stealing a title is not enough? You suborn the very queen of the suns to your debauched cause."

Eldri made a conscious effort not to grit his teeth. "My wife has nothing to do with this."

"Your wife's kin destroyed your castle. The gods have made their displeasure clear." Avaril swept out his hand, indicating the ruins. "Relinquish the title, Eldrinson, before you bring this disaster to all of Dalvador."

"You go too far." Although Eldri would never admit it to his cousin, he feared Avaril spoke the truth, that the sun gods had turned their disfavor on his union with Roca. The last person he wished to discuss it with, however, was Avaril.

"Valdor and Aldan took vengeance on your army." Eldri glowered at him. "They destroyed you because you threatened their queen. Now take your men and be gone. I give you two days."

"And if I don't?" Avaril asked. "You have no more men left than I do."

Eldri lowered his arms, his fists clenching. "I will defend my home. Know this. Whatever I have to do, I will."

"Do not think you have won."

"Two days," Eldri said. "Then the truce ends."

Avaril's jaw visibly clenched. He moved his palm outward, a formal and forbidding gesture of farewell. Eldri did the same, their hands almost hitting. Then Avaril turned on his heel and strode toward the shattered gates, escorted by his warriors and Eldri's defenders.

Garlin spoke heavily. "He will return. Probably not for years, with his army broken. But he will come back, Eldri. He will never rest until one of you is dead."

"Would that it could be different." Eldri rubbed his eyes. "He is our only other kin."

Garlin laid his hand on his shoulder. "Come. Let us see to the repairs."

Eldri nodded, his gaze downcast. Accompanied by Shannar and Shaliece, they continued their appraisal of the castle. He felt queasy. In the days since Roca had gone, and his dreams with her, he had suffered several convulsions, including one Garlin had told him went on and on. Eldri knew only that it left him bruised and sore, and also groggy for longer than usual. He had begun to question why he bothered to keep going at all.

He knew the answer as soon as the thought came to him, knew it every time the survivors of Windward looked to him for help, succor, and leadership. Even if he couldn't find the will to live for himself, he had to be strong for them.

Nor could he forget Roca's words, spoken with desperation as her people swept her away. She had promised she would return. Eldri swore to Valdor and Aldan, the sun gods, that he would be more diligent than the most devout acolyte in performing the proper rituals. If there was more to this business of sun deities than he had believed, perhaps they would forgive his earlier impiety and let his wife come home.

But he had to stop dwelling on this. Shannar was speaking.

"The northern towers are solid." Shannar indicated a wing of the castle far from where Avaril's men had battered the gates. The graceful turrets of three towers reached to the sky. Their foundations also remained solid, but the rest of Windward had fared worse. Avaril's men had only destroyed the gates; the minions of the sun god had brought down the entire front of the castle, sheering through the stone with swords of light. Eldri shuddered, unable to blank the vision from his mind.

Nor could he escape his guilt. Despite his recent seizures, he had suffered far fewer of the big attacks since he started the salts. By chasing the demons from his body, he may have let their human incarnations loose among his people. It was one of two possible explanations for what had happened. The other was that the sun god had come to avenge Roca. Or perhaps the gold man had been a war god. Either way, Eldri knew it was his fault. He had brought her here, daring to love a goddess he had no right to claim in marriage.

Wife. She was his *wife*. She had carried his son. He thought he would break inside with their loss. The gold man had taken both Roca and Brad, but Eldri had no idea where. He couldn't find out anything. They weren't anyplace he or his men had searched in the five days since Dalvador had "won" the battle. The port remained empty, with the strange droids taking care of it. Eldri had never been easy around those little metal creatures, and now he found them positively eerie.

"We can rebuild a portion of the main keep," Garlin said. "But the rest—it seems impossible. How did our ancestors raise these incredible walls and towers?"

"The gods weren't angry at them," Eldri said darkly.

Garlin shrugged. "I don't think any gods attacked Windward. Just men."

"And *women*." Shannar looked alarmed. "Many of those warriors were women."

Shaliece, the Memory, pointed southward. "Look. The metal flyer from the port."

Eldri squinted. A familiar sliver sparkled against the sky, one far more innocuous than the killing vessels from five days ago. His hope leapt. "Perhaps Brad has returned and fixed it."

The flyer grew in size, until they could see it clearly. As it sailed over the mountains, the light of the suns reflected off its silver body, highlighting the blue symbol that indicated it belonged to the Allied Worlds of Earth, whatever that meant. In any case, it was the only flyer on Lyshriol.

Eldri couldn't fathom why Brad liked these "symbols." He had once shown Eldri a most remarkable cup, a mug made out of a material that resembled glasswood, but was more brittle. Brad claimed the symbol on the mug matched the one on his flyer. But it didn't. The one on the flyer was larger and a different shade of blue, and had many other differences despite what Brad deluded himself into believing.

These "holobooks" Brad liked were even worse. He had actually tried to convince Eldri that the marks in them formed patterns you could use to speak. It was crazy. Those symbols couldn't hold meaning, all so different, even those that Brad claimed "spelled" the same "word." They *weren't* the same. They were in different places in the book and surrounded by different patterns. How could Brad think they were the same? It made Eldri wonder if Brad might be a bit strange in his mind about these books.

The flyer floated toward Windward, skimming over the nearby peaks. It settled in the open area before the traitorous bridge that had given Avaril's men access to Windward. Eldri left the courtyard with Garlin, Shaliece, and Shannar. They were crossing the bridge when the flyer opened and Brad stepped out. Eldri's heart leapt to see his friend. Even after having known Brad and his odd ways for so long, though, it still unsettled him to see the flying machine disgorge a man.

Brad looked more like himself now than he had during the siege, when they had all become ragged and tattered. He had shaved his beard and cut his hair in that peculiar style some offworlders favored, so short it capped on his head. He also wore slacks and a "turtleneck" sweater.

Brad had shown him images of turtles and explained the name, which he claimed dated back centuries, but Eldri couldn't fathom the resemblance between them and Brad's clothes. He just couldn't see it. Out of respect for his friend, however, he refrained from saying he thought it absurd.

Brad hadn't come alone. Several unfamiliar men and women descended from Brad's flyer, all in severe clothes. Their garb resembled the coveralls Brad sometimes wore, except these outfits were crisp and snug, giving an impression of authority. They had symbols on the shoulders and chests, not blue, but gold and black. The newcomers all wore boots, sturdy and finely made. Although their apparel would be poor protection in a battle, their manner made Eldri think they were soldiers.

Eldri's group met their visitors at the end of the bridge. Brad nodded with respect and spoke in English. "I am gratified to see you well, Eldrinson."

Eldri wondered at his uncharacteristic formality. "And I you." It was true. He would have mourned even more if Brad had died in the battle.

Brad indicated the people with him, who watched Eldri with disquieting intensity. "This delegation comes from Imperial Space Command of the Skolian Imperialate."

Eldri wondered if he was supposed to know what that meant. "I see."

Brad didn't look happy at all. "Eldrinson, they are military officers from your wife's people. They have inquiries about you. They've asked me to act as an interpreter."

Eldri froze. The war god had sent emissaries. He felt chilled, then hot and flushed. He nodded stiffly, knowing he had to ask the question that had tormented him since the star warriors had taken Roca. "Is my wife all right? And our child?" *Please,* he silently begged the deities he had so neglected during his short life. *Please let them be all right.*

Brad's voice gentled. "She is fine. And you have a strong, healthy son. Your wife named him Eldrin Jarac Valdoria, after you and her father."

The relief was so overwhelming, Eldri thought he would grab Brad right there and hug him in front of everyone. He managed to hold back only because his fear of the war god's minions tempered his rash behavior. They continued to watch him, except one woman who was waving her finger over an object in the palm of her hand. It reminded Eldri of Brad's "palmtop," except this one was gold and black instead of blue.

Eldri inclined his head to the minions, and they nodded back. From their minds, he could tell they found him . . . *interesting*. It made him uncomfortable, as if he were wild prey they wanted to trap. He wished they would leave, but he didn't dare send them away.

So he invited them into his ruined home.


Bewildered, Eldri turned from the strangers and their magicked "holos." The strange pictures floated in the air, diaphanous and untouchable, yet appearing solid. He, Garlin, Brad, and the visitors were sitting at the table in the dining hall. The woman next to him had unrolled a flat screen. Holos moved above it, odd shapes in different colors, pretty but meaningless.

Eldri gave Brad a beseeching look and spoke in English. "I don't understand what they want. Why won't they tell me about Roca?"

Brad seemed troubled. "I think they're giving you an IQ test. It measures intelligence."

Garlin frowned. "Intelligence is not sand or water, that you can measure it."

"I will ask." Brad's mood of foreboding disquieted Eldri. Nor had he realized Brad knew so many languages, though perhaps he should have guessed it from how fast Brad had picked up Trillian. The Earth man spoke to the Skolians in their language, and they answered in short sentences. Eldri could tell, from their minds, that they were guarding their responses.

Brad turned back to Eldri. "They want you to find the patterns in the holos."

Eldri was growing angry. "They have *no* patterns. Why do these people keep asking me such bizarre questions?"

Brad's look was unnerving, as if he were watching Eldri fling himself off a cliff. "The pattern is easy. Can't you see it?"

Eldri glared at him. "If you see it, then tell me, I will tell them, and you can translate."

"They'll know. They're recording this session."

"Recording?"

Brad indicated the woman with the screen. "She is a Memory."

Finally Brad said something that made sense. Eldri nodded to her with respect, but his unease was growing. These strangers were *studying* him. He felt it. They analyzed his every move.

"I think they understand English just fine," Eldri told Brad. "They pretend otherwise because they think it will make us careless with our words, so we might reveal useful information."

Brad spoke dryly. "I wouldn't be surprised."

Eldri turned to one of the soldiers, a man with short, dark hair. "Do you understand me?"

The man glanced at Brad. After Brad translated, the man spoke in his own language. To Eldri, Brad said, "Major Bass can pick out some of my English words because he has a spinal implant with a language module, but he can't follow your speech at all because of the harmonics created by your vocal cords."

Eldri glared at him. "Whatever you just said, I am certain I don't believe it."

Garlin let out an explosive breath. "Brad, it never makes sense. All these words—do you mock us with them?"

"No. I swear, no." Brad sounded miserable. "Eldri, I'm sorry. You must answer his questions. I'm not sure why, but it is important."

"Very well." Eldri gave the Skolians his most implacable look. "Proceed."

They started over, asking him to "identify patterns." Frustrated, he gave up trying to understand and answered according to games he played with each symbol. He grouped them in eights and imagined them reflecting, inverting, and translating through their centers. He varied his responses according to how the images changed color. It made sense to him, though he doubted it was what they wanted.

So they continued.

# 21

# Children of Flame

Roca sat in the dark, rocking Eldrin. Her chair responded to her movements, making her comfortable. She cuddled her sleeping child and sang as she went back and forth. In the three weeks since she had returned to the Orbiter, she had come to love this routine with her son.

She dozed for a while, then stirred enough to put Eldrin in his cradle by her bed. As she tucked him in, the front door chimed. She kissed Eldrin's cheek, then left the room, pausing in the doorway to look at him. He was an angel, sleeping so peacefully. Already she saw his father in him. She missed Eldri so much, it was a fissure in her life.

The chime came again. Roca sighed. Rather than asking the house EI to screen the visitor, though, she went to answer herself. This valley where her family lived was one of the best-guarded places in the Imperialate. No one could enter without clearance. Supposedly that meant no one in Valley posed them any danger, though Roca had her doubts. Security could protect them from outsiders, but no one could protect them from one another. Their passions injured their hearts.

She opened the door to find a slender, dark-haired woman outside in the twilight, the breezes of Valley rustling her hair.

"Dehya! Saints almighty." Roca grasped her sister's arm and hauled her inside. "When did you arrive on the Orbiter?"

Dehya laughed and hugged Roca, her head against her sister's shoulder. "Gods, we were so afraid."

Roca embraced her, grateful to see her. After several moments, they parted and Dehya stood back, wiping tears off her face. "Ah, Roca, I'm sorry. I didn't mean to do that. But when you vanished, we all feared something terrible had happened."

"It did." Roca touched a panel on the wall, making the door shimmer closed. "The Assembly voted to start a war."

"Actually," Dehya said, "they voted to reclaim the regions of the Platinum Sectors the Traders stole from us."

"Same thing."

Dehya smiled gently. "Can I come in?"

Roca reddened, mortified that she had let her sister stand in the doorway while she grumbled. She saw Dehya so rarely and loved her so dearly. "Yes. Please. Come in."

As they entered the living room, with its brighter light, Roca was once again struck by how much her sister resembled an ethereal version of their mother. Unlike the queens of their ancestry, Dehya was fragile, though only physically. But she had the classic hair of a Ruby queen, long and luxuriant, hers glossy black rather than streaked with gray. She also had their mother's green eyes, slanted and large. A shimmer of sunrise colors overlaid hers, a vestige of their father's inner eyelid.

Dehya glanced toward the bedroom. "Is he in there?"

"Yes." Roca's voice softened. "He's sleeping."

"May I see him?"

Roca lifted her hand in invitation. "Please."

They padded into the bedroom, to the cradle. Dehya peered at the baby. "He's beautiful," she whispered.

Roca felt her heart go tender. "I think so."

"Even Kurj thinks so."

Roca scowled. Then she stalked out of the room.

Dehya joined her in the living room. "Sister."

Roca crossed her arms. "What?"

"He is your son. Not your enemy."

Roca grunted.

Dehya regarded her steadily. "Kurj voted the way he did to protect all the babies whose lives the Traders will destroy if they conquer us."

"How can you defend him?" Roca demanded. "You voted against the invasion."

"A mother should not hate her son."

Roca lifted her hand, then dropped it in frustration. "I could never hate Kurj. That's what makes this so wrong. I hate the things he does, but I will always love him."

"You and he must come to terms with this."

"I don't know if we can this time." Her memories of Kurj as a boy eased into her thoughts. "But still, he is my firstborn, my golden child."

Dehya sighed. "Now you have two."

Roca heard the longing in her sister's voice. "Are you and Seth still trying?"

"Not anymore." Dehya walked with her to the couch. "We tried for decades with the best doctors we could find. But finally—well, it just hurt too much to keep failing." As they sat on the couch, she said, "I am happy for you, more than I can say. But—ai, Roca, I envy you, too. Sometimes I long for a child so much, I am breaking inside."

"I'm sorry," Roca murmured. Although she had sensed Dehya wanted a family, she hadn't realized how deeply it hurt her sister that it had never happened. Dehya had married an Allied military officer, William Seth Rockworth, in an arranged marriage, part of an Allied-Skolian treaty.

"Ah, well." Dehya tried to smile. "I have nephews."

"Don't give up yet," Roca said. "It wasn't easy for Tokaba and I to have Kurj. We went to many clinics. The doctors said I could never get pregnant, not unless we were willing to have the child's DNA altered so it wouldn't be a psion."

Dehya sat up straighter. "That is what they told Seth and me! Ruby genes have too many lethal recessives. The combinations that made our family may be the only ones that produce a viable fetus. Artificial methods never worked for us, not even cloning." She shook her head. "Why can't we figure out why Ruby children survive only if they gestate in the mother? It is an injustice."

Roca remembered the difficult time when she and Tokaba had struggled to accept that they would never have a child of their own. Even manipulating their DNA to delete the genes of a psion might have failed, given the difficulties. Nor did she think they could have made such a decision. It would have been like taking away the child's sight.

She spoke in a low voice. "When we found out I was pregnant with Kurj, it was a miracle."

"I can imagine." Dehya's face gentled. "Father thinks Eldrin is beautiful."

"Very beautiful." Roca smiled. "Not that I'm biased."

Dehya laughed. "Not at all."

"Perhaps Eldri and I managed better because his people have been separate from ours for thousands of years. Apparently we don't carry many of the same recessives." She thought of her difficult pregnancy. "It was easier for me to carry Kurj, though, probably because he is more like us."

"What does your husband's DNA show?"

It gratified Roca that her sister referred to Eldri as her husband, a reference most of the family avoided. "I don't know. Kurj hasn't given me the results yet."

"Ah, Roca." Dehya obviously understood what she left unspoken. "He will come to accept his stepfather."

"I hope so." But Roca knew it would never happen.

Dehya was watching her closely. "You hurt."

"I miss Eldri." Softly she added, "And it tears me apart that he can't see his son."

"Why can't he come here?"

"Kurj." Roca put a world of anger into that one word.

"He threatened you?"

"Not me. Eldri."

Dehya stared at her. "This is wrong."

Roca made an effort not to grit her teeth. "Tell Kurj that."

"I will."

Roca laid her hand on her sister's arm. "No, don't. I will deal with it. I don't want you caught in the emotional shrapnel from this."

"I would like to help."

"Support me in the Assembly when I speak of Eldri."

Dehya didn't hesitate. "All right."

"I am glad you voted against the invasion."

She spoke awkwardly. "Kurj has asked for my help on it."

"You said no of course."

"Actually, I agreed."

Roca went rigid. "How could you agree?"

"And if I don't?" Dehya pushed back tendrils of hair curling around her face. "ISC wants me to improve the EI security on their ships. It could save lives. If that is within my capability, I must do it, regardless of how I feel about the invasion."

"I admire your integrity," Roca said dryly. "I doubt I could do the same."

"Work within the Assembly. Be a moderating influence. I will support you."

"*How?*" Roca hit her palm on her knee. "I am thoroughly sick of Kurj blocking my simulacrum from appearing in the Assembly. I am a Councilor, a member of the Inner Circle. Every time he cuts off my transmission, he interferes with government business. It is appalling." She had kept her staff working on the problem nonstop, and they had barely dented Kurj's security blocks. But she intended to succeed, regardless of what it took.

Dehya spoke carefully. "That is a serious accusation."

"I know it's him."

"I had wondered why you didn't attend this last session. I assumed you were busy with the baby."

"I am. But that wasn't the reason." She tapped her fingers on the arm of the couch. "I'm thinking of going to Parthonia for the next session."

"If it truly is Kurj behind these problems, he could have his people there prevent you from attending in person."

"They can try," Roca said darkly.

Dehya's mouth curved upward. "The solution is simple."

"It is?"

"I told him I would design security to keep out Traders." Her eyes glinted. "I never promised to keep out his mother."

Roca gave her a dubious look. "I know you're good at what you do. But *that* good?"

Her sister leaned forward. "Just watch me."

Kurj worked late into the night, reading reports from his top officers. All plans for the invasion were on track.

A comm hummed on his desk. He rubbed his eyes, then flicked his light-stylus through a holo. "Primary Skolia."

One of his aides answered. "Sir, this is Secondary Teller. Your grandparents have received a message from the Eubian emperor."

Kurj lifted his head. *That* was unexpected. "What is it?"

"The message is secured, sir."

Gods. His officers were as bad as his EI. "I'm cleared to see it." He wasn't, but he doubted Teller would argue with him. "What does it say? You have my permission to read it."

"I'm bringing it up—" Astonishment crept into Teller's voice. "Sir, it looks like an offer to negotiate for the Platinum Sectors."

Kurj gritted his teeth. He knew his grandfather; given a false offer of truce, Jarac would weaken instead of keeping the resolve they needed for the invasion. "Say nothing more about this. Forward a copy of the message to my home. I will go over it tonight."

"Right away. Also, sir."

"Yes?"

"We have the results of the medical tests on your father."

Kurj's hand clenched the edge of his desk so hard, the muscles in his hand spasmed. He had to make a conscious effort to control his voice. "Secondary Teller, I want one thing understood and understood well. Eldrinson Valdoria is not my father. You will never again refer to him in that manner."

"Yes, sir." His aide sounded subdued. "My apologies."

"Is the report on Valdoria complete?"

"The medical exam, yes." Teller paused. "But the psychologists are questioning the validity of their tests. They have doubts about the interpretation."

"Interpretation, hell. Just send me the results."

"Yes, sir."

"Anything on his DNA? Is he a psion?"

"Yes, it seems so."

The light-stylus in Kurj's hand snapped. He stared at the gash in his hand where it had cut him. "A Ruby psion?"

"They can't say for certain yet. But it looks like it."

Kurj felt as if the walls were closing on him despite the large size of his office. He wanted to explode, but he pressed down his emotions. He wouldn't lose control, wouldn't let the anger burst free. "Very well. Send those results, too, the preliminaries you have now and the final report, when it is ready."

"I'll get right on it."

"That will be all for tonight. Out."

"Out, sir."

For a long moment, Kurj sat unmoving, his fists clenched so hard that his fingernails gouged his palms. Finally he made himself relax, first his shoulders, then his arms. Slowly he opened his fists. He picked up the broken stylus and turned it over in his hand. Then he moved it through holos on his desk, bringing up images until he found the one he wanted, a holo of his father. Tokaba stood grinning, his rakish stance showing a young man full of vibrancy, his blond-streaked hair tousled from the wind.

"We only had six years." Kurj swallowed. "Far too short a time, yes? But in that time, you taught me more about fatherhood than I've learned in all the years since then."

The memories hurt too much. Kurj closed all of his files. A large part of his anger at Eldrinson Valdoria came because he knew the man would hurt his mother. Kurj could never accept him. He represented everything Kurj loathed: turmoil, wildness, barbarism. Kurj wanted— *needed*—the universe to follow rules of logic and reason. Any other path was chaos, the brutality of the Traders, Darr Hammerjackson multiplied a billion times, on an interstellar scale.


Eldri walked through the nursery. It had formerly been an alcove off his bedroom where he stored clothes and armor. He and Roca had cleared it out together, sharing their dreams of the child who would live here. Instead of rough stone walls, now it had blue glasswood paneling gifted to them by people who had scavenged it from their own rooms during the siege. A beautifully carved cradle stood in one corner, full of plump baby quilts.

He gazed into the empty cradle and a tear ran down his face.

Sunlight filtered through the polarized wall of glass behind Kurj's desk. Sprawled in his chair, intent on the holos above his desk, he lost track of time.

A rustle interrupted his concentration. Looking up, he saw Roca in the doorway. His inner eyelids retracted, taking away the gold sheen they laid over his sight. It had been three weeks since he had found her on Skyfall, but he still felt that deep surge of relief each time he saw her.

"My greetings," he said.

She nodded stiffly. "Teller said you wanted to see me."

"Yes. Please, sit down." He motioned at the most comfortable chair in the office.

She crossed the room warily and settled into the chair. He could tell she was trying to keep her expression impassive, but it had already dissolved into concern. She probably didn't even realize it. He wished she didn't look so lovely sitting there, golden and vulnerable.

"You look exhausted," she said. "You need to sleep."

He sat back in his chair. "I'm fine."

She fidgeted with the sleeves on her white jumpsuit. "What did you want to see me about?"

"This." He handed a holofile to a metallic drone waiting by his desk. It trundled over to Roca and gave it to her.

"What is it?" Roca asked.

"The results of your husband's medical tests."

She tensed, scanning the file. "His DNA?"

Kurj wished she didn't look so hopeful. It made him feel betrayed. "We haven't finished that analysis yet. The one you're holding has his medical and psychological results."

Roca sat reading the report. "So it's true. He has epilepsy."

"His condition is severe." Kurj leaned his elbow on the arm of his smart-chair. "The doctors can control his seizures, but they doubt they can stop them altogether."

She looked up. "You will let them treat him?"

"I gave you my word I wouldn't hurt him." Grudgingly he added, "And denying him treatment would hurt him." He hated to admit it, but it was true.

"Thank you." The gratitude that surged from her mind made him feel small.

Kurj clenched the desk, then realized he was doing it and made himself relax his hand. "Look at the rest."

She continued to read the holofile. As she flicked through the reports, her forehead furrowed. "This can't be right."

"I'm sorry." Kurj wasn't, not about this, but it seemed the right thing to say.

" 'Severely mentally retarded'? That's absurd!"

"They did a full battery of tests." Kurj shrugged. "He couldn't answer even the simplest questions."

She regarded him, her gaze smoldering. "Then something is wrong with the tests."

"Nothing is wrong with the tests."

"This is crazy." She thrust the holofile at the drone. "I lived with him for eight months. I would have noticed if he were as slow as these reports claim."

Kurj spoke carefully. "The doctors do have questions about the results. He may not be as impaired as these tests indicate. But, Mother, no one doubts one thing: he isn't competent to make complex legal decisions involving a culture as advanced as ours."

She turned wary. "I disagree. But regardless, no one expects him to."

Although she was guarding her mind, he knew she had doubts, and he knew why. He had investigated. The Allied resort planners had pretended Eldrinson was competent to give permissions that amounted to handing the cultural sovereignty of his people to a multistellar corporation. Had the man truly understood, surely he would have fought it more.

Kurj leaned forward, crossing his arms on his desk. No matter how he handled this, his mother would be angry. He accepted that. He had to take care now. If he acted without sensitivity, it could turn her against him forever. He didn't fool himself that someday she would thank him. He knew her too well. She loved without condition, with a loyalty that had no limitations. It was why he cared for her so deeply; only Roca would love him despite his abiding, irredeemable flaws.

He spoke quietly. "Mother, are you aware of Eldrinson's age?"

She tensed. "What about it?"

"He is rather young for you."

Although she shrugged, her lack of concern was too studied. "Ruby queens have always married younger men. You know that."

"When Skolia was a matriarchy, yes. It isn't now." That stretched the point; aspects of their culture retained its ancient structure, including the conservatism of certain noble Houses, which was why Dayj Majda never appeared in public without his robes and cowl. "We have laws regarding the age at which people can consent to a lifetime marriage contract."

Puzzlement came from her mind, though it was hard to read more from her, given how well she fortified her barriers. "It never bothered you that I'm older than Dayj."

He touched a panel on his desk, and the drone trundled over to give him the holofile. Kurj motioned at his mother with the file. "We aren't sure of your husband's exact age; his people don't measure time in years, and they have enough differences in their physiology that the medics want to do another check." He regarded her steadily. "But no one doubts he is too young to marry."

Roca frowned. "That's absurd. He's well into adulthood."

"That may be." Kurj set down the file. "But you aren't from his culture. And Imperialate law is clear, Mother. He cannot give his consent to marry you, an offworlder, unless he is older than twenty-five standard years."

She didn't look impressed. "It would be easy to prove he's an emancipated minor under our laws. He's a leader, one well loved and respected by his people."

Kurj tapped the holofile. "According to these, he's not competent to act as an emancipated minor."

Roca clenched the arms of her chair. "You can't make this stick. Anyone who talks to him will know he's competent."

Kurj couldn't believe she was trying to replace Tokaba's memory this way. She had done it with Darr, and that monumental disaster had scarred them for life. Now she had chosen someone even worse. He wanted to shout, but he made himself speak gently. It felt strange, as if he were trying to contort himself. "The medics talked with him for a long time."

Her face flushed. "*Your* medics."

"I'm sorry." And he was sorry, not that the marriage wasn't valid, but that he was hurting her.

Roca stood up, her motions controlled, her barriers raised, but nothing could hide the blaze of her anger. "Why should you care if Eldri and I have a valid contract? I gave you my word I wouldn't go back to him."

"Then why make him a Ruby consort? To what point?"

She spoke bitterly. "To protect him from an Assembly that would wring the joy out of his life so they could control him. You *know* he's a Ruby psion. I won't let them destroy his life by treating him like a scientific and political resource instead of a human being. They've tried to do it to us, constraining and controlling our lives, but we have too much power for them to own us. As long as Eldri is my consort, that power protects him."

Kurj stood behind his desk, rising to his full height. "You are right, Mother. Eldrinson Valdoria is a resource." His rage was getting the better of him. "A valuable *resource*. Nothing more. He will never be my father."

"No, he won't. But he *is* my husband. Nothing you do or say, no test you give, will change that." Her voice quieted, though it never lost its steel. "I wish the pain of our past didn't have the power to devastate our lives. I wish I could take away the anguish you've suffered, as a child, an adult, a Jagernaut. I will always love you, Kurj, and I have immense admiration for what you have accomplished. But if you force this, I will fight you. Is that what you want? To tear apart the Ruby Dynasty?"

He pushed down his rage. "No. But I must act in our best interests—not only the Ruby Dynasty, but all of Skolia. I will not relent on this, Mother, no matter what you tell me." He tried to hide the pain under his words, wanting neither her sympathy nor her pity, but he knew she would always see, always know, how it hurt him. "I regret that it causes discord between us."

Sorrow showed in her gaze. "So do I."

Then she left.


Vaj Majda, General of the Pharaoh's Army, stood at her full height, well over six feet. She slapped the communiqué on the Strategy Table. "It is a trick."

Seated on the long side of the oval table, Kurj studied the others around him, trying to sense where they came down in this "offer" from the Traders to negotiate. Jarac stood at the far end of the table, facing off with Majda across its length, his fists braced on its transparent surface, his knuckles reflected in the bright mechanisms within it. His tension beat against Kurj's mind.

The First Councilor was present as a simulacrum, which left Kurj no way to pick up his mood. Kurj's grandmother, the Ruby Pharaoh, was sitting near him, but she guarded her mind with an expertise gained over more than three centuries. Although he couldn't tell if she still supported the invasion, he doubted she had changed her mind.

All four ISC chiefs were also attending in person: Banner Highchief, Fleet Commander; Marla Bay, Commandant of the Advance Services Corps; General Vaj Majda; and Kurj. Highchief and Bay had shielded their minds, but he picked up enough to have concerns. Bay had voted against the invasion. Although Highchief supported Kurj, she preferred an alternative to invasion. Prior to this, she hadn't believed a viable one existed. But now? He didn't like the signs.

"What is it you want?" Jarac demanded of Vaj Majda. "The territory the Traders took from us—or a war? You claim it is the first, but when offered a chance to regain a good part of that territory without fighting, you urge us to battle." He hit the table with his fist. "It is madness. I refuse."

Majda braced her own palms against the table, leaning forward. "The Assembly voted for the invasion, Imperator Skolia. You have no choice." Her voice hardened. "The Ruby Dynasty may feel it has no duty to honor its promises, but you cannot gainsay our entire governing body."

Kurj inwardly groaned. Majda seethed at the insult to her nephew Dayj. Eldrinson Valdoria had a great deal to answer for if his marriage to Roca had done irreparable damage to the alliance between the House of Majda and the Ruby Dynasty.

Commandant Bay spoke. "If we can achieve our purpose without invasion, the vote becomes moot."

Highchief frowned. "This assumes their offer is genuine."

The Ruby Pharaoh tapped the table, bringing up a copy of the communiqué. "This offer is for only one-fourth of the territory."

Jarac turned to his wife, his stance easing. "We only claim one-third of it."

"They have no interest in negotiating," Kurj said. "This so-called offer is meant to mislead and divide us."

"I disagree," the First Councilor said. "They knew when they claimed that territory that we had been mining asteroids there for centuries. They never expected to keep it. They've been bluffing, seeing how far they could push."

Highchief crossed her long arms, lights gleaming along her cybernetic limbs. "They aren't the only ones who know that game." Her dark smile made her look dangerous rather than amused. "Surely by now they know we have voted to reclaim our territories."

Kurj understood: the unstated specter of invasion could be an invaluable tool in a negotiation. But he had no intention of bargaining.

"It wasn't a vote to 'reclaim' anything," Jarac said. "It was a poorly disguised threat to invade them." He motioned at the communiqué. "They've responded with an offer to bargain."

Majda crossed her arms. "I object to bargaining for what already belongs to us."

"They might have some claim to part of it," the First Councilor pointed out. "They've mined a part of the Platinum Sectors for a long time."

Majda waved her hand. "They are claiming far more than that small region."

Lahaylia spoke quietly. "The day will come when the Traders seek to conquer us all. They offer to negotiate now only because they aren't ready to attack."

Marla Bay pushed back from the table and stood. She began to pace, her dark head bowed, her gaunt limbs all angles and sharp edges. Kurj waited. So did everyone else.

Eventually she stopped behind her chair. "We aren't ready to conquer the Traders. Invade them now, in a year, even five years, and we will deplete ourselves." When Majda frowned, Bay held up her hand. "We may succeed with the invasion. But then? The effort will weaken us. Too much."

"It will weaken them as well," Majda said.

"Commandant Bay is right," the First Councilor said. "The Traders have more resources than we do. They can recover faster. We are even less ready for war than they."

Kurj crossed his arms. "What shall we say, 'Let's make peace today so I can kill you tomorrow'? While we dither, they will attack."

Jarac shook his head. "It is foolish for us to attack when they have offered to negotiate."

"It is foolish to let false offers weaken us," Majda said.

"I say we negotiate," Jarac answered.

The First Councilor spoke. "Shall we vote?" When the others indicated agreement, Jarac, Majda, and Marla Bay sat down. The First Councilor set his palmtop out to record the vote. "We are deciding whether or not to accept the Eubian offer to negotiate for a portion of the disputed territory as an alternative to asserting our claim to all the territories by force. An aye vote supports the negotiations, a nay vote opposes them." He turned to Marla Bay. "Commandant, how do you vote?"

Her gaze didn't waver. "Aye."

He spoke to Banner. "Commander Highchief?"

She answered quietly. "Aye."

Kurj silently swore. Banner's reversal spelled disaster. He was going to lose by one vote.

The First Councilor turned to Kurj. "Primary Skolia?"

Kurj gave him an implacable stare. "Nay."

"General Majda?"

She scowled. "Nay."

"Imperator Skolia?"

"Aye," Jarac said.

"Pharaoh Lahaylia?"

She didn't look at her husband. "Nay."

Kurj glanced at Jarac, wondering how his grandparents kept their marriage viable when they found themselves on opposing sides of issues that affected billions of people. His grandfather didn't project anger, though, only relief that the vote had gone his way.

The First Councilor looked around the table. It was a long time before he spoke. Then he said, "I vote nay."

For an instant Kurj was certain he had misheard. Jarac stared at the Councilor with incredulity. Lahaylia was also studying him, though she looked less startled. Kurj couldn't believe it. In Assembly, the Councilor had strongly opposed the vote.

Kurj leaned forward. "You support the invasion now?"

"No." The First Councilor spoke tiredly. "But we voted to reclaim that territory. As much as I may oppose that decision, it was the will of the Assembly. I won't have the Traders manipulating us into a position that undermines our governing body."

"So." Majda spoke with satisfaction. "No bargains."

"No." The Councilor didn't look happy. "No bargains."

*Never.* Kurj thought. Incredibly, he had won after all.

The invasion would go forward.


In the dim light of his bedroom, Jarac lowered himself into a large chair, feeling heavy despite the lower gravity here in Valley. The only light came from the gold silhouette of a desert horizon on the stone walls.

Resting his elbow on the arm of the chair, he put his forehead on his palm. He was tired. Old. He had lived too long, over two centuries.

"Jarac?"

He lifted his head to see Lahaylia in the doorway. She had taken down her hair and was brushing the hip-length tresses. He had always loved to watch her care for her hair, but tonight the joy was gone even from that sight.

He spoke bitterly. "Are you pleased?"

Lahaylia came to sit on the bed by his chair. She answered in that soft voice she used only with him. "I grieve every time I think of war. But it is our only choice. They will never truly negotiate." She shuddered, showing him the vulnerability she hid from the rest of humanity. "Even now, I remember what they were like. Ice. Pain. Cruelty. They have no compassion. They watch us like predators, waiting for weakness."

Jarac took her hand, knowing the horrors she had lived in her youth. "I would find another way than war."

"I know. I am truly sorry."

He pulled her onto his lap as he had often done long ago, in their youth. She laid her head on his shoulder and they sat in the dark, he with his arms around her slender waist.

After a while he said, "I visited Roca today. Our grandson grows strong."

"He is exquisite." Lahaylia sounded wistful.

"You should tell Roca."

"Then she will want me to accept her marriage."

"Kurj claims it is invalid."

"She will fight him," Lahaylia said wearily.

Jarac stroked her hair. "I would like to think, love, that when we are gone, our children and their children will grow strong and wise, with harmony."

She gave a dry laugh. "Well, yes, and I would like the problems with the Traders to go away, too."

He smiled. "Perhaps that has a greater probability, eh?"

She sighed. "I sometimes wonder."

"Still, I think our children will do well."

"Yes, I do think so."

He didn't add what they both knew—the time was coming when their heirs would have to take the reins of power. He had lived too long. Modern science kept his body young, but he was old inside.

He had few regrets. It had been a life he treasured. For all the pain and grief he and Lahaylia had seen, much joy had blessed their lives. Watching Skolia grow and thrive, building the web, serving as Imperator, and most of all, loving Lahaylia and their family—yes, he had enjoyed a full life.

The time had come to rest.

# 22

# Assembly

People filled the amphitheater, in tier upon tier of seats, balcony upon balcony. Kurj stood behind his console high above the dais, gazing over the assembled representatives of a thousand human settlements. Neither Lahaylia nor Jarac were attending this session, but Kurj had many officers present, either in person or as simulacra. He nodded, satisfied. Life was proceeding in an orderly fashion.

His wrist comm crackled. "Primary Skolia, this is Teller. Foreign Affairs Councilor Skolia has entered the Assembly session."

"What the hell?" Kurj scanned the glyphs scrolling across his console. "I thought Security was blocking her."

"Her simulacrum just formed on balcony thirty-two."

He looked across the amphitheater. Thirty-two was too far away to see clearly. "Give me an image here."

The holo that formed above his console showed Roca standing behind a console at the end of a robot arm, listening to another Councilor speak.

Kurj scowled. "Cut her off."

"We're trying, sir. We can't seem to crack her security."

Suddenly the holo of Roca blurred and vanished. But Kurj's relief was short-lived when he realized she had only moved out of view of the holocam recording her position. The robot arm swung to the center of the amphitheater, taking her into full view of the Assembly.

"Foreign Affairs Councilor Roca Skolia," a voice announced. Consoles lit up as people tuned in to hear what she had to say.

"For flaming sakes," Kurj muttered into his comm. "Teller, *cut her transmission.*"

"Yes, sir. We've almost got it." Given the edge of panic in his voice, Kurj suspected they weren't even close to getting it.

Roca stood tall, her head lifted, her gold hair piled on her head, threaded with a string of rubies. She wore a simple white dress, sleeveless, covering her from shoulder to ankle, form fitting, draped in classical lines. She was magnificent. Damn. That would make her speech even more effective.

"My friends and colleagues." Her voice rang out with melodic resonance. "I come before you with news of a Ruby psion."

Kurj spoke into his comm, his voice low and harsh. "Teller, I want the audio in this amphitheater disrupted."

"Sir! Sir, that is illeg—"

"I don't give a flaming damn. Do it."

"Yes, sir! Right away. As soon as we crack their security."

Kurj extended his mind into the web, sending spy tendrils into every system he could find that linked into this session. Far below, the First Councilor was listening intently, standing on the central dais. He and the Inner Circle knew about Roca's marriage, of course, but no announcement had been made to the Assembly or public. In the last two months, since Roca's return from Skyfall, rumors had spread about her husband and son, but they were vague tales, unsubstantiated. Kurj intended for them to remain that way; the less that people knew, the better.

Roca continued to speak.

She orated beautifully, describing her meeting with Valdoria and why she believed him a Ruby psion. By the time she announced her marriage, Kurj's monitors reported that every console in the amphitheater had tuned into her speech. He was gritting his teeth so hard, his jaw ached. Neither he nor any of his operatives had yet found a way to stop her.

Mercifully, she didn't reveal her ugly bargain with him, that he would spare Valdoria's life only if she agreed never again to see her husband. But she described Eldrinson's medical tests and her reasons for disputing them. On private channels throughout the hall, debates were springing up. Some people felt Valdoria was a resource that had to be confiscated, confined, and controlled. Others were horrified at such suggestions for a Ruby consort. Outrage arose over Valdoria's lack of suitability and the insult this marriage gave to Prince Dayj. By coming here today and revealing her story, Roca had taken a great risk; the Assembly might end up voting to take Eldrinson away from her.

But Kurj could read the undercurrents in the debates. People hesitated to challenge a Ruby heir over her consort. Even worse, Roca was creating a fantasy that captivated them—the incomparable Ruby queen, even though she wasn't actually a queen, with the romantically dangerous king cloaked in the mystique of castles and legends, even though he wasn't really a king. Somehow she had caught the imagination of a governing body famed for its profound cynicism. Pah. How could they find charm in this story?

"I demand justice for my consort." Roca's voice carried like the peal of an exquisite bell. "I demand Eldrinson Valdoria be retested. Will we allow such shameful treatment of a noble man whose ancestors surely descended from pharaohs of the Ruby Empire? A man who carries the blood of the ancient dynasty in his veins? I say no!" Her glorious eyes blazed. "Join with me, my friends and colleagues, and rejoice in the discovery of a Ruby psion, a treasure that will bring new life to Skolia."

"Gods," Kurj muttered. If she kept this up, they would canonize his blasted stepfather. Lights sparkled on consoles throughout the amphitheater as people entered requests to ask questions. At a large console on the dais, the Protocol Councilor was fielding the requests, setting up queues so the discussion could proceed in an orderly fashion.

Orderly. What a travesty. Roca had just destroyed the order he had so carefully rebuilt since she came home. Even now, his security couldn't break hers. Dehya must have helped. He didn't know whether to be furious at his aunt or in awe that she could so thoroughly circumvent his systems.

The tide was flowing in favor of Roca. She had won this round— but he had other ways to fight. If he couldn't stop her from having new doctors sent to Skyfall, then he would make sure those who went reported the correct results. A second opinion verifying the first would strengthen his position.

Nothing would stop him from ending this godsforsaken marriage.


The days were sluggish. Eldri moved in a daze.

Today he slouched in a chair at one end of the dining table, his booted foot on its top, his elbow on one arm of the chair, his head propped on his palm as he stared down the length of the table to the double doors, which the work crews had flung open. The gales of Windward were in full force today, whistling through cracks in the walls. Outside, people were working on the castle. Allied people. The resort planners had sent them to do repairs.

He looked away, disheartened. Despite his gratitude, he felt uncomfortable about this "kindness" from the Allied developers. It demoralized him to be indebted to them.

Figures moved in his side vision. Then Garlin came out of the shadows with three strangers. Eldri knew immediately they were more of these offworlders who had overrun everything lately. They had dark hair and eyes. That unusual coloring, which had once enthralled him, no longer held any mystique. He had no wish to meet more visitors, not now, not ever.

Unfortunately, they didn't go away. Instead, they came toward him. The strangers, two men and a woman, stayed back a few steps while Garlin continued to the table. Eldri glowered at his cousin.

Garlin frowned at him. "This is hardly a courteous greeting to our guests."

"I tire of greeting guests," Eldri grumbled. "We have too many of them."

Garlin motioned at the crews outside. "You should give them thanks. Not surly silence."

"You know why they help us." Eldri lifted his head off his hand. "They want to fix Windward so that when they bring their 'tours,' we will look pretty and quaint."

"Yes, well, perhaps you should talk to these new visitors." Garlin indicated the three strangers. "They are Skolian. Not Allied. You might find what they say interesting."

Eldri swung his leg down from the table and sat up straight. "Is it about Roca?"

"No. It is worth hearing, however."

Eldri sighed. But he motioned the strangers forward and waved toward several chairs. They sat along the table on his left, and Garlin settled in on his right. Eldri glanced at his cousin. "Do they speak English?"

"I do, Your Majesty," the woman said.

He turned with a start. This penchant offworlders had for calling him "Your Majesty" bewildered him. He supposed it made sense here at Windward, which stood so majestically in the mountains, but then, they should address everyone here that way.

"I welcome you." Eldri knew his voice held no welcome. "I am afraid my hospitality is clumsy of late. It seems some of your people decided to destroy my home."

The woman shifted in her seat and one of the men reddened. Garlin spoke in Trillian, with exasperation. "Eldri, behave. Listen to what they have to say."

Eldri inclined his head to the woman. "Tell me what you have to say."

Her relief came to him. "My name is Tyra Meson. I represent the Skolian Assembly, the government of your wife's people."

Eldri's pulse leapt. "You have news of my wife?"

"I'm sorry, but no."

"Oh." He sat back in his chair. "Why do you come?"

"King Eldrinson," she began, using the nonsense title the Allieds had given him. "It appears we have a dispute about who this world belongs to."

He gave her a dour look. "I was not aware it belonged to anyone."

"Well, yes, of course." Tyra rested her arms on the table, trying to look relaxed, though Eldri knew perfectly well she was afraid of him. An image came to him from her mind; she feared he might fall on the floor in a convulsion and foam at the mouth. It so irritated him, he was half tempted to do it just to make her go away. But then he would have to listen to a lecture from Garlin, who claimed he should be interested in what these people had to say.

Eldri made an effort. "What does this dispute involve?"

Her tone turned official. "The Allied Worlds of Earth claim Skyfall as their world, because they discovered it first. We challenge that claim. Your settlements here descend from a colony established thousands of years ago by the Ruby Empire."

Eldri sighed. "And what are 'years'?" When Tyra started to explain, he held up his hand. "Yes, I know they are a period of time. We do not use them here."

She cleared her throat. "I appreciate that it is difficult to understand."

"Very," Eldrin said sourly. "Terribly difficult. Every time the planet goes around the suns, it is a year. But this means little, Tyra Meson. It is an arbitrary period of time unconnected to how my people think of things."

"Uh, well, yes." She pushed back a lock of her dark spiky hair, which had fallen into her eyes. "The crux of the matter is this: we may be able to stop the developers from putting a resort here."

*That* caught Eldri's attention. He sat forward. "It is not so easy. We have a debt to them. They are rebuilding Windward."

"We will reimburse them."

"What is 'reimburse'?"

Garlin answered. "The Skolians will give an amount of wealth to the Allieds equal to or more than what it takes to rebuild Windward."

Glancing at Garlin, Eldri spoke in Trillian. "They claim they can do this?"

"They say they have already begun negotiations."

Eldri considered him. Then he turned to Tyra Meson and spoke in English. "What do you want from us in return?"

"Your agreement."

"To what?"

"To your world joining the Skolian Imperialate."

"And then?"

"Skyfall—that is, Lyshriol—" Her attempt at Trillian was barely recognizable. "Your world will have a status known as Protected. It means no one can come here without permission from our Assembly."

Eldri stared at her, certain he had misheard. "You mean, you would leave us alone?" It seemed too good to be true.

"Essentially." She watched him closely. "The starport will be here, with a schedule of ships like now. But no resorts."

It was a fair offer. More than fair, in fact. It was incredible. "Why would you do this for us?"

She spoke quietly. "It is not I who does it, Your Majesty. The impetus has come from the Foreign Affairs Councilor."

Bittersweet emotions swelled in Eldri, a wrenching mix of love and loneliness that threatened to overwhelm him. He fought it down, not because he regretted his love for Roca or his pain that she had gone, but because he refused to show any vulnerability in front of these strangers.

He found no deception in Tyra Meson's mind. So he said, "Very well. I agree Lyshriol will become part of your Imperialate." Of course he had no authority to make decisions about an entire planet. But if that pretense would rid them of the developers, he would make it. "Can you actually take Lyshriol from the Allieds? Just because you tell them to leave, that doesn't mean they will."

She inclined her head in agreement. "It will take negotiations. But we believe they will agree. It isn't worth it to their government to alienate ours over a matter like this."

"Then do try."

"We will, Your Majesty." She seemed subdued. He had the impression these people didn't usually *ask* if a settlement wanted to join the Imperialate. Their warriors just came in and occupied the place, much as Avaril had tried to take Windward. The need for him to give his agreement came from some battle among the Skolians, something about whether or not he was capable of making decisions.

Eldri spoke with care, uncertain what to think of all this. "This agreement you and I are making—is it binding on all your people? Will everyone on your Assembly accept it?"

Surprise flickered in her mind. She hadn't expected him to know he should ask such a question. "Yes, they must accept it. We voted."

"On what?"

She hesitated. "If you were able to comprehend and respond to the invitation, we would carry out the bargain."

Dryly he said, "Well, I have comprehended and responded."

"Ah—yes. Exactly." She seemed at a loss. Even odder, the two men were studying the holos above their palmtops, as if what they saw there linked to this discussion.

Eldri motioned at them. "What are they doing?"

One of the men looked up. "We are recording this conference, Your Majesty."

Male Memories? How truly odd. "You speak English, too."

"We were chosen for our ability to communicate in a language you understand." The man smiled. "I am Cary Undell."

Eldri inclined his head in greeting. He liked having names for people. But as reasonable as they sounded, he felt uneasy. These people made him feel somehow lacking.

The other man spoke. "Your Majesty, I am ****." His name was sounds rather than words.

Eldri squinted at him. "What did you say?"

He and the woman looked at each other. Then he repeated, "I am ****."

"I cannot understand you," Eldri said.

The man spoke slowly, as if Eldri were a child. "That was my name. I am a doctor. A person who heals other people. Do you know what this means?"

"Yes, of course." Eldri didn't like the way this fellow addressed him. He thought of the destruction wrought by the minions of the Skolian warlord, who was apparently Roca's human son. "What has injured my people is not easily healed." He indicated the crews working outside. "They can make the walls whole but the emotional scars are far deeper."

"Perhaps you don't understand," the doctor began.

Cary Undell spoke up. "I think he understands exactly what you mean." When the doctor frowned at him, Cary ignored him and spoke to Eldri. "May I ask a question about your health?"

Eldri cocked an eyebrow. "And if I say no? Will I fail this test you are all giving me?"

Tyra stiffened, the doctor scowled, and Cary grinned.

"What makes you think we are testing you?" Tyra asked.

Eldri waved his hand at her. "Just ask your questions."

Cary began. "I was wondering if—"

"All right," the doctor interrupted, his gaze hard on Eldri. "Please tell us, Your *Majesty,* exactly what you know about your generalized tonic-clonic seizures. Do you have thoracic contractions? Instances of status epilepticus?"

Eldri considered him. "Why do you want me to fail this test?"

Cary laughed, then shut his mouth abruptly when the woman frowned at him. The doctor's expression hardened.

Tyra spoke carefully to Eldri. "Please accept my apologies if we have given offense."

"You do not give offense," Eldri said. "But you baffle me."

The doctor leaned forward. "What confuses you?"

"I didn't say I was confused."

Cary's lips quirked up. Tyra shook her head slightly at him, then turned back to Eldri. "What baffles you?"

"Why do you want to talk about my seizures?" Eldri was fairly certain "seizure" was the right word, because Roca had used it when she talked about his attacks, and she had also used words similar to what the doctor had just said.

Cary leaned forward. "Then you are aware that what happens to you are seizures? Not possession by demons?"

Eldri could tell he was in precarious territory now, though this enemy was more difficult to understand than Lord Avaril. "I know I have epilepsy." Although he found the word difficult to pronounce, Roca had said it enough that he thought he had it right. "My wife claims you Skolians can treat it. Is this true?"

Tyra answered quietly. "We think so. We need to do more tests before we can give you specific answers."

"When the doctors examined you after the battle here," Cary said, "they found traces of sodium bromide in your body. Do you know what that is?"

"My wife used those words." Eldri had no idea what they meant, but he suspected this wasn't the best time to reveal that. "We hoped it would heal me."

"Did you experience any convulsions during the battle?" the doctor asked. Although hostility remained in his mind, his interest in Eldri's health overrode it for now.

"No, actually," Eldri said. "But I have had two of the big ones in the two months since then. More of the smaller."

"If you consent to an examination," Tyra said, "we can set up a plan of treatment for you."

He stiffened. "What does 'treatment' involve?"

"You will probably have several options. We could give your body a type of medicine called nanomeds. They will release chemicals to control the seizures. Some interlock with neurons and prevent them from firing. You could take medicines orally or with a syringe." She paused. "Sometimes it is possible to operate on the brain and heal what causes the seizures. In your case, we don't think that will work."

Eldri didn't understand most of what she said, but it all sounded horrendous. "And if I don't have this treatment? What will happen to me?"

The doctor spoke, his dedication to healing stronger than his obvious dislike of Eldri. "You may be at risk for status epilepticus. It means the seizure doesn't stop or that you have several without your body recovering in between." Quietly he added, "It could kill you."

Eldri pushed his hand through his hair. He knew, from what Garlin had told him, that he had suffered several bouts similar to what they described, though perhaps not as serious. It had terrified Garlin, and afterward Eldri had felt as if he were coming back from the dead. He never wanted to experience it again.

He steeled himself. "Very well. You may do your tests."

His answer seemed to be what they wanted to hear. The men flicked their fingers through the holos above their palmtops.

Eldri rested his forearms on the table, clasping his hands as he sought to appear more composed than he felt. "And my wife? My son? Have you news of them?" His heart beat hard.

The doctor spoke curtly. "No."

Despite Eldri's determination to project calm, his voice caught. "Surely you must know if they are well. Anything."

Tyra answered more gently. "From what we have heard, your wife and the boy are doing fine."

Eldri nodded, striving for control. "Thank you."

He held back his sorrow, knowing he could only shed his tears alone, away from these unwelcome strangers.

# 23

# Lights on the Lake

---

Kurj pressed the panel on Roca's door again. A chime echoed inside, but no one answered. Trees rustled around him, making dappled shadows on the graceful house, with its peaked roof and intricately carved gables. His inner lids covered his eyes, giving the scene a gilded quality, as if it were an anachronism, an old-fashioned photograph.

"Primary Skolia?" a voice asked.

Kurj looked around. "Who is that?"

"The house EI. Would you like to enter?"

He could imagine what his mother would say if he walked into her home without her consent, especially with the strain between them so great these past four months, since he had taken her from Skyfall. "No. I will return when she is here."

"The Councilor should return soon. She went for a walk. However, you are on the list of visitors I may allow entry."

That surprised him. He had thought she wanted him to vanish from her life altogether. "Perhaps she forgot to remove my name."

"She updated the list this morning."

*Interesting.* "Then I will wait inside."

The door shimmered and faded, offering him access. He walked through the entrance foyer into the airy living room full of sunlight, with high ceilings that created attractive spaces.

A curvaceous girl with blond hair and a pretty face came out of an inner room. When she saw Kurj, she froze, her face paling. Then she dropped onto one knee and bowed her head.

Kurj paused. Why was this stranger here? He couldn't help but notice the way her white dress fit her ample breasts. He went over to her. "Please stand."

She rose to her feet, her gaze averted. "My honor at your presence, Prince Kurj."

He scratched his chin. "Who are you?"

"Callie Summerlet. Eldrin's nurse." She glanced up with a hesitant smile, but her agitation came through clearly. His size frightened her, as did his title and reputation.

Now that he thought about it, he did remember his mother mentioning she had a girl look after Eldrin for a few hours in the afternoon. By using the Kyle webs and VR technology, Roca could do her work as a Councilor from this house, but she still needed some help with the baby.

It aggravated Kurj that Roca continued to outwit him and attend the Assembly. He couldn't even demand someone else deal with the Skyfall situation. Had it already been a Skolian world, it would have come under the auspices of Planetary Development and Domestic Affairs. But no, the accursed Allieds had to claim it. Until the Assembly cut a deal with them, it continued to be an Allied world, which made it the purview of the Foreign Affairs Councilor. Pah. He had to block her transmissions. She was far too effective a speaker.

That was no reason, however, to alarm this attractive person. Kurj found her lovely, the type of woman he favored. He moderated his voice into a friendly tone. "How is my brother?"

Her enthused smile lit up her face, taking away her shyness. "Ah, Your Highness, he is such a delightful baby."

The room lost its gold tinge as his inner lids raised. "I'm glad."

"Would you like to see him?"

He thought of Eldrin, and an inexplicable warmth came over him, a feeling difficult to define. "Yes. I would like that."

Callie led him into a bedroom. A white cradle stood by the bed, rocking under its own power. Designs covered it, soft-looking animals with round faces, smiles, and large eyes.

Kurj peered inside. Eldrin was as hale and healthy as ever, but much quieter than usual, taking a nap. Odd that such a small human could make so much noise when awake and look so beatific when asleep. Kurj felt the same softening inside that always came to him when he saw his brother. Bending over, he touched the baby's cheek. Eldrin stirred and made sucking motions with his lips.

"He is remarkable, isn't he?" Kurj couldn't keep the wonder out of his voice. Abruptly remembering the girl, he straightened up and schooled his face to impassivity. The room turned gold.

"Would you like to hold him?" Callie's blue eyes had a glow that made her even more inviting. Kurj thought surely she must be trying to tempt him, but from her mind he could tell her eagerness came from her affection for Eldrin rather than any interest in him. Disappointing, that.

"I don't want to wake him." Kurj wondered what Callie would do if he kissed her. Probably scream. That was the trouble with being an empath; he couldn't convince himself a woman wanted him unless she really did. If he pressured her, he would experience her fear. It would make him feel like a monster. Like Darr. At times, he became so angry, it gave his passion an edge, frightening some of his lovers and exciting others. It was an aspect of his personality he chose not to examine too closely, lest he find he was no different than the Traders who considered it their right to inflict brutality on the rest of humanity.

What held him in check was the memory of what his father had told him so long ago, that loving a woman meant kindness and compassion. Perhaps Tokaba hadn't actually said the words, just shown them in his every action toward Roca. It had been so long.

"I think he would like it if you held him," Callie was saying. "He seems to like sleeping that way."

Startled out of his contemplation, Kurj reoriented on the baby. Again he experienced that disconcerting warmth. Odd. Perhaps he had caught a virus. But he didn't feel sick. Looking at Eldrin relaxed him, though why, he didn't know.

He lifted up the drowsy child. Over the past four months he had become comfortable holding Eldrin, as he realized his sturdy brother wasn't going to break. He settled in the rocking chair, Eldrin in his arms, and rocked back and forth. He was glad none of his officers could see him. Gods only knew what this scene would do to his reputation.

He knew he shouldn't let himself be so easily affected by this tiny life, this child sired by a man who would destroy Roca if Kurj didn't stop him. Yet whenever he saw Eldrin, a deep, abiding emotion filled him unlike any he had known before. He wanted to give the universe to Eldrin. A fierce determination rose within him: he would do anything to protect this child.

Anything.

Roca paused in the doorway, touched by what she saw in the room beyond: Kurj Skolia, formidable warlord of ISC, asleep with his baby brother in his arms. For a while she simply stood, savoring the scene, knowing that if she moved, Kurj's hair-trigger reflexes would awake him, destroying this rare moment.

Despite her attempts to stay quiet, he soon stirred, his eyes opening, first his outer lids, then his inner. "Mother?"

"My greetings," she said.

He shifted Eldrin in his arms and rubbed his eyes. It reminded Roca of when he had been a small child awaking from his nap. He had always vigorously objected to taking it, then immediately dropped off into a deep sleep. That was before he had grown up and enhanced his body until he could achieve the equivalent of sleep by recharging parts of himself. He claimed he needed only two hours of sleep a night now, but she had her doubts.

"How long have I been here?" he asked, groggy.

"Several hours. I didn't want to wake you."

Kurj stood up, holding Eldrin. "I shouldn't have slept. I have work to do."

"You work too hard." When Kurj scowled at her, she couldn't help but smile. "I'm glad you came to see him."

"Actually, I came to see you. Business matters."

Roca tried to fathom his mood. Usually when they discussed business, they met in his office or hers. Today he seemed pensive, seeking connections with his family. This gentler side of him made her remember his youth, in the days when she could still reach him.

Eldrin began to squirm, twisting toward her. Then he let out a hearty wail.

Kurj winced. "I think he likes you better than me." He came over and put Eldrin in her arms. When the baby nuzzled her breast, Kurj averted his gaze, his face reddening. His embarrassment was strong enough that his mood came to her despite both her own barriers and those Kurj used to protect his mind.

He didn't know how to deal with this aspect of her. It confused and angered him, and it evoked a tenderness he strove to repress. Roca wanted to weep for knowing that he believed having gentler emotions weakened him.

Eldrin cried out again, a softer protest.

"He is hungry," Roca murmured. "Can you wait in the living room?"

Kurj nodded stiffly. "Of course." Then he left.


After Roca nursed Eldrin, he fell asleep. She rocked him for a while, then tucked him into his cradle and returned to the front room. Kurj had settled on the couch, taking up a good portion of it, and was engrossed in the holos above a film he had unrolled on the table in front of him.

"You look so serious," Roca said.

He glanced at her with a start. "I was answering web-mail."

"Bad news?"

He straightened up, rolling his shoulders. "This supposed offer the Traders made to negotiate is draining impetus from my officers."

Her anger sparked. "How can you fault them for wanting peace?"

He frowned at her. "This is exactly the discord the Traders want their 'offer' to create. They seek to divide our leadership and weaken our morale. And they're succeeding."

Roca bit back her answer. She and Kurj could argue this for eternity and never agree. To calm down and keep from saying words she might later regret, she walked into the room and settled into a smart-chair, stretching out her legs. The chair shifted subtly, trying to ease her tension. Usually it only took a few moments to find the right shape, but today it kept readjusting well after she had sat down. Had it come to this, that she responded to Kurj as if he were an enemy in her own home? It grieved her, this winter in their relationship.

She spoke carefully. "What brings you to visit?"

He answered with similar caution. "I thought you would like to know. The doctors have finished checking the DNA for Eldrinson and your son."

Roca had wondered how long he would keep them checking. It shouldn't have taken this much time. She felt as if she were on a precipice. Her love for Eldri wouldn't change if he wasn't as strong a psion as she thought, but it would weaken the support for her marriage she had so carefully built in the Assembly these past four months.

"What do they say?" she asked.

A muscle twitched in his cheek. "You were right. Both Eldrinson and Eldrin are Ruby psions."

"Ai, Kurj!" Her relief overflowed her restraint. "I knew it!"

He had an odd expression. "I was wondering about something."

Ah, no. How would he fight now that she had this advantage? Her shoulders hunched in anticipation of his next salvo. "Yes?"

"Why," he asked, perplexed, "is the son called Eldrin and the father Eldrinson?"

Roca blinked, feeling like a warrior who expected to confront an armored opponent and instead found herself at a tea party. Her shoulders lowered. "Ah, well, I guess it does sound odd. That's how his people do it, using 'son' every other generation." She smiled. "We could hardly call him Eldrinsonson."

His expression turned pensive. "I suppose not." For the second time today, the unexpected happened: his barriers slipped enough to let his mood reach her. He wondered if he would ever have a child. *Kurjson.* The intensity of his longing startled her. Then his barriers snapped into place, hiding his troubled emotions.

"The other doctors say more about Eldrinson," he told her, carefully neutral.

Roca folded her arms. "They've said enough already." She had no doubt Kurj would do everything he could to prove Eldri mentally incompetent. It might be the only viable way now to convince the Assembly to dissolve the marriage.

Roca doubted he would openly take her on in the Assembly. The more popular her marriage became, abetted by her orations, the harder it was for him to challenge her without weakening his own standing. But he was working behind the scenes, encouraging those factions that wanted to control Eldri, the schemers and intriguers who would gladly strip her husband of his title. To use Eldri to father Ruby children; they considered this acceptable, a worthy goal. But to allow him the authority of a Ruby consort, with influence above even theirs—this was anathema. They made Kurj's arguments for him, voicing the inflammatory rhetoric, stirring doubt in the Assembly. Kurj remained silent. Nor did Roca want to accuse her own son in public, especially with no proof except her unspoken sense of him. So they fought this shadow war, both struggling to preserve what they considered right.

"I didn't know the medical team that went to Lyshriol had returned." She had managed to select one of the three experts on the team, but she had doubts about at least one of the others, maybe both. They had too many ties to Kurj. She knew they intended to observe Eldri for a longer period of time before reporting, but the wait frustrated her.

"They haven't made a report," Kurj said. "I meant the medics here, the ones studying his DNA."

She spoke warily. "What do they say?"

"It's interesting, actually." Kurj's posture relaxed a bit. "His ancestors had their hands and feet engineered for that hinged, four-digit structure."

"But why?"

He smiled wryly. "Good question. The medics have no idea."

The shifting of her chair eased as her posture relaxed. "Do they know any more about his seizures?"

"Some." Kurj rolled his computer sheet into a rod and slid it into a sheath in his sleeve. "He inherited an unusually low threshold for seizures from his parents. Apparently that isn't unusual for psions. It probably wouldn't have caused him problems if his brain hadn't been injured when his family died."

The thought of how Eldri had lost his family made Roca tense again. "Avaril Valdoria has much to answer for."

His expression darkened. "If you would only protect yourself with the same ferocity you protect your family."

Roca knew he wasn't talking about Avaril. "I was much younger with Darr. Less mature. Less confident."

"I meant now."

Softly she said, "Did you?"

He watched her through the gold shields of his inner lids. What he saw, she had no idea. She wished he would rage, condemn her for those years with Darr, *respond* in some way. Instead he remained in his mental fortress, behind impenetrable walls.

"Eldrinson's Ruby genes are different from ours," he said.

Roca felt as if she had run into a blockade. He wouldn't talk about Darr, not now, perhaps never. Perturbed, she answered more sharply than she had intended. "We couldn't have had a child otherwise."

"You and father had me."

An old pain stirred in her. "That is because we had the best experts and technology available to help us and geneticists to select the right genes. Even with that, it took years." She ached with the memories. "Kurj, you truly were our miracle child."

He spoke in a low voice. "And now?"

"You always will be."

But they both knew the truth. Too much had happened in the relentless years of his adulthood for them ever to regain the trust and simple affection of his childhood.


Kurj was walking across a meadow in Valley when his palmtop buzzed. He flipped it open. A response had arrived to a message he had sent earlier today, after he left his mother's home.

"Skolia here," he said.

A shy voice came out of the comm. "My g-greeting, Your Highness. This is Callie Summerlet. Your EI paged me."

"My greeting, Callie." Kurj kept walking, his mood improving as he thought of the curvy nursemaid. "I have a houseboat in a lake up here. Would you like to join me there for dinner tonight?"

A long silence came from the comm. Just when Kurj was going to check if the comm had malfunctioned, Callie said, "I—I think, I mean, yes." She sounded out of breath. "I would be honored to dine with you, Your Highness."

"Good." Kurj wasn't sure if she was excited or terrified. He hoped it was the former. He hadn't expected her to decline, though. They rarely did. Some felt honored by his attentions, and even the ones who didn't like him were curious enough for a first dinner. Nor did most want to risk his displeasure.

"I will send one of my aides for you sometime this evening." He wasn't sure when he would be done with his work. "Will you be in your apartment in City?"

"Y-yes. Will. I mean, yes, I will."

"Very well. I will see you. Out."

"Uh—out." In a softer voice, she added, "Until tonight, Your Highness."

He smiled. "Until tonight."

As Kurj continued his walk, a thought formed in the back of his mind. Callie Summerlet could help him banish the emotional demons that threatened his control. She was safe. Simple. Sweet. Maybe for one night he could evade the way his emotions tangled whenever he thought of what it meant to be a father and a son. The roles had snarled in his mind until he could no longer separate them. His emotions fused in the wrong ways. He didn't want this yearning to act as a father to Roca's son, didn't want to remember that a half-grown barbarian held his mother's love. Why couldn't he rid himself of these thoughts that threatened his control?

Callie. Think of Callie. Tonight he would make a normal bond with a normal woman.

If he only could.

A face gradually came into focus, hovering over Eldri. He lay on his side, aware of hard ground under his body. Slowly he rolled onto his back. Garlin was kneeling on his right and one of the Skolians was on his left, the woman, Tyra Meson.

So tired. He felt so tired.

"Your Majesty?" Tyra asked.

Eldri wet his lips. "A . . . seizure?"

"Yes." The line between her eyes was deeply etched today. "Another seizure."

"A bad one," he whispered.

"I'm afraid so."

Garlin brushed the hair back from Eldri's forehead. "It didn't last long."

"That's . . . good." Eldri sat up slowly, aware of the doctor watching him. "We still have the wrong medicines?"

Tyra looked apologetic. "I'm afraid so."

He let them help him stand, but he insisted on walking without help, though he limped for the first few steps. It disheartened him even more now to have the seizures, because these Skolians had given him hope that they could make him better. Instead, the attacks continued, now with "side effects" that left him exhausted and ill. The demons that caused the attacks were surely angered by his attempts to escape retribution.

But even if these healers did eventually manage to help, they couldn't cure his loneliness.


The rocking houseboat soothed Kurj. Callie lay against him, her backside to his front, her curves fitted against his body. The old-fashioned door stood ajar, and colored light from paper lamps on the deck filtered into the cabin. Only the lap of water and the chirps of insects broke the slumbering night.

Callie stirred, turning onto her back. Kurj languorously slid his hand across her breasts. As her eyes opened, her face reddened, her blush deep enough to see in the dim light.

"My greetings," he said in a low voice.

"My greetings, Your Highness." She rolled to face him, and pressed her lips against his chest. "Your beautiful Highness."

Kurj stretched with pleasure. "I've been called many things, most unrepeatable, but never beautiful."

She ran her hand over his torso. "You scared me today, when I first saw you."

"Do I still?"

"A little." She sounded more aroused than frightened.

Kurj nudged her back and covered her body with his, holding himself up on his elbows so he didn't smother her. She groaned when he entered her, and he could tell from her mind that it was real, not an act. He made love to her with the same control he exercised in every part of his life, but at the end he let go, giving in to a rush of sensation that obliterated all pain from his heart.

Sometime later, when alarm surged from her mind, he realized he had sunk down and was crushing her. He slid off, then moved his large hands over her body, savoring the soft skin and curves.

Callie sighed. "You are very robust."

"Robust?"

She yawned. "Very awake."

"Yes." He rolled her nipple between his fingers.

"Don't you ever sleep?"

"Not much." His two hours this afternoon would last another day. With all his cybernetic augmentations, his body could care for itself in many ways that required sleep for unenhanced humans.

"You looked different, rocking Eldrin this afternoon," she said drowsily.

"How?"

"It was sweet."

*Sweet?* Gods forbid. "I hope not."

She curled against him. "That was when I stopped being so afraid of you."

"Oh." Her misperceptions had their advantage. "Good."

"Lady Roca told me they verified Eldrin was a Ruby psion."

Kurj stroked her abdomen. "So they did."

"You must be very proud."

"I suppose."

"Will the Assembly give him bodyguards, too?"

He slid his hand between her thighs. "Maybe."

"Ummm." She moved against him.

"The Assembly may make you have bodyguards."

"Whatever for?" She sounded distracted, her eyes closed, her body responding. It was taking her longer this time, though. Kurj supposed he ought to let her sleep. He had kept her up all night.

He propped his head up on one hand and let his other rest in the triangle between her legs. "They will give you bodyguards because you're important to me." It occurred to him belatedly that she might mistake his meaning and think she meant more to him than she actually did. He did rather like her, though.

"It makes you a target," he added. "People may think they can get to me through you."

She hesitated. "Why does that make you angry?"

"What makes you think I'm angry?"

"Your voice."

It was a moment before he answered. "The Assembly has manipulated the Ruby Dynasty for so long, it is hard to remember when our lives were our own." Even he could hear his bitterness.

"You mean the way they guard you all the time?"

"That. Arranging our marriages. Decreeing when and how we have children. Telling us where we live, how we work, where we go."

Her eyes widened. "They do all that?"

"They try." His voice hardened. "We resist."

"I had never realized."

Kurj blew against her ear. "Let us think of more agreeable things than the Assembly."

Her lips curved in a tempting smile. "With pleasure."

As she soothed him with her passion, Kurj began to think that perhaps, just perhaps, he could come to terms with the anger in his heart. He hoped so. For if it didn't happen, he feared that someday he would lose control of the roiling darkness within him and destroy all that he loved.

# 24

# The Buried Grotto

---

He looks just like me," Jarac decided.

Roca smiled as her father dangled a sparkling cube on a string. They were sitting on the floor, on a blanket, with Eldrin lying on his back between them. The six-month-old baby laughed, waving his hands at the cube as if it were the most extraordinary object ever created.

"I guess he does look like you," Roca said. In truth, her young son resembled his father far more. Eldrin's eyes were still blue, but they were turning violet and they had the rounder Lyshrioli shape. His hair was the same burgundy shade as his father's hair. Roca longed to show him to Eldri, to see his joy.

She so missed her husband: his mischief, smile, scowl, the quirk of his eyebrow, his exasperation with Garlin, his athletic grace. She wondered how he fared, if his seizures had stopped, if he had rebuilt Windward. She feared if she tried to contact him, Kurj would find out she had violated their bargain. Then he would retaliate. Kurj wouldn't kill a Ruby psion, but he would find other ways to hurt his stepfather. He might send his operatives to kidnap Eldri regardless of the uproar it could cause. She shuddered, pushing the thought from her mind.

Eldrin batted the swinging cube out of his grandfather's hand, burbling with delight. He grasped the toy in his pudgy hand and rolled onto his stomach.

Jarac beamed at Roca. "He is intelligent, too. Smart, handsome, and strong. Definitely takes after my side."

She smiled. "Maybe he will also inherit your modesty."

Jarac laughed. "We can hope."

His care soothed her heart. It meant a great deal to her that he visited Eldrin. She wished her mother would do the same. If Lahaylia would spend some time with Eldrin, surely she would love him. To Roca, it seemed especially important now, as her parents aged. Their outward youth was deceptive. They had lived longer than any other humans, and she knew they were tired. She couldn't bear to think of their passing. If only her mother would accept Eldrin, she could see in him the promise of the dynasty she and Jarac had founded. Eldrin was a symbol of new life.

Jarac spoke kindly. "He is beautiful, Daughter. You have given us a gift greater than we ever expected."

Her voice caught. "If only Mother felt that way."

"Give her time."

"Eldrin is her grandson. Why can't she care for him like she does the rest of us?" For all her mother's reserve, Roca had never doubted her mother loved them. It overflowed her emotions. But not for Eldrin. Never Eldrin.

Jarac poked the cube Eldrin was pawing, making the baby gurgle. "She does not know what she misses."

"Do you think she will come around?" Roca asked.

"Perhaps." Jarac wouldn't look at her.

Roca averted her eyes, hiding the moisture that filled them. Her marriage had rent cracks in her family, leaving wounds that might never heal.

Eldri stood at his bedroom window, gazing at the starred night. *Roca, are you out there?* By the reckoning of the Skolians, she had been gone for six months, where one "month" was apparently about four octets of days. She had become part of him; since she had left, his heart had been bereft. He and Roca had melded in ways he didn't understand; he knew only that when she left, she took pieces of him. He kept expecting the passage of time to make it more bearable, but nothing helped. Whatever this bond they shared, its loss went deeper than anything could ease.

It was an irony that his emotions should hurt now, when his body was finally becoming healthy. Incredibly, the doctors had found medicines that helped his convulsions without causing lethargy or nausea. He had experienced none of the big seizures and only a few of the small in the past five octets of days. For the first time in his life he could actually hope he might live like a normal man.

But that gift came at too high a price.

"Come home," he whispered. "Roca, come home."

"I urge you to reconsider," Banner Highchief said. "Even if you don't believe the Traders genuinely want peace."

Kurj gritted his teeth. The Fleet Commander stood with him on the observation deck, resting her long arms on the dichromesh-glass rail. The transparent bubble surrounded them, as if they stood in space itself. The lights were off, so nothing dimmed the splendor of the stars. His heritage.

"They are trying to trap us," Kurj told her.

"Possibly. It is still worth bargaining."

His hand tightened on the rail. "They offer to 'bargain' for what they took from us. I will call off the invasion only for complete restoration of our territory. No half agreements."

She leaned her considerable length against the rail. "They were mining asteroids in that region before we claimed it."

"We had already set up operations." He snorted. "So they were robbing us from the start. This is a reason to bargain?"

She thumped the rail. "I say we settle, let them have part of the territory and take the rest ourselves."

"I will think on it." Kurj had no intention of changing his mind, but if he appeared intractable, it could alienate her. She commanded the largest arm of ISC and had more authority than he wielded as the head of the J-Force. He preferred to stay on good terms with her. Someday, when he became Imperator, he would be her commanding officer. It behooved him to build a strong base now, one that would support him when he took over ISC.

His wrist comm buzzed and he raised his arm. "Skolia, here."

"Sir, this is Lieutenant Opson. We've received a message from Sky-fall. It's the report from the medical team."

Kurj tensed. Gods. Finally. "Send it to my home office immediately."

"Right away, sir."

"Good. Out."

If Highchief had any inkling about the significance of what she had just heard, she gave nothing away. They left the observation bay and walked through the corridors that networked the Orbiter hull, discussing ISC matters. Although she shielded her thoughts, she couldn't completely guard against him. His power lacked nuance, but he could pick up any leakage of emotions no matter how slight. He felt her wariness. She didn't like their impasse over the invasion.

They parted at the magrail station. Kurj rode out into the Orbiter's landscaped biosphere, the car hurtling down the mountains into the Ground hemisphere, past City and back up to Valley. He wanted to read the report on Eldrinson in private. With some maneuvering, Kurj had handpicked the doctor in the second team, and he felt reasonably confident about one of the psychologists, Tyra Meson. But Roca had influenced the Assembly on the selection of the other psychologist, a man named Cary Undell. The fellow was too cussed independent and he made no secret about his dislike of political intrigue. The last thing Kurj needed was a nonconformist asserting his opinions.

Kurj expected the team would have helped Valdoria's epilepsy. He had given his word to Roca. But they knew their job. It would take only two of them to make their conclusions a majority decision. Then their report would verify Valdoria was incompetent to sign a contract with anyone, let alone a Ruby heir.

They had better make that determination. Otherwise, he would have to pursue more severe methods to achieve his goal.


Roca crossed the plateau, which stood high in the mountains, near the horizon where Ground met Sky. The gravity was weaker up here. She felt it especially with the added height of her boots, which made her over six feet tall; each step she took seemed slow and longer than usual.

The cold air was crisp against her face, bracing her for the confrontation to come. On one side of the plateau, cliffs rose toward Sky; on the other, the plateau dropped down into foothills. In the distance, the translucent towers of City sparkled in golden light from the Sun Lamp.

A woman stood at the edge of the plateau gazing out at City, her hands clasped behind her back. Wind tugged her short, iron-gray hair. She had aged formidably well, her austere face lined just enough to add authority to her patrician features, including her high cheekbones, upward tilted eyes, and straight nose. She wore a dark blue tunic and dark trousers with a gold stripe up each leg. Only a discreet insignia on her shoulder indicated her stratospheric rank: General of the Pharaoh's Army, commander of the legendary Skolian army, which claimed five thousand years of fealty to the Ruby Dynasty.

Vaj Majda, the Matriarch of Majda, waited for Roca.

As Roca came up to her, Majda turned. The general spoke with an impeccable formality that offered no welcome. "My honor at your presence, Your Highness."

Roca inclined her head. "And mine at yours, General."

Majda wasted no time. "My nephew sends you a message."

Tensing, Roca gave the response dictated by protocol. "I would be pleased to hear it."

Ice could have formed in Majda's gaze. "Prince Dayj accepts the figurines you sent him."

Roca's shoulders sagged with her relief. Dayj's acceptance of her apology was so cool, frost could have formed on it, and he had taken so long in responding, an ice age could have come and gone, but it was still an acceptance. If he had taken public offense at her marriage, the scandal would have reverberated throughout Skolia. His response left no doubt that relations between Majda and the Ruby Dynasty had suffered grave damage, but it didn't preclude reconciliation between the two Houses.

"Please tell Prince Dayj that I appreciate his gracious message," Roca said.

"I'm glad one of us does," Majda said sourly.

Roca held back her impulse to make a retort. Although Majda had never acknowledged Roca's apology in words or writing, she had taken ownership of the shipping company, which made her acceptance unambiguous.

Majda suddenly froze, looking past her. Puzzled, Roca turned—and stiffened. A tall woman was approaching them, her willowy carriage a graceful contrast to Majda's steel posture. This newcomer had an exotic beauty rather than the austerity of Majda, but both she and the general evoked the ancient queens. The Ruby Pharaoh, it seemed, had discovered that her daughter and top general were meeting in secret.

Lahaylia joined them, standing such that Roca and Majda had to turn to face her, putting their backs to the drop-off from the plateau. A flyer soared far overhead, a speck against the immensity of Sky, undoubtedly the pharaoh's bodyguards.

Majda bowed. "My honor at your presence, Pharaoh Lahaylia."

Lahaylia inclined her head. "General. Daughter."

Roca crossed her arms. "I didn't realize you planned to meet us, Mother."

Lahaylia lifted her hand, a simple gesture that conveyed a world of meaning, making it clear she relegated Roca's words to lesser importance than her daughter intended. "The Assembly soon convenes. Rumors abound of discord within ISC."

Majda met her gaze. "You will find no discord within the Pharaoh's Army. We honor the Assembly vote."

"So I have heard," Lahaylia murmured. She glanced at Roca, then back at Majda. "So I would like to believe."

"As you should," Majda said.

Roca inwardly swore. Her mother had showed up because she believed her daughter sought to sway Majda into support for the negotiations. In truth, Roca had already tried exactly that. But she had made no headway; right now, Majda was hardly predisposed to consider any of her arguments.

Roca scowled at her mother. "And if we can settle this affair through peace rather than war? Still you would fight."

"What affair?" Lahaylia arched an eyebrow. "Yours, perhaps?"

*Pah.* "I have no affairs, Mother." Roca had married Eldri, and she intended it to remain that way. "I speak of the invasion."

The pharaoh answered in her dusky voice. "Peace is a tenuous dream. It appears real to one generation and dissolves in the next. To ignore the survival of our children would be a crime greater than any perpetrated against us by the Eubians."

That gave Roca pause. Thinking of her sons, she spoke in a quieter voice. "Yes, it would. But each generation, when it matures, must make its own choices."

Majda frowned at her. "And its own mistakes?"

"Indeed." Roca knew her eyes were glinting. "Including the mistakes made by those generations that have lived the longest."

Lahaylia spoke dryly. "Wisdom has this peculiar tendency, Daughter. It tends to increase as one matures."

Roca put her hand on her hip. "Vibrancy and innovation also have a peculiar tendency, Mother. They annoy people who don't like change."

Lahaylia's lips quirked upward. "Ah, well, that is part of life." Her smile faded. "But so is the determination in people to fight for what they believe is right."

"And to stand firm in their resolve," Majda said. She seemed intrigued to see an argument between the pharaoh and her heir.

Roca didn't like the way the lines of support aligned here. Her mother and Kurj formed an inflexible bloc, one backed by Majda's support. There seemed no hope for compromise. At the same time, she knew they didn't like this schism any more than she did. They wouldn't back down on the invasion, but another type of bargain might be possible.

"I have other options in Assembly," Roca said.

"What options?" Lahaylia said. "The Assembly has voted for the invasion."

Roca answered in the deceptively quiet voice she had learned from her mother. "Nothing is ever set."

"And what of honor?" Majda demanded.

"Honor takes many forms," Roca answered.

"So your son tells me," Lahaylia said dryly.

"He says a lot of things." Roca wished Kurj would quit doing it, at least when it came to her husband.

"He seeks to protect Skolian honor," Lahaylia said.

Roca met her gaze. "I speak of personal honor."

"Yours?" Majda's sarcasm could have chilled ice.

Roca bit back the response she wanted to make: *I honor my commitments, not betrothals others would force on me.* Instead she said, "I deeply regret if my commitments have caused distress. But my vow to Eldrinson Valdoria is made. I stand by it."

"In other words," Lahaylia said, "if we quit opposing your ill-made marriage, you will quit opposing the invasion."

Put that bluntly, it sounded even more unpalatable. But the invasion would proceed and she would resist a divorce regardless of any bargain. Better a distasteful agreement than this constant battle with her family. "If you accept Eldri, Kurj may moderate his objections."

"I will never accept him," Lahaylia said flatly.

Roca's frustration welled. "Why the hell not?"

"Everything about him is objectionable: common birth, lack of education, age, lifestyle."

Roca was acutely aware of Majda listening. But she had to speak. "He is one of the finest men I've ever known."

"You ask too much," Lahaylia said.

"What, it is too much to ask that my mother be happy for me?"

Lahaylia scowled. "You have duties. How you conduct yourself affects more than this family."

"Eldri is a Ruby psion."

"You didn't have to marry him to bed him."

"What, now you suggest I dishonor him?"

Lahaylia snorted. "Nowadays women go about compromising men's honor all the time and no one blinks. These purportedly despoiled fellows seem to be thoroughly enjoying themselves." She lifted her shoulders in a shrug. "Besides, you wouldn't have been the first Ruby heir to have a man on the side."

Majda gave the pharaoh a sour look. "On the side of what, Your Highness? Her marriage to my nephew?" She spoke grudgingly, to Roca. "It is true that you have treated the Skyfall man with honor, as you did my nephew in your visits to him."

In truth, Roca had never been attracted to Dayj, despite his good looks. It hadn't been hard to keep her hands off him during their constrained visits. But she could hardly reveal that to Vaj Majda. "Whatever the price," Roca said, "my marriage is made."

"And you wish us to stop trying to unmake it," Lahaylia said.

"Yes." Roca's gaze didn't waver.

Majda spoke. "I will not set myself against Kurj Skolia."

*Damn.* Majda knew perfectly well Kurj would never relent. "To cease an offense," Roca said, "isn't the same as setting yourself against an ally."

"Make your peace with Kurj," Lahaylia told her. "Then perhaps we can entertain this compromise."

Roca swallowed. "There is no peace between us."

Lahaylia's face changed, revealing a sadness Roca suspected she had meant to hide. The pharaoh lifted her hand as if to reach out to her daughter, but then she lowered it, her restraint taking over. But she couldn't hide the pain in her voice. "A child and parent shouldn't be so at odds."

"No," Roca said softly. "They shouldn't."

But she saw no way to heal the wounds that divided them.


Anger suffused the Imperator's home.

It vibrated through the stone mansion where Jarac lived, high on a hill of Valley. The house had many windows and spacious rooms to accommodate his large size, filling it with light and air. Given the perfect weather of the Orbiter, the windows needed no glass. The main entrance had no doors.

Today, an inexplicable brooding filled his home. Jarac paced from room to room trying to fathom it. Finally he left. He walked across Valley, past the house Dehya shared with her husband, Seth Rockworth, then past the home where Roca lived with her new son. It wasn't until he had traversed the length of Valley that he reached Kurj's house. In some ways, it resembled his own, large in dimension and simple in style. But it had accents: arched eaves, beveled glass, a slanted roof. Its windows were designed so someone inside could see out, but no one could see in. It reminded Jarac of the inner eyelids Kurj often kept lowered.

When Jarac touched the pager at the entrance, the door shimmered and vanished, offering admittance. This surprised him; given his current strained relationship with Kurj, he hadn't expected his grandson to put him on the list of visitors with automatic permission to enter.

He found Kurj in his office, sprawled behind his desk, studying a document on a screen in front of him, his inner lids lowered. He was clenching a light-stylus in his hand so tightly, his knuckles had turned white.

"Bad news?" Jarac asked.

Kurj jerked up his head. Then he threw the stylus on his desk. "Did you send Banner Highchief to try talking me into negotiating with the Traders?"

"No."

Kurj stood up, rising to his full height, one hand on his back as he stretched. "She wants me to reconsider my vote on the invasion."

Jarac felt tempted to say, *So do I,* but that was the wrong approach with Kurj, reminding him of his subordinate position. He had grown more and more restless these past years, impatient for more authority.

Jarac waited.

"I told her I would think about it," Kurj finally said.

"And have you?"

He crossed his muscled arms. "No."

They faced each other across the desk. Jarac knew his grandson had more to say. He wished he could find a way past Kurj's emotional armor, but it had no chinks. The days when Kurj was a laughing child running to him with arms outstretched were long and forever gone.

After a while Kurj spoke in a quieter voice. "When I was a pilot, I participated in an engagement against a Trader frigate. Its Aristo commander had a psion, a youth he had captured by raiding a Skolian commercial liner." His fingers were pressing his desk so hard, tendons stood out on the back of his hands. "The Traders were using the psion to detect our forces. They had already killed his parents, using them for the same purpose. I picked up the youth's mind at the same time he detected me."

"What happened?" Jarac asked, dreading the answer.

A muscle twitched in Kurj's cheek. "He wasn't revealing enough about our forces. So they 'encouraged' him." He made a visible effort to speak evenly. "While they were torturing him, I couldn't break my connection with his mind."

Jarac felt the horror in Kurj's mind. "What did you do?"

His jaw tightened. "I blew up the frigate. I couldn't free that boy, but I could end his agony." His hand curled into a fist. "And I rid the universe of the monster who had destroyed his life."

Jarac spoke quietly. "If I could free you from those memories by taking them into myself, I would do it in an instant."

"You've never fought." Kurj's voice grated. "You weren't a military officer when you became Imperator. How can you lead ISC when you don't burn inside?"

"And what would you have me do? Destroy us in the blaze of my hatred?"

"You have no right to be a man of peace."

Jarac's voice took on an edge. "It makes no difference, does it? No matter how hard I work toward peace, we will have a war."

Kurj fell silent then. Jarac didn't push. His grandson had said his piece and would add no more. In that rationing of words, he and Jarac were alike.

Then Kurj said, "I received the report on Eldrinson from the medical team that went to Skyfall."

That caught Jarac off guard. "What does it say?"

Kurj jabbed a panel on his desk and it ejected a copy of the report on Eldrinson. He gave it to Jarac. As Jarac scanned the report, his relief grew. Both psychologists rated Eldrinson Valdoria as above average in intelligence. Tyra Meson called his spatial perception "spectacular." Both she and Undell considered him competent to sign a marriage contract with Roca. The doctor's opinion was less definitive, but even he acknowledged that the initial reports on Eldrinson were wrong.

Jarac raised his eyebrow at Kurj. "Even your handpicked doctor won't judge him incompetent."

Kurj crossed his arms.

Jarac sighed. "Why don't you go talk to this man your mother married?" He set down the holosheet. "Perhaps you will find him less objectionable than you expect."

"How can you accept him? That marriage is a travesty."

"Roca loves him. He makes her happy. That makes me happy."

Kurj gave a dismissive jerk with his hand. "All sorts of things make us 'happy' that are wrong."

"You must make peace with this."

"Why? So you don't feel threatened by my anger?"

"No." In truth, it unsettled Jarac to hear Kurj acknowledge what usually went unspoken between them, the tension born of Kurj's conviction he was better fit to rule as Imperator. They both knew it could be decades before Kurj assumed the title, possibly even centuries, given that Roca was next in line.

Kurj pushed his hand across the short cut of his metallic hair, so unlike Jarac's shaggy mane. "I would wish that life could have given us kinder roles to play."

"Yes." Jarac spoke quietly. "I, too."

*DNA molecules rotated, helices in neon colors wrapped around his neck, choking, choking, choking . . .*

Kurj sat bolt upright, staring into the darkness, his heart pounding. As it slowed, he took a deep breath. His biomech web registered that he had held his breath for more than two minutes.

Callie lay on the other side of his bed, asleep. He leaned over her, brushing back her hair, but he didn't wake her. Instead he slid out of bed and pulled on the black robe he had thrown over a chair. Then he left the bedroom and walked through his house. It remained silent but aware of him, always aware, never sleeping.

In his office, he brought up the DNA records for his father, Tokaba Ryestar, and compared them to Eldrinson's genetic map. He *had* to find defects in Eldrinson's DNA, proof it would contaminate the Ruby Dynasty. A way had to exist to negate this last, damning report. But he had to show that whatever flaw existed in Eldrinson didn't apply to Tokaba, who had also brought new blood into the Ruby Dynasty and sired a Ruby son. Surely a dramatic and usable difference existed between Tokaba's DNA and that of a barbarian on a backward planet. He had to prove Eldrinson's flaws.

Kurj had more trouble than he expected in his investigation. Several systems he needed to access were unusually well secured, challenging his most sophisticated EIs. But gradually he uncovered the story. His conception had involved years of work by a team of scientists. The Assembly had set up an entire program dedicated to that one purpose. Desperate to ensure the Ruby Dynasty would provide heirs for the Kyle web, they had insisted the doctors do whatever possible to make it happen, regardless of what that meant to Roca and Tokaba, even if the failures of Roca's pregnancies brought them immeasurable grief.

Kurj clenched his teeth, his resentment hot within him. Yet he understood their desperation. He felt it every time he let himself acknowledge how little stood between his people and enslavement by the Trader Aristos. Only a gossamer, indefinable web protected them, one that didn't even exist in the spacetime universe. But no matter how much he understood their motivation, nothing would ease his anger at the pain his family had suffered as the Assembly sought to control and manipulate their lives.

The more he investigated his birth, the more he understood why his mother called him a miracle child. The odds against his conception had been so high, it made him feel strange, unreal. He followed the trail through ever more abstruse networks, searching out his heredity. Finally he left spacetime and plunged into the Kyle web, becoming a cowled figure striding across a stark grid.

The more he searched, the more puzzled he became. On the surface, Tokaba's DNA map seemed reasonable, but the deeper Kurj delved, the more anomalies he found. The shade of blue it predicted for Tokaba's eyes wasn't quite the same as the true color. His hair should have been a slightly darker brown. He had always joked about how it curled in the fog, but according to his DNA, it should have stayed straight.

Kurj continued to search, probing forgotten nooks in the web, following the oddly confused trail left by the geneticists and Assembly. His cowled avatar climbed down the grid, deeper and deeper, until no light filtered down from above and fluorescent data-fish swam by his body.

Someone had hidden the trail.

At first he thought the files he was searching out had degraded over the years, but gradually he realized someone had deliberately erased them. He sank into areas that even the most adept telops didn't know existed. In a data-grotto encrusted with corrupted files, he found traces of an encryption scheme used by the Assembly long ago. They had retired it just before his birth. He cast about, searching for whatever it had hidden.

Searching.

Searching.

And finally he found what he sought, the barest trace of a file, one that had languished for thirty-five years. The actual data had been erased, but its ghost persisted like a translucent copy. Laboriously, using all the mental tools at his disposal, he reconstructed the file.

It was a DNA map.

Tokaba's DNA map.

Tokaba's *true* DNA map.

In many ways, this vague file matched the robust records Kurj had found at the top levels of the webs. However, it gave the right shade of blue for Tokaba's eyes and the proper traits for his hair. It matched his physical records in every detail. It lacked only one thing.

The genes of a psion.

Tokaba had none of the complex genetic mutations that created a psion. He manifested no empathic traits because he lacked the genes, either paired or unpaired. He just plain didn't have them. Tokaba couldn't be his father. It was impossible.

Impossible.

Nausea rose within Kurj. He refused to believe Tokaba hadn't sired him. It would kill him.

Inexorable now, Kurj slipped through convoluted mazes in the depths of the web, following tenuous leads that thinned and vanished. He continued to probe, search, and dig. What had the Assembly done? What godsforsaken crime had they committed, to make a Ruby psion out of the impossible?

Finally Kurj found the truth they had kept from him, from his parents, from his entire family. They had sabotaged Roca's and Tokaba's fertility treatments. They replaced Tokaba's sperm with that of another man.

And then Kurj found what the Assembly had hidden.

It was the name of his father.

His true father.

Jarac.

# 25

# Sacrifice

---

Kurj lost control.

He ripped his mind out of the web so fast, his disrupted neural pathways registered the process as a firestorm of white light. It didn't matter. Nothing mattered. He had stumbled upon the ultimate treachery. The one moderating force in his life, the memory of his father, was a lie, one on such a monstrous scale he couldn't comprehend its enormity.

The Assembly had destroyed him. And now, in his rage, he would make them pay. The Skolian Imperialate survived because a Dyad powered the web. Kurj knew exactly how he would achieve his vengeance— he would take into his own hands the power of the web that the Assembly so prized, the web for which they had committed this atrocity. He would become that web. He would control it. He would hold the Assembly hostage to his power.

He would destroy them.

A thought far back in Kurj's mind warned of danger to his grandparents, but his fury swamped it out. His grandfather was his father. The betrayal went so deep, he thought he would scream with the knowledge.

By the time he became aware of his surroundings again, he was striding through the War Room. The amphitheater was strangely empty, without a single telop on duty. Kurj stopped at a console and accessed its records. An hour ago an immense spike of power had surged through the systems here. Following it, Kurj had sent an order to every telop, officer, aide, page, and tech in the War Room: *Evacuate.*

He didn't remember giving the order. In his mental explosion, he had operated without conscious thought, ridden the magrail across the Orbiter's interior and come here to the War Room without seeing where or how he went, his mind careening from the shock of his violent withdrawal from the web.

He strode to the Lock corridor.

It began at the perimeter of the amphitheater and stretched back into the wall itself, dwindling to a point as if it reached to infinity. A great arch framed its entrance and its floor flashed, a steel and diamond composite. Set off by pillars rather than walls, the corridor glowed in the otherwise dark War Room. The columns were akin to the Strategy Table, transparent and indestructible. Clockwork mechanisms gleamed within them, active as never before, glittering with light and alive with moving gears, all eerily silent.

He stepped up onto the raised corridor. His boots rang on the floor as he strode toward the infinite point of perspective. The end of the corridor never seemed to come closer, though he passed pillar after pillar.

Suddenly the point expanded into an octagonal doorway. He slowed as he reached the sparkling arch. When he stepped through it, time dwindled. Space became thick. He felt as if he were moving through invisible molasses. A great hum of power filled the octagonal chamber, and a glare of light hid the high ceiling.

The Lock pierced the chamber.

A pillar of light rose out of an octagonal well in the center of the floor, a great column of radiance so bright it made the air shimmer. The Lock was a singularity in Kyle space. It pierced spacetime like a needle, rising from the floor and vanishing overhead in a hazed glitter, back into its own universe. Humanity had lost the technology that created it, but the Lock remained, forever enduring.

Kurj crossed the chamber in slow motion, his steps long and heavy. He stopped at the rim of the octagonal depression.

Then he stepped into the pillar of light.

**Kurj, of the endless Fire;
My one son, forever bright.**

*Escape the blazing pyre;*
*Mute your rage, decry the night.*

Tokaba's voice flowed through his mind. He knew the cadence of
that rhyme; his father had often sung it to him. But the poem had been
about a child's playful life, not fire and rage. Kurj had never heard these
words—and yet, he knew Tokaba's voice. It came from his memory,
and he wanted to weep for the loss of what it meant to him. Caught in
grief and fury, his mind twisted the rhyme into a chant of his anguish.

In this nether land between space and time, braced between two
universes, he relived his life in a million instants, so many moments he
had thought lost and forgotten.

Then other memories began coming to him, recollections not his
own: Lahaylia, Ruby Pharaoh, born into slavery and ascended to rule
one of the largest empires in human history; Lahaylia, who built the
Skolian Imperialate from nothing and would protect it with the same
ferocity she protected her family; Jarac, the only survivor of a dying race
from an ancient Ruby colony that had failed over the millennia of its
isolation; Jarac, whose Ruby genes had revitalized an ancient family and
whose love gave Lahaylia an unexpected gift in the twilight of her life.
Together, they had founded a dynasty that commanded, enthralled, in-
censed, aroused, and mystified the peoples of a thousand and more
worlds.

The waves of thought that created Kurj's mind overlapped with
those of Jarac and Lahaylia, blending, interfering, canceling and adding,
creating wave patterns for three instead of two. Power flowed through
Kurj, filling him with white noise. He stood within the pillar of light,
his face turned upward, his body bathed in the radiance of another
universe.

The Triad was born.

The mental explosion yanked Roca awake. As she scrambled out of
bed, Eldrin cried out, his wail rising in terror. She stumbled to the crib

and lifted him into her arms, murmuring as she struggled to focus. Her mind was reverberating from an incredible surge of energy.

Roca strode into the living room, holding Eldrin. He was sobbing now, his simple anguish filling her heart as she tried to soothe him. Starlight slanted through the windows, silvering the room. The console by the doorway had lit up like a festival tree, including the *page* light and its alarm, alerting her to an urgent message. Shifting Eldrin to one arm, she thumped her hand on the pager.

"Roca!" Her mother's voice crackled. "Are you all right?"

"Yes." Roca's heart was pounding as if she had just run a kilometer. "What happened?"

"Gods only know. Have you seen Jarac?"

"No. He isn't with you?"

Eldrin went still and silent, his small hands hinged in half as he clutched Roca's nightdress.

"He went to see you hours ago," Lahaylia said.

Roca felt the blood drain from her face. She sensed her mother's dread all the way across Valley—her mother, who never showed fear. "He never arrived. Can't your EI locate him?" It could monitor every centimeter of the Orbiter.

"No." Lahaylia took an audible breath. "Something is blocking its signals."

"That's impossible," Roca said.

"I can't find Kurj either," her mother said.

Eldrin began to cry again, taking gulps between his sobs. Cradling him, Roca leaned over the console to hear her mother better. She thought of Kurj—

And her mind *burned.*

*He burned.*

*Blazed like a flame.*

*A pillar of flame.*

"Gods, no," Roca said. "It can't be."

———

Eldri sat up in bed, the images of his nightmare flaming in his mind. If it hadn't been for his medicines, he had no doubt he would have convulsed. His mind was on fire. *Fire.*

"Roca!" He jumped out of bed and strode from the room in his nightshirt, pulling on his robe, headed for the shrine he had erected to the sun gods. In his mind, he entreated them: *Please. Don't let my wife and child die.*

The shrine was a small room with a stand of polished granite in the center. Eldri had laid out dried bubbles and goldstone balls as offerings. He threw open the shutters, letting the gales of Windward tear over him. Their chill bit through the heavy cloth of his robe as he gazed at the stars.

"Take me, if you must," he said. "But don't hurt them."


Roca reached the War Room before her mother. She held Eldrin close, shielding him with her mind. He was no longer crying, but he remained wide awake, his mind swirling with formless nightmares kept at bay only by his mother's arms. Had she put him down now, he would have panicked. Her terror of losing him to forces beyond her control had grown the entire time she had ridden the magrail here. She couldn't lose her son. Her sons. *What had happened to Kurj?*

Impossibly, the War Room was empty. Even this late at night, it should have hummed with activity. But no telops sat at the consoles; no pages hurried among the stations; no techs rode in the robot arms. The only light came from the Lock corridor, its columns blazing. Roca stopped several meters away, holding Eldrin with one arm while she raised the other to protect her eyes against the brilliance. The corridor seemed to stretch forever, diminishing into a point of perspective.

A man walked out of that point.

He was barely visible, a speck forming out of infinity. He seemed to grow as he came forward, until he reached his true size, a giant of gold. His boots rang on the floor as he strode that ageless corridor, his gait never faltering. White light coruscated around his body, and his face had a terrible radiance. Consoles all over the War Room were coming to life, screens activating, panels flashing, comms humming. In the dome far overhead, the Imperator's throne pulsed with light.

Roca became aware someone else had entered the War Room. Lahaylia walked past her and stopped before the archway of the Lock corridor. Light haloed her body. Kurj reached the end of the corridor and stood in the arch, framed by its dazzling energy, its mechanisms glowing and spinning around him. The power of his mind surged, huge, tremendous, and chaotic.

"Go back." His deep voice echoed unnaturally. "Both of you. Go back. Go home. Be safe."

"Kurj." Roca held Eldrin close. "What have you done?"

He lifted his hand, nearly blinding her with the light it emanated. "I cannot stop what is happening. You must go."

Lahaylia didn't move. "Where is my husband?"

Kurj answered harshly. "With my father."

"Gods, no," Roca said. *Tokaba was dead.*

Eldrin had gone still in her arms, but she felt his nascent mind focused on Kurj. He responded to his brother's power. Like knew like. But he had no defenses. Roca shielded his mind with hers, lest the outpouring of mental energies overwhelm him.

Light radiated from Lahaylia's body; whatever surged through Kurj already burned within her. They both called now on the same forces. The Dyad. No, *Triad.*

Lahaylia's voice resonated throughout the War Room. "Your father, Tokaba Ryestar, is dead."

"I speak not of Tokaba Ryestar," Kurj said.

"Darr Hammerjackson is also dead."

"I do not speak of Darr, either."

Roca went rigid. He had only one other "father": *Eldri.* Her anger and her fear blazed. "What have you done to my husband?"

Kurj turned his gaze on her, his inner lids glowing like molten shields. "Eldrinson Valdoria will never be my father."

"Then who?" Roca asked.

His answer dropped into the air like a great weight.

"Jarac."

He had to have gone mad. "You can't mean what you are saying." Roca felt as if she were shattering inside.

"Go." Kurj braced his arms against the sides of the arch. His voice thundered, unreal in its eerily amplified power. "Go now, both of you, while you are safe."

"Kurj, listen." Lahaylia faced him with no sign of fear, though he towered over her, huge and solid, standing on the raised floor of the corridor. Her voice matched his in strength, drawing on the unleashed power of the Lock. She and Kurj were part of a triangle now, aware of space and time in a way Roca could perceive only from the edges of their Triad.

"The power-link is collapsing," Lahaylia said. "It cannot take the power of our three minds. Yours and Jarac's are too alike. They interfere. They will cancel each other. You cannot both survive."

"No!" Kurj let go of the columns and stepped down from the corridor. He faced Lahaylia, the two of them locked in a connection neither could break. Her gaze never wavered. He walked on, past Roca, and her mind felt his passing like the gales of a mental hurricane.

Eldrin cried out and burrowed his head against her shoulder.

The transparent bubble of the observation bay curved out from the Orbiter's hull. The glory of deep space surrounded Jarac. He stood on a transparent platform staring at the cosmos, his hands resting on the rail of dichromesh glass.

Kurj crossed the bay like a mammoth walking in space. When he neared Jarac, his grandfather turned, his motions slowed by his large size. Jarac's face was drawn, strained, his eyes reflecting the same agony Kurj felt ripping him apart. Their minds were trying to fit in the same place, two leviathans superimposed on each other in Kyle space.

Two minds.

One space.

Only one could survive.

Kurj's voice crackled. "Grandfather."

Jarac's inner lids lifted, revealing his eyes. Deep lines furrowed his drawn face. His mental power was crushing his grandson. Kurj had always believed himself the stronger of the two, but he knew now he had been wrong. Terribly wrong. Jarac's mind had more power, more strength, more will than his own. Kurj couldn't endure against him. Jarac would survive and he would die.

Suddenly Jarac's mind receded. Kurj didn't understand—and then realization hit him: his grandfather had relinquished his hold on life. He would let himself die so Kurj could live.

"No!" Kurj strode forward, knowing now, too late, that his grandfather meant more to him than the power of the Imperator. He wanted Jarac to live, wanted it with an intensity that burned.

Jarac sank to his knees, his great back bending as he lowered his head. Dropping next to him, Kurj grabbed his shoulders. "You must not give up! We will find a way to coexist."

"It is not possible." Jarac lifted his shaggy-maned head. "We are too alike."

"No." Kurj felt as if a band were constricting across his chest. "You are a better man than I."

"Greatness is in you. You must find it now."

"You must live." Kurj would do anything, even beg the fates, to stop Jarac from dying. "You must."

"I am too old."

"But you don't know. I found files about my birth."

Jarac answered with infinite, agonizing gentleness. "I know. I see it in your mind."

The words wrenched out of Kurj. "You are my father."

Jarac took a deep, shuddering breath. "I cannot forgive what the Assembly has done. But I am as proud to have you as a son as a grandson."

"You must live!" Kurj would say it a thousand times, until Jarac heard.

"Do you know their minds?" Jarac asked.

"Whose?" But Kurj felt it, what his grandfather meant. The minds of the Ruby Dynasty were linked, all of them. He, Jarac, and Lahaylia flared in a triangle of fire. Less intense, outside the Triad but still bright, the Ruby Dynasty burned: Dehya, intellect instead of force, sensitive, fragile, beautifully luminous; Roca, a blaze of vitality and health, with a love for her family that knew no bounds; young Eldrin, glowing within the circle of her light, unformed, full of promise, so very, very treasured.

And yes, Eldrinson was there, distant but full, a great swelling ocean of light. Kurj wanted to weep for the purity of that radiance, the untouched beauty of a mind that for all Eldrinson's physical suffering had remained unscathed.

Jarac clenched his forearm. "The baby. He has not our strength. Protect."

Kurj felt the wash of Eldrin's terrified impressions. The child was panicked, cowering from the inferno of the Triad, his mind huddled against his mother's, his thoughts instinctively fleeing toward love and warmth, desperate for the father Kurj had denied him. Eldrin was so enormously vulnerable. Jarac's dying, this agonizing pain, could devastate Eldrin the same way the deaths of Eldrinson's family had so traumatized Eldrinson in his infancy. Kurj reached out, swaddling Eldrin's mind in layers of protection, buffering him from the agony killing his elders.

"You feel them." Jarac struggled to speak. "They are yours now. You are the Fist of Skolia. The protector. Lahaylia and Dehya, they are the Mind. And know this, Kurj. Eldrinson and Roca are its Heart. You cannot deny them."

"Father—"

"You must care for them, betraying none." Jarac's voice rasped. "Promise you will do this."

"You are not going to die."

"*Promise.* You will never betray any of them."

Kurj took a shuddering breath. "I promise."

Jarac sagged forward, and Kurj grabbed his shoulders, trying to stop him. But like a great tree falling, Jarac settled onto his side, then on his back. Kurj knelt next to him on the transparent deck, bathed in starlight, moisture gathering in his eyes.

"I cannot heal the wounds that ravage your heart," Jarac whispered. "But I can give you a gift." His massive chest rose and fell with his strained breaths. "Know the family we love . . . as I know them."

And then he opened his mind.

Jarac's thoughts, emotions, hopes, memories, fears, longings, knowledge, loves—it all rolled into Kurj's mind. His brain, so much like Jarac's, imprinted with the neural pathways that formed Jarac's personality. Kurj remained himself, aware of the pain in his heart, but in that instant, he also became his grandfather.

Kurj's voice caught. "Forgive me."

"Yes." His father took a final breath. "I do love you."

Then Jarac Skolia, Imperator of the Skolian Imperialate, passed from life into death.

# 26

# Ruby Heart

---

Lahaylia Selei sat on the floor in her bedroom, against the wall, unmoving. After an age, or perhaps only a few moments, a man paused in the doorway. She made no move to look at him, speak to him, acknowledge him in any way.

Then he spoke. "Lahya."

"Ah, gods." She *knew* that voice. She couldn't help herself; she turned—and saw her husband in the doorway, his posture, his expressions, even his mind so achingly familiar.

Except it wasn't him.

"Don't," she whispered. "I can't bear it."

Kurj came to her and knelt on one knee. He spoke in a low voice. "I thought I knew his love for you, but I had no idea, no hint of how deep it went." His voice cracked. "I am sorry."

Lahaylia wanted to hate him, to cast him out of her sight. But she couldn't. She saw Jarac in his every word and gesture.

"I cannot live with this," she said.

He started to reach for her, but when she stiffened, he dropped his hand. He spoke quietly. "In time, the part of me that is Jarac will recede, I think, and integrate with Kurj."

Her voice caught. "The Assembly has much to answer for."

"Yes."

"You have made yourself the most powerful individual alive, Kurj. None can match what you have done." She regarded him steadily. "Now you must take responsibility for it."

Kurj took a deep breath. "If I can."

"You must." Her gaze darkened. "Otherwise you will destroy us all."


Roca cradled Eldrin.

He slept in her arms, nestled against her, his eyes closed, his face finally peaceful. She leaned back on the couch, too exhausted to move. The grief was too big. She had nowhere to put it. She wished she could be like Eldrin, able to sleep when the storm abated.

Her console chimed.

Roca lifted her head. "What is it?"

The house EI answered. "Imperator Skolia is at your door."

She froze. "*Who?*" Her father had just *died.*

"Kurj Skolia."

She took a ragged breath. Of course. Bitter grief filled her. The son had killed the father and assumed his throne. By joining the Triad, Kurj had bypassed her in the line of succession, wresting the title away from her. She hadn't held any great desire to lead the military, but never would she have wished for this. Damn the Assembly. Damn the Traders for their relentless brutality that drove people to such desperate wrongs. Damn them all.

"Let him in." Roca sat up, shifting Eldrin carefully so he didn't wake up.

A man appeared in the shadowed entrance of the room. Roca drew in a sharp breath. It wasn't Kurj. His walk, his posture, his face—it was Jarac. But he wore Kurj's clothes and had Kurj's hair.

Son, brother, father: to her, he was all three.

He sat on the other end of the sofa, his elbows on his knees. "How is Eldrin?"

"All right." Roca smoothed the baby's wispy hair.

"Did he suffer when—?"

Roca thought of her father's death. "No. He cried, but that was all." Kurj had protected his half brother, doing for Eldrin what no one had been able to do for Eldrin's father, protecting him against the ravages of his family's deaths. Eldrin would live without the torments Eldri had endured all his life. Roca wanted to reach toward Kurj, but she couldn't bring herself to do it, knowing the price they had all paid for his fury.

Kurj looked at his hands. "I have made a decision."

"Yes?"

"I will call another vote on the invasion." He raised his gaze to her. "As Imperator, I can do so."

She went very still. "And?"

"I will vote for the negotiations."

Hotness filled Roca's eyes. She had finally achieved what she had intended when she escaped her bodyguards and tried to reach the Assembly so long ago. But the price was so terribly, terribly high. A tear ran down her face. "I am glad."

For a long time he said nothing. Then he broke his silence. "Mother—go to your husband."

Surely she had misheard. "To Eldri?"

"Yes." He spoke with difficulty. "I don't know if I can ever accept him. But Jarac was right. You must go."

Eldrin stirred in her arms, nestling closer, his face smoothing out in sleep.

"Thank you," Roca whispered.

"But you must come back." Now he sounded like Jarac. "We will see you in the Assembly and on stage?"

"Certainly the Assembly. I have much work to do." She bent her head over Eldrin. "But I think not the stage. I would like to have more children."

"Mother—"

She raised her head. "Yes?"

He struggled with his words. "I am sorry."

Roca knew then that no punishment any judicial body could mete out to him would equal the guilt tearing him apart. The Assembly would fear to take action against him, lest it destabilize the web they all depended on with such desperation. And those who knew what had happened thirty-five years ago would be terrified to do anything that might anger him, lest he reveal their crimes.

But for the rest of his life, her son would live in the hell of his own remorse.


Roca stood in the doorway, gazing at the darkening Valley long after Kurj had left. Eldrin continued to sleep in her arms. She didn't go back inside; she couldn't bear the solitude of her house, not now, not after all they had lost.

Gradually Roca realized someone was approaching. The figure took form out of the night, a woman with dark hair and a graceful walk.

Roca waited until the woman reached her. "Mother."

Lahaylia nodded. "My greetings."

"I am glad you came."

Her mother spoke with a softness she rarely showed. "I thought, if you would allow—I would visit with my grandson."

Roca's voice caught. "Yes. I would like that." She moved aside. "Please come in."

So the Ruby Pharaoh acknowledged her second grandson.

# 27

# Lyshriol

Eldri walked through the rubble piled around the edges of the courtyard. The work crews had said they would move it, but now they were gone and it was still here. He would have to enlist some people to help him carry it out.

He raised his head, inhaling the crisp air. Ever since his nightmare fifteen days ago, he had been in a daze, certain that Roca and Eldrin had died. He had sent riders to ask Brad if he knew anything, but they had yet to return.

Garlin was walking toward him from the rebuilt castle. It looked exactly like Windward, reproduced from "satellite images," whatever that meant. But it had lost an indefinable essence, a sense of age and history he had always loved, though he had never realized it until that elusive quality was gone.

Garlin's smile quirked. "Why do you scowl at me?"

"My apology." Eldri grimaced. "I am contemplating carrying rocks."

"An excellent reason to frown."

"Yes, indeed." A dark speck in the sky caught Eldri's attention. "What is that?"

Garlin squinted. "I believe it is Brad's flyer."

"Maybe he has news of Roca!"

His cousin laid a hand on his arm. "Don't put your hopes too high."

Eldri turned away, unable to bear Garlin's compassion. It felt like pity. He had put his hopes too high over and over, every time one of the offworlders visited. And every time they dashed his hopes. No one would give him news of Roca and Eldrin.

The flyer came on, soaring through the sky, visible now as a silver craft. Eldri walked with Garlin out under the portcullis. As they crossed the bridge, he looked into the chasm that surrounded Windward. He couldn't see far enough down to locate the remains of the battering ram that he and his men had pushed off this arch of stone.

Brad's flyer landed in the open area beyond the bridge, the place where Avaril and his army had camped. Eldri stood back with Garlin, shielding his eyes with his hand as the craft settled down. He tried to contain his agitation, but it seemed forever before the machine rumbled into silence.

Eldri started forward, his heart beating hard. Then the hatch opened. Brad jumped out and waved, a great smile on his face. Eldri blinked. Although Brad always seemed to enjoy his visits, at least when he wasn't starving in a siege, he had never looked this happy to see Eldri and Garlin before.

Eldri came up to him. "Hello, Brad."

"Hello." His smile widened. "I have a surprise for you."

"A surprise?" Eldri asked, perplexed.

A woman appeared in the hatchway of the flyer.

In that moment, for Eldri, the world stopped. He didn't feel the wind blowing or the sunlight on his face; he didn't see the towering mountains or the sky above them; he didn't taste the air. He knew only the sight of the woman.

Roca.

Eldri ran forward as Roca jumped down from the flyer. He almost threw his arms around her, then jerked to a stop when he saw the bundle she carried.

A baby.

"By the suns," Eldri said. "What beautiful child have you there?" His eyes suddenly brimmed with moisture.

Roca extended the baby to him. "Your son."

He took the boy into his arms, holding him the way he had held so many children of his friends and servants. His son looked up at him and gurgled.

"He smiled!" Eldri gave a shaky laugh, his heart filling with an indescribable emotion. "He smiled at me."

A tear ran down her face. "I saw." She came forward, and he moved the baby in his arms so he could hold both his son and his wife. As he hugged Roca close, his tears mingled with her hair.

His family had come home.


Roca and Eldri relaxed on the rug before the fire in their bedroom, Eldri with his arms around her waist and Roca reclining against him. Eldrin was curled in her lap, playing with a ball of polished blue glasswood.

Eldri was finally content. He had been torn in two; now he was complete. But he ached for the tragedy that had devastated Roca and her family. He didn't comprehend all its nuances, but he understood that the truth could destabilize her government. A new Imperator ruled. The Assembly called her father's death an accident, letting the story spread throughout their realms. Her family had to be preserved, lest it weaken this "Kyle web" that held their empire together. But speculation ran wild: the grandson had killed the grandfather to take his throne. Given what Eldri had seen of his wife's firstborn son, it didn't surprise him that no one wanted to naysay that great, metallic warlord.

Roca had been restrained since she came back, mourning for her father, who had somehow died and not died. Eldri wished he could heal the wounds in her heart.

"Will your family be all right?" he asked.

"Someday." She spoke softly. "It will take time."

He bent his head over hers. "If only I could help."

"You do, just by being here."

So they enjoyed the warmth of the fire. After a while, she said, "ISC is going to build a medical clinic near Dalvador."

He still couldn't untangle the mess of relations between her people and Brad's. "ISC is the Skolian army, yes?"

"That's right."

"Lyshriol is part of Brad's Allied Worlds."

"His people have agreed to relinquish their claim." Dryly she added, "It will take much debate and bargaining to settle on terms."

He thought of the Dalvador Plains where he had lived all his life. "Will the starport stay in the same place?"

"I think so. ISC will probably buy or lease it. Brad has asked to stay on, as a liaison for your people and mine."

"I am glad. I like him."

"I too." She hesitated. "What will happen with Lord Avaril?"

He grimaced, acknowledging the unease he hid from everyone else except Garlin. "He has gone away for now. I fear though that someday he will return."

"You'll be ready for him." She closed her eyes. "My people can help. We can do a lot for your people."

He tensed. "You must not change Lyshriol."

"We won't. You will oversee anything we do." She traced her finger along his arm. "Perhaps someday we can understand your people, why you are so different from us."

"These psychologists ask many questions." He sighed. "They say odd things, that we are a living 'computer.' They want to know why we interpret symbols differently than your people, why we can do math but not read. I don't understand a lot of it."

Roca laughed softly. "They don't, either, yet. Pieces are there, like the way you count in octal instead of decimal, or the binary aspects of your world: two suns, two moons, two sets of opposing fingers."

"Do you think they will make sense of it?"

"Someday."

It would be interesting if they did, but Eldri wasn't holding his breath. "Well, perhaps that will make them happy."

She smiled. "Perhaps."

They relaxed for a while, watching the flames. Every time Eldri looked at his son, he marveled anew that this boy was his. Surely no child had ever been so fine. Even his hands were normal, with a hinge and four fingers.

"Tell me," he murmured to Roca. "How many children would you like to have?"

A hint of her mischief sparkled. "A hundred."

"Ai, Roca! It would be bedlam."

She laughed. "Perhaps so. How about ten?"

"Ten. Yes." Although he could tell she was joking, he liked the idea. Among his people, ten wouldn't be unusual. He contemplated a family full of laughing children with gold hair and eyes. "What should we name them?"

"Althor for the next boy, after you."

"If it is a girl, we must name her Roca."

A memory stirred in her mind, one so vivid, Eldri picked it up: the statue of the warrior goddess in the corridor outside his suite, the one Roca had run past when she had gone to Brad's suite during the battle and sent off the fliers.

"Her name should be Sauscony," Roca said. "After your goddess of arrows."

"Not Roca?"

She shook her head. "But I would like her to have my mother's name. Lahaylia."

"She will be strong and beautiful."

"That she will." Roca tickled her finger along the back of his. "Pick another name."

He considered. "For a boy, Kelricson."

She smiled. "Who is Kelric, that our son should also be his?"

Eldri nuzzled her ear. "The god of youth."

"Ah. I like that."

"Roca?"

"Hmmmm?"

Eldri spoke with care. "We must name our children after your family, too." He made himself say it. "Including Kurj."

Her mood turned somber. "Thank you."

"Why?"

"For not hating him."

He brushed back her hair. "I cannot hate those you love."

Roca turned to him, with Eldrin cradled between them. Her voice gentled. "You are my life, Eldri."

"As you are mine."

So they sat together, symbols for an empire that had seen too much death, offering instead, in simply their existence, a promise of new life and a future for their people.

# Family Tree: RUBY DYNASTY

Boldface names refer to members of the Rhon. The Selei name denotes the direct line of the Ruby Pharaoh. All children of Roca and Eldrinson take Valdoria as their third name. All members of the Rhon within the Ruby Dynasty have the right to use Skolia as their last name. "Del" in front of a name means "in honor of."

= marriage    + children by

**Lahaylia Selei** = **Jarac**

**Dyhianna Selei** = [1]William Seth Rockworth III
(separated)

= [2]**Eldrin
Jarac**

**Havyrl** = [1]Lilly
**Torcellei** = [2]Kamoj Arga

**Althor
Izam-Na** + Syreen Leirol

[1]Coop and Vaz Majda

Ryder Jalam Majda Valdoria

= [2]Cirrus
|
son

**Del-Kurj   Chaniece
Roca**
(fraternal twins)

**Taquinil
Selei**

**Delson   Jaqui**

**Akushtina** = **Althor Vyan Selei**
**(Tina)**
**Santis Pulivok**

**Jaibriol III** + Tarquine Iquar          **Rocalisa**

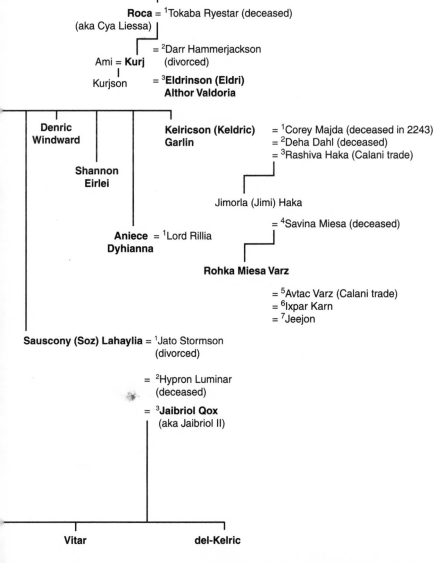

**Roca** = [1]Tokaba Ryestar (deceased)
(aka Cya Liessa)

Ami = **Kurj** = [2]Darr Hammerjackson
(divorced)

Kurjson = [3]**Eldrinson (Eldri)**
**Althor Valdoria**

**Denric**
**Windward**

**Shannon**
**Eirlei**

**Kelricson (Keldric)** = [1]Corey Majda (deceased in 2243)
**Garlin** = [2]Deha Dahl (deceased)
= [3]Rashiva Haka (Calani trade)

Jimorla (Jimi) Haka

= [4]Savina Miesa (deceased)

**Aniece** = [1]Lord Rillia
**Dyhianna**

**Rohka Miesa Varz**

= [5]Avtac Varz (Calani trade)
= [6]Ixpar Karn
= [7]Jeejon

**Sauscony (Soz) Lahaylia** = [1]Jato Stormson
(divorced)

= [2]Hypron Luminar
(deceased)

= [3]**Jaibriol Qox**
(aka Jaibriol II)

**Vitar**                **del-Kelric**

*Genetically, Kurj carries Jarac's DNA

# Characters and Family History

Boldface names refer to Ruby psions, also known as the "Rhon." All Rhon psions who are members of the Ruby Dynasty use **Skolia** as their last name (the Skolian Imperialate was named after their family). The **Selei** name indicates the direct line of the Ruby Pharaoh. Children of **Roca** and **Eldrinson** take Valdoria as a third name. The "del" prefix means "in honor of," and is capitalized if the person honored was a Triad member. Most names are based on world-building systems drawn from Mayan, North African, and Indian cultures.

= marriage

**Lahaylia Selei** (Ruby Pharaoh) = **Jarac** (Imperator)

**Lahaylia** and **Jarac** founded the modern-day Ruby Dynasty. **Lahaylia** was created in the Rhon genetic project. Her lineage traces back to the ancient Ruby Dynasty that founded the Ruby Empire. **Lahaylia** and **Jarac** have two daughters, **Dyhianna Selei** and **Roca**.

**Dyhianna (Dehya) Selei** = (1) William Seth Rockworth III (separated in 2205)
= (2) **Eldrin Jarac Valdoria**

**Dehya** becomes the Ruby Pharaoh after Lahaylia. She married William Seth Rockworth III as part of the Iceland Treaty between the Skolian Imperialate and Allied Worlds of Earth. They have no children and later separate. The dissolution of their marriage would negate the treaty, so neither the Allieds nor the Imperialate recognize Seth's divorce. Both Seth and Dehya eventually remarry anyway. *Spherical Harmonic* tells the story of what happens to **Dehya** after the Radiance War. She and **Eldrin** have two children, **Taquinil Selei** and **Althor Vyan Selei**.

### Althor Vyan Selei = 'Akushtina (Tina) Santis Pulivok

The story of **Althor** and **Tina** appears in *Catch the Lightning*. **Althor Vyan Selei** was named after his uncle/cousin, **Althor Izam-Na Valdoria**. Tina also appears in the story "Ave de Paso" in the anthology *Redshift* and *The Year's Best Fantasy*, 2001.

**Roca** = (1) Tokaba Ryestar (deceased)
      = (2) Darr Hammerjackson (divorced)
      = (3) **Eldrinson (Eldri) Althor Valdoria**

Roca and Tokaba had one child, **Kurj** (Imperator and former Jagernaut). Kurj marries Ami when he is about a century old. Kurj and Ami have a son named Kurjson.

Although no records exist of **Eldrinson**'s lineage, it is believed he descends from the ancient Ruby Dynasty. *Skyfall* tells the story of how he and **Roca** meet. They have ten children.

**Eldrin (Dryni) Jarac** (bard, consort to Ruby Pharaoh, warrior)
**Althor Izam-Na** (engineer, Jagernaut, Imperial Heir)
**Del-Kurj (Del)** (singer, warrior, twin to **Chaniece**)
**Chaniece Roca** (runs Valdoria family household, twin to **Del-Kurj**)
**Havyrl (Vyrl) Torcellei** (farmer, doctorate in agriculture)
**Sauscony (Soz) Lahaylia** (military scientist, Jagernaut, Imperator)
**Denric Windward** (teacher, doctorate in literature)
**Shannon Eirlei** (Blue Dale archer)
**Aniece Dyhianna** (accountant, Rillian queen)
**Kelricson (Kelric) Garlin** (mathematician, Jagernaut, Imperator)

**Eldrin** appears in *The Radiant Seas* and *Spherical Harmonic*

**Althor Izam-Na** = (1) Coop and Vaz
= (2) Cirrus

**Althor** has a daughter, Eristia Leirol Valdoria, with Syreen Leirol, an actress turned linguist. Coop and Vaz have a son, Ryder Jalam Majda Valdoria, with **Althor** as co-father. **Althor** and Coop appear in *The Radiant Seas*. The novelette, "Soul of Light" (Circlet Press, anthology *Sextopia*), tells the story of how **Althor** and Vaz met Coop. Vaz and Coop also appear in *Spherical Harmonic*. **Althor** and Cirrus also have a son.

**Havyrl (Vyrl) Torcellei** = Lilliara (Lilly) (deceased in 2266)
= Kamoj Quanta Argali

**Havyrl** & Lilly marry in 2223. Their story appears in "Stained Glass Heart," a novella in the anthology *Irresistible Forces*, February 2004. The story of **Havyrl** and Kamoj appears in *The Quantum Rose*, which won the 2001 Nebula Award. An early version of the first half was serialized in *Analog*, May 1999–July/August 1999.

**Sauscony (Soz) Lahaylia** = (1) Jato Stormson (divorced)
= (2) Hypron Luminar (deceased)
= (3) **Jaibriol Qox** (aka **Jaibriol II**)

The story of how **Soz** and Jato met appears in the novella, "Aurora in Four Voices" (*Analog*, December 1998). **Soz** and **Jaibriol**'s stories appear in *Primary Inversion* and *The Radiant Seas*. They have four children, all of whom use Qox-Skolia as their last name: **Jaibriol III, Rocalisa, Vitar**, and **del-Kelric**. The story of how **Jaibriol III** became the emperor of Eube appears in *The Moon's Shadow*. **Jaibriol III** married Tarquine Iquar, the Finance Minister of Eube.

**Aniece** = Lord Rillia

Lord Rillia rules Rillia, which consists of the extensive Rillian Vales, the Dalvador Plains, the Backbone Mountains, and the Stained Glass Forest.

***Kelricson (Kelric) Garlin*** = (1) Corey Majda (deceased in 2243)

                                 = (2) Deha Dahl (deceased)

                                 = (3) Rashiva Haka (Calani trade)

                                 = (4) Savina Miesa (deceased)

                                 = (5) Avtac Varz (Calani trade)

                                 = (6) Ixpar Karn (closure)

                                 = (7) Jeejon

***Kelric***'s stories are told in *The Last Hawk, Ascendant Sun, The Moon's Shadow*, the novella "A Roll of the Dice" (*Analog*, July/August 2000), and the novelette "Light and Shadow" (*Analog*, April 1994). ***Kelric*** and Rashiva have one son, Jimorla (Jimi) Haka, who becomes a renowned Calani. ***Kelric*** and Savina have one daughter, ***Rohka Miesa Varz***, who becomes the Ministry Successor in line to rule the Twelve Estates on Coba.

The novella "Walk in Silence" (*Analog*, April 2003) tells the story of Jess Fernandez, an Allied starship captain from Earth who deals with the genetically engineered humans on the Skolian colony of Icelos.

# Time Line

| | |
|---|---|
| *circa* 4000 BC | Group of humans moved from Earth to Raylicon |
| *circa* 3600 BC | Ruby Dynasty begins |
| *circa* 3100 BC | Raylicans launch first interstellar flights; rise of Ruby Empire |
| *circa* 2900 BC | Ruby Empire declines |
| *circa* 2800 BC | Last interstellar flights; Ruby Empire collapses . . . |
| *circa* AD 1300 | Raylicans begin to regain lost knowledge |
| 1843 | Raylicans regain interstellar flight |
| 1866 | Rhon genetic project begins |
| 1871 | Aristos found Eubian Concord (aka Trader Empire) |
| 1881 | Lahaylia Selei born |
| 1904 | Lahaylia Selei founds Skolian Imperialate |
| 2005 | Jarac born |
| 2111 | Lahaylia Selei marries Jarac |
| 2119 | Dyhianna Selei born |
| 2122 | Earth achieves interstellar flight |
| 2132 | Allied Worlds of Earth formed |
| 2144 | Roca born |
| 2169 | Kurj born |
| 2203 | Roca marries Eldrinson Althor Valdoria (*Skyfall*) |
| 2204 | Eldrin Jarac Valdoria born |
| 2206 | Althor Izam-Na Valdoria born |
| 2209 | Havyrl (Vyrl) Torcellei Valdoria born |
| 2210 | Sauscony (Soz) Lahaylia Valdoria born |
| 2219 | Kelricson (Kelric) Garlin Valdoria born |
| 2223 | Vyrl marries Lilly ("Stained Glass Heart") |
| 2237 | Jaibriol II born |

| | |
|---|---|
| 2240 | Soz meets Jato Stormson ("Aurora in Four Voices") |
| 2241 | Kelric marries Admiral Corey Majda |
| 2243 | Corey assassinated ("Light and Shadow") |
| 2258 | Kelric crashes on Coba (*The Last Hawk*) |
| early 2259 | Soz meets Jaibriol (*Primary Inversion*) |
| late 2259 | Soz and Jaibriol go into exile (*The Radiant Seas*) |
| 2260 | Jaibriol III born (aka Jaibriol Qox Skolia) (*The Radiant Seas*) |
| 2263 | Rocalisa Qox Skolia born; Althor Izam-Na Valdoria meets Coop ("Soul of Light") |
| 2266 | Lilly dies |
| 2268 | Vitar Qox Skolia born |
| 2273 | del-Kelric Qox Skolia born |
| 2274 | Radiance War begins (also called Domino War) (*The Radiant Seas*) |
| 2276 | Traders capture Eldrin. Radiance War ends |
| 2277–8 | Kelric returns home (*Ascendant Sun*); Dehya coalesces (*Spherical Harmonic*); Kamoj and Vyrl meet (*The Quantum Rose*); Jaibriol III becomes emperor of Eube (*The Moon's Shadow*) |
| 2279 | Althor Vyan Selei born |
| 2287 | Jeremiah Coltman trapped on Coba ("A Roll of the Dice") |
| 2298 | Jess Fernandez goes to Icelos ("Walk in Silence") |
| 2328 | Althor Vyan Selei meets Tina Santis Pulivok (*Catch the Lightning*) |

# About the Author

Catherine Asaro grew up near Berkeley, California. She earned her Ph.D. in Chemical Physics and her M.A. in Physics, both from Harvard, and a B.S. with Highest Honors in Chemistry from UCLA. Among the places she has done research are the University of Toronto, the Max Planck Institut für Astrophysik in Germany, and the Harvard-Smithsonian Center for Astrophysics. A former ballet and jazz dancer, she founded the Mainly Jazz Dance program at Harvard and was a principal dancer and artistic director of Mainly Jazz and the Harvard University Ballet. Her husband is John Kendall Cannizzo, the proverbial rocket scientist. They have one daughter, a ballet dancer and mathematics enthusiast.

Catherine has also written *Primary Inversion, Catch the Lightning, The Last Hawk, The Radiant Seas, Ascendant Sun, The Quantum Rose, Spherical Harmonic,* and *The Moon's Shadow,* all part of the Skolian Saga; *The Veiled Web, The Phoenix Code,* and *Sunrise Alley,* near-future science fiction; and *The Charmed Sphere,* a romantic fantasy. Her work has won numerous awards, including the Nebula for *The Quantum Rose.* She can be reached by e-mail at asaro@sff.net and on the Web at http://www.sff.net/people/asaro/. To receive e-mail updates on her releases, please e-mail the above address.